Dub Steps

Dub Steps

by
Andrew Miller

JACANA

First published by Jacana Media (Pty) Ltd in 2015

10 Orange Street
Sunnyside
Auckland Park 2092
South Africa
+2711 628 3200
www.jacana.co.za

© Andrew Miller, 2015

All rights reserved.

ISBN 978-1-4314-2220-3

Cover design by publicide
Set in Sabon 11/15pt
Printed and bound by Creda Communications
Job no. 002450

See a complete list of Jacana titles at www.jacana.co.za

You

I am an old man on a hill, and my regrets are generic. To the extent that death can surprise, this has been it. It shouldn't be a shock, but there you go.

I regret, most of all, my shrivelled heart. So focused on the numbers. On the maths of my personal equation. Can a man change his heart? Are there ways to improve the spirit of who you are? Of why you choose? It would be nice to think so. But me, now, I am simply ambient. I must be. Into this air I shall shortly slip. The solvent is this running, jagged brain, all angles and contusions, breaks and falls. The surface shines. Teflon. I slip back, and back, into my stories, ideas of her. Whoever she is now, her, the love I refused. Me, angry little peanut.

I should have loved harder. Generic.
 I refused to let go. Generic.
 I think I will miss the birds, the weavers most of all, but all of them really. (The worker birds more than the exotic. The mynas and the barbets and the robins. The boys on the rush, building and moving, private and fast and swooping.) Generic.
 Blue sky. It starts to taste like something as you get really old. Something powerful. You open your sagging mouth and let the blue pour in. It's fresh and light and it bubbles like an advert. Generic.

I remember a time on the beach. Well, not really a memory. Just the brushstroke of us, down the shoreline. She took my hand. Gave me hers. It was some kind of gift. A human transmission. I flickered with a deeper recognition I couldn't place.
 It all feels like that now. Transmission. Flickers.

It's all on the record, in the archive, on display at the expo. You know what I looked like. What I did. You have the details, the story and all of its bastard children. Still, I must bleat just once.

Look, I was a cunt. Maybe that's it. Maybe that's all I really want to say. I know it now. It's not a regret. You can't apportion blame – even to yourself. It's an observation. Age makes it easier to actually see. (Generic.)

A cunt on the move. A cunt with intentions. A cunt who cried at his own pain, paper cuts and marriage, it never mattered. I lived filled with tears.

So, there it is. That you are reading this, whoever you are, wherever you are, is enough. I have spoken. You have heard.

The rest is up to you.

I

Chapter 1
Failure and I considered each other

I looked into the bathroom mirror and ground my knuckles into the sink.

A face too pockmarked.

Skin: puffy. Eye sockets: grey, pushed in too far. I shoved a thumb into the half-moon beneath the left eye and the white indentation stayed.

Failure and I considered each other, Angie's cackle rising and falling and rising again from the dining room. I ratcheted my knuckles further. Then I punched the mirror, smashed it.

I marched through the dining room as hostess Clarissa, followed by Angie, was clicking in my direction to assess exactly what the fuck.

I mumbled a thank you at Clarissa, then at the rest of the now standing guests, lastly at the seething form of my wife, whose keys I grabbed from the foyer table.

No one moved to follow.

I took Angie's retro Mini Cooper, a vile black-and-cream thing, and aimed it right at the complex boom, as they did in those old movies. We came to an auto American halt inches from the red-and-white pole. The guard hit the button from his booth. I slammed the heel of my palm against the steering wheel and let the blood splatter across the cream leather.

I drove to Eileen's Rosebank apartment, parked the Mini deep under and went to sleep for two days.

Chapter 2

Drunk

The dinner party had been Angie's attempt to get me straight with the Mlungu's ownership. There were rumblings and rumours, talk, mutterings about Roy. The usual. As the business grew I was receding, and I was receding because I had been drinking for the greater part of twenty years.

There were pauses, but they were brief and inconsequential.

Once, I booked into rehab for two weeks.

Otherwise I was drunk.

The dinner had rolled along. We were all wit and astute, analytical asides. The boss boys, Rick and Mongezi, were calculatingly casual, keeping the talk light, shop. The VR legislation, the new drugs on the underground, and so on.

Mongezi, bless his humble little black ass, did his best to stay parallel to me. We had started together, and no matter how far away he grew, he was always loyal.

Which was no easy thing. The bottle tipped and I tipped the bottle and it was too fast, of course it was too fast, the anxiety simmering already, less than an hour in. I was talking too much – I should never talk – and I was messing.

Red wine in all the wrong places.

Chapter 3
The ultimate farce

I only met my mother a few times and my father – despite his many talents and attempts to be something else – was ultimately a useless fucker.

We lived in Greymont, on the cusp of Triomf, a shattered, angry suburb still trying to become Sophiatown again after all these years. She lived on the Westcliff hills, locked into the glimmering heights by her father. Punished.

Their story was the ultimate farce, and I the farcical result.

My father was at the height of a failed international cricket career, and my mother was in London on one of those white South African working trips. She was beautiful. Trim and fit and a dancer, part-time, but good enough at waggling around to be asked to appear on the boundary at one of the night games, where her form caught his eye and ... it's obvious and predictable. They came together full of pills in a club somewhere on the fringes of the West End, he a minor celebrity, she very star-struck. They fell into each other, fingers and blushes, sweaty palms and neck massages, and nine months later I came carelessly into existence.

My most vivid maternal memory is her arriving one evening when I was around five years old. I remember her hand and its foreign dimensions. The length of her fingers. Their restlessness. She had mousy brown hair and nervous eyes. Oh, and she was wearing brown slip-ons. I remember that.

She thrust a present at me. I opened the rectangular gift, pulling red ribbon off patterned brown-and-gold paper. I peeled the expensive sticky tape easily off either side and unfolded the paper to reveal a royal blue box. Inside the box was an overwhelmingly classy pen. Silver, very understated, thin, heavy.

An adult's pen.

She crouched next to me and brushed my cheek with long, anxious fingers. 'It's in case you need to think out loud,' she said. I was busy assessing the gift, clicking the push button in and out, captured by the smoothness of the internal latch, still searching for the right reply, when he kicked her out.

'We gotta go.' Russle Fotheringham stomped into the lounge, bakkie keys in hand. 'I'm late. Next time, yes?' She left the lounge quickly, half looking back. Russle and I drove to the bottle store, then back home again.

Chapter 4
Genital nappies

Even in Jozi – thousands of miles from the celebrity moon shots, from Silicon Valley and the baked bean teleportation parties – there was a belief that we were shifting it.

Life.

Change was the thrill as I left university and entered advertising school. Mankind was, so the story went, finally crossing the threshold into a truly functional existence. If we chose the right combinations we could augment and magnify and enhance forever. The pavement, the sky, the air pushing quietly in and out of our snouts.

Our first copywriting module of the year was delivered by a thirty-something man in wire frames, stubble and a Steve Jobs buzz cut.

The class was twenty deep, all Model C kids with family backing (such as myself – my mother was absent, but her father funded any educational desire) or corporate sponsorship. Mr Jobs peered down on us.

'I believe in change,' he said, deathly career-serious. 'Not that it is often very likely, in a deep, fundamental sense, but rather that it is our true hope as a species. The desire to change is all we have.'

I waded through the hype with as little focus as I had applied to everything else. I drank. I went to clubs. I tried to date girls, and failed, because I drank.

Still, I put my glasses on and marched out to the street with the rest of class as the wise Jobs added colour to the walls. As he raised the elevation of a passing pair of middle-aged breasts. Copywriting, he told us as we walked, was dead. Yes, there would be a requirement for a certain volume of text, but our professional lives would be defined less by our words than by our ability to manipulate the paradigm of experience.

Which sounded fine to me. To all of us, thumbs hovering, eyes rushing. We were the pioneers. Eventually, we would pass the gifts on. To our parents. To schoolkids in Uganda. To the mamas in the rurals.

The year passed, a thin layer of communication verbiage fell over my equally thin arts degree and I stepped into 'the agency'. HHN – Huber Huber & Ndimande – a sixty-person set-up with offices in Hyde Park and an array of young, fiery-eyed executives leading the charge.

Looking back on my first days at the agency, I perceive Mongezi as a friend. He now possesses, via the warmth of an old man's imagination and despite everything to come, a benign and accommodating place in my idea of my story. I see him clearly: a tall, thoughtful young man, prone to empathy.

Before we got into serious business, we were chat partners on the agency balcony. During work hours the rotation of smokers and gossipers and chatterers was ceaseless. But after hours I would inhale tobacco, he would drag on his blunt and together we'd pick the world apart.

In my hood, Mongezi said, there is nothing. At home people fetch water in buckets and walk kilometres carrying it. No one is networked or connected or app-enabled. If we had the net, or credit cards, the goods would still never arrive. There are no deliveries.

I admired him. He had all the southern African tongues, including media and technology. He travelled regularly north, and east, into the landscape that for most of us was just backdrop. Mongezi was aware of the distance between his chosen profession and his philosophical heart. He was not out to save the world, but he knew it needed saving.

In our business that was no small thing.

I remember a time. An episode. On the balcony, leaning on the rail, watching over the unfurling minutiae of the post-rush-hour parking lot.

'I was thinking last night,' he said, releasing a long dribble of spit down onto a Mercedes. 'Labour will not be required. It's redundant. Human muscle has peaked.'

'We rocket past the sun in technicolour glory.'

'Sho. Of course. But I've always thought of it in terms of labour. Elites up in space. Chunks of meat down here, harvesting food. Screwing the lids on Coke bottles.'

'Which are sent up daily, in fleets, unpacked at the Virgin docking station.'

'Sho. But maybe not. Maybe they won't need us. My mother, in Limpopo. Not required. My gogo. Aunts. They'll grow their shit in space. Automagically generating food. Livers. Feet. Rice Krispies.'

'Who? The rich?'

'They won't need us. We won't need them. My grandmother can grow her sweet potatoes in peace.'

'We say fuck off!' I shouted to the dusk.

Mongezi flicked his roach over. We watched it fall, hoping to see it stick in the spit on the Merc's window.

The door to the balcony swung open. A middle-aged traffic lady from Venda scolded Mongezi in vernac, then slammed it shut.

Most of our time together was on that balcony, and it was usually much less philosophical. We smoked and developed, in spiralling increments, our current obsession: our premise for a truly South African slasher flick.

Housewife in car, somewhere in Bryanston. Sandwiched behind the driver's seat is her hedge cutter, which she is driving back from the repair man. She's rich, but sensible too. She fixes the hedge cutter instead of replacing it, even though the rewards are negligible.

'Three hundred bucks is three hundred bucks. It all matters.'

'Even if a new hedge cutter would ultimately last longer than the broken one.'

'Even if.'

A street thug passes her at the traffic light, can't spot a device worth anything, decides to drift by, but at the last second spots the cutter and smashes the back-seat window with the spark plug gripped between his knuckles, the glass spraying all over the baby in the booster seat. He grabs the cutter, which, conveniently enough, is petrol powered, and rips it to life.

The thug has issues. He feels a need to express them. He runs the cutter through a newspaper seller, then lops off the head of a young biker guy on a 50cc. In the midst of the ensuing ruckus he slips away, marches casually to the Bryanston Spar, cutter in hand, looking like a reasonable enough man on his way to do reasonable things.

'He blazes into the Spar at ankle height.'

'Optimum height for chaos.'

'Ankles and baby heads.'

'The chocolate shelves.'

'Mixed nuts everywhere.'

'Screams. Blood. Mixed nuts.'

Before it was serious, before business fell accidentally onto us, it was that kind of thing. Our movie. Our lives. Wild ideas about all the things we were lucky enough to know very little about.

All the while, the media philosophy fell like steady coastal rain. The creative directors and division heads looked over us as they spoke, their eyes locked into the mythical middle distance, where they saw community. Always community. Placing the brand at the centre of a community. Facilitating community interactions. Creating genuine, tangible community value. Bringing the virtual to life within the community. Developing brand equity within the new paradigm of real-world augmentation and the limitless virtual possibilities for community interaction.

That sort of thing.

Juniors spent productive time managing social chat. Agency legend said it would take a small lifetime, most of the rest of one's twenties, to gain the privilege of writing. Until we had the wisdom necessary to write, we were to interact with the public According To The Brand Guidelines Supplied.

I spent my first month tweeting for a dish-wash brand, posting pre-prepared competition content on Facebook and escalating all but the most basic interactions.

Social media was our training ground for immersive VR –

the true front line. The technology was scratchy, the resolution pixelated, the interface prone to breaks, but the kiddies couldn't get enough. The holograms – big-breasted Disney ladies wrapped in cat suits and motherly smiles – beckoned and cajoled at the mall entrance. Moms dumped their kids at the pen, glasses already on, and they sunk straight into it.

I eventually graduated to babysitter at a franchised mall holding pen for three- and four-year-olds, Barney's. The interface was a simple fantasy forest. Castle at one end, playground at the other, rivers in between. The kids picked one of five available avatars and ran up and down from the castle to the jungle gym. Snow White took them all into her arms. Dwarves jumped and blew bubbles into the sky.

The children loved it. But they would have loved anything. The real traction was created by the parents, who spent the bulk of their own time at the mall blinking wildly into their glasses, reaching for virtual specials, chatting and sharing. When they came back to the Barney's virtual spectator deck – always stuffed to overflowing – their eyes thrummed at the site of their progeny.

It wasn't just the parents. We all thrilled. The suburbs reached and blinked and clicked and gawked. The holograms stood proud and fluid and sexy.

And then it changed.

They painted the bottom half of an under-maintenance cooling tower on the N4 to Mozambique and the Kruger Park. The video flashed from a hundred kilometres out, a crudely cut mash-up of squatter camps and mine workers going down the shaft. Gardeners in blue overalls walking dogs. Maids in pastel pink pushing prams, little white heads bobbing inside. Open Free State farmlands, rich with crops. Sandton parking lots, replete with luxury vehicles.

Democracy is digital
the text flashed. Then
Land was taken
… then

People will not be quiet
... then
Reparation | return | revolution

It took close to a full day for the cops to find the cellphone paired to the paint. It was buried in a bucket, underneath a mop, in the tower's maintenance basement.

Meanwhile, the press flocked. The public too. Land Rovers – carrying British and French and German and Japanese game viewers – parked on the highway verge, and then at the petrol-station lots. The khaki tour guides unfolded camping chairs and proffered coffee flasks. They pointed to the tower and its message. Tourists dunked rusks and refocused binoculars. Initially the cops pushed them away, but the scope of the cooling-tower broadcast was so extensive anyone could park on any road – primary or secondary – and enjoy the view. Eventually the scuffles settled and everyone watched it play out, together.

They stayed long after the phone was turned off and the video stopped. They watched the paint being scraped away with wire brushes and solvent, hoses and solutions. The breathless reporters with swept-back hair, the tourists, the government officials, the cops. They all stayed.

Transmission paint was cheap. And simple. Lash the dirty brown onto any surface. Wait for it to dry. Enter pin. Pair. Broadcast.

Post-cooling-tower-show, transmission paint was sold out, restocked and sold out again. The rush was led by street protesters, red berets, political challengers. Behind them the rest: small-time advertisers, the floggers of products, remedies, solutions. The hawkers and preachers and tyre repairmen. If you had a wall you had a stage. If you had a phone you had a broadcast. All you needed was transmission paint.

Back in ad land, the geeks figured out what the paint could mean for the consumer and the brand experience.

Entertainment.

Communication.

Etc.

Paint innovation was mandated and costed and assessed. Strategists plotted. Clients caught their collective breath.

But nothing could match club land.

Club VR had been fine, fun, entertaining in the sense that the future was fuzzy yet tangible. But the interface was inherently fake. The VR clubs were, despite much effort, mall kiddie pens with booze and pills.

Now, painted clubs stitched geolocation to the network, creating an interface with actual, physical depth. Now, once the punters paid and stepped through, the walls fell away. They could be taken anywhere. No matter who you were or where you went, the experience suddenly felt seamless. Limitless.

After years of burrowing down inside ourselves, we poured out of our houses – big and small, brick and tin, flat and shack – into the basements and the warehouses.

To touch, to hold hands, to kiss ... to blow it all up into hyper augmentation and exaggeration. To step inside, then out into the stars and the planets and the true mythical. Well, fuck. It was great.

Genital nappies – naps – became the accessories of my generation.

And yes, I explored as well. I slipped my nap on, zipped up my retro advertising pants, donned my wire frames, descended to the basements, paid my money and did what everyone else was doing.

It was a clear, assumed city agreement. Clubs and drugs and VR sex downstairs. Advertisers and government up top, controlling the veneer.*

Everyone else in the cracks.

'There is appeal,' said Mongezi at the time. 'If they weren't such monkeys with the avatars it could be wild, nè? But I felt a bit stupid

---

* To a degree. See the counterculture section of the Verwoerd Annex for full detail on the graf rebels and the use of retinal-pause subliminals to send messages within transmission-paint messaging.

at the end. You know, when you take that nap thing off and admit you were fucking the same shitty JPEG as everyone else.'

It was an offhand balcony conversation. A flippant comment. But it made both of us rich.

VR punters wanted fantasy. They wanted to fuck the woman or man of their dreams, and they wanted to look unbearably hot doing it.

Mogz's idea was simple: punters should compose avatars, not select them. They should wield the freedom of the four critical categories (face, ass, chest and legs). They should morph and blur identities. They should be able to pull together any mix of face and ass and have the result feel and look and taste right. None of it was new, but his brilliance was the jacking of open-source image software to deliver the fractional file sizes that allowed thousands of users to interact seamlessly within the club network – sexually and otherwise.

I knew none of these things. I barely knew what image resolution was. Nonetheless, about a month after our conversation, two things happened.

(1) Rick Cohen, a university associate, stumbled into my table at a Rosebank coffee shop, drunk, depressed and bemoaning the fact that he was closing down his VR club – the punters were dribbling away ... the fad was over.
(2) The following week Mongezi sent me a message:

It's done. The VR thing. It works. We should sell it.
Mgz

We sold it to Rick, who rebranded his city VR club as Mlungu's. He gave us fifteen per cent each.

Heels clicked through all night, down the concrete stairs, ominous rather than filthy, then into the reception area staffed by rippling Zimbabweans who patted them down, took their cash and pushed the trembling punters in.

Rick Cohen was a true businessman. He knew the underground hype would die, fast, and when it did he was already selling off virtual chunks of Mlungu's to sponsors. The bar counter, the tabletops, the urinals, the waitress's cleavage. He lured the brands with the promise of their own slice of the legend, virtual reality in perpetuity, blah blah.

Smarts aside, he was also connected. Within six weeks Mlungu's had formal office space at HHN. As the 'reputational head' of a new division, I had the job of making sure Mlungu's sponsors looked good.

'Mlungu's changes the VR game,' the street-pole slugs said.*

The door to the top floor of media life swung open, but instead of walking over the threshold I stepped back.

'What is it with you?' Angie taunted. 'When the suits arrive it's like you're back in nursery school.'

I changed corners many times. I logged in from the office, I logged in from home, I logged in at Mlungu's itself, but I always ended up in essentially the same position, just off the bar, on the side, watching the same scene play out over and over again.

'Are you actually drunk if you've been drinking at Mlungu's all day?' Rick asked quasi-seriously, more than once.

Being perpetually drunk was – in the context of Mlungu's – almost the same as being sober. Regardless of location or orientation, getting high and fucking – the combination, the marriage of the two – was the point. The only point. The perpetual point. Without drugs, even the new-generation interface became generic, the avatars recognisable, the stitching on the seams of the interface a little too predictable.

Drugs and fucking. Fucking and drugs.

---

* For full detail on the VR revolution, transmission paint, interface glasses, etc., consult Annex II of the Slovo Library, St John's campus.

Thus, yes, I was permanently drunk, but I was also, within the jagged reality of the club, the sober-minded guiding hand.

Chapter 5
I leaned back casually

By the time I fled to Eileen's flat, I had been running Mlungu's for over ten years and Angie and I had parted ways in every respect except the sharing of a residential address. We lived in the same building but, as in a classic TV series of your choosing, we hardly saw each other. The evening at Clarissa's had in fact been our first out together for months. I worked late, drank late, slept late, and she did the same, but according to a different sequence.

Eileen wasn't an affair and her flat wasn't our love nest. She was a sweet, plain, thin, twenty-three-year-old account manager with a wealthy, concerned daddy watching over her.

She gave me the spare keys to her flat in a rush. 'My grandmother,' she said, shoving them anxiously into my fist, 'in Cape Town. She's … she's … not well. At all. Will you feed Mozart?' She looked panicked, embarrassed. 'Sorry. I don't know who else to ask.'

No problem. 'Dog or cat?' I asked.

'Oh!' she barked with relief. 'Cat. Very self-contained. Female. Sleeps most of the day. This is my address.' She buzzed the details through. 'Parking bay, alarm codes, instructions on how to feed her. Once a day – should be pretty easy. I'll call as soon as I know what's going on.'

'Take your time.' I leaned back casually, pretending I wasn't already worried about fucking the whole thing up.

Chapter 6
I lit a cigarette and thought about my father

Lean. All in black. Daniel Craig beneath a half-smiling, ironic, clubby-cool exterior.

It was important to be clean and straight. Unflappable. They had to be able to recognise me. And they did.

They called my name.

Life passed like that. Me, avatar-black, striding in slow motion, ears primed, waiting for the call.

Years after he had stopped, become adult and all that, Mongezi pulled me aside. Skin bunched up around his eyes. He winced. It had looked like he was about to smile, as if the glory would flicker again. But he winced.

'You haven't had enough yet, Roy?'

'I can't do media management, Mogz. I just can't do it.'

'Sho. But clubs. You can't do those either. Not for so long. You just can't, my broe. It's gonna kill you.'

'Ah, but what a way to die!'

'It's a shitty way to die, Roy. Shitty.'

I had my reasons, then. I'm sure they made sense. Now I think maybe I just fell in love with a time. A place. An idea. For those first few years we thought we had the world in our hands. Planet earth. City of Joburg. We owned it all. We changed it on a whim. I met and married Angie in that place. Ceremony in Rosebank Church, reception at Mlungu's. We hatched the dragon. We hung on as it flew. That it would fly was never a question. Not to me anyway. I would be firmly on its back as we crashed through the atmosphere. It never occurred to me that we were already done. That change had come. And gone.

Year after year, hype cycle after hype cycle, there was nothing new. The revolution stalled at paint broadcasts and geo-located VR. Technologies were turned into advertising. Messages were bought, broadcast, sold. Clubs stayed clubs. The drugs evolved. There were additions to the technology, incremental shifts, but that next quantum leap ... well, it turned out to be a mirage. A myth, forming and swirling in the middle distance.

'You got money, my ninja. Money. You can do anything. Why don't you quit? I know Angie would love a change. Go overseas. France. The south of France. You could write a novel.'

'And Angie could paint.'

'Ja!' Mongezi's eyes lit, then faded, angry. 'Fuck you. Stay cynical like that and life will punish you.'

'Ag sorry, Mogz. Jammer. For real. It's just that Angie and me ... we struggle, nè? Even to be in the same room, if I'm honest, if she's honest, she'll tell you we struggle.'

'Well, fucking get a divorce then, you fuck. Do something. Anything. You have to do something.'

'I *do* do something. You people might need to accept that I am happy doing this.'

You people. Once it was us, all of us, together. We were powerful. Full. Stuffed. Then it was you people. I was the only one left, still at the bar, still zooming and refocusing. The rest were in meetings. Building houses. Having babies.

You people.

How did I get so angry? So lost? Where did that decade actually go?

Mongezi believed it was all my father. His death. My denial.

Roy, he would say. Roy, you can't. You have to. You can't. You must. Look. Look at it. At him. You can't just. Please. Roy. Please. Please.

But I didn't look. I would like to say it wasn't possible. That there was a mess inside that was simply too much. But really I could have.

Still, I chose not to. I turned away. Fuck Russle. Fuck parents. Family. There was never anything for me in that place. I was different. Others might need to look back, down, into the past. Me, I was headed in one direction.

Forward.

And then they let go. Mongezi drifted away. Angie too. Rick. The rest.

Me? I remained in rotation, swirling in tight, personal little circles.

Eileen, and the others like her, were the final evidence of my decade of decline. After I had pissed on my friends, after the wife and I had spat at each other, green and angry, I was adopted by a succession of thin, anxiety-ridden young girls. Girls who liked cats and struggled with men and worked far too well. Organisers. Anxious little beings. Filers of documents. Placers of calls.

And really, it was right. For what was I other than feral? Wild. Hungry. Hunting for affection I would instantly reject.

* * *

Eileen's flat eased my aches and awakened a sense of shame at my own shabby, juvenile existence. The place reeked of adherence to a life regime. From the well-used exercise bike to the bookshelf and its contents (Cormac McCarthy, Josie Blues, Mtutuzeli Matshoba, JG Ballard, Lesego Rampolokeng, Gabriel García Márquez, Vince Khumalo, Gore Vidal, Kagiso Nkuna, Zadie Smith, Zapiro, Calvin and Hobbes), the markers of structure and adult activity were everywhere.

Most attractive was sleeping in her bed, which I did shamelessly, making sure to ruffle the linen in the spare bedroom, where I was supposed to be. Her bed, full of the olfactory pleasures of the female nest, was my sanctuary. I wallowed in it.

I turned off my mobile and dropped naked into her soft, dark-pink bedding. I drained the red wine in my glass, poured another, drank that and went to sleep.

I dreamed of my father. He was chasing me. As usual.

With knives. Belt buckles. Broken bottles. He chased and I ran and it lasted for days, weeks, until eventually he stopped. Hands on knees. Panting. Staring at me. Exhausted. Tears in his eyes.

I woke up.

I sat in the lounge. I'd been out for a long time. I lit a cigarette and thought about my father.

He died when I was twenty, crashing into his coffin with a brain haemorrhage. He warranted a few column inches here and there, a mention on the news scroller, that kind of thing.

> *Russle Fotheringham, who played a single season for the Proteas and three seasons for the Gauteng Lions, and who started a second career as a DJ in the greater Gauteng area, died on Saturday of a brain haemorrhage. Fotheringham's symptoms were consistent with what has become known colloquially as Cell Brain. He is survived by his only son, Roy.*

Towards the end, just before the haemorrhage, my father had fallen into fluffy trance. The last time I had visited him he was spinning Markus Schulz obsessively in the lounge, finger in the air, eyes half closed.

'This,' he said, pulling the cans behind his ears and looking at me seriously, 'is actually very good stuff. People say it's too simple and too happy, but I'm telling you, this is good music.'

I took the Senheissers from him and plonked them on. It was standard four-to-the-floor trance, a simple, never-ending bass underneath a litany of equally simple, rising candy synths. Beats for children, sports back-tracks and junkies. I put my finger in the air. 'Someone pass me my lollipop.'

Russle Fotheringham took his headphones back.

He was all spindly legs and arms. A cigarette burned in the ashtray next to him. There was always one waiting, smoke curling. It was one of the marvels of my father, his ability to keep a smoke alive without ever really smoking it. He would grab it with long, accomplished fingers, toss the butt into his lips, give it the smallest nip possible and then lay it back in the groove.

This is the last image I have of him, the one burned into my brain: a tall, too-thin forty-year-old man in white shorts and a maroon vest, bobbing his head to candy trance, smoke rising from the ashtray, track listings scrawled in an uncontrolled hand on scraps of paper around his laptop.

I asked him how long he had been up. He intimated via a series of nods and eyebrow raises that it had been a long time. A looong time. We did our usual dance around my disapproval and that was that. He died the next day.

I walked through the house with cardboard boxes. The disks and the laptop and the playlists and associated DJ paraphernalia. I piled it all in, randomly lifting interesting items into an old cardboard primary school suitcase. The few boxes went into my boot, and then into my basement. Everything else to charity.

I rented the place to a succession of young families – people too busy creating their own memories to bother about mine.

So there I sat, naked in Eileen's sweet lounge, sucking on a cigarette, taking in the realisation that by smashing Clarissa's mirror I had probably destroyed the last career opportunity open to me in the country. Rick Cohen was a lot more than a club boss. Rick Cohen was a media mogul, an industry general. What he thought radiated out across our business in influential circles. The dinner could have been a reconciliation. It could have been an opportunity. The door had opened. The door had closed.

The sun was setting. My glasses sat ominously on the lounge table. A day and half out of contact was a lifetime. I decided to go all in and make it two. I went back to bed.

I turned on midway through the following day and waited for the messages.
    Nothing.

I opened a new bottle and poured a big glass of red.
    And another.
    I called work.
    No network.

I tried to log in and accept my fate, but there was nothing, not even an interface. Just the click of the lost Google API call. I dialled technical, but the call failed. There wasn't a single bar on the reception tower.

I turned the TV on.

Static.

Chapter 7
The occasional bark of what must have been a dog

Dry brown walls, stripped of their broadcast. Their colour. Their purpose. Dirty brown walls. Simple. Sagging.

I remember them above everything.

First and foremost, the brown.

I stuck my head out the window of Eileen's Tyrwhitt Mansions flat to see two free pigs – strange genetic cocktails, easily over 350 kilograms, big ears, straight snouts and that specifically curious air of anger and intelligence that belongs to the free pig – loping down the hill together, heads swivelling.

As they picked up speed a small street dog – a black and brown brak, compact and wiry, likely full of rabies – fell in behind them.

There was never any quiet in those first days. The air buzzed with the futility of a million abandoned alarm systems – cars, houses, offices – and their desperate, decaying batteries. As the door panels forgot the thumbprints of their owners, as the last of the power trickled out of the grid, the electric yells merged into a crescendo.

And always the brown. The crushing, dirty brown. It had been decades since I had seen a simple painted wall, a wall without movement, without a message. The brown was bad, of course, but it was the uniformity that was so hard to digest. It stretched forever. And the closer you looked, the more alarming it was. Decay. Cracking walls. Rivers of damp, creeping, swelling. Pipes falling off the walls, cable ties and piles of bundled wiring. Slumping angles, falling arches.

As my eyes adjusted to the new vista, they slowly accepted. No colours. No messages. No accents. No shading. Just brown, from sky to floor, top to bottom, wall to wall.

    Brown.

I lost sight of the pigs. The incessant whine of the alarms, the recurring crescendos, shook me awake and forced me to consider. To think.

I ran into Tyrwhitt Avenue, then jerked right and ran uphill for another fifty metres.

No people.

No movement.

Just the alarms. Just the brown. And the occasional bark of what must have been a dog.

Chapter 8
Just one

My name is Roy Fotheringham.

I am a little over forty years old. I walk with a shuffle developed in my twenties to indicate some kind of street/club cool and that I am now unable to shake, even though I know how it looks at this age.

I am wiry and lean. Lifestyle lean, not gym lean. I smoke when they're around, and I don't when they're not.

I drink. Of course.

I am currently in shock.

I have destroyed my life, in small increments, each thoughtless step adding unbearable weight. The framework, the superstructure of Roy, has been knocked and beaten and rendered fundamentally fragile. All it took was one punch. A single fist.

Everything is over.

There is nothing left for me in this city. And therefore this country.

I will never work again.

Yes, there is that curious liberation. I am free in the world, and once the administrative details of my departure are finalised I will be able to go anywhere, do anything.

Problem.

There is nothing I want to do. There is nowhere I want to go. There is, in fact, only an echo at the centre of me. It has been filled for all these years by work, so called, management activities and the rest. Now that these are gone there is nothing but the reverb.

Shock.

Look, from this distance it all comes off as infantile and deluded in a childish, indulgent way. But at the time it was real. The shock. The horror of what I'd done. At Clarissa's, and at the coalface of my pitiful life.

Jozi was empty. The people were gone. There was nothing.

Let me put it this way. Advertising and media and Mlungu's was my life. It wasn't much of a life, and it may not have meant much to anyone else, but it was the only life I had, and in that sense it defined the length and breadth of my personal universe.

The shock radiating through my core was personal. I had pulled the pin at Clarissa's and everything exploded.

It seems deluded and indulgent now, but at the time everything was truly my fault. I had, somehow, caused this.

It was me.

I did it.

Now I would have to deal with it.

I stopped drinking. At first the adrenalin spur was so strong I didn't need a drink, didn't even think of it, and by the time I fully realised that I hadn't had one in hours, I knew well enough. This was the time. My time. There would be no other.

I was as practical as I could possibly be, but I was also driven by a cacophony of competing, self-referential voices. There was the observer taking notes, lining up and prioritising the never-ending series of things that were not right. There was the reactor, the violent screamer who wouldn't shut up at the shock of it, the emptiness. And there was the pacifier, the steady, assuring voice claiming calm and balance, resisting the reality with the understanding that this was all, well, a misunderstanding. Then there was the homosapien – who just wanted to see, to touch, to speak to another human being. Who was constantly clocking the horizon for one. Just one.

Chapter 9
Shotguns falling from my arms

I brushed my teeth. It felt like the right thing to do.

Just a glance. Casual, thoughtless. A quick check-in with my abluting self. But suddenly I was trapped, locked into the return view. My hair was grey. Completely, comprehensively, shockingly grey.

I was a different person.

Older, but softer. New, but decaying.

I examined the hairs, the impact of the colour on the lines and pits of my face. Zoom in. Zoom out.

Stunned, I could hardly look. I peered at the mirror out of the corner of my eye. But still, it was there. Grey.

Eventually I jumped (literally, there was a strange spring in my step) into the shower. The water was warm, but cooling noticeably.

I got dressed, grabbed the keys and let myself out of the flat.

Up Tyrwhitt Avenue. As I broke into an army-type jog I realised I was going to the police station at the top of the road. As I ran I thought of my new grey hair. Then I realised I hadn't run in decades – sweat broke through the freshness of the shower in waves. Will the water stay hot? I asked myself.

I stopped running. Strode up the hill.

Cars lost on the road. One or two piled into walls and street poles, glass confetti littering the street. An ancient 1990s red Volkswagen hatchback in the middle of the road. Empty. I popped the boot but it was clean. No jack, no wheel spanner.

Up to the Rosebank Hotel, then left to the police station, a half-brick, half-prefab oddity. The doors open, reception empty. A stiff breeze ran through it. I felt cool, then hot. Sweat.

I grabbed a set of keys off the front desk and went into the back. The interview rooms were empty, also the holding cells. There were four offices. The superintendent's and duty sergeant's were vacant, but there was a newspaper in one of the desk drawers. I grabbed it to take it with me, then realised I hadn't brought a fucking bag, so how was I going to carry the guns?

I opened the newspaper and spread it on the desk. Tenth of April. The day after I fell into Eileen's flat. The usual:

Behind the global youth. Chasing down the graf rebels. Crime. Violence. Service delivery. Corruption. Soccer. Cricket. Rugby. A double-spread free-pig feature – same old thing. Their intelligence levels. Pig steroids, fat cells and the frontal cortex. What a free pig actually feels. Why they run. Where they run to. Five Things to Do When You Encounter a Free Pig (1. Don't stare. 2 Don't start a fight. 3. Don't laugh. 4. Be respectful. 5. Pigs want to be left alone as much as we do ...).

I crumpled the front page of the paper, stuffed it into my pocket and searched for guns. Eventually I ended up back in the reception area and there it was, a recessed glass-fronted gun cupboard with four shotguns inside. I used a paper spike to smash the window, first with the spike itself and then beating the shards out of the sides and corners with the pedestal.

There were two boxes of shells in the drawer underneath the cupboard. I spilled the shells onto the desk and then stuffed them into all available pockets. I thought about trying to load one of the guns, but I'd never even held a gun before.

I jogged back down Tyrwhitt Avenue stuffed with bullets, shotguns falling from my arms. I realised as I ran and stumbled and dropped a gun, then another, as I bent to pick the second up and a few shells fell from my top pocket, that this was a real risk. I felt eyes watching me. I heard feet sneaking up into the backyard of my mind. As I reached the entrance to Tyrwhitt Mansions I stopped and swivelled. I glared back out at the world, radiating survivor vibes in case someone was watching and thinking anyone who carries guns like that must be an easy target.

I ran up the stairs to Eileen's front door, dropped the guns outside with a clatter, fished the keys out of my pocket and got very confused with a lock I'd opened many times. I felt the eyes watching, again. Eventually I forced the door open, threw the guns inside, then myself, and slammed it.

I stank. Sweat and fear.

I couldn't stop moving.

Tore my clothes off and jumped back in the shower.

I let the water pour over me until it went truly cold, then I dried myself. I caught a glimpse of my grey-haired reflection in the mirror.

I tried the TV again. Checked the lights (dead), then the stove (dead), then the mains board – switches up.

I threw my naked body back on Eiléen's bed and waited for a sound. But there was nothing. Just the smell of Eileen on the sheets, the pillow.

I tried to cry. I felt like I should. There was a slight moistness in the corner of my left eye, but otherwise nothing. I grabbed my dick and my balls in one hand and lifted my legs into the air. A light breeze blew over my exposed ass. It was the calmest I'd felt since I woke up. I stayed like that for a while, in self-defence.

Chapter 10
Five

I took a cold shower, created a seat on Eileen's bedroom windowsill with pillows, and waited.

And waited.

I spent the day there. I watched the pigs and the dogs on their circuit, counted the heads. Five.

Chapter 11
The only reliable thing in the circumstances

Now, dangling over the cusp, I can tell you it was beautiful. I can carve and clip around the edges. I can look into that orange Cresta horizon, at that sagging water tower, and say the end of the world rescued me.

Of course I'm laughing at the younger me; the one who was actually there. The one who filled a cash-in-transit van with ten foraged barrels of diesel and drove south down the M1 crying like a girl.

The van, a vehicular pit bull, was shaped for attack as defence. I found it, door open, half a Tupperware of tripe and rice and morogo on the seat, white and green crumbs spilled on the brown plastic and down under the pedals, parked to the side of a yellow petrol station on Jan Smuts. Both front doors were open. The keys dangled in the ignition.

From a distance it had all the signs of a super vehicle. Of something from another time and place. In my mind these vans had always been something extra-human, apart from the prosaic realties of cars and highways. Up close, however, things were different. It smelled and looked like a prehistoric, atavistic creation, the panels consisting of buckled, reinforced, bulletproof sheet metal. Its snout broad and angled and ready, fronted by a black grill designed to crush and bounce. The thin front window squashed into place. The glass was many centimetres thick and comprehensively bulletproof, its density creating a blue tint inside the driver's cabin, which in turn was tight and defensive – a cockpit made habitable only by a gushing aircon system. The two side-window slits were essentially decorative, and the rest pure fortress. The back section literally a vault on wheels. Impenetrable.

It was a van built to be shot at, bombed and attacked. Built to keep its cash guts from spilling out, at any cost.

It was also the only reliable thing in the circumstances – a vehicle I could use to smash and grind and rip my way through fences, over the spikes and razor wire, and into houses. That the van took diesel was painful, but the pain was offset by its smash-anything ability, and by the fact that no thumb was required to start it.

Also, it had a CD player – an ancient front-end loader that looked too dusty and scratched to ever work, but which actually did. An extreme, and welcome, cultural oddity. There were a few old Maskandi disks in the glovebox, a Zwakhe Mbuli, a Brenda greatest hits and an original copy of Vinny Da Vinci's *Africanism*.

Chapter 12

Tears of ass pain

My grandfather Barnaby Fotheringham had been pathological about miscalculating the N1 slipway out of Joburg. I remembered him freaking out on one of our rare family holidays, as my father drifted left, flirting with Soweto.

'Watch it, Rus, watch it!' Grandfather Barnaby barked.

'Jesus, Dad, we have to go left here. It's Soweto, not the dark forest.'

'Just watch it's all I'm saying. Friends of mine got lost here – ended up God knows where …'

Born into a wealthy family of timber farmers in the Natal Midlands, Barnaby Fotheringham had conspired to lose his farm, his fortune, his self-respect and pretty much everything else thanks to an unreasonable attraction to the fine sport of polo. The great loss of the Fotheringham fortune wasn't much discussed in our family, for obvious reasons, but from what I could gather the nut of it was that Barnaby had underestimated the time his father, and his father before him, had spent on the farming part of running a farm. He left the technicalities to the farm manager, who in turn left much of his load to his manager, and so on. When the timber market collapsed, Barnaby returned from the polo fields to find the outer shell of a business – the insides had rotted away. All he had left was a stable of ponies.

Thus, Russle was born a rich kid. He left high school a middle-class kid, and he dropped out of university to pursue his cricket career the son of a living cautionary tale.

As I headed down the N1 in my armoured van, loaded up with supplies and jerry cans of diesel, Barnaby's voice echoed in my head. 'Just don't go too far left. The Bloem slip road is the same as the one to Soweto. You have to go left, but then straight. Left then straight.'

I let the wheel drift left, then pulled straight. The rain smashed on the van's armoured window, turned into hail and smashed again.

The N1 south was simultaneously reassuring and evocative of all the things I was trying not to think about. Orange Farm loomed up on the right, the township veneer familiar. On the left, Vanderbijl Park and Sasolburg, the cooling towers also reassuring, yet ominous in their lack of vapour. How many times had I travelled this road in my life? Fifty? Eighty? A hundred even?

Just after crashing through the lowered boom at the Kroonvaal toll plaza (another in an ongoing set of satisfying armoured van experiences), I stopped in a sunny post-storm spot on the highway and considered my father's music collection, contained within a very old, brown cardboard school suitcase, my name stencilled in big, childlike letters on the lid.

The loss of the cloud – disconcerting in many ways – was most disruptive in terms of access to music. I was constantly patting my pockets, expecting contact. I carried my mobile in hope, but it lay silent, flashing the connection-failure notice ad infinitum, Bambi looking for his mom. Which meant my life's music collection was scattered across the now dissipated cloud. Few of the cars, players, glasses or devices I had picked up along the way had anything in their memory banks aside from playlists; requests for beats lost to the sky.

The first cover in the suitcase had my father's hopeful spider-writing scrawled over the front. 'Schulz – Demo Mix 1 – Final,' it read.

Two tightly folded A4 email printouts fell from the jewel case as I opened it.

> Thanks Markus. That's exciting. I'll get something through to you asap.
> Best
> Russle

-----Original Message----
From: Markus Schulz [mailto:markus@coldharbour.com]
Sent: Friday, June 19, 2011 4:28 PM
To: Russle Fotheringham
Subject: Re: great

I think send me a sample of what you're thinking. It's best to have the conversation revolve around something tangible – if we're both listening to the same thing we can make appropriate decisions.

Let me know when you're ready and we can Dropbox it. We might need to get you over to Miami to work on it when the time comes ...

Peace
markus

On 17/06/2011 4:05 PM, Russle Fotheringham wrote:
Thanks markus – that means a lot, coming from you. Delighted you enjoyed it as it was a bit of a departure for me.

I'm actually putting together an odd kind of mix at the moment. Plays with some of the ideas that came out in the Cape Town set, but maybe in a more steady, hook-filled way than that gig, which got a little wild and broken.

If you like it, it could be a good project to explore ?

Lemme know
r

-----Original Message----
From: Markus Schulz [mailto:markus@coldharbour.com]
Sent: Friday, June 12, 2011 3:45 PM
To: Russle Fotheringham
Subject: great

russle

just wanted to say wow. Wow wow wow. That set last friday at Immortals. It just blew me out of the water. Completely unexpected and weirdly beautiful. And I see and hear a lot of sets.

I'm looking for something fresh for Coldharbour. Would you consider a project within that realm?

Let me know, and thanks for the experience

markus

19 June 2011.

My father was dead three months later. He had never mentioned the Schulz exchange to me, but then I was simply a son, riddled with emotion and judgement. It would have been safer to keep quiet.

The emails explained a lot. I had always wondered about the sudden swing to trance. More than being annoying, which it definitely was, it was also odd. Russle Fotheringham had always been a deep house man. Throw in a few breakbeats and some of those slower hip-hop thumpers and that was him really. Deep house. And then suddenly, just before the end, he was all trance.

I put the disk in the front loader.

I left the CD box and printouts on the passenger seat, along with the mementos I had culled from Eileen's flat, all stuffed, together with various last-minute additions, into a large green Woolworths carrier bag. A few of her old shirts, a blue skirt, a bottle of old perfume and a newish-looking pair of white panties I had found in the back of her cupboard.

At the bottom of the Woolworths bag was a small chequered wallet I had pulled from behind her underwear while rummaging. I unzipped it. Inside, a stuffed plastic baggie of what looked like very old weed, a matchbook from a hotel bar (the Balalaika, of all places) and a totally out-of-proportion, scrunched-up, king-size Rizla pack.

Weed.

A tingle of excitement, rooted in my early HHN balcony days with Mogz, the only time I had properly engaged with grass ... a time when its jagged whack to my psyche felt more thrilling than dangerous. I zipped the wallet back up and flipped through Eileen's CDs.

Bobby McFerrin.

The Pet Shop Boys.

Bump Volume 3.

Peter Gabriel.

Deep Forest.

Eileen must have been several years older than I had always

thought she was. Either that or she had inherited her father's music collection, in toto.

Fun Lovin' Criminals.

I extracted the weed wallet again and rolled a terrible, mangled joint as the first run of angelic voices came together at the trance crossroads. The girl voice began to sing: 'There's something in the air / Baby, we just don't care / I see you in the mist tonight / Thula thula baby, thula, alright / We sleep / Tonight ...'

There was some relief, I thought as I rolled the joint, in knowing that my father hadn't simply lost his musical mind towards the end, but was rather working on career progression with a famous Germanic-American DJ. It gave him credibility – something he needed a lot of with me. I particularly enjoyed the tiny slip of vernacular into the vocal. The girl sounded as generic as trance girls always did, but that one word – thula – gave the track a touch of something different. Mr Schulz would surely have loved it.

Stalks poked through the spit-addled mess of a joint in several places. There was no discernible end to the construction, so I just stuffed it in my mouth, holding fingers and thumbs over as many of the holes as I could and burning my right forefinger badly in the tussle with the matchbook.

The van erupted in a cloud of green. As did my lungs. The coal fell straight off, into my lap, and I exploded out the door. Four more failed attempts later, I realised I was stoned. I turned the CD player off.

Silence.

Stale heat in my mouth.

I sat in the middle of the highway, the wet white lines dividing my ass cheeks.

I got straight up again. The wet tar was boiling.

Back in the driver's seat, tears of ass pain prickled behind my eyes. I drove, excruciatingly slowly at first, south. I hit play on the CD and felt better located, as if I was suddenly in place. The right place.

I bopped to my father's demo for a while, then stopped it and let the whistle of the wind through the gaps in the van's bodywork take over. I forced my arm through the slit of a driver's window and hung it out while the van weaved back and forth across all four lanes. I tried to stick my head out of the window like a dog. It wouldn't fit.

Off the highway, to Parys.

Green and white coffee shops, waiting. Landscapes and wildlife art on the walls, waiting.

I pulled into a rest stop at the bottom of the town, overlooking the Vaal River. I scaled the old sagging fence, pulled off my clothes and jumped in.

I swam to the middle of the river and lay naked on an expansive black rock, unfolding my whiteness and asking the early afternoon sun to sear it while my mind rumbled on and on and on.

With the sun baking my hake-white body, the faces and the beats and the spikes and the colours bubbled over my mind's eye, the sound of the river and the power of the weed winding it all tighter and tighter until I opened my eyes and let the relief wash over me. Somehow, in the midst of the mess, right smack in the centre of it, I appeared to have been set free.

Back at the van, I put my glasses on again, checked one last time for a log-in screen, then threw them in the river.

Through to Kroonstad. Trucks falling against themselves, waiting.

The sign to Ficksburg. The idea that maybe a few old ravers like my father were still out there at Rustlers, eyes blazing.

I pulled in at the Engen 1-Stop on the Joburg side of Bloem, rejecting the Shell Russle was always loyal to, and rammed the van through the Quick Shop glass doors, running right through to the Wimpy at the back of the building.

I stomped to the toilet, which was clean and expectant, the attendant's folded paper towel peppered with hopeful coppers. I pissed all over the sinks, and all over the floor. I walked the full length of the restroom, steering a spiralling yellow arc out in front of me, spraying the toilet doors and ending with the paper towel, pissing it and the coppers into a mess on the floor.

I zipped up and marched back to the van. En route I grabbed a few bags of crisps, some Jack's popcorn and three warm Cokes from the rancid freezer. I held my nose tightly, denying the rotting braai packs. Outside, I sucked diesel with my hosepipe, a diabolical, exhaustive effort involving an hour-long search for a set of keys able to unlock the underground storage tank.

And so I went. Trying to stay left, swerving always around the stranded vehicles, crying occasionally, thinking of my father and my youth and the life I had abandoned before it abandoned me. I stopped where I felt the need, the urge, and I destroyed as much as I could en route, battering the van into houses, resorts and hotels, bursting randomly into lounges and kitchens. I pissed on floors. I shat an increasingly fluid stool onto dining room tables and the beds of sweet teenage girls.

I spat a lot. The diesel was permanently slick over my tongue. I drank warm Coke and fruit juice and bottled water and I spat.

I burned a twisted trail. Colesberg. Graaff Reinet. Beaufort West. Oudtshoorn. George. Mossel Bay. De Rust. Jansenville. Somerset East. Kenton-on-Sea. Bathurst. De Doorns. Butterworth. Elliot. Barkly East. Kokstad. Pietermaritzburg. Cape Town.

I abandoned the stockpiling as I finished my supplies. All I really needed was the hosepipe for diesel. The rest was on tap. Bags of crisps, boxes of biscuits, cans of beans, etc.

I lurched from house to hotel to garage driven only by an evolving desire to shit and piss on all signs of life.

I ripped the houses apart, developing an addiction to the nuances of the South African suburb in the process. The placement of the kitchen, the type of duvets used, the clothes and underwear and school projects and mobiles and glasses and lipstick. Each was the same, yet ever so slightly geared to its owners. I was fascinated. I took mental notes as to structure and design and composition before I kicked it all apart.

Why was I destroying? What led me to shit on the pages of family photo albums? Even now, all these years later, I can't answer.

Suffice to say I was surviving.

Every now and then I would run across a pack of wild dogs or a cluster of free pigs. The dogs would watch me from a distance, tongues lolling as they considered the anomaly. The pigs, secure in their size and their hunger and their extended frontal cortex, simply foraged. Once I saw a lone cow, suddenly wild, static on the horizon.

But the encounters were few and far between. Reality was empty.

Was it weeks?

Months?

I came to some kind of stop at the Blaauwbosch Game Lodge and Rest Camp, perched on the Baviaanskloof mountains of the Eastern Cape. I swam in the resort's ice-cold pool for days and lay in the sun, letting my skin roast an even dark brown.

I bullied the van through the resort's kitchen wall and, defying the rotten meat and pools of blood on the floor, used the well-stocked larder to cook real vegetarian food on the gas cooker. I drank expensive fizzy drinks and watched the sun set and rise and set and rise and set and rise.

I smoked all Eileen's weed. I muttered and walked. Prowled, resisting the urge to defecate and piss, forcing myself to use a toilet again, dreaming each day that I was working to some kind of plan and that, ultimately, I would emerge better for it.

I started reading: through the Wilbur Smiths and all the other resort pulp and then more widely, into the dusty colonial history, ending, finally, with a tatty, broken copy of Deneys Reitz's *Commando*. I remember sitting perched on the low front wall of my suite's private patio overlooking the Klein Karoo, following Reitz and his Boers in my mind as they ran up and through the country in search of a battle they could win. Eventually they ended up at the foot of the Zuurberg, not fifty kilometres from Port Elizabeth and, I calculated roughly, not far at all from where I sat reading. They considered how far they had come, straight through the British lines, to a point where they were looking down on the sea, the literal edge of things. They could hardly attack the city, but as the British moved around them they thought seriously of it.

I closed the book.

I needed a war.

I needed an enemy.

I needed to fight.

CHAPTER 13
Suddenly claustrophobic

I ran at her. We hugged furiously, wildly. Even when she felt my erection she didn't pull away. She clung, instead, to this last thread.

We fucked immediately, our hands finding each other with a deeper desperation than the need for names or stories. Against the black grill of the armoured van. She yelped at the heat. I rammed it home like a wild animal. She responded in kind.

Her name was Babalwa.

'It means "Blessed",' she said, filling the space as we pushed away from each other. 'I was the second. And the last.'

I looked over my shoulder, wondering suddenly if we were alone.

'There's no one else,' Babalwa said. 'Just us.' She leaned against the grill, her brown skirt pulled back down to above her knees. She looked in her early twenties. Thin. Head closely shaved. Neutral brown T-shirt to go with the skirt. Gentle acne bumps across her skin. A girl in a young boy's body, her small breasts and big, rounded eyes accentuated by the shaved head.

'So ...' She leaned back further, posing a little. 'Would you like to step into my parlour?' She waved behind her, at the row of semi-detached houses. Whitewashed with green-and-black trim and red-and-white stoeps, the units started at the top of a savagely steep incline and rocketed half the way down to the city streets. She gave me the tour.

'Since I was a little girl I always wanted to live here, in this house, with the view and everything. Long before the dealers took over again,' she said as we opened and shut doors. 'When it happened I thought, why not? I'm the only person left, I can just take one. So I did. The one I always looked at when I was a girl. Took me a few weeks to clean the fungus out but ... time's not an issue, eh?'

We stood in the neat pine-and-white kitchen, considering each other in the afternoon light.

I had driven into PE spurred by a new, Reitz-inspired understanding of the place. By a sudden desire for adventure; movement and action and all those things.

I came into the city via the modest highway leading in from the northern beaches. At what looked like the beginning of the docks, at the big red watchtower, I caught site of a very large flagpole at the top of a hill. I turned right, on instinct, then right again. At the base of the hill was a spiralling, climbing path, surrounded by mosaic art and the placards and historical-info signage of a public space. Above the path, up the hill, was the flagpole, surrounded by low walls and more education props. The pole and its walls fronted a squat pyramid and a lighthouse. They crowned the hill, and were surrounded by the bright colours and graffiti scaffoldings of a community skatepark.

I skirted the lower perimeter, then turned left up the hill, and up at the top was a living, breathing female.

Simple as that.

Babalwa pulled a chair from under the kitchen table and shoved it in my direction.

'Tea? Coffee?' she asked.

'Jesus. Really? Yes. Uh, tea. Tea would be fantastic.'

She opened a cupboard door and extracted a silver camping kettle. 'Water stopped ages ago,' she said, taking the kettle out the tiny back door onto the small metre-square back stoep, where a gas cooker and water tank lay waiting.

'Nice set-up. Take you long?' I leaned back in my chair to get my head around the door.

'Food?' Babalwa ignored my question.

'Nah. I'm full of shit already. Been eating Engen 1-Stop all day.'

'Ah.' She walked back into the kitchen, pulled her chair out and sat down. Then she reached a formal, bony young hand out to me. 'OK, so, I'm Babalwa. And you are?'

'Roy,' I replied.

'Roy ...' She tittered as we shook hands. 'Great. Roy. Roooy.' She stretched my name out between us. 'I have definitely never met a Roy before. And where does Roy come from?'

'Joburg.'

'Damn. And you drove all the way down here—'

'Well, kinda. I mean, really I've just been driving, you know. Looking. For something. For somebody.'

'And now you're found her.'

'I guess.'

'And what did Roy do before all this?' Babalwa waved at the world surrounding us.

'Um, advertising. Writing ads. And then recently running one of the VR clubs. You know, with the glasses.'

'Wow. Nice.' Babalwa gushed a little, with no obvious sign of irony.

'And you?' I ventured. Our eyes had been skirting the periphery of contact since we came inside, avoiding the intimacy already forged. Now she looked at me directly, smiled vaguely, then adjusted and gazed past me, at the wall.

'Nothing as fancy. Sorry.' Her fingers toyed with a splinter of wood that had come loose from the tabletop. 'Call-centre agent. "Ngqura Development Project, how may I assist you?"' Babalwa stood to attend to the kettle. 'You stink, by the way,' she said on her way out to the stoep. 'Either I'm going to have to move upwind or you're gonna need to take a bath.'

'Uh, sorry, I kind of left the lodge where I was on impulse. Didn't think I would find anyone to offend.' I was shy. Suddenly claustrophobic. I considered bolting back to the van and hitting the road again, then swallowed the reflex. 'So, do you know what the fuck happened?' I asked.

Babalwa came through the back door with two steaming mugs of tea. Mine read 'World's Best Dad', the words held aloft by an overly round brown bear of the generic Paddington/Pooh variety. Hers bore the word 'Love' in a large font, surrounded by a forest of red hearts in receding sizes.

'Later, Roy, let's talk about it later. But no, I don't know what the fuck happened.' She sat down behind her mug, voice shaky. 'I woke up and I was alone. That's it.' She blinked the beginnings of a tear out of her left eye. 'But we've got plenty of time. Tell me something fascinating. Tell me about Jozi. I've never been. They say it's got everything.'

And so we sat at Babalwa's pine kitchen table and talked about nothing. About Joburg and PE and work and advertising and call centres and lovers and salaries and mothers and jealous aunts – our stories overlapping hopelessly, both of us embellishing to ensure we travelled as far away as possible, for as long as possible.

Babalwa Busuku was born and raised in PE, on the southern edge of the New Brighton township, into the same compressed poverty as everyone else. Her mother was a maid/manager at a B&B on the beachfront, her father a shop steward at the Volkswagen plant. Her grandmother worked as a maid for the headmistress of Erica Girls Primary School. 'I got to go to Erica for primary, hence the accent, the coconut vibe and the call-centre gig,' she offered sarcastically. 'Of course, Gogo got too old to clean just before I hit high school and the head lady moved to Cape Town so back I went – ekasi.'

The call centre was her third job after school, her university applications terminated by money. And the rest, as she told it, was typical. Too many responsibilities, not enough money. So many dreams, not enough hours in the day to add them up.

She was sparing, letting each sentence out carefully, but the words flew free once released. I thought suddenly of Angie and her verbal violence, the way her words attacked a room, any room. I thought also of the agency people, the theatricality with which they delivered the simplest sentences.

Humility, I thought. Maybe that was all it was. Nonetheless, it made her pretty. Her face shone from the inside, a glimmer rising from below the surface. The fuck against the grill rushed sneakily across the my brain, the urgency of her fingers on the elastic of my boxer shorts.

She stopped.

'You can't keep looking at me like that, please. You're scaring me.'

'Jesus.' I jumped a little in my chair. 'Fuck. Sorry. I can imagine.

You've got a strange-smelling gorilla in your kitchen giving you the eye. Sorry. Sorry sorry sorry. Listen, should we get out of here? What's the friendly city of PE got to offer?'

She deflated at my apology and I realised just how wound up she had been. 'Um, shit, I don't know. I mean ... we can do anything we want. Anything. That's what's so horrible.' Tears flowed down her face. She held her hands in her lap, her gnawed fingers flipping the splinter of wood over and over.

'Excellent!' I said, a few of my own tears also making a break. 'Goddam. You just don't know how great it is to see someone else's pain.' I grabbed her hand and pulled her from the table. 'Let's go to the beach.'

We drove down to the beach in the van and I was suddenly very aware of the chaos that reigned inside my vehicle. The shotguns piled up in the back, the stench of sweat and lingering piss and petrol, the hosepipe curled like a snake, the scattered Simba packets and baked bean cans.

'Seriously, Roy. When we get back I'm gonna run you a proper bath. For shiza. Then we need to clean this pit or trade it out for something else. It's disgusting. You've let yourself go.' Babalwa clipped her seat belt in and glared at me. 'You stink. Sies.'

She directed us down to Kings Beach in embarrassed silence. Ours was the only car in the parking lot. 'Only car here,' I offered pointlessly.

'Race you!' Babalwa leaped from the cesspit and ran down the footpath to the beach, disappearing over a small dune. I ran after her to see her pulling her clothes off at the shoreline and jumping into the waves in underwear she must have snuck on at some stage.

The water was flat. Tiny waves rolled in and released themselves humbly onto the shoreline. The beach was about three-quarters of a kilometre wide, sandwiched between a small harbour wall, where the loading cranes hung limp in the evening breeze, and the entertainment zone, where the fast-food outlets sat waiting. After my swim I lay wet in the sand, watching Babalwa bodysurf. I thought of a hot bath while I pondered the girl in the waves, already an inscrutable force in my life.

'Look,' she said, eventually flopping down on the sand next to me. 'It's too much. I'm gonna help you run a bath and then you and I are going to retire to our corners. May I suggest, before your bath, you find a mattress or something to sleep on. I need space. I haven't spoken to a human being for over a month.'

* * *

She was gone when I woke on the minuscule lounge couch the next morning. There was a note on the kitchen table.

Roy
Gone for a walk. See you later.
Tea and long-life in the cupboard.
The rest is up to you.
Me

I made myself a cup on the tiny back stoep and eventually found the bread bin tucked away in the far corner of the kitchen, under a shelf with four mugs dangling off it. I carved two slices off the crumpled home-made loaf, which was surprisingly fresh, given its almost total lack of form. I opened the unplugged fridge in instinctive hope, looking for butter or some such. Inside there was simply a collection of durables. A blizzard of jams from Jenny's Farm Stall, Bovril, Marmite and then spreads and spices. Oregano. Mixed herbs. Woolworths spicy dessert crumble. An open carton of long-life milk. I considered the Bovril, decided against it, and went out onto the front porch to eat my dry bread and drink my tea.

The morning cast a benevolent light. I could see why Babalwa the child had fallen so heavily for this particular cottage. The sheer drop down into the city on the left created a panoramic view of the bay, a view of the world really. The blue world. The sea air was fresh and clean, light ripples of wind creating a salty texture on the tongue. Directly across from the porch was the Donkin Reserve, a chunk of lawn, maybe a hundred square metres, with a large triangular monument and what looked like a small white lighthouse perched off to the right.

I sat on a small, rickety fold-out chair on the porch – a chair I was pretty sure wasn't there the day before. Had she put it out for me?

The bread was good, peppered with herbs and fresh spices. I sipped the tea and wished that long-life milk tasted less like a school camping trip.

The reserve lawn was scrappy, scattered palm trees holding their form against thick, rising clusters of harsh Eastern Cape grass. Soon, I thought, the grass would win.

Babalwa's head appeared to the left, rising quickly up the slope.

'You found the bread. Good.'

'Ja, morning, thanks.' I raised my tea mug in mock salute.

She was wearing white shorts, a white Castle Lager T-shirt and slip-slops. She leaned carefully against the white picket fence.

'Look, sorry, I've been thinking and there are a few things I need to clear up.' Her eyes were fiery.

'Sure. Shoot.'

'First, what happened yesterday.'

'What, on the van?'

'Yes, that.' Her eyebrows arched. 'What you—'

'Ay, no, you mean what we—'

'Oh fuck, it doesn't matter. It's fine. The situation and everything. All I'm saying is, it won't happen again. Please. Just stay away from me physically. Try not to touch me. I mean, not touching, eish, not that kind of touching. You know what I mean. Yes?'

'Well, fuck. I mean, Jesus. It takes two to—'

'Oh please. It takes one. It takes you.'

'OK. OK.' I fell into the furthest corner of my chair and raised defensive palms. 'I stay away. Totally away.'

'Thanks.' Babalwa folded her arms, looking ludicrously serious in her cricket clothes. 'The other thing is, I would appreciate it if you moved in next door. Made a place of your own and all that. I would ... I would just feel easier. You know?'

'Sure. I know.' Tears welled. I stood to return my mug to the kitchen. 'Don't worry,' I called back over my shoulder. 'I know how freaky this is. I know exactly how freaky.' I placed my mug overly carefully into the sink and turned on the red tap. The pipes groaned, then screamed. I turned it off, then hung my head over the sink.

Babalwa's feet flopped down the ancient wooden floors to the kitchen doorway.

'Look, it doesn't mean—' she offered eventually.

'Leave it,' I said to the sink. 'Trust me, I know what you mean. I'm as scared as you are.'

'I just need—'

'Trust me, Babalwa, I understand. I really do understand.'

'I'll help you move?'

'Sure. Let's do that.'

Chapter 14
I hopped around on my other leg

I kicked down the door to the adjacent semi, carving up the skin on my right ankle as it caught on the edge of the broken Yale lock. 'Fuck! Fuck fuck fucking mother of God! You got first aid?' I bellowed at Babalwa, who was standing in the street behind me, arms folded, amused.

'Actually I do, Chuck. Stay there. I don't want you bleeding in my house.'

She came back carrying a full see-through medical box with a red cross on the top. She dropped it next to me and retreated.

'The cross glows in the dark. Found it in a 7-Eleven just after—' She broke off mid-sentence.

I opened the box and used some of the contents to bandage the wound, which wasn't as impressive as I had first thought. A scratch with some blood really. 'Where do the larnies live?' I asked. 'Clearly nowhere around here. I need supplies.'

'Walmer. Big walls. Swimming pools. Golf.'

'Perfect. How do I get there?'

'Seriously? You're not even going to clean that out with salt water or anything? You're just gonna wrap a bandage on like that? Damn, who raised you, boy?' Babalwa knelt down next to me, unwrapped the bandage and said, 'Wait – I'll be back.'

She returned with a bowl of salt water and proceeded to clean and bandage my foot as I hopped around on my other leg, painfully aware of the sparse nature of my boxer shorts.

'Roy, you stink. I mean, you really, really smell. You should have bathed last night. When last did you actually wash? Like, with soap?'

'A while back, but chill. Chill.' I felt defensive. 'Soon as I'm done here and I've got some supplies I'll clean up – proper.'

'Bullshit. I'm getting you a bar of soap right now and when you find one of those larny swimming pools, you use it, right?' She was laughing as she looked up at me. 'And see if you can find some actual underpants. I've seen too much of you already.' She patted my freshly dressed ankle wound and packed up the first aid kit. 'I'll draw you a map to Walmer. It's easy. You won't get lost.'

Babalwa's map included these directions:

> *Up parliament*
> *into cape road*
> *left into roseberry*
> *which becomes Target Kloof ... follow the loop*
> *right into main*
> *township on your left*
> *larnies on your right*

'Target Kloof?' I asked as I stepped up into the van.

'It'll make sense,' Babalwa replied. 'Big S bend. People always wrapping their cars around the poles.'

'Sounds exciting. See you now now.'

I drove away, up Parliament Street. At the top of the road I looked in the rear-view mirror to see Babalwa waving goodbye.

I waved back.

Target Kloof was as she had described it, a sweeping downward S bend ending in a little bridge over a valley, the road dividing two lush halves of suburban jungle. I drove at a crawl. A troop of monkeys watched me from the tops of the trees, a large male scratching his balls as the van passed. I waved at them.

Once through Target Kloof I took the right where Babalwa suggested, although at this stage I was already where I needed to be: fences, signature gates, walls, swimming pools, satellite dishes. I cruised, looking for easy targets.

Eventually I settled on River Road, a strip of double- and triple-storey houses facing onto a golf course, a few of them gabled, a few done out in mock-modest homey style and a few completely walled off. I smashed the van through a relatively humble black-and-white gated entrance, and then straight through the wall of a family entertainment area. A flat-screen TV – a relic or family keepsake of some sort – fell forward from its cabinet and shattered on the van's bonnet.

I kicked through the thin, locked inter-leading door with my good ankle and headed into the main house. This, the bills on the entrance hall table said, was the residence of the Cotton family. Mr Ken Cotton. His wife, Barbara.

Hallway family photos. Their two girls, bright teenagers, arms around parents, themselves content in plastic pool furniture. The girls playing tennis in all-white, alluring outfits. The wider Cotton family on Christmas Day, lined up in two rows, arms linking, each combination telling its own story.

I pissed over the photo collection and the bills, soaking the Cottons as thoroughly as possible. Then I walked, dick out, as far as I could into the lounge proper, hosing the off-white lounge suite and the expensive wooden coffee table. It was a relief to be able to slip back into my habit. I zipped and thought of Babalwa's request that I secure clothing, and then of her wrinkled nose at my stench. Too lazy to go back to the van, I searched the Cotton house looking for soap, finding a spicy underwear collection in one of the girl's bedrooms instead. Pink G-strings. A studded bra with fake gems on the rim. Suspenders. I stopped awhile on her bed, running my hands through the teenage fabric, my erection throbbing half-heartedly at the loss.

The wall above the bed was covered in photos stuck onto the wall with Prestik, the montage carefully constructed to portray the life of a young PE debutante and her beau, who looked, in almost every respect, like a fool. He posed in each shot – sometimes pulling muscles overtly, or simply beaming far too intensely into the camera. Throwing a rugby ball to his mates. Running. Jumping. Pointing. He was on the ugly side and wouldn't have aged well at all; but in the pictures the ugliness was light, a hint beneath the dominant, metallic veneer of youth.

I spat at him first, then at her, both lugs finding their mark on the wall and slowly dribbling down over their young faces.

In her cupboard I found a bar of Reece-Marie herbal soap (coarse rosemary, sage, lemon grass, teatree oil, aqueous cream and glycerine). The packaging promised it would lather exceptionally well.

I turned into Ken and Barbara's bedroom, a typically dull set-up attempting to mimic magazine style. Creams and off-whites, wooden-framed pictures of Cotton life through the ages. Young Ken making his way in the world with a fishing rod and a smile – about twenty years old. Young Barbara gazing with measured effort to the horizon from what looked very much like the same beach Babalwa and I had visited. Ken and Barbara must have been, I guessed, around my age: the grain on the photos matched the scant remains of my own past.

I found a fluffy off-white bathroom towel in the en-suite bathroom and, even better, a key to the door leading out to the pool.

The back garden was ominous. Vast lawns tracked away from the pool, down a series of mini rolling hills, but they were out of control, the grass wild and angry. Shrubs and bushes created a barrier between the kitchen and the pool which, back in the day, would surely have been cut back weekly. But as I stood there the Cotton family entertainment zone hummed with decay, reinforced by the green skin on the pool and a layer of aqua-bugs and insects dancing on the corpses of drowned colleagues.

I sucked in a deep breath, dropped my towel and my threaded pants, and jumped.

Ken Cotton, it turned out, was pretty much my size. I pulled everything he owned out of the cupboard and onto the bed and selected a hardy range.

8 pairs of boxers
hiking boots
slip-slops
7 x coloured Ts
2 x blue jeans

1 x black jeans
3 x khaki shorts
1 x international carry-on bag
4 x socks
2 x secret socks
1 x pair white Reeboks

I stuffed the lot into the carry-on bag, save for a pair of khaki shorts, a brownish-red T-shirt, long white socks and the hiking boots, which I wore as a joke I hoped would impress Babalwa. As I stood in front of the mirror, now more Ken Cotton than myself, I wondered what she might find funny about it, other than my shockingly grey hair, which looked, well, funny. My long, freshly clean, grey flyaway hair, the big grey beard, the hiking gear ... I was a caricature of myself and Ken.

I loaded up a second bag on exit. A printed photo album from the saucy teenager's room; the bra, G-string and suspenders from the same; her mobile and Kindle; a bunch of toothbrushes and toothpaste from the bathroom. I dumped the bags in the hallway and went back to clean out the kitchen.

Next I reversed the van from the rubble of the family room and rolled it around to the edge of the front garden, where the garage adjoined the kitchen. I put my seat belt on and smashed the van through the reinforced garage door. Reversed, and smashed again. Reversed, and smashed again. Reversed, and again. The van was shrill now, the engine and chassis moaning together. I parked in the driveway, walked back and checked out the Cotton garage, which contained, predictably, a BMW and a ladies' 4x4, a RAV4. My heart leapt. The RAV's metallic-blue shimmer was evocative. Neater than the cash-in-transit van, far less aggressive, it probably handled better on the road too. My heart still lifting, I stomped through the rubble in my new hiking boots to look for keys, which were hanging dutifully on a hook on the side of the kitchen cupboard, but which, of course, also had the biometric logo on the ring.

I went back to the saucy teenager's room, pulled her queen

mattress off its base, dragged it out to the driveway and pushed it into my beaten van.

'Honey, I'm home!' I shouted as I hopped out in front of my new apartment: 1B Donkin Terrace.

There was no reply.

In my charged and refreshed state, I had expected Babalwa to come out and greet me. To laugh – possibly – at my bizarre new attire. Instead, I dragged all my new stuff into the flat on my own. I pulled the hiking boots off when I was done and sat for a while on the white rail of my flat, which was really a stinking ghetto apartment with a teenage girl's mattress and bedding dumped in the hallway.

I had, I now realised, neglected to bring any cleaning materials from the Cottons.

I wondered where Babalwa was.

I waited most of the morning for Babalwa's return, dawdling around the front entrance of 1B, but there was no sign of her. Eventually I drove all the way back to the Cottons' house, emptied out their cleaning cupboard, and then went back and scrubbed my new flat. Or at least the important parts of it. I would not, I suspected, be entertaining vast crowds.

The rooms were mostly empty. One had what looked like the remnants of a mattress on the floor, an overflowing ashtray, and a litter of broken and abandoned quart bottles. What passed for the lounge was really just a collection of beer crates, bits of wood and other odd seating devices on top of a morphing, interlocking spread of floor stains. I threw all the shit as far down Donkin Hill as I could, then went back to deal with the toilet, which I treated initially by hurling three buckets of Babalwa's collected water over everything in the place, and then attacking it with Handy Andy and rags until it looked like somewhere I might be able to shit.

She returned a day later, by which point I had been back to the Cottons' place too many times to count. Towels. The family book collection. A pillow. Another pillow. Another swimming-pool bath.

'Nice,' she said, using her big toe to mark areas still needing attention as she walked through my renovated digs. A mouldy corner of the bathroom. A light tickle against the grime on the bottom row of the stack of bean and tuna cans. 'Not bad. Like a home, nè?'

'So where you been?' I trailed expectantly behind her.

'Ah, I went home for a bit, you know, just ... just to see. I dunno. Had some thinking to do. You know ...'

'We haven't talked about it yet. I mean, we need to. I need to. I need to find out what you know. Jesus. I need to tell you what I know.'

'Sho.' She opened the door to the spare bedroom, then closed it again. 'Limiting your range. Fair enough.'

'So, fine. Can you tell me what happened? What happened to you? Or should I tell you what happened to me first? Maybe that's better. Me, I was going through a bit of a life crisis that involved a serious need to sleep, which I did for a few days, and then I woke up and—'

'Everyone was gone.'

'Ja. All gone.'

'Did you dream?' In the kitchen now, Babalwa turned to face me, arms folded. 'I dreamed.'

'No – nothing. But, I mean, I wasn't really in a condition to dream. Or maybe I dreamed and didn't remember anything. Totally possible. One thousand per cent possible. In fact, very likely. What do you mean, dream?'

'Let's go to church.' Babalwa marched out the front door.

I followed her over the crest of our hill to the Hill Presbyterian Church, an 1800s classic, replete with huge spire and broken front door.

'Took me days to get this open,' Babalwa said as she pushed the oak door gently forward. 'Beat the lock with a hammer. Tiny thing. Took forever.'

We headed into the interior carefully, respectfully. Babalwa lead us to a front pew, where we sat in full view of a struggling Jesus.

'I don't know why. It makes me peaceful, this place,' she said softly, still not looking at me. 'Silly, I know. But—'

'Christ, there's no silliness left any more,' I offered.

'Sho. Sho.' She folded her hands into her lap, priest-like, and looked me in the eye. 'I was really tired that night. You know, beaten. It was a Thursday; I remember being rude to my mother and going to bed early. I was in that way, you know. Just kind of hating everything, but I couldn't sleep either. I remember lying there and looking at the ceiling and questioning whether this was it. You know?' Her eyes darted between me and her lap. I nodded encouragingly. 'Anyway, do you know what lucid dreaming is? Ever had a lucid dream?'

'Babalwa, I was a bad drunk. To be really honest about it, I can't remember dreaming at all, ever. I passed out every night for over twenty years, so ... no. Until it happened, nothing. After that, of course, I've been dreaming like a wild man. All over the place. But I can't say any of them were lucid. The normal stuff, hard to keep a handle on when you wake up.'

'I've heard the term before,' Babalwa said, 'so I've been wondering since I had the dream if that was what it was. A lucid dream. Anyway, I couldn't sleep so I just let myself drift, wallowing in being awake, or half awake, or drifting. Whatever.' She looked up at Jesus, then back down at her lap. 'So at some stage I'm definitely not awake any more, I can't be, but I don't feel like I'm dreaming either. I'm alert. Even now, when I think back I can remember the small details, which is strange, because who can ever remember the details of a dream?

'Anyway, in the dream I was sitting in a wooden chair. I remember the chair especially well, 'cause it felt out of context. Wrong. Then this face appears. Oprah. Not old Oprah. Young Oprah. Her voice was really warm. Gentle. Like it actually took hold of me a bit, like in my stomach – it gripped me. Anyway, ah fuck, I should just say it. She told me it was up to me now. That the key was love, not hate. That there are reasons for everything. Even the smallest things. Like a bird sitting in the tree. He's there for a reason. She told me that, and not to panic. That I need to think of the family and grow it. Shit, it sounds stupid now, but it was so real, so vivid. When I woke up in the morning, I took ages to get out of bed, just remembering it. The texture of it. Her words. How warm she was.'

'And when you got up?'

'Gone. Everything. Everybody.'

'People, and pets,' I said. 'And livestock. I've seen a few dogs around, a couple free pigs, a wild cow, but other than that, nothing. Farms are empty. And it must have been at night, 'cause everything is locked up at night. Like the car park at the beach.'

'I know.' Babalwa looked up at Jesus, back at me, then Jesus again. 'The dream, Roy, it was too much. Too real. It must have been something else. It must have been ...'

I left the church.

Jesus was freaking me out.

I strolled back over to the pyramid and lighthouse; odd, incongruous structures. The pyramid especially, with a neat bench attached to the front of its skirt, welcoming sea-view visitors. I found a plaque on the reverse side, which read:

To the memory of one of the most perfect of human beings who has given her name to the Town below.

I sat on Elizabeth's bench and stared out, over the skatepark and educational graffiti walls, at the sea.

Chapter 15
Just look at this grass

I tried to woo her.

In writing it sounds different – teenage and constructed. But at the time it was real, the attempt wrapped around the weird fact of the two of us. Around the days we spent together, or near each other, circling from a middle distance. So call it love. Call it what you will, at the time and in those moments there was a pull towards her.

Why would I resist?

And what is to 'woo', anyway? It, the word, has all the hallmarks of a plan, a trap. But really it was the typical flutterings of a human heart. I saw her see me, and in the process I began to see myself, feel myself, become aware again of my feet on the ground; my grey, flying hair.

Or, put another way, my chest began to swell. So I pushed it forward. One does these things. One doesn't always know why.

Often, one turns to jazz.

I had this idea. A vision, really. A dream.

Babalwa's in the kitchen, stirring something light and non-taxing. She's wearing a summer dress. It's blue and a little bit yellow and every now and again it puffs out with the wind and you know there's another form in there, a presence, waiting. Me, also in the kitchen, chopping and guiding, the master planner. Bill Evans or Moses Molelekwa is playing and there is wine in our glasses – metaphorically in my case (I'm sipping Appletiser maybe; regardless, the bubbles dance like champagne). The sun is thinking of setting, there's that rich orange lightness in the air. She's a little tipsy, but only a little (OK, maybe I've smoked the tiniest bit of something, just for mood's sake). The air is rich with the smell of onions frying. It's that smell as they hit the pan, the fizz and that first rush of it, then of the garlic and the simmer. The piano carries us and she looks over, just a functional glance really, maybe she's checking where the pepper is, and she catches a sideways slip of me and she smiles, instinctively.

And pause.

The generator – an old red thing requiring bicep force and much gas – delivered power, but proved surprisingly hopeless at charging the battery for longer than ten minutes.
 The jazz, therefore, was tricky.
 I initiated searches for inverters and other, better batteries, but we had, between us, a fool's understanding of what we were doing, and why we were doing it. And the hard fact is that jazz doesn't matter that much.
 Still, there was a piano tinkling in my heart that evening. And the sun was actually right, just on the golden side of going down. She was in the kitchen, stirring something. I was alongside, chopping, and it felt, for a few moments, like *it*.

A little later, my heart still quietly whistling, she screamed from the back porch. 'The water! Roy, the water!'
 I dropped my wooden spoon into the garlic and onions and bolted, to find her, jaw chattering, eyes hysterical, pointing at the water tank, the receptacle for her strange and amateurish – yet effective – network of roof rainwater pipes. She was pointing at a crack, seeping and leaking, stretching before our eyes.
 'What do we do?' She turned to me.
 'Pray.'

In the minute of our watching the crack raced across the plastic tank, which then exploded over us.
 I took her hand as we stood there helpless, drenched.
 She took it back.

Inside, the onions and the garlic had turned to a heap of hot black mush, billowing fire and smoke. Babalwa grabbed the pan, ran out front and threw it all, everything, down the hill. It skipped a few yards and landed in a pile outside my front door. She turned and marched past my helpless presence, muttering something about useless and men.

As the sun set we sat in candle darkness, each with our own can of beans, each with our own thoughts and ideas about time and space and water and onions and garlic. She apologised, of course. It was no one's fault, nothing to do with me per se, just frustration, and I accepted, of course, but we both knew that real men don't say pray.

We scooped the beans, the hopeless beans, and said goodnight.

Later that night Babalwa vomited on my front door. She knocked and vomited and ran back. I followed slowly, grudgingly, then held her hand and her head while she spewed those bad beans back into a bucket, and then another, and then another. All of which I intended to wash, but eventually just kicked down the hill to join our other failures.

'Roy,' she called weakly from the shithouse, where her other end balanced over another bucket. 'We need a plan.'

* * *

We settled after that. Each in our semi-detached flat, we coexisted gently for days, then weeks, then months. Water. Power. Food. Water. Power. Food. It was, ultimately, a simple equation.

Babalwa's rain-catchment system was restored, rickety and yet ultimately effective. Trouble was, it didn't rain too much, so every second morning I would drive around the suburbs and fill two twenty-litre barrels from the swimming pools.

I didn't talk too much about the dream or her telling of it, and neither did she. We talked, instead, about our old lives. And then, the mirror image, our new life. The plan.

The grass on the reserve grew thicker, inching skywards in a knotted mat. I suggested trying to cut it, but Babalwa scoffed. 'What,' she asked snidely, 'you're gonna mow this hundred-square-metre lawn every week? Why?'

She was compelled by Joburg, by the VR clubs and naps, by the music scene and the graf rebels. In her mind they were all rolled up into a single metropolis where big things happened. She would pick at me with questions, one after the next, the links between each query leading me on to greater descriptive heights. I tried explaining that I had never even seen a graf rebel and that their lives were hard as stones – they were arrested and beaten, their nails were pulled, their balls shocked.

'To do what they do ... to repaint and rebroadcast, eish. It's heavy. No glamour.' She looked at me blankly, expectant, as I explained. 'People like me never even got close. I wrote ads for those walls.' She deflated, but recalibrated quickly. Kept me going for hours with demands for stories about the clubs. The naps. What is it like, VR sex? Better or worse or completely different? What kind of people? Where did they all end up, the ones in the early scene? Were they literally orgies? How many people did you fuck at one time? Just one nap for the whole night or did you have to log out, change it, then log in again?

I answered as honestly as I could, and realised in the process how detached I had been from the whole thing. To me it just seemed a bit silly. Pretentious. Messy. The dumb stuff ad people do because they need to feel rough, alive, edgy.

But to Babalwa, down in PE, it was the revolution. The very same revolution as the service delivery protests and the graf rebellion. As the global youth.

I did my best to set her straight.

The plan – Babalwa's plan, really – started with power.

We collected portable solar panels, inverters and batteries. The idea was to build something akin to a home grid, a power source able to do more than boil the kettle or light a bulb.

The bean incident was a reminder that our raider-gatherer lifestyle had a limited time frame, and would have to morph into food production. A life of chickens (presuming we could catch the wild ones) and crops – plucking and hoeing and growing. Soil and harvest.

'That means,' said Babalwa, 'there's no way we can stay here. It's all sand. We'll never grow anything.'

Day to day, I foraged and raided. I drove ceaselessly, peering into the cracks and corners of Port Elizabeth from my obscene, crushed and dented armoured van, flipping ceaselessly through an always evolving stack of raided CDs and sticks and players. Even with all the musical foraging, I spent most of the time in my father's dance space – not Schulz, but the old boys. The ones who had got him started.

Digweed, Tenaglia, Fatboy Slim, *Africanism*, Fresh House Flava et al.

Babalwa developed her own orbit. We inched into a mutual ritual that accommodated our disparate paths, our innate need for human contact and our permanent state of metaphysical terror. Seldom, if ever, did we join forces. The raiding was private – each person's way of communicating internally, of addressing the context and the place and the situation.

I dissolved, for the second time and through calculated effort, my pissing habit, displacing it with an expanding collection of teenage girls' photo albums, iPods and mobiles. I picked them carefully, cultivating an archetype to which I attached my lusts and dreams.

The girl – my girl – was between fifteen and eighteen years old. She wasn't a rebel, but she wasn't a nerd either. She was that quiet girl, still to be properly unveiled, especially to herself. She sat in the middle of the class and her mind drifted as much as it paid attention to geometry, biology and equations. She felt stirrings in her heart and her loins when she thought of him, but she was only just becoming aware of how to deal with them practically, firstly, and with him, secondly. Her underwear was, of course, crisp white. She listened to alternative indie-style sounds. The Canadian scene, but with old-fashioned hip hop and newer broken beats thrown in. She was conversant in local music – she knew her deep house from her kwaito from her trashy Eurobeats.

She read a lot of books. Any book really. Pulp fiction. Poetry. History. She was open. She was waiting. Every now and again she wrote poetry.

She had friends.

Boys.

Girls.

They gathered in groups. Hugged. Held hands. Smoked illicitly, around corners.

Took photos.

And I collected them. I snuck them, presuming Babalwa was ever looking, into my flat. Pored over them gently, some days. Pawed them on others. Pulled the printed pictures out, examined them, put them back. Thumbed my grubby way across screen after screen after screen.

'Roy,' she said. We were sitting on the pyramid bench, looking out over the skatepark and the memorials at the sea, our toes tickling in the knee-high grass. 'Just look at this grass. And think about it. We are going to run out of cans. The roads are already growing over. It's going to get harder and harder to move. The animals will keep coming. It will get more dangerous. Harder to find food and, if we don't make a serious plan, harder to grow it, to hunt it. If we just stay here, if we don't build, we'll be swallowed up.'

She leaned forward on her arms, lifting her backside slightly off the bench, and rocked. I considered her profile and realised how well I now knew her features. Her always shaved head. The clouds that hovered in her eyes. Her boyish body. Her ridiculously conservative clothes. Shorts, T-shirt, sandals. The incongruity of her. Of the two of us. I looked back out to the sea, all flat and benign.

'Where do we live? Why? How do we live? Why? What do we do about power?' she asked in a rush. 'I mean, electricity – it must be possible to get much more than we have with the portable panels. We can't just pile them up, we need to make them work. How do we farm? 'Cause we know nothing about farming, do we? Do we become hunters? Where, why and how? All of it, Roy. We can't wait any more.

'We can't just collect portables and pretend it will be OK, that someone will sail in off that fucking sea and rescue us.'

'Power,' I said. 'We have tools. If we have the power to use them, we can build. We need power.'

We would become farmers, in one sense or another, but most probably in the sense I dreaded. Actual farming. Planting and reaping. Harvesting and watering. Tilling.

'But Roy' – she was earnest, pleading almost – 'you need to think more widely ... of why we would be farming. If we set it up right, if we get the tools we need and sort out the power, we can be pretty efficient, and the power wouldn't only feed us, it would free us. Regular hot water. We could fry a steak—'

'Who would kill the cow? You? Butcher it? Turn it into steak?'

'OK, sho. Bad example. But you ken mos. You can't think of it as farming. Think of living some kind of life in this place, in this situation.'

Babalwa insisted our current home wasn't it. That the life we were destined for couldn't possibly take root on the bare patch of scrub that was the Donkin Reserve. 'Come!' She dragged me by the arm and pulled me down onto my knees, then started clawing her fingers into the earth. 'It's fucking beach sand with a layer of evil, hard grass on top, Roy. Nothing can grow here. Nothing.'

'We need to think of more than simple farming,' I said, my fingers mirroring hers, pulling clumps of sandy earth up and letting it all spill back down again. 'There are only two of us. If we want to get this right and not spend every waking hour until we die with a fucking hoe in our hands, then we need something better than a farm. We need more control. Greenhouses. Plant food, fertiliser and those artificial steroids. We need layers and layers of great soil and fresh compost and all that shit.'

'What, like, import a nursery?'

'Sho. We just load the shit up in a truck, and if we don't have enough we get more from somewhere else and we keep going until we've got an artificial environment that meets our needs. We need control. And we can have it here – if we just look to control this patch of land. Look.' I stood up and pointed to the four corners of the reserve dramatically, like a settler. 'We've got about, what, eight hundred square metres here to control. With the right tools – one of those lawnmowers you can drive and a set of greenhouses – we can control that pretty easily. Beyond the square, there's not a lot to worry about in terms of vegetation.

'We look to control the reserve as a clear area we can manage, and there's enough concrete in this place to make sure that the jungle can't close in on us. Where else can we find something like this?'

'Well ...' Babalwa, doubtful, remained on her knees. 'There must be plenty of similar places around the country, nè?'

'Possibly. But how long will they take to find? How much work will they take to settle to the point where we are now already? How many will be right on the sea in case of miracle sea rescues and to service our need to fish?' Babalwa snorted. Fishing had not, as of yet, taken place. 'Seriously, I've been thinking about fishing quite a lot lately.' I rolled with it. 'It will probably end up being easier than trying to keep cattle.'

She nodded, head down, the corners of her mouth twitching.

'Laugh, but if not here, then where? It's going to be fucking tough to start again. And, like it or not, we have started here. And other people chose to start here too.' I waved at the Donkin pyramid. 'There was surely a reason why these people decided to start this city here. Right friggin here.' I jumped slightly on the turf, issuing up a little puff of sand.

I had forced her. Bullied her. Or maybe she had conceded strategically. Not immediately, of course, but as I heaped the pressure on she gave a little, and a little more, and within an hour or two we had – by mutual agreement – decided to stay where we were, peering over the sea into an empty horizon, farming in the sand.

We had a cup of tea.

'So what do you know about solar?' Babalwa asked me as we sipped.

'Less than fuck all. You?'

'I know that you can only stack three panels to a battery before it blows.'

'So I guess the question is, where? Where will we find more power than portables? We need better batteries.'

'When we get the solar thing right we should rig up a player.' Babalwa topped up her teacup, holding the lid and tipping from the pot in classic English style.

'Home entertainment? We'll need to be careful with the movies. When we've watched them all it's repeats for the rest of our lives.'

'Music would be wild though – somewhere to put all those sticks and things you been hording.'

'Agreed. Agreed. Movies. Music. Stuff of life.'

'Roy,' Babalwa said, pulling out her chair. 'Can I ask you something personal?'

'Shoot.'

'How scared are you? I mean, just like day on day. Are you scared?' Her voice got a little higher. 'Because, honestly, some days I can't get out of bed. I have to pull myself out piece by piece. I mean, you're out there all the time in your van, with that machete, doing whatever you do. So to me you look fine, but I feel awful. I just want to cry all the time.' Tears rolled down her cheeks.

'Come here,' I beckoned. She rounded the pine coffee table, littered with the patchwork of A4 pages that constituted our farm plan, and sat on my lap, her arms around my neck, like a child.

'Listen,' I whispered into the nape of her neck. 'I keep moving to stay alive.' She pushed her chin into my collarbone, tears and snot smearing onto my cheek, mingling with mine, creating a mutual river between us. Then she pulled back.

'Will you bring your mattress this side tonight? I don't want you in my bed, but I don't want to be alone either.'

'Sure.' My heart skipped, dropped, then picked up again. I didn't want to sleep with her, per se. Sex was a peripheral consideration. I badly wanted to be wanted, though. To be held, also. To mix energy with her – to dilute myself and gain a little bit of someone else. 'No problem. No problem at all. I don't feel like flying solo either.'

Babalwa folded her arms around me again, leaning properly into my neck with her shaved head. She smelled slightly of sweat. Sweet sweat.

'You got anything decent to read? I got a whole library over there, you know.'

She mumphed snottily into my neck.

I stroked her back slowly, my hand moving in ever-widening circles over the Castle Lager logo.

The next morning the air was thicker than usual, and spotted with smiles. I had dragged my mattress into the kitchen and slept there.

Her toe woke me, prodding against my forehead. She looked down on me, the length of her dramatically extended, my view deep into the inner thigh of her shorts.

'Hey,' she rubbed her head and yawned. 'You a tea or coffee person?'

'Uh, tea, I guess.' I grabbed her ankle and gave it a playful twist. She yelped and jumped free. 'Today we find power, nè? That movie thing has really got me going.'

Our next target was All Power EP, in Kempston Road.

'Easy, right near our family home,' said Babalwa. 'I'll show you where I grew up.'

II

Chapter 16

Refugees

'Smoke,' Babalwa said as we caught our first sight of the Jozi skyline. 'There's smoke.'

We were about seventy kilometres out. There was, indeed, a small spiral of smoke curling over the right-hand side of the city.

'Looks like it could be coming from Ponte,' I said casually, while my heart leapt, fists in the air. 'Could be anywhere, I suppose – can't tell from this far.'

'Where there's smoke ...' Babalwa wriggled excitedly.

'There's something burning,' I finished coldly. 'Could mean anything.'

'Could mean everything.' Babalwa laughed at my caution.

I ran my tongue through the guillotine gap in my front tooth and grimaced behind closed lips.

The smoke toyed with us over seventy kilometres, shifting the source of its dance as we threaded our way through the splatter of empty cars blocking the highway. Babalwa squirmed ceaselessly, thrilled at the idea of Jozi. My tongue matched her vigour, probing relentlessly, excitedly, for the missing half of my front tooth.

'There'll be nothing to see,' I kept saying to her in the build-up to the trip. 'It's not a big city any more. It's an abandoned pile of glass and brick.'

'Still,' she said, refusing to concede, 'it'll be fun. Better than pretending to be farmers. We can go shopping. Looting. Whatever. Sandton City.'

As much as I tried to deny it, I was with her. Jozi, as always, held the lure of change.

Once we had the player working, once we had watched that first movie, our PE lives slid into a shambolic routine. We mowed the lawn and trimmed the edges of the reserve. We erected a greenhouse. We decided what to plant. We watched our seeds sprout, and rot.

Theoretically, hydroponics had seemed like the answer. In practice, however, we couldn't get even the simplest elements of the process right, and after three months we had grown sick, thin and very tired of farming. We roamed further and further, seeking out homesteads and nurseries and smallholdings and farms with vegetable patches. We didn't score often, but when we did we scored big. One farm in the Gamtoos Valley yielded a truckload. Spinach, carrots, green beans, potatoes – all waiting neatly in a lush garden, right next to the farmhouse.

But that was the exception. Generally we reached far and worked hard for little – the drooping, dying greenhouse mocking us each day when we returned.

'We have to learn,' I would insist to Babalwa. 'How are we going to survive if we never learn to produce our own food?'

She agreed on the imperative but differed fundamentally on the rest. Babalwa saw clearly how bad we were at food production, and how much help we needed. Soil. Conditions. 'You know, Roy, you know …' She would stare and hold it until I walked away.

And really, I did know. Our few attempts to secure meat had failed badly. We had one or two surprisingly wild chickens cooped, providing eggs and, supposedly, meat. But we were as terrible at butchery – even something as simple as a chicken – as we were at farming. We never even thought of trying to find a roaming sheep or cow, the subject avoided by mutual silent agreement.

We survived, but in no comfort. Eventually, as the daily grind took proper hold, we fell back into a reliable rhythm of rice and canned beans. Rice and canned stew. Rice and spinach.

Perhaps most indicative of our state of decline was our inability to watch movies. After weeks and weeks of fiddling with panels and batteries and portable solars, we set up enough power to fire up genuinely warm water, as well as the entertainment system in Babalwa's lounge. That first night she scattered the small room with cushions and prepared popcorn. I made coffee. We stacked the table with chocolate and argued over the first movie, eventually settling on *Spanglish*. Something soft and old to start, please, she begged. Just to get going. Something American and stupid.

I conceded, then ruined the evening by crying.

Adam Sandler reaches into Téa Leoni's bathrobe and cups her breast to calm her. It's a mock funny scene, nothing really, but I was judderingly reminded of Angie and myself. It was exactly the kind of thing she would have done to me, had I had breasts. It was our kind of fight, comedy or not. Their weepy hysteria felt so much like home I crashed under the memory. We tried again, but the weight of the films was too much. Their ideas, their people, their references, their beauty all spoke of subjects too rich. So we walked through and around and over our home entertainment system, playing music on it occasionally but generally leaving it fallow.

'If it's people, what d'you think they're burning?' Babalwa asked as we slid past Gold Reef City. The column of smoke had drifted further back as we approached. Now it looked like it could be over Midrand, possibly even Pretoria. It thinned while we drove, threatening to disappear totally into the late afternoon clouds.

'Who the fuck knows?' I grunted, irritable now with the idea that coming back to Joburg would somehow alter our circumstances. 'Probably just an accident of nature. Leaves burning through broken glass or something.'

Babalwa pulled her knees up to her chin and stuck her tongue out at me. 'Poes! It better be fucking people. I'm not sure I can spend the rest of my life with a sulky pants like you.'

I laughed, then clamped my lips back over my half tooth. I managed to forget about it most of the time, but every now and again it came back to me how ridiculous I must have looked with this massive angular chunk missing from my face. Despite the fact that I was the only man on the planet, I still wanted to impress and please Babalwa in the way that men impress and please women. But I found myself keeping my mouth shut and looking away as much as possible. Dentistry was now my constant ironic companion.

'You should just laugh. Let go, man,' Babalwa said, eyes

twinkling. 'I think it's cute, anyway. Broken teeth are sexy in lotsa places.'

I grunted and made a pretence of refocusing on the road.

'Don't be grumpy, Roy. It's my first time in Jozi. I'm excited.' She reached a bony little hand over and patted my knee. 'Tell me what it was like,' she said, gripping my kneecap in encouragement.

'Full. A lot of fokken traffic. Angry people.'

'Liar.' She tried to lift my patella, pushing it painfully around its socket. 'You were probably the angry one. I'm sure there was lots that was great here. I wish I could have seen it ...' She trailed away and focused on the industrial landscape as we looped into the spaghetti junction.

I allowed myself a couple of flashbacks. Images of shiny cars and the glinting Highveld sun, traffic jams and metro roadblocks. Fat cops hustling for lunch. Maybe she was right, I conceded to myself. Quite possibly she was right ...

Initially Jozi seemed little changed. The dry brown walls were still slumped and decaying and hopelessly wrong, but now the transmission paint was peeling, doubling up the ghetto atmosphere. Inside the easy lines of the skyline, the city had faded, was fading.

As we crested the hill to Zoo Lake we entered a teeming jungle. The birds had taken over. The hadedas perched in throngs on treetops, rooftops and garden walls, the packs on high supporting ground troops drilling the earth with prehistoric beaks. The hadada shrieks bounced against the softer calls of the loeries, also obscenely abundant over the forest tops. Then the weavers, the shrikes, the robins and all the smallers, crying and yelling and calling and hunting.

I stopped the van as we passed the zoo.

The houses and converted office-houses facing Jan Smuts Avenue had fallen so far back into the shrubbery they were barely recognisable. An old-school billboard had fallen completely off its wall mounting, the vines and creepers pulling it easily and slowly down. Windows were covered in vines. Where once the tops of the oak trees had merely brushed fingers to create a light canopy, now they had threaded together to form a complete roof, filled in by shrubs and tendrils and leaves.

And birds.

The forest stood tall, as in a fairy tale. Grass poked up through General Smuts's tarmac, challenging the dominance of hundreds of years. Soon it would be the tar that was repressed, and rare and alien. I knew the forest would end in less than a kilometre and we would emerge in the glassy shine of Rosebank. Still, I searched for breath.

'Jesus' was all I said to Babalwa. 'A complete fucken forest.' I felt like a twelve-year explorer, previously bulletproof, suddenly lost, realising the true worth of my meagre experience and supplies. 'It can't have closed off completely,' I added, ostensibly to comfort her, but really speaking to myself, the one with the memories. I pressured the accelerator, urgent in my need to get us through the few hundred metres to Rosebank. Babalwa gawked happily at the hadedas and loeries, shrieking properly when she spotted a zebra grazing next to the road. 'Must be from the zoo,' I said.

She commanded me to stop so she could look at it properly. 'Never seen one before,' she muttered, her chin resting on the half-raised window. 'Check how fat its ass is. That's wonderful. Really wonderful.' She laughed and her little paw came out again and patted me on the knee. 'Thanks for bringing us, Roy. This is fun. Much better than PE.'

We burst through into Rosebank, which had all the hallmarks of a conventional concrete jungle.

We entered Eileen's apartment like we were returning from some kind of prolonged holiday. Me, the father, carrying our baggage and supplies up the staircase from the basement. Babalwa running up the stairs to see if she could find a view of the smoke column, then running back down past me again, yelling about not being able to find it. I dragged the bags and the boxes of food, grumbling to myself. We had become an odd pair. A husband and a wife. A father and daughter. A mother and her lost, toothless son. My tongue slipped through the gap again, seeking out the sharpest edge, playing with the idea of blood.

'Absolutely fuck all!' Babalwa thumped up the last steps to land next to me as I left Eileen's flat for the last load. 'Can't see a damn thing. Maybe it was just a natural fire. Like on *Survivor*, before they get given flint.'

I grunted and turned for the basement, soothed in a strange but significant way by her chatter.

'Can I go in?' Babalwa half stepped over Eileen's threshold.

I dumped the last box (canned beans, long-life milk, canned tuna, canned tomatoes) on the kitchen counter and heaved. As strong as I had become, the carrying had still taken it out of me.

'Who was this chick, anyway?' Babalwa bounced into the kitchen. 'Girlfriend?'

'Office associate.'

'Not very creative though.' Babalwa hoisted her narrow ass onto the counter. 'Check out this flat. It's like she was still sixteen and her mom did it for her.'

'In many ways she was,' I replied. 'Look, it's pretty dark now. We need to decide what we're gonna eat, how we're gonna heat it. We've got shit to do.'

Babalwa grabbed me by my hair, pulled me into her and locked her legs behind me. 'You need to chill the fuck out, baba. There are no deadlines here.' She kissed me carefully, like a wife, probing my mouth with her tongue, reassuring me with her hands and her legs and her grip. Just as I began leaning in, she slipped her tongue through the hole in my front tooth and burst out laughing, pushing me back, the heels of her palms against my chest. 'Sexy!' She laughed, looking me in the eye. 'Sexy like a meth addict. Sexy like a crack pipe.'

I pushed her back, harder than I intended, almost slamming her head against the corner of Eileen's smoke extractor. 'Fuck you. You're in Roy country now. Show respect.'

'Pretty hard to respect a man with a gap like that in his teeth, mister!' Babalwa slid off the counter, hugged me quickly and trotted into the lounge. 'Seriously?' she called out. 'You woke up here, in this flat? Must have been freaky. Seriously freaky. I mean, just being in a space like this, it's like going ...' Her voice disappeared as she entered the bedroom.

We slept that night in Eileen's bed, our stomachs grinding away at the beans and the tuna, Babalwa farting gently as she slumbered. I let my arm curl over her, like we were lovers and not lost, lonely refugees.

Chapter 17

Genuinely enamoured

'Do you even know how to shoot one of these things?' Babalwa laughed at me as she picked up the weapons, then laid them carefully back down again, one by one.

'Blasted a few rounds. Landed on my ass.'

'We should probably give ourselves lessons ...'

We carted a shotgun, an AK and an R1 out the front entrance of Tyrwhitt Mansions. Guns, it turns out, aren't that complicated. You open them up, shove in the bullets where it looks like they're supposed to go, find the safety and fire.

If you're a scrawny girl, you avoid the shotguns.

We blasted the stop sign at the bottom of Tyrwhitt Avenue to pieces, moving closer and closer as the reality of our talents became obvious, Babalwa burying her elbows in the tarmac with every shotgun effort.

The birds scattered with each shot, then came back down again. They were clustered in the trees, on the street signs, on the balconies. Egrets, eagles, loeries, hadedas. They made me think of the free pigs, and I wondered if they were still around.

'Be a bit careful,' I said as we packed the guns back into the basement armoury and selected a personal pistol each. Babalwa chose a Vektor SP4, a Russian thing, far too big in her baby hand. I took the Vektor CPZ, all rounded edges and *Star Wars*. 'There was a pack of free pigs and dogs around when I was here. Big enough to tear up a young girl from PE.'

'Thanks,' she said caustically. 'I'll keep that in mind. Oh, we should look for solar or a generator while we're out, nè? This water thing could screw us up. I know you don't want to move from your cherry's flat, but we might have to.'

'We need to plan a route?'

Babalwa flicked her safety off, then on again, and shoved the

Vektor into the rear waistband of her gym shorts, where it sat, enormous and devoid of context. 'Let's just drive.' She winked at me. 'I can feel there's something out there.'

She loaded the CDs into the van's player as we searched the edges of Gauteng. Randfontein, Roodepoort, Krugersdorp, Daveyton, Vosloo, Magaliesberg, Midrand, Centurion, Tembisa, Pretoria, Benoni, Brakpan, Katlehong, Springs, Soweto. We pounded the speakers, not stopping, not talking, our heads bumping along, teenagers absorbing a new, morphing landscape.

The plants were pushing the houses back, each millimetre of growth adding to each tendril a new triumph of organic force. In the townships progress was slower but still real, clusters reaching up and over the roofs, sporadic grass patches spiralling upwards and sideways simultaneously.

'We're just starting summer rains, right?' Babalwa asked rhetorically. 'It's October, right? And it rains hard up here?' We were driving through the matchbox houses of Katlehong.

'Very.'

'What you reckon – two years? Three? Before everything is gone?'

'Depends. At the zoo it'll be less. Soon we'll have to cut a path out, if we want to go back the way we came.'

'Show me where you grew up,' she said. 'There's no smoke.'

I pointed the van to Greymont Hills.

Babalwa took great interest in my childhood house, firing off a string of probing questions about my father as she shot away the locks to the front door and the security gate.

'Did he beat you? You ever remember him sober? What about your mother?'

She roved through the house, picking up things – coffee mugs, pots, bowls, couch cushions – as if they represented me and my family rather than my tenants, then sitting on the front step contemplatively when I told her how many hours I had spent there myself. She cut an incongruous figure, there on my childhood front step. A scrawny girl in filthy white gym shorts and a vest, shotgun hooked over her arm and a pistol jutting from her hip.

I was becoming genuinely enamoured.

We started having sex regularly after the PE movie debacle – after I had cried through *Spanglish*. She would hug. Rub my head. Hold my hand. At night – only ever at night – she would pull me towards her and take me in, guiding with authority, climaxing with a fierce grip and complete silence. I, in turn, made a habit of collapsing into her, of passing out in her arms, of harvesting the small doses she offered, as fully as possible, as often as possible.

Around that time, she began raising the idea of children.

If we are really the only ones, she would say, then our children are going to have to sleep with each other to breed. We'll be inbreeders.

I would shrug. Grunt.

'Seriously, Roy! D'you think about it? I mean, at some stage we're going to have to breed, nè? We have to try, don't we?'

Once she had forced the idea into my head I did begin to think about it. But inevitably my thoughts would end with the idea of Babalwa as wife – as partner. As family.

I stayed as quiet as she would let me, offering titbits, basic ideas, technical prods along the line of genetics, cross-pollination, and so on. I would research occasionally, presenting her with whatever facts I thought would add to the debate playing out in her head. Personally, though, breeding was an abstract notion. I knew that once she had decided, I would follow in the wake.

Still, my resignation wasn't entirely passive. As the days passed I allowed myself to consider the idea of her in relation to me, in relation to family. I considered her form more deeply. Her child hips. Her adult eyes. Her details began to etch themselves on my brain, and my heart. Soon there would be no wiping them away.

For her part, Babalwa seemed only to grow used to me. Her touches, though warm, were calculated; they sought to heal, to help, to improve. She reached for me through genetic necessity. Through circumstance.

I wondered whether I would be informed of the child decision or simply caught up in it. As we roamed the streets of PE, looting for health, activity, entertainment, smashing locks and walls and doors, I tried to imagine us as a family, but the images refused to form. She was too young. I was ... I didn't know what I was. But I knew I wasn't exactly right.

'Tell me,' Babalwa said, still perched on my childhood step, the shotgun, now resting between her legs, making her especially dominant, 'about being a drunk. There's booze everywhere. You tempted again?'

The tooth episode hung thick between us.

'Always tempted. But I have the fear. Keeps me in line. 'Specially after the tooth.'

'So if we find others ... you'll drink again? Moments of joy? Excitement?'

'I hope not. I'm a proper junkie though, so I know enough to know that I might. You know, the day-at-a-time thing. All standard twelve-step shit applies.'

'Lately I've been feeling like just getting out of my mind. Completely fucked up.' Babalwa peered over the shotgun muzzle at me with hooded, plotting eyes. 'Whaddya think of that?'

We decided on sundowners at the Westcliff.

Splattered on multiple levels against the face of Westcliff ridge, the Westcliff Hotel hovered directly over Zoo Lake, an off-pink series of plush, interlinking five-star units. As we smashed through the front gates, I explained to Babalwa about the foreign tourists and their plastic-surgery safari holidays, with the hotel utilised as recovery venue, about the prostitutes snuck through the gates at night, about the Sunday afternoon high teas for the Parkview ladies and their daughters.

Unable to jump-start a golf cart, we skipped down the enormous staircase three at a time.

Babalwa blew away the security bars on the restaurant window. She had adjusted quickly to the power of the recoil, and was firing the shotgun as regularly as possible now. We clambered in.

The serving trolleys were waiting for us, lined up in perfect threes, knives and forks at the ready. Cakes moulded to the point of crumbling. Proud mounds of green and moss trapped within blithe, unknowing glass cases.

Babalwa pulled a bottle of champagne from the kitchen wine cellar. The kitchen itself looked recently flooded. The floor was slick and sticky, a dirty high-water mark some two inches above the skirting rail. It was actually, she insisted, a high-blood mark; the apogee of fleeing freezer and fridge juice. I turned my head, unwilling to broach the idea of what might have happened to it, the blood and the muck, since.

Babalwa took care of another set of windows and security bars and we clambered out onto the terrace overlooking Zoo Lake and the northern suburbs. She cracked the champagne, took a long swig and spat it out. 'I think it's off?' She handed the bottle over for testing.

I declined.

'Sorry, my bad,' she said. 'But I really think it's off.' She slapped her tongue loudly between lips and teeth, testing.

'Probably just French. Is it really bitter? Dry?' I took the bottle. The label said Champagne. 'Ja, it's French. You might wanna look for something that says sparkling wine. French shit is hard.'

Babalwa hopped back through the window to the kitchen.

I rolled a small joint from my stash and considered Joburg's north.

Trees. Trees. Trees. The forest almost pulsing it was growing so fast. I smoked and wondered. Inhaled and dreamed in reverse. Agency offices and houses of colleagues – their names already blurred and distant. Clubs and girls and campaigns. Media. Marketing. Copy. I was, I decided, looking over the metaphorical forest of my past. I could see nothing but a closing roof. A green, leafy mat.

Babalwa returned with the cheap stuff, cracked it, sat between my legs and leaned back against me.

She drank. I smoked.

We fucked ourselves up.

Chapter 18

Six

We crashed through the front door of Eileen's flat chattering and laughing and collapsing in and out of each other's arms.

There, flat out on the couch, was Fats Bonoko, creative director at TWF something something and something. A shotgun lay on the floor, waiting.

Babalwa swooned and fell to the floor in a heap.

I stood swaying, attempting to compute the fact that not only was there a live human being in Eileen's flat, but that I knew exactly who he was.

Fats, for his part, grinned dangerously, his mini-afro wobbling slightly on top of a laughing face.

'Good people,' he said, pulling his torso lazily to the vertical. 'I've been waiting forever. You, sir, look pretty wasted. Your young lady friend' – he looked happily over at Babalwa's slumped form, which mumbled something muffled and incomprehensible – 'eish.'

'Fats,' I replied eventually, cautiously. 'Howzit hanging?'

'Not bad, Roy, not bad. I mean, I think I enjoyed advertising a bit more overall, but I've kind of taken to this survivor thing.' He was dressed in combat pants, and an army-type shirt beneath a munitions vest. Army boots, sheepskin bangle on the wrist. Muscles rippling under all the gear. All in all, typical of Tšhegofatšo Bonoko, a man who had always been overtly – and frequently unreasonably – styled.

'Jesus. I need to sit.' I dropped onto the couch next to Fats.

'You, Mr Fotheringham, I know pretty well,' he continued blithely, billowing out his usual mock confidence. 'But your young friend here' – he glanced again at the lump that was Babalwa – 'I haven't had the pleasure.'

I was speechless, trapped by a flood of realisations and remembrances. I had never liked Fats Bonoko. He was arrogant, under-talented and over-powerful. Off the top of my shocked, stoned head, I could think of at least four people he'd knifed on his way up the ladder. It didn't seem right, or possible, or logical, that he was where he was, sitting next to me on this couch, grinning with inane self-satisfaction.

'Babalwa,' I said. 'Her name's Babalwa and she's drunk.'

'Ah, a celebration. Nice. I've had a few myself since this shit started.'

'What shit? Do you know what happened?'

Fats looked at me, his face deeply serious. 'I woke up and it was like this. Empty.'

'So you know nothing?'

'Nothing at all. Other than advertising is a pretty damn useless business without a target market.'

'Are there others?' I asked. 'Alive?'

'Plenty.' Fats issued a patronising pat to my shoulder. 'At least six. Maybe more.'

'Six,' Babalwa groaned from the floor. 'Six.'

Chapter 19
The pain did numb, eventually

'Roy, my man, what the fuck happened to your face?' Fats stirred sugar into his cold water and tea bag as we stood around Eileen's impotent kettle. 'The tooth thing. That's a powerful look for you.'

'Ja,' I mumbled, lips closed. 'Know any dentists?'

Fats sipped his cold tea and grimaced. 'On the real though, what the fuck?'

'Let's just say I had an encounter with a rock.'

As the time in PE dragged I found myself slowly, creepingly, thinking about alcohol again. I had run out of weed and the rawness of being stranded – initially a strange, fixating high in itself – was fading. I began to pick my toenails viciously, vacantly, at night. Unable to watch movies, tired of listening to music, listless and disconnected from my sole companion (who herself was drinking increasing volumes of white wine and gin), I was bored.

As we roamed and foraged, I began to look for booze cabinets. Not that I was digging into them or anything, but I noticed myself noticing myself paying attention to stock levels. I began to fantasise about good red wine, about that first sip, something deep and woody, something with the power to slip me up a notch, to refocus my view. My abstract passion for red evolved from observation to actually extracting bottles from the cabinets or shelves, examining them for potential, turning them over in my hands and feeling the weight. Then I would put them back, carefully.

Eventually I found myself in a Bianca's bedroom in Summerstrand, on the beachfront. Her room looked out on Marine Drive, over a few scrub-covered dune humps and then onto the sea. Thin raindrops were tearing into the shoreline at forty-five degrees, the southwester driving perfect, glassy waves which peaked and rolled and peaked and rolled, an occasional dolphin the only surfer taking advantage.

Having stashed her mobile, I flipped through Bianca's photo albums, which were meticulously ordered and maintained, and which stretched right from early childhood through to the end. In pink sleep shorts and a vest, arms around mother in the backyard. Father teaching her to sail a yacht on the Sundays River. Sixteenth birthday with friends at the Pizza Hut. Hair short and styled for the occasion, light make-up, all smiles, friends and lipgloss.

I went for her father's 2019 Zonneblom Shiraz.

I returned with a corkscrew and the bottle and lay down on Bianca's unmade bed.

And it was beautiful, while it lasted. The warmth of the wine, the blurring, evocative safety of her photos. She was ordinary, Bianca. Dark hair. Careful smile. Eyes that sparkled and evaded in equal measures. Bianca with her sailboat. Bianca and dad chasing older brother in fancy-dress masks. Bianca baking, silly hat on head, floury hands in the air.

The wine poured through me and healed me, touching gently, reaching into all the corners. My head went warm, then cold, then warm again. As the bottle died the red crust grew on my lips. I ground it off with the heel of my palm, examining it like it had some deeper, metaphorical meaning. Which it did.

I drained the bottle and passed out, Bianca on her bike in my lap.

I woke in the dark, throbbing drunk, the wind and rain pulsing outside.

Back to dad's rack, another Zonneblom, back again, stumbling. Suddenly I was reaching for destruction or damnation or something similar and opening the third was impossible. I couldn't get the screw into the cork.

And then out the front door and to the car and over a rock and smashing my face into the ground and the black wet darkness of being out cold in the rain on some stranger's driveway. Then the waking and the pain needles all through my face and my torn lip and my ripped cheek and the sight, the awful, pathetic sight of my shard of tooth on the driveway, pointing like a compass in the direction of home.

I laughed when I saw Babalwa the next day but she didn't return it. Her face fell, her eyes hooded and careful and a little bit scared.

'What the fuck?' She shouted like a mother. 'What the bloody fuck Roy?'

'I got lost.'

'Your face.' She shook her head and then snuck another look at me. 'Your lips. Jesus, Roy, your tooth!'

'I won't do it again, promise.'

'What?'

'Drink.'

'That's what this is? You went drinking?'

She closed the space between us down to a millimetre and slapped me, through the cuts and scabs, through the broken lip and tortured gums. As the pain shot through my mouth I groaned and fell back a step or two. 'You stupid fuck,' she said, crying now, tears running down both cheeks. 'Please, please, I'm begging you, Roy. You're all I've got. You're the only hope there is. If you turn into this ...' Her head twisted away from the horror. 'If you turn into this, you're pushing me out, totally alone, into the world. You can't do that. Jesus Christ, you can't do that, Roy.'

'I said I won't.'

'I don't believe you.' Babalwa walked away.

I saw her again two days later.

By then my mouth had started the healing journey, healthy parts reaching for each other over the volcanoes. The remaining half of my tooth throbbed constantly. Babalwa insisted I extract it, but I refused. The pain would fade, or the nerve would numb, or something like that. She shook her head and walked away again.

The pain did numb, eventually, ratcheting down from a scream to a throb, from a throb to a pulse, from a pulse to an annoying dull ache. I sliced constantly on the guillotine that now hung from my gum, tiny, almost invisible trickles of blood forming repeatedly in the curl of my tongue.

It was weeks before Babalwa could look at me directly without her own countenance crumpling completely.

I stopped smiling.
I eliminated the smile from my life.
The very idea of smiling, gone.

Losing a back tooth is unfortunate. Losing a front tooth is life-changing. I would catch glimpses of myself in shop windows and stray mirrors and every time I was shocked; the combination of hair and tooth had created a reflection I didn't recognise. I turned the van's rear-view mirror far left, cutting myself out entirely. I withdrew from Babalwa, and from myself. I lay awake at night, fizzing in sobriety, frogmarching myself into dreams of magnitude. I whipped and whipped and whipped. But while the scars slowly grew closed, the damage remained.

'Boss.' Fats sipped his tea and blinked rapidly. 'That's about the most fucking tragic thing I've ever heard.' He wiped back a tear. 'Serious. Since all this shit happened, this is the most pathetic, disturbing thing ...'

I shrugged, picked a tea mug off its stand, reached to turn on the kettle and then put the mug back. 'Imagine how I feel.'

'That's the point, nè?' Fats locked me in for a while, eyeball to eyeball. 'That's exactly the fucking point.'

'What's the point?' Babalwa slurred, having appeared at the corner of the kitchen door. She was wiping her eyes.

'Hai.' Fats shook his head. 'We were just discussing your mlungu here and his dental problems.'

'You drinking tea?' Babalwa asked Fats hopefully.

'Ice-cold. Straight out the barrel. You want?'

'No. Yuk'. She shivered in the doorway, hugging her elbows.

'Where you from, anyway?' Fats asked, managing to sound simultaneously serious and slyly suggestive of something unnamed.

'Port Elizabeth. PE.'

'Ah. Land of the defeated. Askies.'

'Not so bad.' Babalwa glared at him. 'It wasn't so bad.'

Fats carried on the conversation in a mix of bad isiXhosa and tsotsitaal. Babalwa replied rapidly and within seconds I was gazing around the room looking for something. I tried to hang onto the one or two familiar words, but it was useless. The conversation shifted gear several times and I felt myself become the subject, discussed rapid fire, followed by an awkward silence.

'Sorry, Roy, my man, you know, it's good to connect. Authentically.' Fats drained the last of his tea and thumped the mug down into the sink without looking at me.

Babalwa backed out of the kitchen, still hugging herself.

Fats turned and beamed at me blankly. 'Well, I must tell you, it's fucking good to have some more faces on board. And one that I already know – I would never have thought it was possible.'

'How long you been following us?' I asked on a whim.

'Tebza and I heard the shots – when you were testing your cannons. We followed the sound, tried not to get pinned by stray bullets, and here we are. Tebza was supposed to follow you from a long distance but I presume you lost him at some stage. He's not really the following type.'

'Where's he now? Tebza?'

'Not sure,' Fats replied, three-quarters of an eye seeking Babalwa's vanished form. 'That will have to be our next move, before we go back. We'll have to find him.'

'Back where?'

'Home, my half-toothed friend. Home.'

There were a million reasons why I had never liked Fats Bonoko and they all came flooding back as he marched through Eileen's flat calling the shots. Firstly, he was an arrogant son of a bitch. Secondly, he was extremely skilled at putting that arrogance to work. Fats invariably emerged shining from the rubble of his business interactions. He launched the hand grenades, picked out the prizes and stepped around the corpses. Hardly a unique paradigm in our business, but extremely frustrating for the foot soldiers.

He was, to top it all, good-looking, fit, muscular and possessed of a powerful, annoying wit.

'I've just remembered,' he offered as we waited for Babalwa to gather warmer clothes. 'That chewing gum thing you came up with. Awesome. Quality work. What was the line again?'

'Counter revolution.'

'Counter revolution.' He slapped the butt of his rifle. 'Counter revolution. Love it. It was rare, that one. Perfect timing. Fantastic.'

'I like to think I made a contribution.'

Fats burst into a guttural laugh, slapped his rifle again. 'Ah man, too much. So dry. You always were so dry.'

We headed out. Fats in front, leading us down the stairs. Babalwa behind him, then me.

'There are seven of us,' he called out as we descended the stairwell. 'Me, Tebza, Lillian the American – don't even fucking ask me how we ended up with an American – sis Beatrice, Gerald the mercenary and the twins – well, that's what we call them, they're inseparable. Thus far, just so you know, we have no agreement on what happened. Tebza has his very own ideas, which no one can understand; the rest of us are split somewhere between the apocalypse, a virus and godly intervention of some kind or another.'

Our feet thumped in unison down the last stairs.

'Me,' Fats continued, 'I'm scared shitless, but I'm also glad I'm not in advertising any more. You feeling me, Mr Fotheringham?'

I grunted.

Teboho appeared as we left the building. He was a tall, sloping kid of about nineteen or twenty, one tiny white earphone dangling over his heart, the other plugged in. There was a faint scar next to his left eye, which squeezed and wrinkled when he smiled or squinted. Basketball clothes: shorts cutting off below his knees, fat white sneakers, red Nike vest. An R1 wrapped uncomfortably around his left forearm. He stepped forward and shook hands politely, repeating his name to me and Babalwa.

Teboho.

Teboho.

He turned after the greeting and led us down the block and

into Jan Smuts, where their gleaming black Toyota 4x4 was parked beside an abandoned bus stop.

'We did a big campaign for them years ago. Don't know whether you noticed it, Fotheringham,' Fats said, not bothering to look at me or wait for my participation, 'but it was massive. Fell in love with these beasts then.' He patted the Toyota's bonnet. 'Just can't resist.'

We got into the car in silence.

Fats waved his thumb over the reader, started his beast and kicked it into first with relish.

'For as long as there's petrol, I think this is my baby.'

Teboho, front passenger, popped the dangling earphone in and stared out the window.

Babalwa took my hand and squeezed it.

Fats blitzed us over Bolton, then over the highway, and cut a series of sharp rights into the upper side of Houghton, where the mansions lined up on the ridge. He didn't stop talking, rattling off random snippets like a tour guide, ranging from reminiscences from his ad days to broad reflections on the apocalypse and specific insights on the current practical difficulties in their community.

'Our focus at the moment is on security – obviously – and the solar bank. That's the big thing, for now. With enough power we can do pretty much what we want into the future with the farm and regularised production. That's why we are where we are, on the ridge. We're picking up wicked sun pretty much all day ...'

Fats spoke in the classic manner of the project manager, the we's and us's flowing seamlessly into each other, pulling Babalwa and myself immediately into the centre of things. A de facto integration had already occurred. His mission was ours. Their challenges already belonged to me. I wondered what Teboho thought about it all – about Fats and his assumptions and directions. I looked for some kind of expression from him in the side mirror, but his face was completely blank. Zoned out.

'Don't mind him,' Fats offered, letting me know he was observing as well as rambling. 'He's totally addicted. Don't think I've ever seen him without at least one ear plugged in. It's disconcerting but you get used to it.'

'Music?' Babalwa asked. 'Is he listening to music?'

'Ja, that and scanning for communiques from the aliens, and pinging, always pinging. He can't let go of the idea of the network.' Fats chuckled, then added, 'On the real, though – this boy's on completely another trip. Personally I think he's just got monster withdrawal, but there you go, we all cope in our own ways, nè?'

Teboho's head bounced gently up and down to some kind of beat. He could have been agreeing with Fats's assertions, or he could have been completely otherwise engaged. It was impossible to tell.

After we'd crested a steep series of S bends, Fats turned the Toyota into a plush lane, mansions on the left and the classic stone British public school buildings of King Edward High School on the right. Just past KES we pulled into an anonymous driveway fronted by Joburg's traditional upper-class black gangster gates. The gates swung open.

'Look,' Babalwa poked me excitedly in the ribs. 'They've got power.'

'Not a lot,' gushed Fats. 'But enough to cover all the basics and we're growing the bank every day. Soon we should be able to juice up anything that needs it.' He steered us through a driveway designed to impress and maybe even humiliate its visitors. We rolled down a steep slope, stone walls on either side fighting a barely controlled jungle.

'We haven't got to regular gardening yet,' Fats added, in reference to the foliage. 'But soon. The way these fucking things are growing, very soon.' He stomped hard on the brake and guided us down an especially sharp slope before parking in a garage area littered with 4x4s of various colours and sizes and featuring a long, extended turning loop. On the left of the parking area was a multi-levelled stone mansion behind an enormous and surprisingly clear swimming pool.

The mansion rolled out across the property in several different directions. Each wing looked like it could have lived a full life on its own – creeping vine covered the central hub and stretched out to each arm, but the four quarters could have worked as stand-alone buildings. At the far end of the garden, near the front gate, stood a separate house, a cottage for the help. Also built from stone, it had its own small swimming pool, a tiled veranda and four or five rooms.

'Previously owned by the Minister for What, What and What, I believe,' said Fats. 'The Right Honourable Jackson something. Also, obviously, a member of the King Edward High School governing body, et cetera, et cetera.' He waved in the direction of KES. Babalwa looked at me blankly, seeking elaboration, but before I could get going a tall, incongruously made-up and polished lady clipped beaming out the front door. She fit well into her mid-range stilettos, blue jeans and neat black vest. She sported gold hoop earrings and maroon nail polish, her hair swept into a tight set of braids running in parallel lines over her skull and down into a funky yet neat tail that rested, mullet-like, on the back of her neck.

'And that,' Fats bellowed as we walked awkwardly towards each other, 'is our ever impeccable sis Beatrice.' He gave her a fake advertising hug and introduced us all. 'Beatrice is never, ever, caught out,' he observed as I shook her hand and Babalwa fell into her arms in a child's hug. 'Regardless of the circumstances, even in the midst of the apocalypse, sis Beatrice is impeccable. It's the CEO in her' – he was unable to stop – 'she brings style, grace and a little bit of sexiness to every occasion.'

Beatrice shot him a look, blushed a little and told us how happy she was to see us. She joined the tour as if she was also new to the place, listening intently to Fats's explanations and introductions. We wandered through the property, picking up new members with every stop. The greetings ranged from wild hugs and yells from Andile (the loudest noise, it turned out, we'd ever hear from her) to a smile from Javas, and a gentleman's handshake from Gerald. Fats marched us through the facilities in the dark, waving his torch around a series of vague shapes and forms. Eventually the group wound downstairs to the deck area overlooking northern Johannesburg, below which was a glimmering solar bank. The panels covered the entire slope underneath the deck, a space of about three hundred square metres. The panels blinked a confident silver in the moonlight.

'This, really, is it.' Fats waved his hand in a full arc around the panel area. 'This has been our mission since we found each other. Power, people, is everything. And what makes this lot work are the batteries. They are the latest, the very latest, in fact, from Germany. These babies can store for over four days.'

'It was all set up when we got here. That's why we chose it,' Lillian, the plump white American, whispered at me conspiratorially. 'All we've done is add more panels.'

We stood in silence for a while, blinking back at the panels.

'Anyone hungry?' Beatrice asked, looking at Babalwa with motherly concern, then at me. 'You must be hungry.'

'Starving, thanks.'

'OK, a lightning pass over the rest then, just so they can get their bearings!' Fats pulled us back upstairs, through the cavernous foyer and into one of the other wings. 'This is Tebza's domain, eh, Tebza?' The first room in the wing was packed with old-school flat-screen monitors and blinking green and red lights. Teboho blinked at us from the back. 'Tebza is pinging wildly at the walls, hoping to find a connection to something somewhere. Like those people who send radio signals to space looking for aliens. He's also setting up a WAN* to cover this house; then we'll move it out to wider areas. The idea, obviously, is to get to a point where we start connecting to other terminals in the city, the country, the continent and then the world. The hope, obviously, being that some people somewhere else are doing the same thing. The other hope, more localised, is that re-establishing some form of net will help deal with Tebza's digital withdrawal. Eh, Tebza?'

Teboho pulled a very slim silver something out of his pocket, clicked twice, and returned it without looking up.

'The other thing,' Fats continued blithely, 'is the whole flying

---

* The beginnings of the WAN are well documented in the digital section of the Malema Library, St John's campus. This section is well worth exploring on historical and technical levels. Tebza's role in digital development is often overlooked.

bit. But I'll let Lillian tell you about that.'

Lillian stepped forward, cleared her throat and began talking like she was presenting a conference paper. 'Drones are the starting point, obviously. We have secured three from the Waterkloof Airforce Base, but the relationship between the drone and the software is complex – hence the WAN work Teboho is doing. If we can't set up a link between the plane and the software, we won't be able to capture the imagery and then there's no point. But the drones, really, are a stepping stone to the larger aim of flight.

'There are planes and fuel we can access, but what we don't have and what we really need are pilots. So that machine there' – she pointed out a large PC box with an ancient sixty-inch screen attached – 'is our pilot training machine. At the moment we've only got a kiddy-game simulator running, but we're aiming to source a proper training simulator and to learn how to fly. Then it's a question of being brave enough to try it in the real world.' She took a deep breath. 'Then the next—'

'Thanks, Lillian.' Fats cut her off. 'Good summary. OK, kids, last stop before food, the garden. This way.'

We trooped behind him, obedient. As we walked I thought more about Fats. Ad Fats. With effort, I remembered him as less headmaster and more free radical; most people were jealous of him because it was never clear exactly what he did. He wasn't practical. I never, for example, saw him cook anything up on Photoshop, or write a line of copy, or sketch out a brand idea or a conference map. Fats Bonoko was the ideas man, the guy who breezed past your shoulder saying, 'Love it' or 'Nice, but maybe try a softer green for the housewives'. He was, I remembered, also an experiential specialist, which meant he created events for brands. Parties. Boat trips. Cooking tours. VR extravaganzas. Experiential campaigns equated essentially to brand-activation projects – Fats was the guy who took 'it' off TV, whatever 'it' was, and delivered 'it' to people in the flesh, so to speak.

'This,' Fats boomed as we trooped out the kitchen door, 'is our day-to-day survival patch. There's a lot more going on food-wise outside the house, but this is where we go when we need quick stuff for cooking.' We gathered around a vegetable garden – much of it protected by various combinations of green netting.

'Beans, spinach, carrots, potatoes, lettuce, cauliflower, herb garden, et cetera. Obviously, our major long-term challenges are meat, milk and any kind of dairy. But the vegetables are the foundation. Andile, care to explain?'

Andile snorted. 'It's mos a veggie patch, Fats.'

'Right, thanks.' Fats brushed through the insult and rounded on myself and Babalwa. 'Any questions, guys? We're pretty much an open book here. I know this must be a bit overwhelming for you after all this time alone, but if there's anything specific you want to know, hit me. Or anyone else.'

We glanced at each other. Babalwa shrugged, shy.

'Um,' I piped up uncertainly, 'I guess the only one for me is, like, are there rules or something? Who decides who does what and why … all that kind of stuff?'

Andile and Javas coughed simultaneously. Lillian smiled. Gerald frowned and scuffed the garden soil with a toe. Beatrice stared straight ahead, unmoved.

'It's a collective,' said Fats. 'We all do what needs to be done. We agree on what we can. But really it's about everyone taking responsibility, nè? Ubuntu, et cetera.'

'It's like *Survivor*,' added Andile, giggling out of the corner of her mouth.

'Only no one gets voted out,' Fats said as he herded us back through the kitchen door.

The evening rushed on. We gathered and regathered in small groups, discussing 'the situation' and sharing anecdotes and experiences, most of them revolving around waking up to an empty world. Beatrice set to in the kitchen, making lettuce and tomato sandwiches – from our garden, Fats stressed, all from our garden.

Disquiet rose from my toes, trickled through my gut and into my aching tooth and my head.

Conversely, Babalwa lit up slowly with social fluorescence. I had never heard her voice this light, her laughter this floaty. In small but definitive ways I was already no longer her primary reference point. As for me – despite my better judgement, despite everything I knew to be sensible and right – I wanted to go home.

Chapter 20

My entire life on that fucking cloud

Lillian, the American academic, was typical of her kind – always in the middle of the 'narrative' and prone to wholesale, orchestrated redirections of the conversational ship. She explained a lot, unknowingly talking to us as if to children. She looked, at first glance, to be between twenty-five and thirty years old. Of dumpy build, she had the whiff of cash about her; there had certainly been enough around to have expanded her backside with disproportionate weight, most likely the heaviness of supermarket muffins and cappuccinos. She smelled, also, of roll-on deodorant. The smell would take on a particular sharpness when she was angry and had her arms folded in attack mode. She was also prone to adopting calculated poses, which she held for inordinate lengths of time, until she was sure someone had taken note. She would sweep her hair up into a ponytail and then hold it there, elbows parallel to the ground, as if she were a model, or a socialite on the make. It was like she wasn't quite sure who she was, or who she needed or wanted to be, on any given occasion. Bottom line: when she wasn't carefully cutting a silhouette into the skyline, Lillian talked a hell of a lot, and appeared to believe her brain was a repository of all things worth knowing.

Gerald was quiet, older, very black and very muscular. He came from the north-east – Mpumalanga somewhere – and spent most of that first night watching Fats and mumbling his own unheard replies to the questions bouncing around the room. Barefoot, in jeans and a loose, striped pink golf shirt, he radiated a strong potential energy. Possibly he was desperate to be heard. Possibly he was just desperate for some silence, like me.

Teboho sat nodding, still staring off into the corners, the single white earphone dangling politely over his heart.

Andile perched on the kitchen counter next to Javas and they brushed against each other with easy frequency. Javas looked every inch the artist he apparently was. There were light paint splatters on his jeans, which were also torn at the ankles. He wore a faded dark-blue Standard Bank T-shirt and a Scottish-style golf cap, perched high on dreads. His face was leathery and crinkled and his eyes glimmered like those of a travelling man. Andile, in turn, was all eyes. Her ocular equipment was markedly bigger than average, and she had an unnerving ability to lock you into their big brown pools. She was, relatively speaking, lightly primped. She wore a very light brown lipstick, two neat silver teardrop earrings, and a knee-length frock neatly suspended over blue jeans.

At this early stage, Beatrice was the oddity. She was fully dressed and ready for the office – all she had to do was reach for her bag on the way out.

Babalwa talked on our behalf, dribbling out the details of our misguided PE stint and sudden compulsion to flee. Beatrice and Fats punctuated the flow with humour, ideas and plans. Always plans.

I let the words fly past. I looked at my feet. My filthy, filthy feet, still caked in the debris of our flight from PE. My equally damaged jeans. My dirty fingernails. I looked, I knew, like a lost bum. Babalwa, at least, was more together. No longer completely pissed on the champagne, she cut a reasonable, less bum-like figure in her T-shirt, jeans, sandals and socks.

'So!' Fats clapped his hands and brought us to order. 'If we can just get practical for a few minutes. Any suggestions as to which rooms they should take?'

Lillian offered up two rooms in the left wing. 'Ja? Guys?' Fats beamed at Babalwa and me in turn.

'Fine by me,' said Babalwa, glancing in my direction without actually looking at me.

'All good.' I smiled, and fought an animal urge to run.

My room was clearly a spare. A decently wide single bed and a large bookcase filled with technical books: governance and leadership manuals, MBA study materials, policy guidelines and frameworks.

A map of the world in a thick, black wooden frame on the wall.

I traced my finger over Africa, then America, down to South America. Brazil.

I considered going over to Babalwa's room. I wondered whether she was thinking of knocking on my door. Our separation had been surgical and subtle. Fats was slick, I had to give him that. I missed her presence already. I counted the number of consecutive nights we had spent together in the same bed. Seven.

I probed the guillotine with my tongue while I lay on the bed and stared at the map.

I waited for her knock.

Hours later, in the dark of the early morning, I conceded defeat and wandered the mansion, strolling up and down the staircases, running my hand over the oak banisters, contemplating what kind of life the minister had led. Whether he had, on the odd occasion, paid attention to the same railings, run his hand down them, waited for his thoughts to catch up with his body.

Eventually I landed at the doorway to the computer room and there was Tebza, clicking and nodding. He turned, telepathically, pulled an earphone out and greeted me.

'Come inside.' He waved at the machines. 'Feel free ...'

'What you up to?' I tiptoed to his desk.

'Ag, just network stuff, you know, trying to figure out the last of it. Jesus, even just a WAN that reaches past the gates. Mission.'

'You in computers? Before?'

'Nah,' he scoffed. 'Broker. Stocks and shit.'

'Ah.'

'And you? Advertising, nè?'

'Ja, kinda. Initially anyway. Then I ended up in VR. You know, the clubs ...'

'Ah. Ja, I heard something like that in the kitchen. Mlungu's, yes?'

'My claim to fame.'

'Had a few nights there myself. Good place.' Tebza leaned back into his screen while keeping his nearest shoulder blade open in conversational invitation. He slammed the enter key through a never-ending string of IP addresses as we talked.

'You think we'll get it back? The net? A net? A cloud?'

'I fucking doubt it. The cloud is now in a gazillion tiny pieces.' Teboho leaned fully back in his office chair, the springs holding him at a dangerous forty-five degrees. He locked his hands around his head. 'You have no idea how much shit I had on the cloud. So much shit. My entire life on that fucking cloud. Everything ...'

'Eish.'

'It always worried me. To have everything that meant anything sitting there. So I made sure I backed it all up, twice.'

'Onto the cloud?'

'Onto the cloud.' Teboho laughed and made genuine eye contact with me for the first time. 'I dunno, maybe it's just panic. A defence against everything, but I feel like if I could get just something back, a few albums, some photos, that would be a step. An important step.' He shrugged, flapping his elbows a bit, and considered me.

'Eish.' I couldn't think of anything else to say to indicate the sudden warmth I felt for him. 'Jammer, nè? Hardcore. Me, I had nothing up there that meant anything.'

We shrugged together.

'You smoke?' I asked hopefully, my heart accelerating.

'I do.' Teboho sprung his chair forward, pulled a small bankie from his pocket and tossed it at me happily. 'I most certainly do. Roll it up, son, roll it up.'

We sat on the brick stairs guarding the swimming pool and smoked.

Teboho was a middle-class kid. 'Straight outta Midrand', as he put it. With Model C schooling followed by an average BCom stint at an average university, he went straight into finance, banking and trading. There were constant hints, however, that he was more than a collection of banker parts. His music references were more complex than I expected. His technology obsession was genuine as well. Real geeks always had a certain manner about them – a particular way of describing life and ambition and the tools at our disposal as a lush, expanding horizon. Tebza fit the bill. He spoke easily, unthinkingly, of time-lapse nanotech, the importance of getting the raw vector designs right in the VR clubs, of algo trading and new beats emerging from somewhere in remote Russia that, by all accounts, were about to turn current notions of X, Y and Z on their heads.

And the boy was genuinely, seriously pained by the loss of the cloud.

'Dumb-assed.' He shook his head slowly. 'Just dumb-assed. I thought about hard backups so many times, but I was lazy. Told myself I was being paranoid. But fuck ...' He tailed off. 'All that's gone now. No use dreaming. It's a long, long way away. I'll always miss it though, you know. As shallow and cheesy and stupid as it was, our life, I'll miss it. The clubs and the music and the people. Maybe there was a kind of security in the triviality?'

'That's my life,' I grunted in affirmation, mesmerised by the glow of the moon on the pool. 'Security in triviality.'

'Ha.' Tebza flicked the roach into the hedges. 'I suppose we're learning now, nè?'

Our conversation drifted back and forth across the landscape of our past. Together we reached as far back as we could go, pushing into the jelly of what was. Of times that were sweet and green and simple.

Eventually we fell to quiet, and then back into the present, and Fats.

'He's obsessed, just so you know,' Tebza warned. 'He has this master plan. Pretty freaky. He can be forceful, you know? It's tough, 'cause he also seriously gets shit done. He's got the farm and the food and the power moving, and so, you know, he can be hard to deny.'

According to Tebza, Fats aimed to fence off our block completely, including not only the entire grounds of King Edward High School, but also St John's – an even bigger and richer stone institution, adjacent to KES, at the end of the lane we occupied. If Fats had his way, our enclave would feature controlled access points at the beginning of our lane and in key areas: the top of Munro Drive – apparently the name of the steep S bend we had travelled to get to the ridge – the outer edge of St John's School, where the property linked with the main road, and others. Fats, apparently, was obsessed by the idea of invasion. The idea of a pack of others the same size as us.

'Dunno, could have merit,' Tebza mused. 'I mean, a posse with big enough guns could just come and take it. Take us. So that's his thing – the fencing. He's pushing hard on it, got district maps and everything all up on the wall, the perimeters marked out. Red pins, little marker pens and the whole bit. Jesus. All in his control room.'

'His bedroom?'

'No, the control room. Next to his bedroom he's converted this study-type room into a control room, centre, thingy. Put a few computers in – for atmosphere more than anything else at this stage, I think – rigged up a two-way radio, that kinda thing. Massive map, red pins, bits of linking string and such.'

'Bit freaky.'

'Bit, ja. But you know what they say – fattest stomach wins, eh?'

'Ja …' I mulled over the idea of Fats The General. He had spent a lifetime designing and managing events – for forty thousand people and more. He probably needed a way to carry on with what he knew. Didn't we all?

'I guess he could have a point. I mean, we can't be the only nine people left on the planet.'

Teboho patted my knee and stood. 'My friend,' he said, 'we could be anything at all. Absolutely anything at all.'

Chapter 21
Cow experience

The sun rose the next morning, and darkness fell.

We were drifting awake, emerging from our bedrooms, mumbling quietly in the kitchen, when the clouds blacked out the day. Drops hit the ground like mortar rounds, each shattering into shrapnel. The dark was ominous, and complete.

'This is too weird for me,' said Lillian, who headed back up to her room.

The rest of us – save Tebza, who was still asleep – sat on the expensive porch furniture with our toast and black coffee and tea. Babalwa sat next to me. She pulled her wrought-iron chair up close, made eye contact and dropped a few direct conversational threads. I felt grateful and oddly patronised, but ultimately any kind of contact with someone familiar was settling. The stilted conversation and forced eyeballing of new people was like a trip back to junior school.

'What's on the agenda for today, kids?' Fats asked the group, trying to make eye contact with each of us. Heads stayed low.

'Javas?'

'Dunno, boss.' Javas bit a chunk off his toast and chewed. 'But I have a feeling you're about to tell me.'

'I was thinking about a cow – a resident cow. As we've agreed before. For milk. It's the next step. Can't speak for y'all but I'm sick of this long-life shit.'

'A. Resident. Cow.' Javas repeated the words slowly, individually. 'And I am the man for the cow, yes?'

'Sho.' Fats leaned back in his chair and pulled an oversized hunk off his toast. 'You have cow experience, do you not?'

'I do,' Javas replied slowly. 'I do.'

Chapter 22
It could be good once it's done

The mansion operated completely off-grid. Tucked into the tailored shrubbery beyond the driveway's turning circle, the borehole was the philosophical and practical centre of things. Deep and plentiful, it fed a stocky, black plastic fifteen-thousand-litre tank. A criss-crossed trellis surrounded the tank, hosting the concealing shrubbery. The pump was noisy – wherever we were on the property, the random thwuuump thwuuump thwuuump reminded us of its service. We soon forgot it, how to even hear it, but it was nonetheless omnipresent – the subliminal functional soundtrack to life.

The solar bank supplied most of the power required, most of the time. For emergencies, there was a generator the size of a small caravan. A sick, old-looking thing on wheels, which only Tebza and Fats were technically familiar with, it was rarely required, because the erstwhile minister had also ensured that the septic tank, rather than draining away into the soil, fed its methane into the system.

'We shit power,' Fats announced proudly.

The miracle of it – the technical set-up – faded over time, but for Babalwa and me the breadth of the accomplishment was shocking, given how much we had struggled to establish even the most basic power in PE. For weeks after we arrived I would flick light switches on and off. Or stand wet and amazed in the bathroom post-shower, gazing at the geyser. One afternoon I found her tapping the borehole tank while hovering her ear over the black plastic, as if it held a secret.

The resonance within the house itself was that of money. Thick red carpeting, Persian rugs, oak panels and leather-backed armchairs – the smell of wealth was threaded into the structure of the place. Layered lightly over the booty of postgraduate decision-making was the evidence of our more flippant, plastic existence. We each kept to our own residential quarters faithfully, but in the communal areas our collective presence steadily stained, moved and altered. Inconvenient Persians were rolled up and shoved to the side. Ring marks spread on the arms of the furniture. Stains and nicks and chips in the expensive wood. Mould.

One day Andile tramped garden mud through the entrance hall, initially unknowingly, then unapologetically. Beatrice tried to protect the carpet with a plea for immediate cleaning but was vetoed. Instead, we ripped up the lush red and brown and washed down the concrete underneath. The hallway echoed weirdly forever after, the floor stripped of all possible pretence.

Fats ordered and prompted and planned, and the rest of us, each for our own reasons, followed dutifully. With my meagre possessions packed into my oversized room, I lived a life in neutral. I completed my allotted tasks in their allotted time, and otherwise I drifted across the empty city, looking at full bottles of liquor through the closed store windows.

Lillian lectured anyone within earshot on the history of the area. Untouched by the irony of being the only foreigner, she lashed us repeatedly with her knowledge of the ridge: how it was occupied by the mining magnates and the original colonisers, back when Jozi was just a scrappy piece of dust with a lot of gold underneath it. It – the ridge – was occupied for all the obvious reasons. It allowed its inhabitants to perch on top of the city and observe the movements and machinations below. Lillian explained how the ridge was a slow starter as a residential area compared to Parktown, that it was only in the 1930s that it really took off with the larnies, when the so-called International Style of architecture came around and allowed the rich to feel like their Upper Houghton houses would compete with those in France, England et al.

Of course we all knew all this; the knowledge was threaded into our genes, and so Lillian was shrugged off and smiled at and tolerated with varying degrees of annoyance, frustration and amusement. 'These people,' Gerald would occasionally mutter under his breath while being educated.

Word was that our arrival gave Fats the energy burst necessary to finalise his mission to enclose us. Our farming area occupied the King Edward High School sports fields. Some of the fields were being grown over to provide grazing for the cattle Javas was sourcing. Others were tilled and prepared to grow stuff. Corn. Vegetables. Sunflowers.

The school buildings were less important. We used them, classroom by classroom, for various functional ends – the closer the classroom to the fields, the higher its utility level for tool storage and such things. The outer third of the KES buildings, those facing towards St John's, were left alone.

St John's, Fats decided, should be treated as our moat. Our security façade. It was crucial, according to his strategy, to have a bulwark in place. He mounted a South African flag on the school's outer pole, facing north, looking over the highway off-ramp.

His control-centre map marked off, with red pins of course, the areas where the already robust fencing could easily be repurposed. The southern fencing simply needed to be joined – each institution was already carefully cut off from Louis Botha Avenue, the historical divide between the schools and the real/ghetto worlds of Yeoville, Berea, Hillbrow and the city. The western fences around St John's required only a moderate additional stretch to close off the small St Patrick Road entrance. Munro Drive twirled up in steep loops from Lower Houghton and could be easily sealed at the top, as it joined St Patrick. Here Fats planned to install a primary guard hut, our key defence post, which would protect the top of Munro Drive and the only entrance to St Patrick Lane, where our residence was located. Beyond our house, St Patrick died off into a dead end of ridge mansions overlooking the eastern city. All that remained, according to Fats, was to restructure the crime-prevention fencing that blocked off eastern suburban access via smaller roads leading off Louis Botha, and we had a secure area of more than a square kilometre.

There were questions, of course. Mutterings and mumblings. Lillian was the most prone to seeding rebellion. She cornered me a few days after our arrival, as I was pacing the artificial turf of the KES hockey fields trying to assess and understand. I saw her coming, shuffling aggressively across the field, the mousy intervener. Beatrice had coined the phrase and it stuck. Lillian moved like a mouse, always scratching, always ahead of herself, twitching, eyes on the move. She pulled her heavy ass around at high speed, accentuating the general impression, and once her mouth had started moving there was no stopping it. She was in every sense mousy. Equally, it was her essential nature to intervene.

She flicked curls away from her eyes with a pointed hand.

'Fats's thing' – she moved to the point via an introduction on the extremeness of these public schools – 'to tell you the truth, I'm not so sure. We could be wasting a lot of time and resources. I mean, there is no sign of anyone else, let alone invaders.' She dropped onto her haunches and tried unsuccessfully to pluck a blade from the artificial turf. I wasn't sure if there was more to come or if this was my cue. I let the silence settle, then initiated a stroll through the KES buildings.

I had, like most South African kids, walked into adulthood through the shadows cast by the country's boys' schools: KES, St John's, Michaelhouse, Parktown, Grey, St Andrew's, St Stithians, Bishops ... Whatever city you were in, there was at least one school cut directly out of nineteenth- and twentieth-century England, dropped into the southern African bush. The names differed but they were all fundamentally linked in their structure, their uniforms, their architecture and their ability to push out generation after generation of CEOs, opening batsmen, fly-halves and marketing managers. My father was a product of one of these institutions, but his dalliances with fate ensured that I navigated a different channel. Me, I attended Northcliff High, a more common brick-and-prefab organisation devoid of national sporting, political or business ambitions. At Northcliff, graduate successes were the accidents of fortune likely to befall any institution that held its doors open long enough. At places like KES and St John's, however, the school legacy was threaded into the very edifice; every brick, every blade of rolled grass or every inch of carefully maintained artificial turf.

We walked into KES through the heavy stone arches of the hockey-field entrance, past a bronze statue of Graeme Smith leaning into an ugly, manly cover drive, then to the main hall, lush with rows of dark wooden chairs, honours boards, and stained-glass badges at the top of the double-volume glass windows, which shed bright light over the hall. The hall was, in the same manner as Big Ben and the old churches of Europe, undeniably magnificent.

I had always skirted around these buildings. Even on those occasions when our shoddy school bus would broach the gates, there was never enough space or time to truly observe and take it all in. We were always rushing through the process, through the event, eyes down, trying not to make any mistakes that would too obviously disclose the awe that the structures created.

Now, with Lillian rattling off facts at my side, I was able to step back and observe, step forward and run my fingers over the honours boards: Graeme Smith, Bryan Habana, Ronnie Kasrils, Donald Gordon – the list was endless. The wood was old and ever so slightly ridged under the fingertip. You could, if you knew what you were feeling for, actually touch the texture of the upper classes. I was, of course, an indirect descendant of this same lineage. The Maritzburg College boards featured several generations of Fotheringham success, not least of whom my father, national cricketer, DJ, oddball.

Lillian powered on as we bridged over to St John's. 'A World Class Christian School in Africa,' the foyer brochures said. She informed me that the institution had maintained this motto for many decades. She snorted derisively as she parted with the information and, despite my general irritation, I snorted too. While KES was a brat factory of the highest order, St John's was in a different, higher league. To anyone looking up at its multi-tiered stone immensity from the bottom rugby fields, it was at least as impressive in scope as the Union Buildings themselves. But its true magnificence lay in the details. Even after close on a year of natural growth, the lines of the almost nuclear green grass held steady along the stone paths and walls, and pointed decisively to the stairs. St John's, the grass said, maintained its lines. Always.

A single road separated the two primary segments of the 'campus'. In the middle of the road stood a statue of a young boy, an eagle on his arm. The boy is releasing the bird to flight, a powerful metaphorical summary, according to Lillian, of the opportunities created by such institutions for those lucky enough to be well born. Further on, the 'David quad' featured a similar type of slim boy, but this one was simply looking outward, hand resting on a cocked hip covered by a boy skirt, creating a camp Peter Pan feel.

We climbed the bell tower. The view at the top was all-encompassing, pulling the breadth of the city easily under its wing, likewise the horizons of Sandton and Pretoria. The enormous sheer drop down to the front façade and the northern sports fields via a series of stone staircases, swaddled in upper-class creepers and surrounded by benches, pristine resting points and quaint yet classy alternative paths, was the kind of descent only those with permission would dare attempt.

The silence would have been an important, magnificent accompaniment were Lillian not still booming on, this time about her master's thesis on how the Native Indian idea of photographs stealing your soul had finally come to fruition in the usage by NGOs of photos of indigenous locals, vital to securing the funding necessary to pay for upper-middle-class suburban Western lifestyles and a metaphysical lust to save the planet.

Which was all good and well, and possibly true, but the sound of her words was nibbling at my sanity. I reverted to Q&A format, speaking as slowly as I could to try to balance out her verbosity.

'Where are you from in the US?'

'Atlanta, Georgia. Can't you tell from the accent?' She looked serious.

'Uh, nah. Skies. Hate to say it, but you all sound pretty similar to me. But ja, I guess now that you say it, it fits.'

'Yeah.' Her accent grew thicker. 'Well, I'm a Georgia girl.'

'You missing it? Home?'

Lillian blinked a few times and looked to the Pretoria horizon.

'Beyond explanations. That's how much I miss it.' She locked me into eye contact. 'But what do you think, Roy? About Fats's gating thing. I mean, I know you haven't been here long and all that, but I just wanted to get an idea of what your thoughts are—'

'I knew Fats before, you know,' I dodged, 'and he was a pretty forceful guy then too.' I laughed.

'Sure. You can tell he's used to getting what he wants. I'm not so sure that this is the same thing though. I don't know, I just have doubts.' Her eyebrows formed a McDonald's arch.

'Ag, I don't see the harm so much. I mean, it could be good once it's done. Then we'll know that we're safe, you know. But fuck, I haven't really been here long enough. Haven't got through the honeymoon yet, so what do I know?'

'All I'm saying is there could be other, better things to do. And' – her voice took on a sharp edge – 'I seriously doubt whether we would ever be able to maintain such a big perimeter if there was an angry horde out there. There are nine of us. Just look at it. The fencing is like a square kilometre. It's never going to work.' She swivelled slowly, taking in a full view of her subject.

'I think you need to understand, though,' I said to her back as it turned, 'that we've got a thing for fences, you know. They make us feel better. Secure.'

'Thanks, I'll bear that in mind.' The mousy intervener dragged her ass down the bell tower stairs, through St John's and back over the KES hockey fields. I trundled obediently behind as she further discussed the dichotomy between the global aid system and development of narratives within non-profit organisations.

Chapter 23

Shangaan in many ways

My guillotine tooth was an emblem for many other shortcomings, its jagged edges thrown into relief by Fats and his relentless march towards organisation, development and security.

Babalwa fell, inevitably, into his orbit. She didn't fawn over his every move – well, not completely, anyway – but she was certainly increasingly guided by his alpha force and his big-ape vibe.

Beatrice and Fats had once been entangled sexually, and Babalwa's presence thus generated the recurring sparks of low-level community conflict. The three circled each other in a wary triangle during the initial months. Innuendos, double meanings and flashes of sharp eye contact spiralled, without ever getting completely out of control.

But even outside of the Babalwa context, Beatrice looked perpetually out of alignment. Her frown was fluid, her eyes restless. She wrung her hands like washing, eventually ramming them into her pockets, then pulling them out and starting the cycle all over again.

She was a profiler and a networker. Her corporate career had been carefully shaped and crafted to brush over the fact that she grew up in Beaufort West, and that she was the offspring of no one at all. She had achieved her elevated corporate status through a careful construction of virtual profiles, which she maintained with diligence and care. While Tebza was always clicking and checking, jumpy and seeking to plug into this socket or that, it was Beatrice who, of all of us, was the most distraught at the digital detachment – specifically the separation from her profile. Her make-up, her new jeans, her cultivated look – all of these were dysfunctional proxies for her deeper compulsion to maintain her identity.

'It's tragic,' Lillian stated authoritatively. 'You can see she's actually physiologically stressed by the whole thing. I guess that's what working in marketing does.'

Teboho spent all of his time in front of a machine, or clicking on a device, or removing or inserting that dangling white earphone.

Our evening joints grew into a ritual (he was farming a huge plantation down in the far bottom corner of St John's), which meant I got to know him best of all.

He released snippets of himself to me around the pool, and I slowly patched together the image of a young stockbroker who spent most of his time doing other, more interesting things. We slotted into the druggie-techno lingo of his generation easily enough, but his references were more nuanced than mine, and many times I found myself bumbling along while actually adrift. I had no practical experience of hack, a substance of some importance to him in his pre-life. Even given my considerable Mlungu's experience, I was sadly out of touch with the VR and nanotech mix, my frame of reference limited to glasses and transmission paint. Already, and somewhat surprisingly, I came from the old school.

He didn't offer much beyond slight references; how hectic the brokers had got with the illicit algos, which had veered far, far beyond trading and weather and customised movie predictions. He dropped small clues regularly enough for me to know that I didn't really understand how the boundaries of his world were shaped, nor even what they were made of.

Some nights – frequently, in fact – he didn't offer anything at all. Neither did I. We sat in silence next to the pool and contemplated the universe that had unfurled over the city now that the lights were out.

Now, looking back, it's clear to me that Babalwa had broken some part of my heart, and that I was suffering. The mirror had shattered. At the time I simply felt numb, and tired, and sad. I was navigating mostly through stubbornness. There were so many conflicting forces at play I wasn't able to discern the true source of any of them. I was simply surviving. Babalwa, for her part, was clear about the course of things and made regular attempts to recalibrate the dynamics of our relationship. Punches on the shoulder. Warm friendly hugs. Etc.

I considered pulling the guillotine tooth and living with the gap, but that felt like even more of a defeat than the half tooth itself. Instead, I spent an inordinate amount of time staring in the mirror at the disaster of my mouth, pondering its meaning, the social consequences of facial misfortune and other such indulgences. When I could no longer cope with my reflection, I retired to my room, locked the door and sat with my photo albums, a final and necessary refuge. I spent many hours leafing through them and constructing detailed stories for each girl and each family, stitching their lives together in my imagination. The albums were my true sanctuary. I buried myself in them gratefully.

Of course everyone had been untethered from their lives and their loves. Husbands and fathers, children and families. None of us had even a single mooring left and so we were all wafting across each other's emotional paths. We came together successfully over the tasks and functions of the farm, but there was a cloud hanging over St Patrick Road that no force could move.

Fats's obsession with project management, food production, setting up the slaughterhouse and gating off our enclave gave us a critical series of focus points. Food was food – it was governed by its own logic – but the gates were especially important practical pillars. They were our unspoken way of telling each other that we hadn't lost hope, yet. It took special circumstances for discussions around our real plight to take place, and they seldom arose. Instead we worked on the gates and allowed ourselves to be led by Fats's energy and vision, by his grand plan for our new city of nine people. Each gate closed was also another sign that we believed there could be other people out there.

I regret now, though, that I was so cut off. That I engaged so little. That I spent as much time as I did with my tongue running through the guillotine, or in my room indulging in neurotic (and, yes, erotic) fantasies.

One afternoon, about three months into our arrival, I was assisting Gerald with one of the last gates. Lacking any real technical skills,

I was, quite literally, his 'hou vas'. I would cling onto whatever needing stabilising. I would pass him tools.

'My skill set is a little limited for this kind of work,' I offered in thoughtless ad language as he dismantled another set of wrought-iron spiked gates from one of St John's inner fencing lines, his forearms rippling with pleasure.

'Sho,' Gerald grunted. He flicked his blowtorch off for a second. 'We all live in our place, nè?' He flipped his helmet back down and carried on.

Gerald's pre-life in the army and security business gave him an edge. His latent talents, while thus far unexpressed, clearly lay in the area of shooting, muscling and enforcing. He had the air about him of a man who had messed with the bigger stuff. I probed while we piled the fencing onto the back of the bakkie.

'You experience a lot of fire, then? Like fighting?' I asked.

'Fire? Ja, sho. Not in the army; there we were just running around with clipboards. But after, when I had the security company. Sho. Fire. Often. Translation …' He gave me a long blank look. 'You would like to know if I have taken a life?'

I was surprised by his interpretation. 'Well, not really what I was thinking – well, not yet anyway.'

'Maybe I'm just in front of you 'cause I already know where it's going.' He softened, let his forearm muscles slacken. 'Anyway, the answer is yes. I have killed.'

'Ah …' Now I was even more intrigued, but unable to further what I had started. 'It changed you? As a person?'

'There is no describing death. All you know is, it is on your shoulder. It won't leave.' Gerald fished a pack of cigarettes, Peter Stuyvesant reds, out of his pocket. I had never seen him smoke before.

'Smoke?' He shook the packet at me and a single red came sliding out to meet my hand. I wasn't a big smoker at all, but this seemed like an appropriate moment.

'I didn't know—'

'I don't. But Lillian brought a carton from Spar. It has been many years. Now I'm finding it's making me feel alive. For now at least.'

We leaned against the bonnet of the bakkie, and Gerald released parts of his story.

He was born on the cusp of the Kruger National Park in the township of Mkhuhlu. His great-grandfather was one of the original 'police boys' hired by the white man setting up the Pretoriuskop Camp in the park. The police boys were drawn from all over. The tourists loved them because they were such exotic photo subjects, and the white rangers – whom they trained and educated – loved them because they knew the bush. They all came from different areas, and they were all called Shangaans.

'So I am Shangaan in many ways,' Gerald said, pulling reflectively on his smoke. 'Properly Shangaan, but also like a toy. Tourist Shangaan.'

Gerald's grandfather and father both worked on the Jozi mines, his father ending up as an alcoholic boss-boy. 'Better pay, worse father.'

Determined to avoid the fate of his elders, Gerald joined the army at seventeen and put in a decade of administrative work before leaving with two partners to set up a security company to guard a Pretoria-north industrial complex on a cooked tender deal. The company lasted five years and then collapsed on its rotten foundations. Gerald started his own thing, which he grew, inch by inch, over the course of the rest of his life, starting small, guarding little shopping complexes and the like. 'A business,' he said as he dropped his cigarette butt onto the dirt and ground it out with a heel, 'is like war – but harder, and longer.'

We spent several gate afternoons together and I came to be an admirer of his technical ability, his pure muscle and his willingness to be quiet. Before we set out, he would quickly knock off a sketch of the project in his little notebook with his clutch pencil, estimating rough lengths and widths and sizes. When we arrived at the installation point, his first action was to relook at his sketch, measure up whatever he could and finalise the numbers. Only then did he take off his invariably striped golf shirt and get to it. His skill, I realised gradually, was rooted in his focus on getting the numbers right first. It felt like a valuable lesson to me at the time.

In fact, it still does, although I can't say I ever learned to apply it.

I had assumed Lillian and Gerald were together – if not sexually then certainly practically. As I spent more time with him on the gates, I realised that this wasn't necessarily the case. It was more like Lillian had attached herself to him, and Gerald, in turn, had silently agreed to allow her into his range. The two of them were, in fact, many miles apart in important ways. Lillian, for example, had already been to the Kruger Park three times. Gerald had spent his life looking in exactly the opposite direction.

'I've never been,' he said. 'There were school trips but I missed them all – this week I was sick, that week there was family business, sometimes I just didn't go.'

'Do you regret that?'

'Maybe the animals. Not the people. The animals I should have seen. Leopard maybe. They should be part of our culture but they are not.' He shrugged.

'We should go someday,' I offered. 'At some stage Fats is gonna run out of work for us. Could be fun.'

Gerald grunted and powered up his drill.

Chapter 24
By the time we had meat in the freezer we hated each other

As is the case for many academics, Lillian's empathy gland appeared to have been severed at birth. She just didn't have that thing a person needs to get along with other people. In her pre-life there were plenty of opportunities for her to fall into books and colleges and universities and working groups designed to accommodate such deficiencies. Now, her Achilles heel was painful to us all. We were forced to endure the ongoing pain of her stilted contact, her addiction to factual accuracy and her wont for entering into meaningless verbal conflict. And, she and I were the only whites. The two without a single indigenous tongue. We were thus often circumstantially lumped together on the outskirts of conversations whose meaning we could only guess at.

Over the years at Mlungu's I had developed my tsotsitaal skills just enough to build the bridges I needed between people and conversations. I could greet and laugh and joke colloquially. I could ask for a rephrase. I could crack a joke at my own expense.

I had, of course, like most whites, lived a full life with people carrying out private conversations in front of me. I knew how to keep a steady face and pretend not to be bothered. In fact, most of the time I truly wasn't bothered, even when I was clearly the subject. Call it a genetically inherited trait.

Lillian lacked such a fortunate inheritance and her resentment at being cut out of conversations – and, even worse, becoming the subject of them – grew. She fretted constantly: over the quality of the water, over potential snakes in the yard, over the future and the past, over the idea of never being able to return to her homeland. And over language. The conversations drove her a little bit more nutty every time they happened. She launched several formal protests, gathering us together as a group to discuss her grievances and attempting one-on-one interventions with each of us in turn. She never seemed to realise that her attempts merely dribbled steady fuel onto the fire.

'You seriously want us to stop speaking our language because you can't follow the conversation?' Babalwa mocked her openly. 'Nxa!' Laughter.

'But Lillian, look at your fellow mlungu here,' Fats climbed in. 'He doesn't give a shit – and we mock him in front of his face all day!'

'Hayi suka, you poes.' I did my best to roll with it. 'I'm not as clever as I think I am, but I'm not as stupid as I look.'

'See?' Javas added, patting Lillian patronisingly on the arm. 'All you need is to do is hint that you might be picking up a few words. Then everyone will be more careful. It's a masquerade, darling. Everyone in Africa must play.'

It was a drinks session around the pool. An attempt at normality. Pool furniture and gin and tonics. The booze had blown the seal on Lillian's pressure cooker and she was taking the fight to Fats via a thinly linked series of bleats about respect and human rights. The backfire was long and painful, but Lillian was nothing if not a fighter; well over an hour passed before she left to cry in her room.

The conversation spilled over as she left, a hodgepodge of tsotsitaal, isiZulu, English, Afrikaans, isiXhosa and Sesotho. I shifted in my pool chair, wishing it would stop.

'Just for the record, boss.' Gerald cracked a rare smile. 'We're saying that the thing about good mlungus is they know that they don't know, and will admit it. That's all anyone wants anyway.'

'Sho, skhokho. Sho.' I raised my gin in mock salute.

Andile trotted over drunkenly and gave me a hug, Javas rattled off an incomprehensible insult and we all got drunk while Lillian cried.

I was free.

But only just.

The next day Lillian, puffy-eyed and wary, enlisted Gerald, Teboho and me to make a trip with her to the CSIR in Pretoria in an attempt to leapfrog the stalled flight-simulator/drone mission. Her theory was that somewhere on the CSIR campus we would find the kind of high-end simulator software required for her to get the fuck out of Africa. Something we could either dump onto a hard drive or just bring back in its box. Or, at least, we would locate the silver bullet needed to get the drones going.

The CSIR consisted of acres of carefully cultivated indigenous bush scrub with hints of concrete peeking out at strange, unexpected angles. The front gate was a typically South African façade, ten metres high and made out of the stuff they protect gold with. A face-brick security check-in building on the left held aloft a disproportionately large Council for Industrial and Scientific Research sign, while a smaller guard-point building between the entry and exit gates held up its own sign. While the rest of us tried to plot an entrance strategy, Gerald was circling the complex in a bakkie. He soon skidded back up to the front entrance. 'Got it,' he said, leaning out the driver's window. 'Two hundred metres up from here. A good spot. We can get the bakkies in. There's an old path. Take about half an hour to cut.'

Teboho said, 'Thank God for men who can do shit.'

We scraped noisily through Gerald's freshly cut fence holes, ripping up the paintwork on the side of the vehicles, and then drove up a small hill into thick bush and out the other side over what used to be a verge surrounding the roads that linked the various CSIR units. We parked facing each other around the main traffic circle. Gerald jumped out of his bakkie, followed by Lillian. Tebza and I just shouted from our driver's seats.

Lillian took charge. 'I guess the first thing would be to follow the road signs?' She issued the command as a question.

'Anyone see a sign for flight simulators?' Tebza asked, deadpan.

'How 'bout Defence, Peace, Safety and Security?' I asked, only half joking. 'Buildings 11, 12 and 13.'

'Biosciences.'

'Materials Sciences and Manufacturing.'

'Department of Science and Technology.'

We called them out one by one, in turn, hopefully. As if the answer would echo back to us.

Lacking logical options, we decided on Science and Technology.

Water features, paths, carports, pot plants and building entrances had all been carefully cocooned in trees and flowers and indigenous semi-forest. Each day, no doubt, twenty or thirty gardeners would have set to with their mowers and clippers to keep the frame in place and the buildings functionally foregrounded. Now, a year's worth of cutting back having gone by, the bush was the foreground. Tendrils and branches and leaves all stretched towards each other, relentless in their quest to convene across the paths, roads and walkways. Grass climbed up the base of the signs, branches reached for windows and doors. The road signs and metal sculptures of miners stood tall, but the revolution grew, unstoppable, at their feet.

'How long, you think, before everything is gone?' Tebza asked no one in particular. 'A year? Two?'

'About a year,' offered Lillian authoritatively. 'Can't see us being able to hack our way around much after a year. Maybe only the bigger buildings, with enough equipment.'

Gerald grunted and walked to the rusted metal sculptures of Marikana miners, scratching his back awkwardly through his golf shirt. Lillian, Tebza and I stood facing building 52. The Department of Science and Technology.

'Roy, consider this.' Gerald was hunched over a miner's foot, pulling a vine loose from the rusted boot of one the five central figures – a group which watched over a central paved memorial installation of plaques and pictures describing the Marikana killings and how they impacted the South African mining industry and society, details quaintly out of context to us now. He showed me the head of a thick organic rope. It was flat and spiked, each spike potentially a new rope of its own. 'I've always loved this thing, this plant,' he said. 'It sends out these shooters, these flat things. They move fast, man, metres in a week. You'll see, when we come back again this will have moved on and on and on. Maybe to another structure or just around the leg. Whatever's easiest I suppose. It's amazing, nè? 'Cause the rest of it, the bush, is not flat like this thing. It's normal. It's like this part is a special advanced force. An advancing force. Very similar to the army.'

We stood together and considered the progress of the creepers over the set of metal sculptures. Up close, we could see the death grip on the feet; all of them were covered, wrapped in layers, the thick ropes reaching sideways but also extending up the leg.

'Rampacious. Is that a word?' Gerald stood, hands on hips.

'Close,' I said. 'Rapacious. You're looking for rapacious.'

'Rapacious.' He said it reverentially, hands still on hips, head swivelling, taking in the implications.

The hopelessness of our mission was obvious as we broke through the front door. The reception area was wide and empty, cigar-lounge chairs awaiting occupation, surrounded by magazine racks bravely holding up a variety of in-house publications, themselves surrounded by long-dead pot plants, now just collections of rank soil. The red reception carpet cut off at the corridors, which stretched cheap grey arms out in all directions. The offices leading off the corridors were a uniform five by five metres; cheap pine desks, red-backed office chairs, and pinboards decorated with cuttings, clippings, photos and printouts. Divisional newsletters and project photos adorned the passage walls. Each corridor ended in a scatter of small meeting rooms with pine seats and dangerously old coffee machines.

'Ridiculous,' Tebza said to me as we moved together from office to office. 'We should be at the air force base or something.'

We entered Super Computing via a common room dominated by a photo-montage pinboard, each shot showing the same group at different stages of a marathon. The tall, thin white guy, a little younger than me and clearly the boss, was at the forefront of most of the shots, grinning manfully, leading his sweating charges through the ABSA charity 10.4-kilometre race. The last shot showed them all arm in sweaty arm at the finish. The girl to the right of the boss had shoulder-length black hair pulled back into a ponytail and a fierce, highly charged look in her eye.

I pulled the photo from the board and put it in my pocket.

'You go on, I'm gawn somewhere else,' Tebza announced in a droll fake Jamaican accent, turning for the door. 'Der havta be more interesting places than this.'

I grunted in affirmation. I wasn't sure where Lillian and Gerald had got to and I was now loving the trawl, digging into the uniformity of it all, wondering exactly what kind of thinking and progress and imagination were locked into the machines on those desks. Equally attractive was the haul of photos. Wife and child. Husband and dog. Lovers and parents. I pocketed the best ones.

Of flight simulators, predictably, there was no trace. I backtracked from Super Computing and followed another corridor from the reception area. This one led to a more scientific set-up – the smell of formaldehyde and a hint of laboratories down at the bottom end. The plaque on the first door read Department of Bio Sciences.

I tiptoed my way through, opening and closing doors, looking at photographs, reading more divisional notices. Unlike the other divisions, the Synthetic Biology lab at the end of the corridor seemed empty and devoid of even a hint of prior activity. The counters were wiped a glimmering kind of clean. Equipment was packed tightly away in glass-fronted cupboards. Whoever ran the place was either bored or exceptionally organised.

And so the afternoon went, the four of us breaking doors, smashing locks, poking through filing cabinets and folders and printouts. I crossed paths frequently with Gerald and Lillian, both on missions similar to mine. Tebza, however, I lost track of. Eventually I sat on the wheelchair slope outside the front door of the Department of Science and Technology centre and listened to the birds sing and the forest hum. I closed my eyes and lay down.

The birds sang some more.

I listened.

Gerald shook me awake, wanting to know where Tebza was, issuing instructions on how and where we would all go to look for him.

That way lay more of the same. Scientific-looking buildings, some older than others, names outside like Materials Sciences and Manufacturing, or Defence, Peace, Safety and Security. A few minutes' walk down 'Karee Road' (really just a path for the occasional maintenance vehicle) was a distinctly newer-looking glass centre, the National Centre for Nano-Structured Materials. Unlike most of the other buildings, which were at least sixty or seventy years old, the Nano building had the ring of early twenty-first century about it. The glimmering glass was not only more stylish but also clearly constituted an attempt at more effective utilisation of natural light – the phrase came winging back to me from a brochure I had written decades ago. I admired the design for a few seconds, then walked on. As I moved I heard the tinkle of glass breaking. I headed around the building and found a smashed entry point at the back. It was a tiny hole, only just big enough for a man to fit through, glass jaws still hanging open.

I squeezed myself through, scraping the skin on my cheek and cutting my forearm, which bled. I followed the sound of things breaking through a series of corridors and eventually, after a host of wrong turns and dead ends, came across a lab titled Recreational Nanotech. Tebza's form moved behind the swing door. He was hurtling stuff left and right, even over his shoulder. He examined each of the items one by one in quick time, engaged in a personal battle of discovery. My hand stopped on the swing door. I stood and watched. The speed and intensity of his movement were totally out of whack with the Teboho I had known thus far. He looked desperate. I pushed through.

'Tebza, dawg. Wot up?'

He turned fast, shocked at the intrusion, and said, 'Forget it, there's fuck all here. Let's move.'

That was the first of several CSIR trips. We moved through the bottom half of the complex building by building, searching for additional salvation beyond the notion of a flight simulator, the thought of which seemed sillier with each journey. Tebza hauled in excess of fifteen computers back to Houghton with him, clucking happily each time he came across a machine with superior specs to the last. Lillian remained steadfast, her jaw set with determination to find a simulator and a way out of this fucking country.

I started packing picnics for the excursions. Bread and juice and fruit and some jams. Each trip, I spent a little longer lying on the thickening lawns or walking around the perimeter, examining the trees and foliage and talking to the birds. Tebza was present but absent. Ever since I had surprised him in the Recreational Nano lab, our tasks and functions were in polar opposition – where I was, he wasn't.

Eventually, though, we gave up on the CSIR and admitted our inability to maximise its potential energy. None of us were intellectually equipped to understand the machinery or the technologies the place contained. The computers, powerful as they were, were also detached from the cloud. Their power was latent and waiting, just like us.

Back at the farm a stodgy collective depression was setting in. The shoddy treatment of Lillian by the group, myself included, peaked and then settled into a general unspoken dislike of the foreigner.

We retreated further and further into small sets of confusion. Fats's gates had blocked off our farm in an impressive and impenetrable way. Once that mission had been completed there was little left to focus on, save for setting up the slaughterhouse, which wasn't really on anyone's priority list.

'Just fuck off, Fats,' Andile snapped as he tried to convince her that electrifying the perimeter should be the next strategic priority. 'There. Is. No. One. Left. On. This. Continent.' She eyeballed him angrily. 'You can fucking electrify whatever you want, it's not going to change it. Leave me alone.'

Fats stood silently next to the kitchen table, an electric-fence manual stuffed uselessly under his arm, pen flicking between his fingers.

Me, I took up jogging.

I couldn't sleep at night. Worse, the days were becoming harder and harder to fill. I started talking to myself – too much. I also started stalking Babalwa, obsessed with her movements and her growing attachment to Fats. I thought seriously about booze, again.

One afternoon we stopped at the Bookdealers of Rosebank. Books were the theme of the day – grist in the mill of our still flickering consumer lust. The Bookdealers had been my old haunt, and so there we were, in one of the ancient, deep submalls of Rosebank. I grabbed a clutch of books at random and then drifted away down the dead escalator, past the business bookshop (*Social Investment as a South African Business Paradigm*; *Management Theory in Practice: A Guide for the Emerging Manager*; *Contact Centres and the Service Challenge*; etc.) and down to the underground parking. Even in the old days the mall had a weird, abandoned ring to it – now, it was freaky. On the right, just before the underground parking, was a clothing and shoe store, one of those last-century establishments that specialised in school outfits and such. I stood in front of the window and remembered. My father had actually brought me to this very store. He bought me a school tracksuit and, as a rare treat, a new stationery set. It was one of those odd memories, a hawk flashing through a dream.

I put my books down, kicked over a medium-sized pot, let the rotting soil spill out and smashed it through the window.

Posters of surfers and rugby stars and tennis players adorned the walls. It had been Kim Clijsters in my day, and the old classic Steffi Graf. Now it was a bunch I couldn't recognise. Young and lean and leaning forward, asses rock-hard and full of fight. The school clothes hung pitifully off their circular racks. To the right of the blazer rack there was a line of sports stuff, takkies and so on. I lifted a pair of bright yellow Nikes off the shelf. They were featherlight. I tossed them into the air a few times, then tried on the right shoe. It fit perfectly. I kicked off my second slop and walked back to Bookdealers in a new pair of bright yellow running shoes.

Back at the house, I ran up the driveway and then down again. Totally out of breath, I hung around the garage with my hands on my knees, panting, then went back up the drive again. The next day the shoes, an even brighter yellow in the morning light, lay waiting at the foot of the bed. I put them on, grabbed a gate buzzer from the kitchen and started running.

South first. Over Louis Botha Avenue and into Yeoville, heading for Rocky Street. It had been many years since I had been to Rocky Street. As I ran I remembered going there in my university days with some hippies who needed weed, in bulk.

I stopped running as my legs denied me. I walked up Cavendish Road. Yeoville sang with empty character. Unlike the suburbs and unlike the townships, it felt like there was a dimensional depth to the place, its little rundown houses the repositories of silent stories. Stories from the old white ladies, stories from the African refugees, the Zimbabweans and Nigerians, the musicians and drug dealers, artists and pimps and agents and journos. My Nikes flashed against the voices as I walked. I started running again. Stopped. Leaned over my knees. Turned around and walked back.

In running I finally found a meaningful weapon in the insomnia fight – the exhaustion drove me easily into the pillow. And so my runs stretched out until I was often away from the house for most of the morning or afternoon. It was a good escape.

As we embarked on the gritty business of putting together the slaughterhouse, our residence felt suffocating. Now, from my old man's perspective, I understand that many of the strange feelings of the time were rooted in the challenge, which evolved slowly over a period of months, of setting up a system that would allow us to kill and eat other living things. Javas and Gerald were the lone sources of expertise when it came to butchery and slaughter, and following their guidance was traumatic for the rest of us, who had only ever faced meat through a layer of cling wrap.

Philosophically, there were two key elements to our programme.

(1) Establishing a slaughterhouse that was close enough to the cows to be logistically convenient. (Debate as to whether the cows would sense the slaughter of their colleagues and be emotionally or behaviourally affected by it arose, led by Lillian, of course, but also

entertained by Andile and Beatrice, of all people. The notion was, eventually, dismissed.)

(2) Three slaughter sessions a year. One midwinter, and one on either side of the cold. The meat generated would have to last us the year.

We built the slaughterhouse in the semi-underground cricket nets that ran off the side of the KES fields and that ended with a set of burglar bars looking onto the street separating the two halves of the school. The area offered good, easy access and, once the artificial turf was ripped up, the concrete was easy to wash down with buckets of water. Javas created a drainage furrow in the cement which led to a small portable swimming pool that could be punctured at the end to release the blood but contain the gunk – the bits of ear and hoof and so on.

We created a trestle table out of a large door, about three metres long and one metre wide. It stood on two empty oil drums. Javas and Gerald put together a slaughter-equipment inventory, locked up neatly in what used to be the kit room adjoining the nets. This included knives (conventional and the curved, strap-on variety, which locked to the wrist via Velcro and allowed the ladies and the weak – such a myself – to make big, decisive cuts), dishes, drying clothes, muslin to wrap the meat in, a generator and, finally, a Meatmaster 2020 Pro bandsaw.

Adjacent to the trestle table we erected a tap, fed by the biggest barrels we could find and pressurised as much as possible by extreme height. Filling the eight barrels – which stood back to back on an elevated scaffolding, the front barrel attached to the tap – was an exercise in patience and brute force. In the far corner was the chain block-and-tackle, set in a high frame strong enough to hold a fully outstretched carcass.

In the last corner an iron ring was set into the concrete floor. This was where the animal died. When we eventually got to the slaughter, we did our best to con the beast into calmness with cooing noises and patting of the snout as we separated it from the herd and walked it to its fate. Then we jumped it as fast as we could: secured the horns and pinned its head to the floor with rope fed through the ring.

At this point Javas or Gerald, the designated executioners, would step up with a loaded 9 mm, place it just above and right between the eyes, and pull. The nostrils would flare. The eyes went wild. The power slammed off.

The cow would collapse onto the concrete in death spasms and kicking fits and then someone (in the early years it was Gerald or Javas – later, myself and Fats and Beatrice also embraced the challenge) would slice its neck open while the rest held the head. It required a messy, collective effort. Once the knife opened the jugular, a fountain of red blood would gush out onto the concrete and we would try with our hose and much desperation to get the bulk of it down the gutter while the beast gurgled and its still beating heart pumped the blood out. Gerald and Javas insisted that the throat-slitting happen fast, so that the heart could pump as much blood as possible, thus preserving the quality of the meat.

When the legs stopped kicking, it was time for cutting and slicing and dicing. Someone would cut the necessary slit through the skin on the Achilles tendon while the boys would use a hacksaw to take the head off. The rest of us would skin the legs and the rump as fast as possible. The carcass was then hoisted onto the gallows, and the rest of the skinning would happen.

We were terrible at it. Lillian wept profusely through the first two slaughters, and while her tears went well beyond irritation, they also articulated the dislocation I felt at the gore of the process. Fats, too, was green and quiet while following instructions.

We were particularly bad at the skinning. Gerald and Javas had to patrol around us like schoolteachers to make sure we were at least getting the core elements right. I was the chief culprit when it came to amateurish snipping of the connective tissue that held the leather and the meat together. Invariably Javas would nudge me aside and finish it off, denying me the final pleasure of balling my fist and ripping off the skin completely. I think he also denied me that pleasure to make sure I wouldn't have to deal with getting the guts and entrails out – not out of any kind-heartedness, mind, but to avoid the tragedy of getting shit all over the meat with a slip of the knife or a shoddy tying-off of the rectum. Dealing with the entrails was an expert's business – we would all step back and watch as the boys slit the stomach open and poured the guts carefully into the two large zinc tubs. Lillian would be sniffling and snorting. The rest of us were quiet and respectful.

By then it had already been a long, bloody day. But the skins had to be dealt with – Gerald insisted on working them into homemade shoes, etc. – as did the entrails, guts and organs, which were turned into tripe and liver and kidney meals for the next few nights.

And, before we could drag ourselves back to normality, for the night at least, the carcass had to be quartered, a process requiring the precision and muscles of three men to ensure the cut was accurate, right the way down the side of the tail bone. Eventually, years on, the girls and Fats and I became skilled enough and strong enough to deal with this heavy dismantling of the carcass. The strap-on knives were useful – we all started using them, even those of us with muscles. But that was all much later. In the early years, by the time the quartering came around, the stress and muck of the day, the physical exhaustion and Lillian's tears had rendered most of us useless. I would collapse onto my haunches, watch the boys do their thing, and offer tools and rags and other such supportive items.

Setting up the slaughterhouse, sourcing our beasts (Javas drove all the way to the Eastern Cape to find the beasts he was looking for, five free-roaming cows and an ox that had – like us – somehow ducked the scythe), and actually killing and butchering our first victim took something on the order of three months. By the time we had meat in the freezer we hated each other, each in our own special kind of way.

And so I ran.

The flight-simulator failures saw Lillian voicing bolder plans, such as driving up through Africa until we got to the top and then simply boating over to Europe. This idea gained little traction, the response morphing quickly into a critique of American bias from

Babalwa and Andile, who pointed out – with satisfaction – the assumption inherent in Lillian's plan that getting to Europe would be some sort of inherent progression or achievement.

Beatrice offered an alternative to Lillian's quest, suggesting an ongoing sub-Saharan African relay team of alternating twos, heading out at regular intervals in various directions. Her logic was that if there were nine of us here, there surely must be at least one other similar group below the Sahara. So seven could remain in Houghton managing the essentials, the farming structure and so on, while two could head out for a week, and then come back and swap with two others, who would go out again, then back.

Teboho said, 'The twins will never be separated like that.'

'Typical,' said Lillian. 'Nine people left on the planet and two of them actually fall in love.'

'If they really are in love, that leaves seven of us for interbreeding,' Babalwa said to me later as we perched on the edge of the swimming pool, which had grown a thick green skin while we were busy setting up the slaughterhouse.

I wasn't yet ready to grapple with the notion that the nine of us constituted the future of humanity. Babalwa, on the other hand, had developed her calculations since our PE days. She said, and I was ready to agree with her, because what did I know anyway, that eight – four men and four women – would be just enough to get some genuine genetic diversity going, as long we ensured sustained cross-breeding. The twins' blossoming love threw her approach into variable headwinds. 'It's an open question,' she explained, 'whether they would be willing or able to cross the line as many times as will be required to get it right.'

I pulled the laces on my Nikes tighter and thought about how I could expand my route.

Chapter 25

Fats took increasingly to his room

Everyone had their own idea of what was necessary, and the ideas were often in direct opposition. All we needed, Fats said, was four people to actually physically commit to their own plan and we were all completely fucked.

But Fats also needed the group. For him, it was the nucleus of our potential, our survival, our effort. In one of many attempts to re-establish unity of group purpose, he started calling house meetings.

I missed the start of the first one. I had been running and miscalculated, again, the uphill return.

I threw my sweating self between Andile and Babalwa on the lounge couch. They both leapt up, squealing and retching, and I ended up by myself in the far corner.

Fats launched proceedings with an unnecessary sermon on the necessity of planning, and followed it with an equally unnecessary outline of the various plans on the table:

> *Drive to the top of Africa and boat to Europe.*
> *Build a community and colony here in Houghton.*
> *Get the drones flying.*
> *Learn how to fly – and fly away.*
> *Dragnet South Africa again to search for more survivors.*
> *Dragnet Africa to search for more survivors.*
> *Get breeding to ensure perpetuation of the species.*

The last item was Babalwa's. She forced it onto the agenda amid the first genuine laughter we'd had as a group for a while. Within the mockery and the explosive fission of general sexual tension, she stuck to her guns. 'You can think I'm crazy, but I'm telling you that if there are only nine of us, we can't grow a community without inbreeding. Unless we purposefully cross-breed.'

And so our first formal house meeting dissolved into a farce of verbiage and theories. Lillian and Fats – representing the two truly polar views – put out the majority of it, facing off with argument and counter-argument. Halfway through the twins moved to sit together on the couch, articulating their own motivations and loyalties.

Gerald was quiet, voicing opinions only on technical matters. The likelihood of boating successfully over the Suez. The true benefits of drones unable to hook into satellites. The technicalities of dragnetting South Africa, or Africa. Tebza sat silent, his dangling earphone the only sign he was even thinking of participating. Mostly he stared at the intersection of wall and roof in the top corner of the lounge. I wondered again what he might be on. His blankness was not, I was sure, a passive-aggressive attack against the group. His brain seemed simply to be otherwise engaged.

I floated along, thinking occasionally about my downtime (I had reached Alex in record time) and my uptime (I was still dying completely going up Munro Drive) and only occasionally focusing on the conversations swirling in front of me.

Between the plan-making and life-dreaming, the daily demands reared up, relentless.

Gerald installed a nifty new guillotine at the back of the chicken run, located at the far end of the fields (to minimise annoying squawking). The guillotine was essentially a funnel bolted to the wall with its tip pointing down. It offered a far better and cleaner way of slaughtering fowl than the axe-and-block method we had employed thus far.

'You keep them as calm as possible,' Gerald said. He held the bird gently under his left arm and stroked its feathers rhythmically with his free hand as he explained to Tebza and me how the guillotine worked. 'You don't want to stress them out, so you just stroke and stroke.' He ran his hand over the bird's head and down its throat, then turned it upside down and pointed the head at the top of the funnel. 'If you are calm it won't even notice what is happening.' Gerald inserted the head of the impressively relaxed chicken down the funnel. 'Once the head is out the bottom, you just take the knife and do it.' He sliced the chicken's head off like a gentle uncle. 'Then you just leave it there to drain.' He stood back admiringly and wiped off the blade on the grass. The blood poured from the chicken's neck into the waiting bucket while its legs and backside wriggled in final protest at the wide end of the funnel. 'Adrenalin,' he mused while we watched the body twitch and the blood drain. 'It ruins meat.'

'Ah,' I said, transfixed by the pouring blood.

'That's why game can taste so bad,' he carried on, warming again to one of his favourite subjects. 'If the person does not know about shooting and can't get the bullet through the head or the heart, then he has to chase the thing down. Lotta adrenalin. Bad meat.'

'Ah,' I added again. Tebza idled blankly next to me, staring right through the chicken's gaping neck.

We returned an hour later and Gerald showed us how to soak and pluck the carcass properly. Complaints had been coming from the kitchen, Beatrice specifically, about quality.

Teboho, once finally focused on the task at hand, was surprisingly successful. He had watched his gogo pluck birds for much of his young life when the family visited the Free State rurals. I, on the other hand, found the task repulsive, and I was bad at it. I snatched poorly at the wrinkled wet skin, grabbing only small handfuls of feathers, sometimes getting nothing other than wet bird.

After the slaughterhouse was up and the farm was producing what we needed at a relatively regular rate, Fats took increasingly to his room. He would stand at his third-floor window and look north for long periods. From my own special places in the garden, I would see him standing with his hands behind his back in a military pose. To me he looked like he was urging the general inside him to deliver a better strategy, tighter execution, more predictable results. I once timed him at ninety minutes. Rooted to the spot. Eyes bolted on the horizon.

Later I realised he was probably not thinking about any of these things at all. He was, surely, debating Babalwa.

During this time I received more personal attention from her than I had since we'd first found Fats waiting for us on Eileen's couch. It was, I surmised, a typically youthful female double play – the leveraging of the weaker male as a point of necessary tension through which to force the alpha into action. She needed him, in other words, to be jealous. Not raging, pull-the-walls-down jealous. Just enough to get him going. To inspire commitment.

At the same time Lillian pulled Gerald, Tebza and myself into her own agenda. The CSIR trips were followed by raids on other buildings and complexes in the same area. We went along, doing what we were told. Searching for flight.

Teboho's behaviour had also become increasingly erratic – he was drifting away from all but the most necessary contact. He kept up with the trips to Tshwane, the CSIR and all that. Otherwise he slept through most of the day and sat behind his machines at night, occasionally disappearing altogether for long stretches. Once he was absent for a full forty-eight hours. He had also stopped eating regular meals, choosing instead to snack perpetually on crisps and Coke.

And so we circled.

Babalwa would sit alongside me, next to the pool, rabbiting about breeding and genetics and cross-pollination and on and on and on. Fats would watch us from on high, his eyes slipping down compulsively from the horizon, then back up again.

One afternoon, after she had bent my ear for an hour or so and then made an exit, Fats descended.

'I just thought I should let you know,' he said after an interminable, uncomfortable pause, 'that I know.' He let the sentence hang, ominous.

'You know what?' I asked, annoyed and threatened.

'What you did. To Babalwa. In PE.' He tried to find my eyes. I ducked.

'What? Sorry?'

'Come, Roy, she told me. There's no point being evasive.'

'I think you'd better spell it out for me, just in case.'

'The rape. Clear enough?'

'The rape?' I spluttered, jolted. 'The rape? Jesus Christ, that girl's ...'

'That girl's what, exactly?' His fists were balled.

'More calculating than I thought. There was no rape, Fats. We fucked, OK? We fucked then and we fucked many times afterwards. Two adults. Fucking. It happens.'

'That's not how she tells it.' Fats stood, looking down on me. 'And from what I know of the two of you, I'm inclined to go with her version.'

I stood up in rebuttal. We looked into each other's mouths. 'Well, that's your choice,' I said. 'But she's lying. I don't know why, but she's lying.' I turned to leave, but I walked the wrong way – to the bottom of the garden, where I stood and stared at the stone wall, Fats watching my back. I stayed that way, trapped, not knowing why I was staring at that wall, or where I could go from there.

Chapter 26

Cloudy with a hint of yellow

The following days we experienced a rain assault. Flying bullets and shells, swirling pools of water and flooding of unexpected places. A Jozi monsoon.

We stayed indoors for the better part of two days, watching the battery from within the mansion and avoiding each other strategically. Fats stayed upstairs for the most part, which suited me fine. Babalwa skipped around as if nothing had happened, and perhaps for her nothing had. I had no idea exactly when she dropped the pearl onto Fats – it could have been the day before or weeks ago – or whether she intended him to challenge me with it.

The twins broke out the movies, slobbing on the couch to an endless run of decades-old sci-fi adventures and special effects.

I took to my books, smoked on my bed and, stoned, flipped page by page through a few Wilbur Smiths, an aborted attempt at Dostoyevsky and a surprisingly interesting biography of Sol Plaatje. The rape accusation bothered me intensely, my subconscious rabbiting away at itself, probing and pushing at my thoughts and also at Fats and Babalwa, issuing counter-accusations and rebuttals, reviews of the evidence, cross-examinations, and so on. The weed forced the weight of the diatribe to the back of my mind but also increased the frequency of the chatter, obliterating in the process logical, linear thought.

Rape.

Rape.

Rape.

I struggled, even in my darkest moments, to associate myself with it. In the best and worst of my memories, what Babalwa and I did on the grill of the cash-in-transit van was very far from rape. A lustful, violent fuck? Yes. Confused, wild sexual fumbling? Yes. But rape? I couldn't even consider it, primarily because I remembered specifically and in detail how wet she was as I went into her. That kind of lubrication was a clear rebuttal. Or was it? I recalled magazine articles, TV shows, Oprah reruns that explained victim arousal as the deeper conundrum. One of the aspects that caused so much confusion and pain for the victim, over and above the violation of the act, etc., etc.

I decided I was going to have to talk to Babalwa. But I evaded it, brushing past her during our monsoon incarceration as quickly and efficiently as possible. A man with things to do. A man too busy to talk.

On the second evening, the rain still battering us inside and out, I walked past Teboho's room and fate revealed him to me: crouched over an Energade bottle and pissing extremely carefully into it. I should never have gained the view I did, but his bedroom door had swung open accidentally, and in one of those double twists of destiny the door to his en-suite bathroom had also cracked open at just the right angle. My view was thus through a double-hinge crack. It was a flashing glance, and if he had been wiping his ass or beating one off I wouldn't have thought twice about it. But there was something furtive in the manner of his crouch that made me stop and take a second, longer look.

Even then I walked on, deciding to file it under 'Strange and Weird', an already brimming category.

The next day the sun broke out. The clouds rolled back and we all ran from the house to escape each other; our recycled breath and farts, the sexual tension and betrayals, the mood stuff. I laced up my Nikes.

I had developed special routes. Straight down Louis Botha to Alex and back for strength work. Through the full breadth of the Houghton suburbs for endurance, and occasionally through Patterson Park for a light, head-clearing run. Given the claustrophobia of the last two days I chose Patterson Park, and there, as I entered the gates, was Teboho off in the distance, sitting with his back to me and leaning against a big oak tree.

He had the Energade bottle against his lips. The liquid was cloudy with a hint of yellow. I walked towards him as he drained the last of it.

As I approached he slumped. His torso lost its form. Then his arms, their willingness to resist gravity gone in an instant.

The bottle dropped from his hand. His chin fell onto his collarbone.

'Tebza?' I walked up noisily. 'That you? Tebza? Tebza?'
Nothing.
'Teboho!' I tried the angry mother voice. Then I shook his shoulder, hard. He remained folded in on himself, lost in a personal sinkhole.

Instinct said I should pick him up and carry him back to the house (thereby morphing my light run into an extreme strength session). But his breathing was normal, light but steady, and whatever he had drunk (his own piss, surely) must have had a lot, if not everything, to do with his state. In addition, he had chosen a faraway, quiet place for this. Somewhere he would never be seen, save by a manic runner.

I sat down in front of him – about two metres away – and waited. The grass was wet – deeply so. The damp rose quickly into my ass.

Every now and again, maybe every twenty minutes, I would probe at him with my toes. Lacking a watch, I had to guess at the strings of time looping themselves together. I marked off estimated periods of twenty minutes, promising myself that after seven such units I would pick him up and carry him back.

The extraordinary thing about his state, I realised gradually, was its rigidity. There were no eyelid flutters. No slight twitches of the leg or the arm. No sighing. No snorting, no changes in breathing. He was still in the absolute sense. Completely motionless.

Somewhere in the middle of the fourth twenty-minute block he sighed, stirred, snorted and rubbed his eyes. After the rubs he opened his eyes and saw me. His eyelids were heavy – dropping, then pushing open, then dropping again – weighed down by an obvious force. He recognised me, comprehended my presence, but was unable to address it. He leaned forward, rubbed his eyes again, then fell back against the tree, asleep.

I let him drift a while longer – this time he was making the noises and movements normally associated with sleep. Then I stood and kicked him hard on the leg. 'Heita!'

Tebza's torso shot forward, his eyes panicking as they shot open. He stared at me, wide-eyed and shocked. 'Jesus, Roy, fuck, man. You should never do that. Never when someone's ...'

'When someone's what, Tebza?'

'Uh, when someone's been sleeping,' he covered clumsily.

I sat back down next to him. 'Tebz, you're gonna need to explain this to me. Because it looks a lot like you've been drinking your own piss.'

Tebza pointed at the heavily gated door of flat 743, Slovo Mansions. 'This is it,' he said. 'Shit, I didn't remember the gate. We never gonna get in. This shit is unbreakable.' He rattled the two-inch steel deadbolt. It rang firm.

'Ag, maybe it doesn't matter,' he said, disappointed. 'I wanted you to get some of the experience, but ...' He shrugged.

'Let's just walk,' I offered. 'I'll use my imagination.'

True city sight was impossible, unless you lived right under the waterfall. For people like me, there was never a city to see. The city people, the flats, the shops, the hawkers, they lived and breathed beneath the gushing digital revenue. The poets and the lit students wrote about them, the shadows. The shadow lives. Me, all I saw was the outdoor revenue models: the chopping and slicing of space into money, of street frontage into monthly rentals, of air into brand experience.

Street names and important buildings were the necessary

poles between which lay shocking colours, campaign points and enticements to act. To get to Mlungu's from Louis Botha, I would take Joe Slovo to Pepsi corner, where the three chicks shook it for years, urban sexy-sumo style, in camouflage G-strings and Fidel hats. Then right at the bottom of Ponte, through the pink insurance strip for about half a kilometre, right again at the detergents, through the penis extensions, then left at the bottom of Carlton, left again at Black Like Me, and about fifty metres on, just past the Neo Afrika Theatre, was Mlungu's. Each citizen had a similar yet personal experience of 'getting there'. A lifelong gathering of tricks that allowed movement through the wash of mega brands and supersized churches and colours and exhortations. Of course the 'where' was always central to the experience of movement. If you turned left at Pepsi corner, it was all Maboneng art, city culture and coffee beans. High-colour fast-cut advocacy for sexual heath, democracy and creative thinking.

Then, once into the faster turns, the blizzard of smaller colours and faces and messages, the voices of the thousands of privates who – for whatever reason – hadn't yet had their street frontage allotted to a greater outdoor advertising share scheme. The barber and the one-man loan sharks, the gurus and the prophets and the preachers, always the preachers, the little ones, growing nascent empires up to the heaven of high-impact roadside frontage.

The joy was always in the graf; the paint-over, the fight for control of the city canvas. The deeper the brands went, the more vulnerable they were to the paint-over, and therefore to the streaming rebel puns, the kiddie-war corpse feeds, the flashing art, the repeat challenges.

The agencies made the big money on public sites – but they pulled almost as much with the personalised, privacy-off stuff.

I only ever switched to privacy off when I was ordered to – when we were testing a new interface or some such mission-critical event. When I did, I came face to face with my public self. My aggregate avatar. For example, a shot from decades back: Roy the young advertising postgrad, leaning casually on a Wits Business School wall, talking to ... who? I had no idea. I left it because, well, why not? Let the average live. Truthfully, I was helpless in the grip of my public profile, a force which insisted on an alternative me. A Roy I could barely comprehend, let alone modify to more suitable proportions.

Privacy off was a junkie's experience, a digital game that belied the walls and the streets and the concrete underfoot. The addicts feasted on the perpetual motion, on plotting a path through the hall of personalised mirrors. No generic camo hip-hop G-strings for them – they customised those asses to their exact desires, picking each thong out, personally, from the Pepsi gallery.

Of course every time they chose – with every click or command or slide – they fed the third mouth of the beast. Customisation. Each wall talked to, each service portal accessed, each colour changed was an implicit request for more.

Even choosing not to choose was, eventually, a choice. **Roy Fotheringham**, the gantry scanner walls would beg. Take a journey into a **new** Jozi experience. **See** the other side of life. We **value** your privacy, but we know you're going to love this.

Zoom here for selective privacy override.

Choose STOP to opt out.

Now, as we walked, the versions and requests and options were gone. The colours no longer existed.

Now, ghettos.

Now, brown.

Cracks carving through walls. Collapsing gutters.

We climbed into a few Hillbrow buildings, enticed by the opportunity to look, finally, at our own pace, with our own eyes, behind the curtain. The hallways were uniformly dark, dank wells. The art deco flats divided and divided and divided into sixteenths or more, each a quadrant for a family, each mattress shared, each view out to the north a taunt, a tease.

While we walked, west, towards Newtown, Tebza painted his story.

He had been getting seriously into hack.

'I had this girlfriend, Joy. Hardcore algo freak. Physics at Oxford and all. Trader. She was always going on about it. Hack. The next level of human experience. She seemed cool. Healthy. Not strung out. Happy. Enlightened, possibly. So she took me to that flat, which belonged to a guy who worked for ... I dunno. Government? Global youth? Graf rebels? I never really figured it out. Anyway, he was deep down there somewhere – wherever people like that live, that's where he was. Where he came from.

'There was no money or anything. We never paid for the stuff. There were just a few of us. We let him guide us, introduce us.' Tebza stopped several times while we were walking for eye contact, for reassurance. Now he led us up a Rea Vaya bus ramp, into the scabby old bus station hut. We sat on opposite benches inside the glass container, our backs against the faded black-and-white city art, Tebza's head framed by the outline of a beaming teenage African mouth.

'So the guy gave us the pill. Nanobot. I was nervous as fuck, but Joy looked very chilled so I just followed her. He – Joel. That's it, nè? Joel. His name was Joel.'

First the bots took the central nervous system – rerouting signals from the brain to the limbs, hands and sensory devices (tongue, ears, nose, etc.), and vice versa. Second, they linked to the WAN, superseding the physical context. The brain took in signals from the WAN, via the bots, and the arms and legs and eyes responded to those. The environment could have been anything, depending on the programs on the server.

'We would obviously be able to run and jump and fuck, yadda yadda yadda. All the basics. Also fly. Run as fast as a car. X-ray vision, if you had enough points, et cetera, et cetera. But Roy' – Tebza turned teary – 'it changed everything. This wasn't some rough glasses thing with bad joins and blur. This was real. Everything you know about the world, every touch and feeling and instinct, repackaged. Every basic physiological fact wiped away and replaced.' He swatted the air with his free hand, flicking at non-existent flies.

'You OK there, Tebz?' I asked,

'Sho, sho. We walk again?' Tebza walked and talked in an

increasingly fragmented fashion, looking up at the sky every so often and still swatting at the imaginary flies. Me, I will never forget it, him, the compulsive swatting, the rising sweat on his brow. And also the city, which, despite its lack, despite its sinking brown walls, seemed to be suddenly brimming with energy. With potential. I have a snapshot safe in my mind, the two of use walking west on Jeppe, alone yet powerful, confused yet profound, on the verge of something special. Something new.

Tebza babbled fast, rattling off descriptions of his hack experiences and insights, most of which sounded to me like standard (if very entertaining) drug fare. He was also sweating. A lot.

'Am I sweating?' he asked suddenly, dropping the monologue.

'Sho. Fair bit.'

'Shit, where's that bottle? In the car? Fuck fuck fuck. I'm gonna lose them if I don't piss now.' His face crumpled.

'Here, you told me to bring it.' I pulled the Energade bottle from my pants pocket, where it had been sitting uncomfortably for the last few hours.

'Oh sweet baby Jesus, thank you for that.' Tebza whipped out his dick and pissed into the bottle. 'You've seen this before so I'm not going to get all coy on you. The only way to save the bots. Disgusting, I know, but I can't let go.' He crouched carefully over the bottle. The level rose rapidly.

'What happens if you overflow?' I panicked on his behalf.

'Doubt it, I don't drink anything before for that reason. Soon as you start sweating, that's the sign the bots are ready to jump ship. You got five minutes and thirty seconds before you actually start sweating them out.'

'And then what, you drain the piss to get them back?'

Tebza shook off, zipped up and let his face take shape again. 'Askies. No.' He winked at me. 'They're molecular, nè? That's one of the things I was looking for at the CSIR nanotech lab. A fucken nano sieve. I'm getting very tired of drinking my own piss.' The wink had died away. He was serious.

'Serious? You been drinking your own piss all this time? And the bots are still active – they don't fade?' I was incredulous.

'Ja. There's only a one to two per cent loss factor.'

'Shit. And it's that good?'

'Actually no, it's pathetic,' he said shyly. 'It's just a blank canvas. No other players. No software, no functionality. With the nanobots I've got all you can do is bounce around between four templates. Desert, nightclub, bedroom and forest.' Tebza rubbed the bottle between his hands as if trying to warm himself, or start a fire.

'So why, then?'

'Because ... you need to understand, Roy. Because hack could explain this.' He waved a theatrical hand at our empty city.

Contrary to his declared where-were-you-when-it-happened story, Tebza had been on hack in the Slovo Mansions flat. During the last few minutes of his trip – a clubby thing, he said – he was suddenly alone; the interface had emptied out. When he came around at three in the morning, the flat was deserted. It was doubly confusing because they had loaded up on MDMA, along with the hack.

Hack, while cognitively revolutionary and of a higher order to anything that had gone before, eventually took the path of all narcotics. It became expected. Slowly you recognised the parameters of the software and the experience, and the limitations – initially so far out on the horizon as to be irrelevant – became tangible. 'Obviously people want to take it further,' Tebza said. He was sheepish again, the scar on his cheek crinkling in an endearing embarrassment. 'You know – humans must. We must take it on.' According to my stockbroker friend, who was now considerably more than that in my eyes, the street had been making steady inroads into the initially glass-office hack scene. Traders were joined by dealers. Financial administrators by DJs. Artists – replete with piercings and tattoos and strangely coloured hair – started popping up outside the Sandton stock exchange, just kinda waiting. Tebza shook his head. 'People were really starting to go off. Whoonga. Nyaope. Tuk. Buttons.* The mixes created a video game that was completely real and mad violent. Bad stories. Terrible shit going down in some places. People were getting damaged. Out of this

---

* See the street-culture section of the Malema Library, St John's campus.

world, Roy. Out of this world.'

'OK, so, why are you now drinking your own piss to go play on a blank VR canvas?'

'It might be blank but it's real, mfana. Completely real. As real as the ground you're walking on right now.'

'I get that. A very real experience.'

'Completely real. One hundred per cent real. As real as what you're thinking and feeling and experiencing now. As real as this step on the ground.' He hopped slightly for emphasis, then again. 'Come, Roy, I'm leading you to the obvious.' Tebza moved ahead at a trot, then turned and faced me dramatically, the Energade bottle swinging from his fingers. 'So, when I came around and saw that there was no one left in the flat, in the city, my first thought wasn't that everyone else had disappeared—'

'But that you had.' The penny clanged on its way down.

'Exactly.' He fell back in next to me. 'My first thought is the same one I keep on having now – that I hadn't come out. That something had happened. That I was stuck.'

'You still think that's possible?'

'Possible, yes. Likely, not so much. The group of us would have had more common experiences. Our frames of reference would have been more in alignment. I think, anyway. That's what I've been thinking.'

We crossed over Simmonds Street. The sun blazed over the city. Late February. Lunchtime. Light wisps of wind ruffled our hair. Bright blue skies to our right, to the north. Purple thunderclouds rising up from the south.

We walked in silence, our footfalls echoing in the streets. Tebza swung the bottle carefully yet casually from his right hand.

I stopped, knelt and undid the shoelaces on my Nikes, then retied them, slowly. I felt the texture of the laces carefully with my fingertips, the combination of a million tiny threads. This lace could not be VR. It was too nuanced. Too subtle. The rub of it between my fingers too complex. I placed my open palm on the pavement and ran it across the gravel and the city dirt. Again, too textured. Too literal on my fingertips.

'So, what?' I remained kneeling, my laces now very well tied, Tebza hovering above me. 'You're saying that you and I – theoretically – could be flat out on our backs somewhere, not moving, and this' – I rubbed my palm over the pavement again – 'could all be interface?'

'It's possible. But I can't find evidence, anything to support it. The glitch. The thread to pull on. If we were navigating via software there would have to be an outer edge. To the interface. You know this from Mlungu's, where the edge is soooo obvious.'

'More than. You have to pretend it's not there.'

'Exactly. Even with hack – I was told, but I never experienced it myself – there are limits, edges. Finely threaded and completely invisible, but if you push the right corner the interface will break and you end up back at the entry point. Problem with hack is that it's seamless. I've been pushing at a lot of corners and have never found one. I still don't know what they look like.' Tebza flopped down next to me. We sat side by side on the corner of Simmonds and Anderson, facing a McDonald's.

'How does one push at a corner – practically speaking?'

'Run hard at it. Drive fast at forty-five degrees until you smash into the koppie. That kinda thing.'

'And nothing. No thread?'

'Not here. And nothing on hack either. Which is why I keep on with the piss. I had one pill left.' Tebza shook the Energade bottle sarcastically. 'Which is now at about eighty-nine per cent strength, in this bottle.'

'How does strength impact it? Does dilution create threads? Interface breakdown?'

'It just shortens the duration. Designed that way. At the flat the pills would knock us out completely for two hours, and then we would come down through a set of screens designed to make re-entry easy. In total the whole thing would be about two and a half. Now, with just this pill and no network, there are no re-entry screens and it's a rough jump back. Time is down to somewhere just over eighty minutes.'

'So in there and out here you're just looking at – pushing at – corners?' I felt a little high all of a sudden. Tebza's profile was cut out against the purple sky building steadily behind him. The thunderous backdrop made his skin look blacker, sharper.

'Sho. Kinda. At some stage the system has to break down, and I want to know what the breakdown looks like. How to recognise it. Otherwise I don't know what I'm looking for.' He paused. 'But it could also just be because I'm homesick for it. The last time I was there – genuinely there – I was having the craziest sex with Joy. It was extraterrestrial. Like we were aliens. Non-human. Past human. Maybe I want to relive that. I don't know.'

'And the others? You haven't told anyone?' I thought of Fats, hands behind his back, staring out of the third-floor window.

'Nah. I mean, I wouldn't have told you if you hadn't bust me.' He looked sheepish again. 'I mean, it's just too much, you know? Too far-fetched. Turns me into some kind of cyborg in everyone's eyes, for no real reason.'

'I get you. I'd like to try it though, for my own sanity.' The words were out of my mouth before I had thought about creating them.

We talked and talked and talked on that pavement. It was the first emotive, heartfelt conversation I had had with anyone for years – certainly since the people disappeared, but also since well before that, stretching all the way back to that uncertain point in time when I withdrew from people, and from my life. The most obvious thing about our conversation – and I realised this fully at the time, and relished it – was the clarity. The smell of the impending rain. The burn of the afternoon sun on my skin, searing it. The silence. The way the absence of sound actually enveloped our voices. Each word had weight, fell down on top of the last and clattered.

Tebza's emotional tap was wide open thanks to the comedown. He explained in passionate detail the intensity of the experience, his hand forming explanatory circles, his fingers drawing words and ideas in the pavement dirt. The cracking open of his cognitive horizon, his falling in love with the girl and the alien sex and, finally, his tipping over the edge of experience into compulsion and, yes, ultimately, addiction.

I followed Tebza intently, my tongue sliding in and out of the guillotine, slicing gently, evoking the smallest dribbles of blood. Slowly I began adding, telling, agreeing, and revealing those parts of myself that, well, that I had spent many years pushing down.

The clouds moved over us. Suddenly we were covered in rolling purple.

'That is the point, isn't it?' Tebza said, rising to his feet. I remained sitting, knees tucked into elbows. 'The desperation. We need people. Even when we hate them. Especially when we hate them.'

I stood.

We decided to walk it. To use our feet all the way back, through the wet.

Despite the intensity of the day, despite the revelations and the change of view and the confessions we had engendered, despite it all – I could not mention rape.

I did not mention rape.

I would not mention rape.

Chapter 27
I also imagined her in his arms

During our time in PE I had grown to love, for my own reasons, Babalwa's emotional distance from me. Even when we were at our closest, even on those rare occasions when we rose together to the heights of actual lovemaking, we were far apart. The distance was comfortable. It fit easily with my own abstracted state. And so I rendered her form in easy, hard lines. I constructed Babalwa as a simple PE girl. I never really considered other possibilities. Now I had to broach the notion that she may not have been that simple. That her dry, withdrawn PE state may have been tailored around my presence rather than being an inherent part of her personality. That she had throttled so far back in self-defence in reaction to an impossible situation in which she could not tolerate me, nor life without me.

After we arrived in Jozi, she began to express herself in ways I hadn't seen before. And since she had taken up sexually with Fats, what I had known as her natural silence had morphed into a quiet, assertive confidence. Now she was allowing herself to think, and then to communicate her thinking. The white shorts and Castle Lager T-shirt had slowly disappeared, replaced by fitted jeans, vests and the occasional skirt. In group conversations she sat back and forward in equal measures.

I suspected that Fats was particularly successful at making love to her. That, instead of twisting and rubbing mechanically (as I now was forced to admit I may have been doing), he enticed her out into the world of active expression. Maybe that inner process was translating into her external life.

I felt shamed.

I looked back with half-shut eyes at our sexual encounters. I saw myself humping and jabbing, fucking and grinding. I wished now that I could erase it. Take it back. Reconstruct.

I also imagined her in his arms, exhausted and raw emotionally and otherwise, confessing, letting go of that terrible first memory of me on the heavy black grill. I pictured the creeping tears, his strong black thumb pushing the first one back, then massaging its companions from their hiding places.

I was shamed.

But was it rape?

Did I overpower her and force her?

Did I hold those wrists in a lockdown, pin her so she couldn't move, break her open and stab and stab and stab?

Chapter 28
Allowing myself to dream

We stomped home through the monsoon. Initially talking, but when the thud of the drops drowned our voices out, just stomping, walking, stomping. We were wet – soaked through – but refreshed, in a childlike, druggy way. Up to the top of Rissik Street, round Constitution Hill, up past the park, past Joburg General and east into Houghton. By the time we got to the St Patrick gate, clouds had wiped the blue away completely and it was pitch-dark. And the gate was locked.

The spikes on top of the wrought-iron fencing were not to be fucked with. Fats had made sure the fence was impossible to climb without a genuine risk of impalement.

The idea of walking back in the rain seemed suddenly very stupid. The drops drove into us like industrial knitting needles. We ducked into a decaying wooden guard hut that stood a few hundred metres back down the street. The thudding of the monsoon prevented all but the most basic communication.

'That fucker Fats.'
'Who locked the gate?'
'They knew we must be coming.'
'These fucking gates.'
'Stupid, stupid shit.'

The hut was rank with decay and wet wood. The floor planks had curled in protest and most had ejected the nails trying to hold them down. An ancient radio tape deck sat helpless on one rising piece of wood, surfing in perpetuity. A small pile of *Houghton Times* and *Daily Sun* newspapers, held down with a brick, rotted neatly underneath a single dirty-white pool chair.

'Jesus, imagine spending your work night in one of these!' Tebza bellowed, hunched up on the sliver of a bench running along the left inside wall.

I nodded. Imagine.

We sat soaking in the hut for ten or fifteen minutes. The rain was going nowhere. The sun was gone, and we had no way of getting back inside the laager. Tebza hugged his knees, shivering, the balls of his feet jackhammering against the pine floor.

Suddenly there was a thud against the rotten wall of the hut and an angry wet snout, flanked by two shortish, chipped brown tusks, burst into the space between Tebza's legs. I jumped vertically. Tebza tried to climb the side wall with his elbows. 'Jezuz fuck! What the fuck!' The snout pulled out, ripping some of the rotten wood along with it, then snuffled back into the vacant space. Tebza tried to kick it, missing completely.

'Tebz Tebz Tebz. No no no,' I hissed, grabbing him by the arm and trying to smother the wildly flailing limbs. 'Kicking pigs in the face. Not a good idea. Not good. Sensitive. They are very sensitive there.' His eyes were wide as dinner plates. I put my finger to my lips and shushed him. Outside we could hear wet snorting and foraging. There were a few more bumps against the hut.

'How many?' Tebza mouthed at me.

It sounded like there were at least three. My immediate worry was that the other two had tusks as big as the first, who, going by snout size, was a certifiably big bastard.

Generally we lived in a state of amicable cohabitation with the pigs, who watched us as much as we watched them. In daylight and with the free run of the land in front of them they didn't pose much of a threat, but now, at night, all sodden snouts and long tusks, it was a different story. It felt like we were being hunted.

The snout came back a few more times, but in a less aggressive manner. We decided in fearful whispers that they were probably just curious.

About an hour in, as the torrent eased, we walked. The pigs followed, snuffling and grunting in the shadows around us. We looked for holes in the fence, or a small road or alley that would get us back inside the perimeter. Although lighter, the rain pounded us at every step. With each blow our enmity towards Fats grew. 'Change in gate policy!' Tebza screamed into the sodden night. 'Complete change!' A pig snorted in agreement, just out of sight.

We eventually found a gap on the Louis Botha side of St John's, and after six or seven tragic wrong turns we made it back. The pigs dropped off once we were through the perimeter fence, but not before two of them, both males, came into full view and watched us as we poked around. Tebza was more disturbed by the pigs than I was. In the full wetness of the night it seemed obvious they meant us no harm. They were observing, and looked, to me anyway, a little hurt at our fear of them. One male lowered his head slightly as we considered each other, in deference, perhaps. Or maybe just to let me know ... what? I couldn't quite get a handle on the communication. After some time he kicked the turf twice and he and his buddies turned and left.

Tebza stormed into the lounge screaming murder about gate policies and the threat of pigs and consideration for others. I quietly deposited the Energade bottle in my bedroom cupboard and took a shower.

When I came downstairs the pot was still simmering, Tebza confronting Fats, who sat unmoved, arms folded, mouth resisting the invading creases of a smirk. The others, looking bored but nervous, tried to wind the subject down with apologies and promises.

The air was thick. Beatrice, hopefully unaware of the rape subtext shimmering beneath, cleared her throat as if to speak, but no words came. Babalwa was seated on the couch next to Fats and picked at her toenails nervously. Fats folded and unfolded his arms and stared into the middle distance as Tebza raged on.

I was all subtext. I watched Babalwa pick her toes and wondered again what her agenda was. Whether she had an angle on the rape thing, and, perhaps more importantly, whether she was in concert with Fats or not. My earlier reflections had led me to conclude it was against the odds that she had an agenda. More likely the memory had slipped out while she was in his arms and he, typical alpha, could not help but chase me down.

But if that was the case, it meant Babalwa truly believed I had raped her.

I would have preferred an insidious agenda.

I would have preferred a plot.

But she just picked at her nails. Pick. Pick. Pick. Fats staring ahead. The rain bombarding the roof. Beatrice clearing her throat, expectant.

The end of the world.

Beatrice clearing her throat one last time, standing, leaving.

Fats and Babalwa sharing a glance.

Me looking down, allowing myself to dream of another reality.

III

Chapter 29
We did our chores

With every sunset another cry echoed out and new predators arrived: feathered, clawed, horned. We watched the world reshape itself. The free pigs prospered quietly, growing in numbers and confidence, their enormous forms staking out swathes of turf, concrete and grass, which they now called their own. The predators followed them, of course. We slept listening to lions cough and hyenas laugh. We woke to the call of raptors. Vultures circled, and sometimes – often, in fact – I had the feeling they were waiting right above our property. Above us.

I tied a small, ladies' revolver in a holster to my ankle, safety firmly on, when I ran.

We did our chores.
> We fed ourselves.
> The canned food went bad.
> The bottled water became sour.

We became truly lonely.

We became alone.

Chapter 30

Just spectators

Teboho drank his piss regularly, the nanobots leaking out every time until he was scrabbling for five minutes, three minutes, one minute more.

He couldn't let go of the idea of finding the door to our prison, nor of the hope that someone in a white coat watching over us in a location beyond our comprehension would take pity, let the bots in our system drain out and grant us exit. I would often catch him running for a corner. Ramming his shoulder hard into a wall, veering his car to the left or suddenly accelerating into a blind rise. When we were alone he would simply crash into objects and areas without pausing. One minute we were talking, the next he was thumping into a tree, a door, a piece of shrubbery.

Once he had revealed his secret to me, Tebza appeared to worry less about exposing his eccentricity to the others. 'Sorry,' he would say, mid-conversation. 'I just, I just need to.'

He would target his spot, line it all up with eye and brain, lower his shoulder and bust into it. It was disturbing to me, who understood the rationale, but to the others it was plain crazy. Each attempt, each hard cement or brick encounter, doubled the confusion, which compounded again as the air was forced from his lungs and he groaned, sometimes falling to the ground, righted himself and then carried on, rubbing the shoulder, wincing abstractedly, adjusting his little white earphone as if the pause, the halt in the conversation or interaction, had simply been one of those things. As if he had merely been coughing, or wiping his nose.

When confronted he would duck, brazenly denying the reality just seen and experienced. 'Thing I read,' he would say, for example, deadpan. 'The gym people reckoned you can harness the adrenalin of pain for muscle growth blah blah. Hurts like hell.'

His behaviour was so bizarre, so out of whack, they had little choice but to let it go. To confront him would be to challenge his essential sanity. And we were all a little too unhinged in ourselves for that.

Tebza, Fats decided, simply had a problem in his head. No one, he said, could possibly rack up that many cuts and bruises without some serious wire-stripping going on inside.

My heart ached a little more with every bump and crash, every trickle of blood, every scab formed. I was the only one who had an idea of where his dreams actually lay and how hard he was striving to reach them. And yet even I found it impossible to wake Tebza from his snowballing internal reverie. He took to his computers for longer and longer stretches, days at a time sometimes, pausing for only the briefest periods to piss or to wander outside for a late-night joint.

Tebza was roaming across two frontiers. He was desperate for a gap, for that hole in the fabric to finally stick his finger through, but he was also clicking and pinging constantly in search of the cloud, waiting for that single, telling beep that would change everything.

But it never came.

I drank his piss a few weeks after the Patterson Park discovery and our walking tour of the city. I expected the atmosphere of androids. The taste of outer space. What I got was a clear, simple canvas. A park with trees, like a golf course but without the fairway up the middle. A set of birds chirping and swapping places on the oak trees. A dam in the distance which I walked up to and drank from and swam in. Grass between my toes, tickling slightly.

I lay around. I rolled in it. Took off my clothes (the same clothes I was wearing in the real world, a nifty hack-programming trick). I held my dick in my hand and jerked it a little until I had a free, natural hard-on. I did a cartwheel. I pinched myself and felt the pain. I contemplated breaking a bone – a toe maybe – to test the outer limits. I climbed a tree.

'Going in,' Tebza said, 'don't expect anything. There's no software other than the basic OS, and it's very basic.' But our earlier conversations dominated my expectations, and I would be lying if I said I wasn't disappointed, given the barriers I'd had to hurdle to get there. Tebza's piss tasted, well, like piss. It was tangy and urinary and all the things I expected. The taste lurked on my tongue for weeks after, a subtle yet compelling reminder of our hidden world.

Blank as the experience was, however, technically there was no questioning the hack accomplishment.

At Mlungu's you always knew you were in an interface. The ground was blurry, the walls were blurry, everything was blurry, thanks to compression needed to keep the stream moving. The trick was never to focus too much, to keep your eyes in the middle distance, the range at which the imagery held best. You needed to keep moving too. If Lady Di approached you seductively, for example, peeling off a layer here, a bra strap there, reaching in your direction, there was an art to making the most of her invitation. The first trick was to get your dick out of your pants and into an orifice as soon as possible. The mixed rush of dopamine, serotonin and adrenalin would override your brain's questioning of the JPEG stitching and enforce a kind of physiological suspension of disbelief. VR sex took off the way it did not only because everyone wanted to fuck, but because sex was the best way to enjoy the nascent VR experience. The sexual fizz provided the cognitive compression necessary to make the sketchy technology behind the whole thing work. As long as you were in a semi- or fully erect state, it was compelling. The final trick was to wet your nap – to use the popular phrase of the time – only when you were ready to leave. The vasopressin released by the brain during orgasm was short-lived, and after it had drained off you were left with the blurry JPEGs Mongezi had detested so. His innovation had vastly improved the paradigm, granted, but the basic limitations still dominated. Only the teenagers and the perverts were willing, or able, to keep going and going.

Hack was fundamentally different. I spent the duration of my time marvelling over the seamlessness of the thing, once I had resigned myself to the awful influence of the music. (I had been intent on taking my own music with me, but there was no way to integrate an external feed and the bots without exactly the right kind of high-end wireless router.) I was stuck with four preselected back tracks – a problem Tebza had circumvented much earlier in his life. While prepping me, he confessed that his little white dangling earpiece was a fake – a prop to support his real, physiological audio system. Encouraged by Joy, Tebza had gone deep, implanting an audio chip onto both eardrums, effectively internalising his home entertainment system. He kept the white earphones in his ear and dangling over his chest to cover for the fact that often he was listening to his own internal music or, in the days before the disappearance, to his operating system.

Lacking his internal magic, I was bolted to the four provided tracks for the duration, dire generic downbeat things. Perversely, I was unable to turn the sound off, or even down. The default system settings could be modified only through the software running off the router – which we didn't have.

At the high end of the park, up past the dam, there was a gate. An old, Boer-style farm gate. I walked around the dam to the gate, opened it, stepped through and emerged where I had started, at the bottom of the park. A virtual loop.

I ran to the left, straight at the far row of pine trees marking off the park's boundary. I got to about three metres from the trees and then was caught treading water, the pines stubbornly out of reach. Unlike my walk to the gate, there was no progression, no sense of movement or change – this was a holding pattern, an edge that refused to come any closer. But even under this system stress, the visual seam held firm – again in complete contrast to Mlungu's, where the walls crumbled at the slightest pressure.

And that was it.

A park.

A pretty, green park.

I lay in the middle of grass and let the birds sing to me until, without warning, the sky dissolved, clouds puffy then white then strands then gone, and I was back in my bedroom, dislocated and regretting I hadn't explored one of the other three interfaces.

I returned the full Energade bottle to Tebza the next morning. Aside from the bummer of the comedown, my mind was consumed by the potential of thing.

'So?' he asked.

'Eish ... so much ...' I struggled for the words. 'The possibilities.'

'Ja, I knew my life had changed when I first took it.' He shook his head. 'Who can ever guess, eh? What happens, happens. We are just spectators.'

I was tempted to go back to it, but I was also wary of becoming as attached to the calm and otherness of the park as Tebza was to the escape. Or the nightclub. His lure was the spacey, empty floor and the mirrorball. Also, I presumed, the lingering, almost tangible hope of more punters arriving. I guessed ultimately I would have taken the park pretty much every time, but the detachment of the experience was too much, the return to life too edgy and jagged.

That, and the taste of piss, which was just hard to stomach.

Chapter 31
None brave enough to stop

I discovered around this time that my father was an authentic beat master. It's a simple fact, but it had eluded me.

I had always fallen into the trap – understandable enough, I suppose, considering the circumstances of our lives – of judging him by the primary layer: according to the visible evidence. I failed to look seriously beneath the business end of his suitcase, and so I missed the cluster of hard drives that captured the true scope of his musical interest, and, yes, I'll admit it now, his talent. Buried beneath the stupid trance and the club mixes and remixes, underneath the devices that stored his ability to make money, and a career, was jazz and breakbeat. Hip hop and jungle, drum and bass and old-school crooners, dub (reggae, dubstep, German ambient, etc.), classical by the bucketload, the full range of singer-songwriters, rock, and a staggering, confusing depth of pop.

It was an accidental discovery. I was rooting through the case looking for a particular Thievery Corp mix that Tebza and I had been discussing and that I knew lay within, when, on a whim, I decided to plug one of the anonymous hard drives into my machine. And there, folder after folder after folder. A cornucopia. A lifetime.

The depth of the collection – its whimsical range, its sheer adventurousness – sent me into an extended spiral of reflection. From the perspective of my grey hair and formally declared alcoholism, from the view of a lost man with a jagged tooth and few prospects – spiritual, physical or otherwise – my father now cut an entirely different figure. A figure of loss and pathos. A figure of farce, of course, but also of hidden dignity.

I had never allowed myself to consider what it must have felt like to travel the strange and distorted road he had. Now, I thought seriously of cricket. Of the smell of the game that occupied so much of his life and his consciousness. How the Velcro of the pads must have felt when he pulled the straps tight. The insane nerves and stomach-rumbling that would have overtaken him as he sat waiting in the hut, heel slamming against the floor. The ball in his hand. How it would have fit so neatly. The roll of his fingers over the seam, the vision of it twirling in flight, alternately shiny red and broken-skinned. All these things, so alien to me, would have been threaded into him and the way he understood and interpreted the world.

I remembered something long-forgotten, or buried, or whatever. The whole Fotheringham hot-spot thing. My father had, for some unknown, unidentifiable reason, cut a very striking figure in the negative TV-replay view. There was something about the sharpness and angularity of his jawline, in combination with his subtle retro sunglasses, that made his X-ray hot-spot profile incredibly dashing and attractive – far more so than that of any of his peers. *You* magazine actually ran a double-page photo feature of Russle Fotheringham in a series of hot-spot frames titled 'The Sexiest Sportsman in SA?'

He didn't like it at all. On the few occasions it was mentioned, he referred to the tyranny of the negative. Of the black-and-white cut-out. He had this idea of himself, post-cricket fame, as only ever successful in the negative sense, when viewed in the simplest terms of black and white. He disliked the metaphor, but he latched onto it well past his cricket days. Maybe – and who can ever truly know these things now that they are gone? – it was this idea that pushed him to let it all go.

He moved from the smell and the texture of fresh-cut grass to the smoke and grime of the clubs. It must have been, I always assumed, a deep and hard fall indeed. And yet, I had never properly considered the possibility that the choice took him by the neck. Trawling through his folders (Amy Winehouse, Josh Rouse, Cassandra Wilson, Taj Mahal, Stimela, Tananas, Gito Baloi, Mad Professor, Brad Mehldau, new jazz, old jazz, country, Jim White, TKZee, Mapaputsi, Neko Case, Professor, BOP, the folders just ran on and on and on), I broached the idea that trance and house weren't so much his new love as his recalibrated and recalculated hope – that he didn't run to the clubs in a misguided high passion, but in search of a viable way out of the rabbit warren. His star had risen and fallen, and having brushed the outer heights it simply wasn't possible for him – for his heart, for his buzzing, intense head – to spend a decade or two foraging on the commons. He needed something new, and dance and trance offered it. Did that make him a dance-and-trance guy? Possibly not. Based on the evidence of the suitcase, probably not. Now he started to make a kind of sense. He became stark, a man forced by circumstance and unfortunate choices into the simple negative. A man forced to dance. A man tapping incessantly on the walls, hoping for return sound.

I filled up with regret. I lashed myself with it. If I had been paying more attention, if I had been less obsessed and internally riveted by my own life, I might have seen more of this man. I might have recognised and realised.

I started refiling and recategorising his collections on my machine. I set up the biggest speakers I could find and played his music in huge, thumping beats that shook the house. I lay back on my bed and thought of spinning cricket balls, recalling the smell of leather, sweat and linseed oil that always somehow lingered in our house, over and above – through even – the cigarettes and club sweat.

I also allowed myself to imagine my mother. Young and rosy-cheeked, eyes ablaze, heart ripping through her ribcage as this man – all muscles and smiles and fame and magnetic, hypnotic charm – pulled beats from the sky and fed them to her. I drew sketches in my mind. I watched two young beautiful fools fall into each other's arms and, for the first time in my life, I allowed my heart to beat in time to theirs.

* * *

Fats's obsession with locking us into a secure complex evolved along with our situation. Now the focus was less on the idea of defying raiding hordes and more on keeping out the animals, specifically the pigs, who effectively surrounded our world. So much had been made of them in the newspapers that we were all a little in awe of their intelligence, their steroid-enhanced raw power and their emotional drive. Free pigs wanted to escape. They wanted to be free. And they had the brains and muscle to make it happen. That single fact made them different from any other animals – ourselves included.

I had always considered the free-pig hype to be, well, hype. The kind of stuff journos can't help but crank up. Yes, their snouts extended and straightened the longer they were free, a freaky instance of instant evolution. Yes, they seemed to grow bigger and more powerful the longer they were out. They swelled, by all accounts, with a kind of atavistic juice of the jungle. But I was always sceptical. Now, having come to face to face with so many of them, having shared post-apocalyptic space with them, I finally understood that, if anything, their immensity had been downplayed. When you stare a quarter-tonne monster right in the eye, like we began doing on a regular basis, when you speak in tones they understood and work with – well, you realise how quickly hierarchies can be restructured.

So we all kept our respective distances. The pigs didn't need us in any specific way. I think maybe they hung around us for the company as much as anything else. They were passive and distant during the day, but at night, while the meat eaters roamed, they were quicker to move, more likely to rush and charge. We took a group decision that anything weighing over three hundred kilograms and possessing tusks and/or wire-brush hair should be kept out.

Fats had, thankfully, begun to slowly let go of his ideas of himself as a leader of men. I suspect Babalwa had a direct as well as circumstantial role in the change, but of course we'll never know for sure. Pillow talk dries on the pillow.

His control centre grew stale. The red polka-dot maps of Gauteng, the complex electricity-enhancement diagrams and schematics, the grand plans of extension and establishment were allowed to yellow and age. He would bring them out when asked or when necessary, but he was no longer frogmarching pieces across the board. Something soft had crept into his demeanour now that Babalwa's fingers curled through his hand. They were expecting.

One day she ran her hand over her stomach and smiled silently. Javas caught my eye, and winked.

I laced up my stinking yellow Nikes and hit the road.

I exited our compound down Munro Drive, a thirty-degree slope about half a kilometre long. The trip down Munro was jarring, and the return run a complete, recurring punishment. Together the two halves tore at my calves and my thighs. I imagined myself as one of those masochistic emo teens nipping away at their wrists with a blade, desperately needing to finally feel something, anything. I tore my muscles apart one by one, until one day I realised that I felt most alive, most ready for the world, on that upward crawl past the stone walls of Munro Drive.

I had become a jogger.

Lillian sketched things on pieces of paper. She listed possible pilots and calculated flight durations, petrol requirements and flight paths. Her dream continued to take shape, at least in her own mind. She conducted excursions across the province, to the Lanseria airport, then out to the fringes, Germiston and Benoni and beyond. Gerald, who, I believed, was suffering as badly as I was in the stultifying atmosphere of survival, allowed himself to be pulled along, as did Javas, as did Andile, as did I. We took turns really. None of us admitting to believing, but none brave enough to stop.

Chapter 32

German Valium

The Kruger Park trip had its roots in my conversation with Gerald while doing gate work. It was my initiative. Quite possibly, now that I think about it, it was my one and only attempt to drive something. To engineer.

I felt a sense of karmic wrong at the fact that Gerald had never experienced the bush in the white man's sense – that he had only ever broached the extended reaches of his homeland, the place of his birth and childhood, by looking over the fence.

Initially it was only going to be myself and Gerald. The twins were a late, surprise addition to the party. Javas slung a backpack each for him and Andile into their Toyota as we started packing ours.

'We'll follow,' he said casually. 'Been a while since I was that side.'

Tebza jumped into our back seat at the last second with no bags or luggage at all. 'Please get me the fuck out of this place,' he said.

We drove like real tourists. Gerald had secured several pairs of binoculars and we were stacked past the rooftop with wood and firelighters, even a cooler box with ice bricks. We were a fully stocked tour party.

It was a quiet trip, but not deathly quiet. Quiet as antidote, rather. Quiet as relaxation and holiday. Gerald looked genuinely happy. The corners of his leathery face tweaked frequently in what approximated a smile, and there was a looseness in his form that ran contrary to the tight barrel of the man I had always known.

The road opened up as we came over the escarpment past eMalahleni, past the heaps and heaps of coal, the rudderless conveyor belts and black dumps of stuff. We turned to Dullstroom to find six shiny 4x4s stranded outside a pseudo English-style pub. We smashed through a few lodges for trout rods and made a pretence of fly-fishing.

The dams were overrun.

'Be easier just to grab one,' said Javas, and Andile did exactly that, squealing with triumph as she wrestled the resistant fish into the air. We built a fire and braaied the trout with onion and garlic, then slung ourselves out on the five-star balcony, beers in hand.

Gerald belched. 'The rich. So few ideas ...' He shook his head and wiped the lemon-butter sauce from his lips. We all agreed, without understanding. Our dynamic had become very much like this: a series of vaguely linked comments and assertions, expressions of mood really. We were feeling each other instead of understanding. Words were irrelevant.

In Hazyview we found an enormous yellow Hummer in the parking lot of a single-storey strip mall that stretched around four different streets, all cheap face-brick and peeling transmission paint.

The Hummer was a triple-cab beast. We dumped our vehicles and loaded everything and everyone in it. I played DJ. We left the town with Brenda Fassie, and then Andile started requesting.

'Any dub?' she asked.

Tebza sought clarity. 'Reggae dub, dubstep or German I've-been-taking-Valium-for-three-weeks dub?'

'The stuff in the middle,' Javas said. 'You know, big Eurobeats and the reggae feel. Crossover stuff.'

There followed an extended two-day debate of the technical specifications of the various dub genres. I took them on the widest journey possible, reaching into the far corners of Russle's musical armoury. Gerald didn't participate, of course, only smiling ironically at the nuances of a conversation he would never understand. We explained dubstep to him as best we could, but the blankness of his face always pushed the lessons back to the essential basics.

True dub, Tebza maintained (and I was with him), required a repetitive beat – a steady rhythm that resisted the drift. Where the Germans always got it wrong was with the beat – they let the pacing go, and as soon as it did the dub was over. Javas defended the Germans, we all laughed, and then somewhere along the way we realised we were laughing, really laughing, and we did it some more.

We entered the park at the Kruger Gate. It was appropriate, symbolic somehow, to go past the man's granite bust and to enter at the front, such as it was. We stopped the Hummer at the statue and had a good look. Javas squatted on his heels, ran sand through his fingers and considered Oom Paul. The dub – German Valium – rumbled on from inside the Hummer.

'What you thinking?' Gerald asked him.

'A doos ahead of his time,' Javas said, rocking back lightly on his heels as the Afrikaans expletive rolled awkwardly off his tongue. 'The park was a good call. Can't deny it. In a time when people just shot everything.'

It was one of the longest sentences I had ever heard him produce, and it was impressively decisive.

There was nothing to add.

In keeping with the spirit of visionary ecological decision-making, as we travelled we decided to open the park's gates, which were all in the night-time lockdown position. We started with Oom Paul. It was initially a flippant suggestion from Tebza and we laughed at the idea of it, like we were kids trying to open up the zoo at night, but then, as we collectively put our hands on that red-and-white boom and pushed, it felt profound and metaphorical and important.

Of course the animals had already been drifting across the borders of the park on their own accord. No longer bound by humanity, they took natural advantage of existing gaps in the fencing, and of the fact that the front gates – really just simple, symbolic booms – were always intended to be protected by humans. We had started seeing the first herds from the town of Sabie. Packs of zebras, their fat asses glistening in black-and-white health, followed by wildebeest and impala. Plenty and plenty of impala. Grazing on the lawn outside the Sabie Spar, grazing on the hills. We stopped to examine them in their new context, peering and leaning.

'Weird, eh?' I asked.

'Sho,' Gerald said. 'Won't be long before there's nothing but animals.'

'What I want to know is, what was the big deal with the Kruger Park anyway?' Andile asked, her question floating in search of a respondent.

I, the most frequent visitor to the place, tried to explain. 'It was a culture. For Afrikaners especially, but also the English. Everything about it. The huts, the camping, the camps, each camp with its own identity and way of being. A family thing. Driving all day, looking for game. Going to the bush without having to go to the zoo.'

'No blacks?' she queried knowingly.

'Plenty washing and serving. A few scattered tourists. But no, no blacks.'

'As a black,' she giggled at her boldness, 'I always wondered about it. Looking at animals. We just never had it. Nè ...' She shrugged.

'It's peaceful,' I explained. 'Watching animals being animals.'

'Let's go learn,' Andile said, thumping the back of Gerald's headrest excitedly. 'Teach me to be white, Roy, teach me.'

I had believed, down in the place where we assume and hope for such things, that Gerald would be revealed on this trip. That the bush – the real bush – would bring him, a local boy, out of himself, and that we, myself especially, would gain insight into who he really was.

But Gerald remained inscrutable. We drove to the Kruger Gate, past his hometown of Mkhuhlu, in silence. He pointed at a cluster of houses set at the base of a hill, four hundred metres back from the main road. 'Scene of the crimes,' he said.

'Should we stop? Wanna pull over?' I asked, wanting him to want to.

'I know what it looks like, thanks.'

'Must have been a weird place to grow up, nè?' I prodded, half to try to get him going and half in genuine reflection on the road we had just travelled, a blizzard of eco resorts, game resorts, golf resorts, getaways and hideaways. Jams and biltong and carvings and breads. Maps of the park, hats and sunglasses, signs for game meat, dried wors and fruit. Bananas and mangoes. And, filling in the cracks, the townships and shacks, homes of the servants and game rangers, receptionists and cleaners. Barbers and petrol stations.

'More than you can imagine,' said Gerald. Later he pointed out a lone buffalo grazing outside the gates of the Protea Hotel, on the public side of the Sabie River, just before the Kruger Gate. 'I've never seen a buffalo before like that.' He stopped the Hummer and half leaned over me for a better view.

'Beautiful.'

And that was it. Gerald was on a game drive. He wanted nothing of his past.

We camped the first night at the completely off-grid Tinga Game Lodge, outside Skakuza. It was as typical, eco-themed and high-end as a lodge could get. A flat wooden deck overlooking the river, with what once must have been a crisp-blue swimming pool sunk into the far right corner, now green and festering with life. Low-slung cane furniture stacked and waiting at the back of the deck, along with loungers and sleepers and general sun-worshipping equipment. A thatched roof, generic African landscape prints on the walls, wooden sculptures from across the continent. Big rooms with yawning double beds and en-suite bathrooms.

We cracked all the windows open and the winter sun poured in.

We had beer. We had vegetables. Bread. Potatoes. But no meat.

'Someone will have to go hunting,' Gerald cracked. He pulled a lounger to the deck railings and put his feet on them. 'Meat,' he mumbled. 'Fucking meat. I lust.'

Twenty minutes later we heard the crack of a rifle shot, and about forty minutes after that Javas marched across the lawn in front of the deck covered in blood, a skinned, gutted buck carcass draped around his neck. 'Let's eat,' he said.

Javas crouched on the grass in front of us, a green Amstel bottle propped next to the carcass, and delivered what can only be described as performance butchery, carving the prime chunks off the impala and stripping the rest of the easily accessible meat off onto biltong hooks he had prepared who knew where or when. Andile sat next to Gerald and myself, grinning.

'You okes take a break,' Javas said. He stood up, sipped on his beer and paused to check out the setting orange sun, the buck and the giraffe drinking at the dam. 'This one's on me.' I laughed at his sarcasm – we were all completely slumped in our chairs – but realised as the evening grew that he was serious. He built his fire casually yet methodically, creating a small oven with firelighters and twigs and bringing a cooking flame to life within half an hour. At his invitation, we jumped down as the sun set and added logs to the flame, creating a bonfire. When we were good and drunk and the sun was completely gone, Javas built a set of brick walls, pulled a spade out of nowhere and shovelled hot coals into his new oven. Andile threw foil-wrapped potatoes into the fire and organised the vegetables, and then we burned and ate the impala steaks.

And they were delicious.

Better, really, than anything I had eaten in my life. This was meat in its original sense. It made me want to learn how to hunt.

When we were fully gorged and rubbing our stomachs and listening to the bats and the bugs, Javas told us his story.

Javas was not his real name. South Africa was not his country.

Art was a recent flourish.

He was born in a small village on the outskirts of the Tsholotsho district in Zimbabwe, and it was there that his father told him how his great-grandfather had been hung by his feet from the rafters of the shed and cooked alive by Mugabe's Shona. It was one small episode. A tiny, almost forgotten sliver of tragedy in the wider river of blood that was the Ndebele extermination.

The image was etched into his father's heart. The story was told and retold, the details sharper and clearer with each telling, a small boy's horrified view through the corner cracks growing more stark, casting brighter, clearer light on the savagery every time.

The death of his great-grandfather was the crux of Javas's family.

His father rolled in it, in his anger towards Mugabe and the Shona. But he wasn't a man able or willing to turn to politics. Instead he veered inward, rotting in booze and recriminations, losing his family along the way, his wife and offspring drifting away in ever-widening circles, without him.

Javas – Jabulani actually, at that time – grew up a quiet, unobtrusive middle child. Like all children of his geography and generation, by the time he hit puberty his ambition had expanded to incorporate Jozi as a logical antidote to living the rest of his life on, as he put it, a 'sinister, abandoned farm'.

Even after Mugabe's death, Javas wanted nothing more than to leave the country of his birth. While waiting, he turned himself into an adult in the bush, tracking and watching game, making fires, climbing trees, observing. Retrospectively it was, he said, one of the happiest times of his life.

Gerald grunted at this. I couldn't tell whether it was affirmation or rejection. He slipped a few notches further down in his lounge chair, his face a mask.

Aged sixteen, having nursed his father out of his frothing, bitter deathbed and into his grave, Jabulani hugged his mother, punched his younger siblings on the arm and hit the road. Before he even got to the border crossing – he had intended to take the through-the-Kruger route – he met up with two teenagers en route to a game farm balanced on the tip of the triangle joining Mozambique, South Africa and Zimbabwe, the furthest point of the transfrontier game reserve. They claimed work was available there. He followed them, and so began his five-year stint as a game ranger. He lasted less than six months at the first park ('It was like school, but the pay was worse') but developed the contacts necessary to get a gig at the Mukato Reserve, on the South African side. Here he became a genuine ranger, ferrying foreigners from camp to camp, leading night drives and bush walks, answering questions, and explaining spoors and nesting habits and who kills who and why. He stayed at Mukato for three years, and then was poached by a new reserve further south. Now working in the area of the Groot Letaba (he laughed again at his Afrikaans pronunciation, at the impossibility of rolling his tongue that far around anything), he was part of a more commercialised set-up, one of a crew of twenty or more rangers.

The hustle for clients, the constant push and pull over tips and pay, the strange and often bizarre divisions of labour (blacks carrying and cleaning, whites guiding and talking) ate his love for the bush and created a new and growing set of resentments and frustrations. It was, of course, never as simple as black and white. Instead, he had to negotiate a convoluted maze of relationships and vested interests, alliances and partnerships. He never quite figured out who was with whom, nor who owed whom what. What he did figure out was that he didn't understand enough of what was going on.

Jabulani was paid half the wage the white rangers were earning, and less than what most of the blacks were making as well. He was also being cut out of the lucrative personalised bush tours for the German and Japanese tourists. A confrontation with management ended with his fist on Franz Calitz's nose and a fast, calculated trot through the reserve and out over the fence, into Limpopo. He faded into the background of migrant farm slave labour, inching his way south-west to Jozi. They were looking for him, of course, but only with the lazy South African half eye. Still, Jabulani decided it would be prudent to change his name. He adopted Javas, and along with it a fictional Zulu heritage.

'If you really want to vanish, like in the movies, you must be committed.' He spoke directly to me when he said this. 'If you really wanna keep a secret, you can't tell nobody. Ever.' As he told his story, I realised that Gerald and Tebza already knew, or had surmised, a lot of it. I was the only one who had no idea.

Slamming Franz Calitz on the nose was merely the spark. Something bubbling down near his toes drove him not only to get out of Zimbabwe but to leave his life, in its entirety, for good. Javas was hell-bent on starting from scratch. With the right approach he could redefine himself as South African and get away, permanently.

So he worked his way down to Jozi and into Hillbrow and the life of a nightclub bouncer and knee-breaker. He gymmed at the right place in town, he fought when necessary, he collected debts, he ducked knives and he broke bones, not only as part of his job, but also as part of his professional identity.

'I never fought unless I had to,' he said. 'But when I did I made sure I klapped them proper.' Javas snapped his fingers through the air to indicate the severity. 'People have to know. Everyone must know.'

It was terrible, he said. The city. Life was dark and dangerous and filled with the stink of humanity. 'Jozi is fucked. If you gonna survive, you have to become fucked too. Crazy like the city. Otherwise you go home.' Eventually, though, once his credentials as a lethal cunt had been established, most of the hard work was done via inference. 'The phone is your most powerful weapon. Once you have created the fear, you keep it, you own it, with the phone. Late night. Early morning. Lunchtime is worst. People are very afraid at lunchtime.'

We were like *Out of Africa* gone to Mars. Me, Meryl Streep, the confused Euro observing the locals, my impassioned white skin glowing while my mind failed. I was stretching, reaching hard to follow Javas's story and his descriptions of his transition into Jozi life, constantly aware of the subtleties I had missed, and was still missing. Gerald's and Andile's – and, to a lesser extent, Teboho's – laughs and clucks echoed tellingly. I didn't have the experience or the language to appreciate the full scope of Javas's humour, nor the true darkness of his venture.

But I could imagine.

And in my imagining, my perception of Javas, and of the people I was living with, morphed. I now saw the deeper lines on his face, the etchings of a man who had truly travelled. I also suddenly saw the lean muscle beneath his clothing. I watched the way he moved and realised the economy of his motion. Javas was a big guy. Javas was a tough guy.

And I had never noticed.

Art, I subsequently realised, is like that. It softens by association and implication. It renders the hard pliable. It creates gaps, gaping holes really, in possibility. As he released the last parts of his history, I began to see Javas himself as a work of African art. A fluid, changeable and dynamic form. A self-sculpture. A muscled metaphor for everything that is beautiful and fucked up on the road from Harare.

Javas kept rolling. 'What I learned is that there is only fashion. No one decides on their own whether they like art or not. They are taken to art by the winds, they are told what it is, and what it's worth, in whispers.'

Javas told a good story. He also knew how to make a print, having been trained in the art of spoon printing by a benevolent teacher in his early childhood. A few years into his stint as city knee-breaker, he began an affair with a Zulu girl of a similar age, an artist who had moved through the Jozi system, studying at UJ and then going on to be mentored by bigger names at bigger venues.

Thus the artist life of Javas Khumalo was born. Funded by his knee-breaker savings, Javas's career followed a remarkable upward curve. A few months into producing cheap but innately sellable prints, he took a studio space in the inner city and began welding scrap metal together, creating massive, demonic, disturbing figures. Towering events really, more than sculptures.

'Remarkable for their combination of size and form, for their ability to both mimic and reflect the fluidity of African life,' said Andile.

'She's quoting a brochure,' Javas added. To hear him tell it, his works were simply collections of scrap metal welded into each other and given names, stories, faces – and a big fucking selling price.

Gangster connections and art connections were not as mutually exclusive as one might think. Kentridges and Makamos and Sterns and Ngobenis and Catherines were always in underground circulation, alongside diamonds and gold, sewage tenders and IT systems, and teenage girls from Thailand or Swaziland. Art, as well as the influence and fame it evoked, was a sought-after commodity. Above ground and underneath.

Javas's connections dovetailed powerfully. The girlfriend's crowd of teachers and mentors and buyers were awfully impressed.

The zing of hard gangster money reinforced the magic, creating an elixir of success, excitement and ego. Men from across the continent, afro mamas in dashikis, tight young girlfriends in super-high heels. The sunglasses and the BMWs and the pink shirts. His exhibitions created the slippery, high-tension buzz that advertising people dream of and that art buyers are powerless to resist.

And so the drug dealers chatted smoothly to the professors, who rubbed shoulders with politicians and DJs, and the hype grew and the prices went up and the girlfriend was overshadowed and outstripped by her find: Javas Khumalo, game ranger turned refugee turned debt collector and club bouncer turned artist turned sculptor. Javas was moving his pieces for well over thirty million each when ...

When ...

He shrugged and threw a log onto the fire.

When I actually saw Javas's sculptures, deeper dimensions emerged. Despite his story, even recognising and respecting his claim of being the incidental recipient of the winds-of-art fate, there was magnificence. The sculptures towered six metres in the air. The heads – sometimes made of engine cylinders or even complete car radiators – balanced easily on top of tortured metal bodies twisted with movement and potential. Tractor wheels and driveshafts and bearings and God knows what else combined to create an immense parody of humankind. Monstrous, delicately balanced, vulnerable giants on their last legs, reaching out for hope, for stability, for one last step before the fall.

I saw Andile's art too, in later months, and it was more technically accomplished, more thoughtful and nuanced. But it was small and usual and, ultimately, expected. A1 Fabrianos have been lining up, side by side, across Africa for generations. Her work was simply unable to match Javas's brute force. His ambition. I wished that I could have seen just one of his events, could have just once been in the city to witness his giants surrounded by the cloying ambition of man perfume and chequebooks.

And that, in a three-hour session of beer and fire, laughter and complete seriousness, was Javas's story. At the end, deep into the night, when we finally dragged ourselves off to our respective lodge beds, I was overcome by the desire to hug him. To embrace him. To enfold him in my arms.

And I did.

CHAPTER 33

My school name

We spent the next two days roaming the park in the Hummer, braaiing meat and eating it, opening gates, looking at game and swapping positions. It was, structurally speaking, a classic Kruger Park trip.

After the enlightenment of his life story, Javas was good company. Not only did we pick up on many of the personal threads he'd let loose, but he was also a mine of wildlife information. He would force us to get out of the vehicle and make friends with a zebra, a buck and even an elephant – none of whom cared about our presence. He explained the details. What they wanted to eat, who they wanted to fuck and when, spoors and tracks.

We drove up from Skakuza through Letaba, Satara, Olifants and up to Pafuri, the dry north. Every time we opened a gate it felt like a grand, important action. We did it ceremoniously, in recognition of our fundamental inversion of the order of things. Often we weren't opening much at all. The bigger gates were really just booms fronting empty guard huts. We swung them nonetheless.

Once we reached the top of the park we contemplated keeping going, up through Zim. Suddenly Lillian's let's-drive-through-Africa vibe didn't seem that weird. There was easy fuel wherever we went, and there we were on the border of Zim with no problems whatsoever.

Gerald nixed the idea. 'Risk,' he said. 'The odds are wrong. We make decisions as a group so we all understand what's happening. It wouldn't be fair to the rest. Which would be bad for us. Risk.'

And that was that.

Still, it was enticing. Point north and vok voort. I couldn't quite shake the idea, even as we turned back south.

We took a lot of pictures.* Well, Andile did. She wanted them for her paintings – source material and such. It wasn't something I had considered before the trip, but on the occasions I had a camera in my hands I shot with relish. I realised months later, looking over my animal photos, that I had developed the habit of always positioning someone in a far corner of the frame, nearly, but not quite, out of the shot. Just a hint, the tiniest hint, of humanity.

We only took one full-group picture, tourist style. Andile balanced the camera on a table and the five of us linked arms and beamed at the lens like we were Germans. I still have that shot now, pinned up on my wall. We all look so young. Young and bedraggled and bush dirty. My top lip had slipped up in the heat of the moment to reveal my guillotine, making me appear the most hobo-like of us all. Andile looks alarmingly young in that shot – just a girl really, just coming into the world. And beautiful in the way only the young can be.

Her own story slipped out piece by piece, in the shadow of Javas's epic. Even at the end of our excursion I saw her within the context of him, although by then I had begun to perceive the outer edges of her shape.

I only truly considered Andile and her trajectory once Javas had shocked me with his. Before, I simply perceived them as the twins. As a singular entity. I was comfortable with them sitting neatly in the middle distance of my consciousness. I'm still not sure whether I was the only one to be so slow, so self-obsessed and wrapped up in my own ideas, or whether the rest also suffered from a similar blinkered state. I remember asking Gerald at the time how much he had known of Javas's story. He gave me the Gerald sigh and beady eye and said, 'I am the same. I have two names. Gerald is my school name. My real name is Mudyathlari. I have also travelled and disappeared. Javas's story is mine. It's just that he had borders and passports.'

I retreated, suitably scolded, and still unclear. I turned to Tebza,

---

* The best of these have been archived in Annex III of the Slovo Library, miscellaneous section – which shouldn't be underestimated; it contains many minor gems.

who said he had suspected and/or surmised the basics without ever knowing the details and that I should really track down this incredibly racist yet accurate book by some colonist who had mapped the different types of sub-Saharan African races by facial type.

Andile grew up a Zulu girl in a Zulu world. She went to school (her school name was Prudence, and she ditched it age ten) and dodged the boys until she found one she liked. She ran the family shop – a small spaza – through her teens and was set to marry when the boy was killed in a car accident. Shattered by the loss, by the idea of loss, by the suddenness and severity of the change, Andile packed her bags.

Washed up on the concrete shores, she remembered art. At school, aside from being successful in dating that boy, that one single boy, she had been pretty good at sketching. She picked up her pencil and in those crucial three months after beaching at a friend's place in Vosloo, those months when you'll take anything, do anything, be anything, she stumbled across an arts college. The tutors noticed a freedom in her lines and she lucked into a full three-year sponsorship, stipend and all. After years of dutiful attention, after months of wracking grief, after weeks of urban confusion, she was riding at a particular pace in a particular direction, and it all seemed to make sense, like someone had planned it.

The art training led to graduation, with no particular honour. Andile ended up running the office of the NGO that had trained her. She managed student stipends and training programmes, secured funding for arts events and herded the artists together for whatever was required. 'I am skilled in chowing the budget' was her sardonic summation. 'I know how to eat. And how others eat. I understand the shipping margins for arts fairs. I know how to overbook hotels.'

It was the inflections, the small hand movements, the gestures and flickers of emphasis that did the real telling. The eyes flashing, sometimes tearing up. A belly laugh. I began to try – while listening to her and following her, while starting to paint my own pictures of her life in KwaZulu, then Vosloo, then the city – to seriously piece it together. Her story, like Javas's and Gerald's, was that of the refugee.

I too had some of the refugee in me, although the troubles I had fled through my life were largely of my own making. Nonetheless, I had perfected an ability to stay away from the core of things, to float myself off, slightly to the left, keeping as silent as possible and as participative as necessary.

Artists could never, would never, harm anybody. They're too busy painting. Same with ad drunks. They might be a bit useless at functional tasks, they may break things (small objects, precious objects, door handles, car accessories, and such), but they're too pissed to get seriously involved in anything.

While considering Andile, I pondered how I was viewed, and how the others perceived me. I had had few conversations of this sort with anyone other than Tebza. The usual chatter and basic information sharing, of course, but I could recall precious few occasions where I had told my story with my hands and my heart, like Andile and Javas had done.

And then, of course, the bigger questions. Had my decades of retreat and personal isolation rendered these skills void in me? Was my heart rusted shut? Was my tongue beyond any meaningful redemption? Could it even tell what needed to be told?

For the moment, the questions were moot. No one had asked for my story yet. Not that story.

We headed back to Jozi enriched, enlivened and imbued with a sense of movement, with notions of hope, change and progression.

'It makes me think,' said Andile as we bulleted down the N4 in the Hummer, chasing Javas and Tebza and Gerald as they led us home in the Toyota, 'that anything is possible. That maybe we're hiding in Jozi. We should move. We could move, if we wanted to. We could go anywhere we liked. Why not move up here? Even if there aren't people, there's places out there, nè?'

I agreed. I imagined. The roadside swept past at pace, the smokestacks on the left horizon teasing with the suggestion of utility, power, progression.

Chapter 34

Hungover, shamed troops

Tebza had finally delivered. Suddenly we had a WAN that covered three square kilometres. Not just any WAN, but one that locked into the IP address for the transmission-paint receptors. We were able to talk to the walls, to command and broadcast. In time, we would be able to create interfaces.

The WAN gave us partial drone ability – just enough to show how distant the real deal was, and would forever be. Without a satellite link the essential function of the drones was void. Images couldn't be fed back to the controls, and so the things could never be sent out of human sight. They were little more than toys. Even if they could have ventured beyond us, we would never be able to see what they saw. They would be out there seeking, seeing, assessing all on their own.

Still, the WAN allowed Tebza to control a drone from a laptop hooked up to something akin to a PA system mixing desk, out of which extended a joystick. Using a combination of wireless signals and radio frequencies that was beyond our understanding, he gave us sight control over the planes, which he set to shoot video and store on the internal hard drive. Long after the little brown bullets were parked back next to us, we all pored over the laptop, peering hopefully into a video stream of vacant land.

We climbed the St John's tower for the best view and reach, and flew the things for days. We flew them into trees and buildings, hovered them incessantly in fear of landing and then crashed them repeatedly in the attempt to bring them down.

The drones, secured from the Waterkloof Airforce Base, were the size of small seagulls. Some were even as small as large insects. They were observation devices and lacked guns and firepower, a fact which disappointed the boys but, Tebza educated us, at least ensured we would receive decent-quality video. You can only fit so much equipment onto a seagull.

It was thrilling, getting those things into the air and then letting them run through the blue. Infused in the thrill was the idea of our own flight, and thus it was Lillian who bounced and bobbed and squeaked with the most force. 'I'm telling you!' she shouted into the air above the clock tower, American fist raised. 'I'm telling you, world! We will fly! We will not be beaten!'

'Just focus, dear.' Tebza reached out to steady her grip on the joystick, then retracted, his hand hovering nervously. 'We don't have an endless supply.'

Andile laid her body carefully on the tower's thin stone ledge, suntanning, hands behind head, ignoring the sheer drop. 'This blue sky,' she said, to no one in particular. 'The sky has just gone mal blue. Crazy blue. Imagine how blue it would be, to be a drone, floating in the sea, just you, just me.' She rapped thoughtlessly, stumbling onto a hidden beat. 'Baby, it's life, baby, it's a bee, it's the drone, it's you, it's me, free in the deep blue sea ...'

Lillian plunged to the right, the joystick pulling her body down as the drone flipped up in the sky, lost itself and started to crash. She yelled theatrically and thrust the stick in six different directions. The drone, tiny insect, dropped helpless onto the rugby field. 'Wait, I'll get it!' she yelled and bolted down the stairs. We watched her shifting across the turf, lost in the simple thrill of the search.

'I'm having a feeling,' said Gerald carefully, 'that this is the beginning of something.'

Drones aside, there was much debate around what use to make of our new ability, which, although exciting, was not immediately practical. Eventually we settled on painting the corner façade of the St John's building, the bit overlooking Houghton Drive. We did a bad job, just a straight up-and-down lashing of the dull brown, but it was enough. After a week of energy and effort, we stood proudly below a twelve-metre-wide and thirty-metre-high rotating slide show. After we grew bored with pictures of ourselves, Tebza loaded up a static, shimmering South African flag and it sat there, humble during the day, insanely colourful and neon at night. It was, we decided, important. It marked our presence. At night, the neon could be seen from Tshwane.

'You'd swear by the size of the thing,' said Andile, 'that we would be thousands.'

It was an achievement. A clear and obvious accomplishment.

It deserved celebration.

We drove to the coast in three vehicles, drinking from early in the day and ending up on the Durban beachfront, wasted and crazed.

Fats shagged Lillian on the beach.
Babalwa wept.
Gerald punched Fats.
Tebza disappeared.
Javas punched Fats.

The drinking actually started before we left Houghton. Beatrice produced two cases of cider. 'Before this shit really does go off,' she rationalised. But really it was the tequila Fats pulled into his 4x4 that sent it all to shit. I rolled a self-defence joint for the journey, and by the time we had passed Heidelberg it had all pretty much collapsed. Joints were being passed between moving vehicles; the cider and tequila and beer smashed head-on into much pent-up energy and scattered into the winds.

I took the Édith Piaf out of the CD player and replaced it with Fresh House Flava's Volume II. Lillian and Fats were in my vehicle on the first leg and I watched in the rear-view as the spark of their eventual encounter flickered. The tequila had made them silly. The joint added a subtle kind of hysteria. A hand moved to the left. Another hand brushed a knee. Someone needed to lean somewhere to get something and suddenly the air was thick and sweet and about to explode.

The problem, we discovered on arriving in Durban, was that we had nothing to do.

Unlike Kruger, where the animals in themselves are an agenda that can roll out peacefully for days, now there was only the sea. Of the nine of us there were only four swimmers (myself, Andile,

Lillian and Beatrice), and in any case the waves were rough and churning and brown.

We swirled around the parking lot. Ran up and down the pier.

Lillian and Fats kept brushing against each other, and Babalwa started getting scratchy. I sat with Tebza on the low brick wall dividing the esplanade and the sand.

'Heard there was hack going down here.' Tebza spoke from the corner of his mouth. 'Somewhere near the harbour.'

'Lemme guess.' I couldn't resist. 'A flat somewhere.'

'Exactly.'

'Nothing more than that?'

'Blue,' he added, laughing at himself. 'A blue block of flats. On the beachfront. Near the harbour. That should narrow it down.'

'Name of block? Owner?'

'Nope. Blue block near the harbour. All I got.'

'You gonna check it out?'

'Why not?' He glanced at Beatrice, who was doing drunken, misguided cartwheels on the sand. 'I think I know where this is going.'

We watched Andile try to guide Beatrice's legs through the last phase of the cartwheel. Beatrice yelped and shook her foot free, kicking Andile in the jaw in the process. Andile clutched her jaw in tequila drama and they stood in a sudden face-off, accusing each other.

Tebza drifted away. I joined Gerald on the pier, where he was fishing like an old man. We sat there for an hour without a real bite. The sun dropped fast behind the beachfront flats and hotels.

Gerald looked at the parking lot, at Beatrice, Lillian and Fats sitting on the wall talking animatedly, at Babalwa walking alone in a dramatically sulky fashion down the shoreline. 'This,' he said, 'was a bad idea.'

Pause.

I sipped on my flat Coke.

'Be dark soon. They're too messed up to even walk.'

'Gonna be a long night.'

'Where'd the twins go?'

'Dunno.'

'Tebza?'

'Said something about the harbour.'

Gerald sighed, and played the line out of the reel, bit by little bit.

Gerald was right, of course. They were too messed up to walk. Despite earlier plans to find suitable lodgings, we slept in the cars, like we were on some kind of school trip.

The twins parked their vehicle as far away from the rest as they could get. There was frequent vomiting, mostly from Beatrice.

After dark Fats and Lillian did what they were always going to do, right there on the beach.

Fats must have been punishing Babalwa for some transgression, such was the proximity of the coupling to the parking lot. It wasn't close enough to watch, but it wasn't far enough away to ignore either. Babalwa's sobs, and her pseudo-attempt to muffle them, issued constantly from her 4x4 – regular little yelps of pain, anguish and tequila.

A few hours into darkness, the sobs had become too much to bear. As had the giggles emanating from Lillian and Fats, still cynically scooping handfuls of sand through entwined fingers. Parked in the passenger seat of my Toyota, I watched as Gerald marched up to Fats, yanked him to his feet and slugged him on the nose. Gerald tried to pick him up again and repeat the process, but Lillian had covered Fats's shocked body in a fit of protesting arms and legs. Gerald stomped back to the Toyota, got in next to me, folded his arms and feigned immediate sleep.

The fight sparked a cacophony of drunken protests from Fats and, finally, the appearance of Babalwa, who stood confronting the cuckolding couple until eventually, like an avenging angel, Javas appeared, issued a few curt words to them all, ducked the two swings Fats sent his way and then knocked him out with a single, brutal shot to the snout. Fats slumped into a heap on the sand. Lillian and Babalwa screamed. Javas picked Fats up and slung him over his shoulder like a carcass. He carried him to the back of the Toyota and dumped him inside.

'I think this might belong to you.' He winked slowly at me, once, and marched back to Andile.

The next morning we couldn't look at each other. I drifted over to the twins, who were, as usual, smiling and calm. Andile suggested a rapid departure. We engineered a quick round-up of the hungover, shamed troops, searched for Tebza for an hour or two and then decided to leave one of the 4x4s at the beachfront with a note on the dash.

We drove back to Jozi in silence.

Intimacy, finally, had got the better of us.

Chapter 35

Guinea pig in the air

The fighting and fucking and embarrassment of our collective behaviour finally saw the gods rain change down on us. After many months of stagnation the dam wall broke.

Everyone got wet.

We parted ways as we arrived home from the beach. I went running, coughing the smoke out of my lungs as I pushed along Munro Drive, through Upper Houghton, into Louis Botha and the slow drift lower into Alexandra, right into London Road and up a last, punishing hill to join the N3 highway. I sat on a large rock by the on-ramp, a strange, out-of-place thing lost on the side of the road. I looked down on the shanty city. From up high, with the Sandton skyline as a backdrop, it was a truly ridiculous sight. The shacks began at the grossly confident feet of the glass horizon and lined up on each other interminably, never-ending rows cascading all the way down to the brown banks of the Jukskei River, where the last abodes hung impossibly over the water, destined to fall.

Running through Alex was an existential exercise I never got used to – which was why I did it so much. As alien as it felt to be stranded in Houghton, Alex reminded me of the essential alienness of my wider life. My pre-life.

There was anger and regret and tension and bruising back at the farm. I avoided it all.

When I eventually emerged ready to talk, make eye contact, and so forth, it was to greet Tebza as he pulled into the drive in the 4x4 we had left for him on the Durban beachfront.

'Thanks for the note,' he said. 'Very considerate.'

'Sorry, things got out of hand. We had to leave. Fast.'

'Fine, fine.' He shrugged. 'Little freaky being abandoned, but I cope.'

'You find the blue flat?'

'Nah.' He shook his head, clearly disappointed. 'I mean, ja. Crack, coke, pills, weed. But not what I wanted.' The scar wriggled as his cheek moved. He looked like a dealer, or a hard-times man – one of those guys who could do anything, be anything. He looked older than he had before, and even less like a broker.

'Shit. Really?'

'All of the above. But nothing else. I went flat to flat for a full day, mfana. Fokol. Nix.'

* * *

Two weeks later Lillian and Gerald roared up next to Tebza and me as we were walking up the driveway to check on the cows. Lillian leaped out of the Toyota. 'Guess what?' she asked excitedly, bouncing on her tiptoes, hands behind her back, beaming beaming beaming. Tebza and I looked at each other suspiciously. He sighed. 'What?'

'We have just found' – Lillian made a sweeping, unveiling motion, a matador fooling the bull – 'a complete flight simulator! Like the ones they use in the movies!' She pulled me by the sleeve and I expected her to show me the thing in the back of the bakkie, but there was nothing – she was dragging me to the vision in her mind. 'At fucking Waterkloof.' Her American drawl was suddenly marked. 'Same place we've been a hundred times. Don't know how we missed it, it was in this shed type of thing. I dunno ...' She was babbling at high speed, her hand still clutching and pulling on my sleeve, tugging me in no particular direction. 'When I think back, I guess I must have thought it was a shed or something. It looked like it should have had tools in it.' Gerald had disembarked by this stage and was standing next to her, quietly radiating a similar high energy. 'You know what this means?' Lillian was bouncing on her toes again, her boobs and ass moving in excited asymmetric harmony. 'Do you know what this means, Roy?' she repeated. I smiled, wishing she would calm down. 'It means we can fly!'

I looked at Tebza, all question marks.

'All we have to do is hook up some power and we can start using it.' Lillian was still firing at a million words a minute. 'We thought about trying to get it into the van, but it would never have fit. I reckon we'll only need, like, twenty portable panels and we can power up that whole section.' She stopped, cast her eyes to the heavens like a Brazilian soccer player and ran off to the house.

Gerald shrugged. 'Here we go,' he said as we followed her to the house. 'Here we fucking go.'

Days later, once the excitement around the simulator had ebbed, Babalwa told me she was pregnant, as if I didn't know.

She knocked softly on my door one night, hopped onto my bed and let the tears run. I asked her what type of tears they were, and she said after the Durban trip she wasn't sure. Only thing she definitely knew was that at a higher level it felt right, even if the father happened to be a domineering prick who fucked other women on the beach pretty much in front of her.

'He know yet?' I guided her over the age-old, rocky path.

'Sure. We found out properly a while back. I went to the chemist and found a pregnancy test and—'

'So what happened with the Lillian thing? What's going on?'

'Eish. I mean, I dunno. I mean, I think I know ...' She took my hand. 'Roy, I just wanted to apologise. For the rape thing. I don't know, I don't know what it was. It just frightened me, I guess, the whole thing, the animalness of it. But I know, in my heart, I know you're not a rapist. You didn't rape me. I know that.' She pushed at the cuticles on her entwined hand with her free one, sorrowful. 'I think I just scared myself, that's all. You know? With what I was a capable of, and then I started to rationalise and ... you know ... you do know, don't you, Roy?'

I tipped my head.

'You told Fats this? Is that what the Lillian thing was?'

'He won't believe me.' More eyes, more regret. 'He thinks I'm in love with you or something, or, like, I'm addicted to you as a father figure. Shit like that. Every time I try to explain he just talks over me. Like I'm a child.'

'A naughty child.'

'Ja. A naughty child.' She batted teary eyes at me and waited for redemption.

I gave her the platitudes she was looking for and she eventually squeaked back out, pulling the door shut like a teenager. The latch clicked, and I was alone. I felt suddenly like I had on that first night in Houghton, pitifully small, stuck in a spare bedroom like a little boy. I looked around my room. After all this time I had barely occupied it. It was essentially in the same condition as when I had arrived, save for the addition of a computer and speakers. The MBA books sat waiting still, as expectant as on my first night.

Pitiful.

The others had all fully occupied their parts of the house. Beatrice, for example, had converted her wing into an empire. One needed permission to get through the front door, behind which cascaded various rooms and offshoots, all with specific functions. Her hallway included framed copies of her MBA certificates and company awards. Her bedroom lay recessed in the far corner, north-facing, naturally.

But me – I was just waiting. Marking time as usual. I thought of my corners of the house I had shared with Angie, the little areas clearly my own, which were just as spare as my current abode. As if I was denying the most basic human need to nest. As if nesting was just never for me. Maybe that was why Babalwa had jumped ship so fast. Maybe I just couldn't provide the nest.

I was still at least partially in love with Babalwa. Our PE time had faded, but part of my half-toothed, jagged consciousness was still locked into her, especially after I was let loose for the mighty Fats. I was jilted, and I still felt the pain. I found myself dreaming odd thoughts about a life together with her, alone again somewhere, coexisting quietly, holding hands occasionally. That sort of thing.

For her part, Babalwa was clearly comfortable using me as a counterpoint (physically, emotionally, intellectually) to Fats. While patting her hand I wondered what the hidden agenda of her visit was. I also questioned how in touch she was with her own agenda-setting. The best liars, they always say, believe they are telling the truth. How much belief was there in Babalwa at any one time?

* * *

The next morning I took off in the opposite direction of my traditional route, heading this time for the Drill Hall, in the city. Javas had his studio space there. It was where he built his monsters. Since the Kruger trip I had visited the studio several times. I was compelled by his creations. Being in their presence gave me a kind of metaphysical comfort.

The Drill Hall was an old military station converted into a quasi-cultural space featuring careful brickwork and commemorative plaques telling struggle and other stories. It sat in the middle of Noord, the biggest and most aggressive taxi rank in the country.

Javas and Andile took great delight in telling Noord stories. The incredible hooting, the grinding crush of perpetually angry taxi drivers. The tsotsis and pickpockets. The mamas and children and students and artists and hawkers. The kieries and hidden guns. The crush the crush the crush.

Devoid of its humans, though, Noord was just a few intersecting streets. Well worked with rubber stains, yes, but just a few streets with a past, history bouncing around helpless, waiting.

On my first trip to the Drill Hall I followed the twins. I stood next to the Chicken Licken and watched from a few steps back as they processed a reality that had little bearing on me.

'Unless you were here before,' Javas explained, 'you could never understand how this feels.' He squatted on his heels. Andile stood separate, looking up at the flats, hands on her hips, shaking her head slowly.

Being inside the gates, on the Drill Hall square, was to be on a ghetto picnic island. Surrounded by towering, crumbling, white art deco buildings, the complex was crisply marked off by a serious set of gates, the bars of which had been decorated with African symbology, creating a curiously resonant vine of safety and art. The fences were children running, animals moving, ladies carrying wood and baskets on their heads, the motifs literally wound into the fabric of the iron. The island effect was enhanced by the sea of surrounding sleeping taxis. Twist Street was only pockmarked by the occasional midnight ride, but the surrounding streets and intersections were stacked four and five rows deep with waiting half loaves.

'Blue, yellow, red HiAces, silently rejoicing,' Andile mumbled.

'Eh?' I asked, still mesmerised by the ghetto art deco, especially the spooky extended vertical ovals on the left, which Javas said used to be a cinema.

'Ah, nothing. Just an old song my uncle taught me – about taxis.'

Now I was back by myself in Javas's studio, which used to be a library run by an NGO. It was a cavernous double-volume hall filled with five six-metre metal beasts, each staggering towards the other. I sat at the foot of the biggest one. Its absurdly square head (a radiator perhaps?) was bolted and/or welded onto rusty shoulders, the fringe of the weld purposefully messy and bold and orange, the function of the bolt and screw ambiguous – possibly aesthetic, possibly structural. The giant was reaching out, its right arm three-quarters extended.

I pulled my knees to my chin, Babalwa-like, and waited for something to happen. I examined the complex scaffold-and-pulley system that was rigged around the piece.

Now that I had seen his art, Javas's general state of silence and passivity made much more sense. He had no need to displace or channel his energy – it was all being funnelled into this.

When I visited his studio I invariably talked to my Nikes. I tied and untied the laces. Patted the toes. Asked them where they would take me next. I felt as attached and friendly towards those shoes as I did to anyone in the house. The shoes took me places and never asked questions. They were simple and comfortable and friendly.

'So.' I spoke directly at them. 'What now? What the fuck now?'

There was no answer.

I pushed the same question at Javas's beasts, but they were silent.

I smacked my knees together. It hurt and made a loud, hollow noise.

I stood.

I wrapped my arms around the leg of my host beast and hugged. A spot of sun beamed in from the window on the upper side of the hall, forming a natural spotlight on the ankle and foot. The rusted metal of the calf (a car chassis? some kind of tractor part?) was warm and rough on my skin. It felt good.

I held on.

The others had rushed out to Waterkloof at first light to start powering up the simulator. Excitement had fanned across the house (bypassing myself and Babalwa, each immune for our own reasons) and great dreams were being sketched of transcontinental flight. Of trips to America and Europe. Maybe Russia, Lillian said.

I wasn't sure we would ever be able to get a big enough aeroplane off the ground to fly to another continent. A few joyrides across sub-Saharan Africa, maybe, but full-on flying? The agreed-upon goal felt like it would be beyond us. Aeroplanes, even the smaller jets that business moguls and sports stars used, seemed to me to be inherently complicated. Runways and tyre pressure and lift-offs and wind speeds and landings and all those things were being funnelled in Teboho's direction, and he was displaying more and more signs of coming unhinged. Our late-night joint conversations had become more speculative and wistful, his language and ideas drifting off to extraterrestrials and harnessing star power for proper energy, and then suddenly back to inner space and nano flights and the biological dimensions of internal infinity and such things.

I humoured him. I even went with him, as far as I was able to in my own more restricted, linear mind. But I also suspected that as the hack percentage in his piss was dwindling, Tebza had been topping up with things secured on his Durban scrounging session. I knew the symptoms well from the ad bunnies, who oscillated similarly between bright-eyed interest in and sudden hypersensitivity to the basic stimuli of life.

From a distance the Waterkloof Airforce Base looked like a poorly executed attempt at a school. The architectural signage at the sagging entrance gates announced structural redevelopment. Stabbed into the red earth next to the technical information was a logo mounted on a single steel leg: a sun rising over a generic horizon, beneath the header 'Watching Over South Africa's Future'. The sign had fallen dramatically to the left, the edge of the W hovering inches above the ground.

The base consisted of a collection of vaguely interlinked facebrick and temporary prefab buildings. A cluster of elderly, dirty-brown military planes were parked around the runways, waiting patiently behind a single, more prosperous white jumbo jet, which was aimed directly down the runway, ready to take off. Surrounding them all was an army of construction machines: yellow front-end loaders, trucks and others born to drag and move.

Lillian and the rest hovered in and around the simulator hut. (As Lillian had suggested, the building, based on appearance, shouldn't have housed much more than detergents and brooms. According to an A4 laminated notice which had fallen from the door, it was the temporary flight-training facility.) Meanwhile I walked around the complex a few times, poking my head into offices, running my fingers over the many prefab walls, marvelling at the structural transience of a place that had been there since long before I was born. And of course it was all khaki and brown, the colours of the desks and files and folders and photos matching eerily with the cargo planes at the back, all of it mirrored by the deep orange of the Highveld soil, which swarmed around and over my peripheral vision.

It took a little over a week for us to set up the power for the simulator hut. I provided as much muscle as I could and tried not to think about anything specific. I carried and dropped off, and plugged and unplugged things in and out of various holes, obeying Fats and Gerald and Lillian in turn, sharing sighs and grunts with Beatrice and the twins, feeling Babalwa's pregnant eyes on me as she sat and watched like a representative from the UN.

Once the power was set up and the simulator was fully

operational, I fell back. I dedicated my early mornings to a long run, which generally ended with me sitting at the top of London Road and looking down over the shacks of Alex. After the run I made sure I managed the farm as best I could while the rest were occupied. I milked the cows, slaughtered whatever small creatures needed to die, and skinned and plucked and butchered as was necessary. I maintained the vegetable garden, turning the soil gently, picking dead leaves off here and there, talking to the plants, encouraging them in the way I myself needed encouragement. After the farm maintenance I allowed myself to drift into the mid-afternoon.

Sometimes I would dream while lounging on the pool furniture, arms behind my head, eyelids heavy and falling. Other days I would read, stocking up on South African history. Joburg history. The miners and the slaves. That sort of thing. Sometimes I would just stare out at the northern horizon and wonder how they were getting on with flight.

The twins operated in a parallel orbit to mine, staying chiefly housebound and focusing on food and maintenance. Andile and Javas would take turns in the kitchen, and often one of them would join me for a period in the garden or – when necessary – in wielding the knife on a chicken. Javas spent nights in his studio and woke just before lunch. The three of us maintained a pleasant mutual quietude.

Then the rest would arrive back from the base: Tebza looking frazzled and disturbed; Lillian and Fats arguing some point (take-off trajectory, flaps or fuel); Gerald trailing behind, arms full of the day's supplies and equipment; Babalwa at the back, belly cupped in her hands.

I made sure I visited the base every few days. It felt important to be seen as part of the venture – as part of the team and all that. In truth I was relieved the farm had to be maintained and that there were viable tasks for me back home. The simulator hut was hot and cramped. With two people in the available seats and three more hovering around the edges of the plastic bucket that housed the dash and screen, it was a stuffy, hot and bothersome gig. The less I participated, the fewer reasons there were for me to be near the action, and so when I did visit I generally ended up kicking it with Babalwa just outside the hut, the two of us perched awkwardly on plastic pool furniture.

Cheers would rattle the hut after hours of silence. With each roar we grew closer to the idea of actually taking off. Even I, the sceptic, felt myself occasionally roused at the thought of the ability to break free of our domain. I pictured other small packs of people in different parts of the world attempting similar things. I imagined us crossing paths in mid-air, waving at each other.

Even when we were fighting – and there was always an argument of some sort on the go, to say nothing of the lingering Durban resentments – we were driven by an intention, by a goal. This was in marked contrast to earlier months, which had felt like a steady march towards complete stagnation or death. As a group we were now imbued with meaning and a larger purpose. There was, in a word, progress.

I don't think Tebza felt very much of that. Towards the end of training, when regular touchdowns and landings were being achieved, he began to openly question his position as pilot. He had never wanted to be the pilot. He felt that Lillian and Fats had bestowed the position on him because of his computer addiction and his drive to establish the WAN – hardly, he said, the same thing as wanting to fly. He also said to me privately, on several occasions, that he was feeling extremely pressured. He would have preferred to be the training guy on the ground rather than the guinea pig in the air. I couldn't fault his argument, but Fats and Lillian shut him down with the brute force of a fait accompli. Fats would pat him on the head or fake punch his shoulder and say, 'Too late my son. You're our pilot now. You're our man in the air. The guy with the skills. Sometimes destiny is undeniable, eh?' Or some other such fatuous rubbish.

Some nights I would push my head into his room to see Tebza slumped and drugged in front of his machine, listening to old broken dubstep beats, eyes drilling into the fractals on some retro reconstruction of a '90s-era Windows Media Player. I would call his name, but my voice was unable to spark even a grunt of acknowledgement, let alone a reply.

So, at Javas's Drill Hall studio I found peace of the sort I just couldn't get my hands on anywhere else. As often as was logistically possible, I began to reverse my routine. Laundry first, then cow milking and general farm maintenance, followed by a run to Drill Hall and a long session in the midday sun, letting the warmth of the metal sculptures broil me as I leaned against the legs of the biggest one – who I had come to call George. I talked to George, running him through events in the house and preparations for the flight. He was a good confidant, always listening, always neutral. As the weeks of preparation drifted into months, I relied on him more and more to keep my mental balance in check.

'You never know, Roy,' Javas said as he stepped out from wherever he had been listening. 'Miracles do happen. They could just as easily figure it all out as fuck it all up.'

I shot to my feet, shocked, and gulped a few times. Thankfully I hadn't been gossiping.

'Ag, moenie worry, mchana. I talk to them too. All the time.' He drifted between iron legs, patting a thigh, kneeling occasionally to inspect the weld on a foot. 'They're like that, nè? The more you get to know them, the more they want to get to know you – your story.'

'Strange shit' was the best response I could come up with.

'Ja. Strange shit.' Javas took a seat at the feet of Julius, a fatter, squatter, meaner-looking creature. 'This one's my favourite,' he said. 'He's a bit fucked up. Quite ugly. He lacks the abilities of the others.'

It was odd to hear him refer to the creatures so personally, as individual humans, in just the same way as I had been interacting with them. I sat back down at George's feet. 'George is my man,' I said. 'Something about him, I don't know. He's just ... my guy.'

Javas smiled and leaned back against Julius's fat, ungainly foot. 'So, Roy, what the fuck is going on with you, son? Everyone is talking about how you're drifting. Not involved. Et cetera, et cetera.'

My heart thumped. 'You're not exactly in the middle of things either, are you?' I said.

'Well, you're right there. But I think, and forgive me, I don't mean to insult' – he smiled warmly to reinforce the non-insult – 'that I'm a bit smoother than you. I don't make people jumpy like you do.'

'I make them jumpy?' I wasn't completely shocked by this, but still, it was strange to hear it out loud. 'Must be this bladdy tooth.'

We roamed for a while around the flight and its potential for success or otherwise, and then further out to art and the Drill Hall and life and advertising and all the things we had, respectively, left behind. Javas talked straight at me, his words bouncing lightly off the roof. I was struck again by how articulate he was, by his ability to warm me up with words. Mostly, I was struck by his interest in advertising, a subject of little worth or interest to anyone else. He questioned me repeatedly about what I had worked on before getting involved with Mlungu's, what my job actually was, who controlled me, who controlled the process, how much I got paid, and so on. I self-expressed, as we used to joke at the agency while mimicking a lactating breast.

Eventually I reversed the Q&A. 'So you were famous?'

'Depends on your definition,' Javas said. 'I mean, no one outside of these people' – he indicated the statues and, I assumed, their associated industry humans – 'would know who I was. Just artists. Buyers, you know. That stuff. So no, not famous. Not in the real way.'

'But on the up, yes?' I pressed on.

'On the up. Ja. I like that. I was on the up.'

'How much were you selling these for again?'

''Bout three bar, sometimes four, five, six even.'

I whistled.

'Not a lot, Roy,' he countered. 'Each one takes more than six months to build. Hard cost is about eight hundred thousand rand. And a million today's not what it was.'

'So you weren't rich.'

'Eish, no. Just bought my first car. Tiny BMW.'

'But happy?'

'Crazy happy. Crazy happy, boss. It was a miracle, for someone like me to fall into this stuff and find money in it. The shock of my life.'

'But you're good, hey. I mean, it's so obvious. You're a really talented artist.'

Javas laughed. A good, long, cynical laugh. It came right from his belly. 'I'm not an artist's ass, Roy. I'm a guy who learned how to weld and met some people in sunglasses.'

Chapter 36
Kids and grannies scrambled

So that was it. The ability to weld and the good fortune that arrives with people in sunglasses. The critics called it his 'genuine humanity'.

I agreed with the critics. Javas was humble and thoughtful, and both characteristics found form in his art, in his creatures, his monsters, who weren't trying to prove anything, or win any competitions, or better anyone else working the block. They were complete and confident on their own, and that was thanks to their creator.

Javas forced me into a reciprocal effort. Tired of 'I was an advertising drunk' and the crass simplicity of my time as Mlungu's manager, I scratched around for something a little more genuine. Eventually I settled on cheese.

Our agency was hired on the Dairy Board account, and I was given cheese. I stole a very old idea from the Americans, tweaked it a little and got the credit. It was simple enough. We put the Dairy Board and a pizza house together. The board subsidised the development and promotion of an uber-cheese pizza – with twelve times more cheese than a regular. It was a giant success, in every sense, and changed the standard across the country. Cheese volumes went through the roof, kids and grannies scrambled for the giant pizzas, and the fattening-foods debate only sparked more exposure and more sales. The Dairy Board was ecstatic, and I was personally responsible for adding at least two extra inches to the national waistline.

'Cheese,' Javas tutted. 'Cheese.' He was only half laughing. 'I had no idea things like that happened. Cheese.'

We left it at that. His monsters. My cheese.

Chapter 37

Picking and biting

The excitement grew. Like one of those really old movies about going into space. The ones with Clint Eastwood or Ed Harris or Burt Reynolds, where the wives flutter around making sandwiches and staring up at the moon, kids under wing.

With every successful simulator trip they (we) allowed themselves (ourselves) to crank it up a notch. Plans were laid for which plane to use, a not insignificant question. They (we) settled on something small (but not too small, pleaded Tebza), but when they got into the cockpit it bore almost no resemblance to the simulator.

The simulator turned out to be for a fighter jet – but it took over six weeks to discover this. It seems bizarre in the telling, but this is how things actually happen. You jump in the simulator, learn how to fly, presume the best and ask the important questions later. Only once Tebza was successfully taking off and landing regularly did anyone think to question what kind of plane he was learning to fly.

And so we stalled. None of us were foolish enough to think Tebza could fly a fighter jet – even a small one. We would have to find another simulator, and another method.

The failure sent Lillian into a crushing decline. I frequently found her in strange corners, peering into the middle distance, picking and biting at her fingernails. Once I made the mistake of enquiring after her mental health and in reply she delivered, in shocking and extended detail, an exposition on the fundamental differences between the USA and South Africa. It was a searing monologue, born of a great deal of frustration. The only thing the two places had in common was their obsession with God. Otherwise, it was extreme contrasts and damaging mirror images. She rattled them off (ethics, innovation, music diversity, national planning, tendencies towards a feudal state, physical security, consequences for actions, entrepreneurial culture, etc., etc.), but while she began the tirade powered by a tart, ironic sense of humour, this ebbed as the list grew and eventually she was, knowingly, and semi-ashamedly but still unable to stop herself, dragging me through a pool of her own bile.

She tailed off eventually. 'I'm sorry, Roy, I am,' she said. 'I just want to go home.'

'But Lillian,' I replied, squeezing her shoulder tentatively, 'do you really think there's a home to go to?'

'Well, I've got to, don't I? This can't be it. We can't be it.'

I went running.

I milked cows.

I slaughtered chickens.

Fats eventually emerged from his rejuvenated office to pronounce that, based on his reading and research, a commercial Boeing was our only option. A simulator was unable to replicate the physical forces involved in piloting a small plane, which ultimately required hands-on-the-stick experience. Fighter jets and other types of army planes were too powerful and risky. Commercial passenger planes like Boeings, on the other hand, were almost completely automated. Once you knew what you were doing, it was simply a question of telling the on-board computer to follow the flight plan.

'How do you create a flight plan?' Gerald asked.

Fats brought the answer back from the OR Tambo International pilot-training centre, which included a full simulator, instructions on how to file flight plans, and everything else anyone wanting to learn to fly a Boeing could possibly need.

Yet again, none of us could figure out how we missed it. Lillian accused me of a lack of thoroughness and/or vision. I took the blow, although we had all been to the airport several times, and

none of us had come close to the training centre.
We moved out to Kempton Park to repeat the process.

Chapter 38
A month

A month to rig up the solar panels.

A month to get control of the simulator and figure out how to program a flight plan.

A month to fuck around nervously.

CHAPTER 39
No emergency vehicles

Tebza and Lillian were dead in a second.

We watched.

We gripped each other, thrilled at seeing the plane fly, unable to let ourselves believe it was true – that they were up there, in a Boeing. The plane lumbered into the air like there was a real pilot in it and disappeared through the clouds. To me the angle looked steep, like they should have levelled off at some stage, but they kept climbing and disappeared into the thickness and we all jumped a bit on the spot and hugs were shared.

The plane looked good coming down, from what I could tell, and then just as I expected the thing to float onto the tarmac, its nose dipped forward and it lurched hard to the left and completed two shattering cartwheels. It's an image I will never be able to erase, the jumbo flipping over and over, twice, like a child's toy, then exploding.

We watched.

There were no emergency vehicles. None of us rushed forward or backward or called for help. We sat. We watched it go. Watched them blaze away in an orange sky.

Beatrice was the first to start screaming. Fats slapped her face hard and she throttled down to an ongoing series of wrenching sobs. The rest of us were silent.

I stared at my hands. My old man's hands. My advertising hands. My confused, useless hands. The plane roared. The flames boiled the sky. The metal hissed. We remained in our seats on the towing machine – that squat yellow thing that pulls aeroplanes – that we used to pull our Boeing into place.

Andile ran. Back to the cars. She gunned it out of the airport alone, tires squealing.

The rest of us ... we sat for a long time, watching the wreckage burn down. Listening to Beatrice bubbling and frothing.

The next day a weaver bird arrived on the big leafy tree down at the bottom of the garden. He looked young. He started on his first nest, stripping pieces from the adjoining property's palm tree and flying back over to his construction, threading it all in an intricate, instinctive pattern. I watched him the whole day, from various vantage points. It was so natural, his process. So opposed to the idea of an aeroplane. The threading of matter into nest was very complex, yet innate to the bird. He knocked it off without thinking, whistling and chirping as he went. This strip here, that strip there, weaving and pulling, hanging underneath the bowl for long stretches as the first crucial structural layers were pulled tight.

I dragged a pool chair under the tree, rolled joint after joint and watched.

The house was silent.

The weaver chirped and burped and worked, alternating between his nest and clearing the tree of its leaves so he could see enemies approach. All day the leaves twirled to the ground, gentle little helicopters. The section of the tree that would house him grew sparse, more suited to a bird needing a clear view. By dusk he was damn close to done. The nest wasn't fully stitched, but the frame had already received several layers.

I left the pool chair under the tree, grabbed a bottle of wine from the cellar and took it to bed.

I lay hugging it under the covers, a forty-something-year-old red, 1996.

It grew hot in my arms. The minutes ticked. Its heat grew steadily and somewhere there, somewhere in the middle of it all, I moved from jumping off the cliff to actually holding the fucking thing, embracing it, clinging to it like a lover. Right before I fell asleep I remember thinking that this bottle wasn't really my crutch, nor my nemesis. It was my fucking baby. It was my small, innocent child.

The weaver bird was at it again from dawn.

I woke with his first chirp and I could think of nothing else to do but watch him and so I went outside and sat in the cold dawn on that white plastic pool chair and watched.

It took him the better part of the day to finish off, fine-tuning and fine-tuning, leaves twirling, always falling, even as he wove. I began to see him as one of those magicians with their spinning plates. From nest to branch to palm tree and back again.

And then he finished.

I stood and applauded. Whistled a few times. Stamped my feet.

Fats came out of the house in his shorts, stared at me and went back in.

That night I held my bottle of red again, felt its warmth wash me as I lay awake, unable to move, unable to think, surrounded by feathers and wings and falling leaves.

The next morning the nest was in a million torn-up strips on the ground.

Chapter 40

Weeping into the basil

I berated Lillian while I pounded Louis Botha, running repeatedly through her list of stupidities and crimes. First was her ambition, her desire for more than we already had, her inability to accept the reality we all, at some stage, should have come to terms with. Lillian just couldn't let it settle. Her nationality was surely at the root of that thing in her that just had to fly a fucking Boeing off the continent, that just had to smash through the horizon. It was so typically American.

I was also pissed at Tebza, for other reasons, but whenever I thought of him, whenever his face (that crinkling, smiling scar) took form in my mind, I let go and refocused on something simpler.

I shoulder-charged door frames and lounge corners and even the occasional tree – anything that might have caught his own attention. It felt like a mark of respect, a sign of deference and remembrance. My shoulders bruised heavily, a complex purple and yellow weave extending slowly down my back. Each connection with the wall or the door or the pole added weight to the last and the pain built satisfyingly until I could detect a slight but definite chipping of the bone on certain contacts. I relished the bruises, the grinding sensation that had developed when I swung my arms, which I did frequently.

Gerald's inner soldier needed to take responsibility.

The vibes coming off him were so strong I could almost hear him torturing himself for not ... well, for whatever it is he thought he didn't do. I didn't see him for days after the crash, weeks possibly. He disappeared. When he returned he was an almost complete blank; there was only the smallest flicker in the far corners of his eyes, when he managed to raise the lids.

Of course we were all blank. We were completely stricken by the reduction in our numbers, by the collapse of our horizon.

Now we were seven.

Fats worked in the gardens and with the cows, supported by Beatrice, with Babalwa looking on, still holding her belly. Gerald drifted. I ran. The twins were around but hard to find.

Two or three days in, Fats collapsed in the garden. I found him weeping into the basil, his feet kicking in a childlike rhythm against the carrots. I wanted to console him, but I was inconsolable myself. I had no words. I stood over his body for a while, reached out to pat his shaking shoulder and then retracted.

As much as Lillian's obsession with flight ran against my own instincts, as dangerous as I thought her dream was, it was, after all, still a dream. It was a potential future, for her and for us all. It was something to look towards. To sketch out and plan, to calculate and recalculate.

It was something to do.

Now, there was nothing.

We tended the gardens, we milked those fucking cows, we ate and farted and slept and woke up and ran and did it all again. We walked and worked and tended. We did it in the absence of light. In the absence of hope. In the absence of anything.

I kept the bottle of red in my room, on the bedside table – a memento, a monument, perhaps, to a bad, bad time. Sometimes I would just look at it. Sometimes I would take it to bed with me, hugging it for warmth. It was my thing. My one little thing.

My other little thing was the weaver bird, who spent the rest of the summer building nests and tearing them down, obsessively clearing the space around his construction area until a full quarter of the tree was devoid of leaves. I couldn't figure out what the deal was. The nests all looked good to me, but each one came down in a shredded mess. He built and built and built the whole summer, but never moved in.

An unsettling sadness grew in my gut in relation to that bird. I began to hope actively for each nest. I watched the progress carefully, talking to him as each one went up, advising him as best I could.

But the nests never made it.

With each nest that came down my own sense of futility deepened. Did the weaver know pain? Failure? The tearing of futility against his bright yellow heart? Was he truly content doing this, building nest after nest after nest? Did he question what the fuck he was doing this for? If he did, I felt sad for him, for his failures. If he didn't, then it was even worse. Then he was just like me, an automaton moving by instinct and genetic force alone.

Babalwa had her baby three months after the crash. Gerald delivered it and cut the cord and slapped its pink ass and it cried and all was well. There was laughter. There were tears. It was a relief to experience it, the joy, to go high before another low. Up before down. And all that.

They named the baby Roy Junior, which was pretty damn odd.

Despite all her planning and her deep desire to perpetuate the species, initially Babalwa was a confused, nervous mother. Roy Jnr did not sit easily on her hip, nor on her tit. She looked bewildered a lot of the time, and Beatrice and Andile – neither of whom were mothers but both of whom had grown up in baby-heavy families – stepped in to guide and coax. Hold him like this. Head like that. Pat like this, on the small of the back, gently.

Fats emerged. He beamed. He made fatherly noises. He scuttled around trying to help without being able to. On occasion he just sat with his feet up, arms behind his head, looking like he had achieved something. Javas called it his dream phase, and we laughed. But below the laugh lay the understanding that we would all have to get breeding soon. Babalwa had been on point all along, even way back in PE. Now that we had lost a pair, the maths was dangerous. Three females and four males. We would have to breed vigorously and frequently across all possible combinations.

Babalwa sketched it out for us: four to the power of three was just enough to get a compounding dynamic going, but we would all need to cross-breed. There could be no exceptions.

'It's not about fucking,' she asserted as we clucked nervously over her diagram. 'It's about our species. We need to breed.'

'They can just jerk off, then we pour it down,' Andile offered sensibly. 'I knew a few lesbians who did it that way. It works. You don't need a lab and you definitely don't need to fuck. Sorry, Roy.' She laughed and patted my hand.

'The only thing left is a decision,' I said. 'Are we now a breeding colony? Not that I'm opposed, but if we're going to run a baby farm we're all going to need to be involved for the rest of time. Our time anyway. It's a big decision.'

'Are there any other options?' Babalwa rocked Roy Jnr in her arms.

'There are always options. We could take Lillian's plan B and go through Africa to find Europeans. We could just let ourselves die off. We have options.'

I was alone in my diffidence. The others had accepted their duty. We ended the discussion. Andile was already pregnant. The fences were up. The farm was being populated.

After a shaky start, Babalwa took well to motherhood, and the collective of mothers was effective. The three shared little Roy and the infant-care duties, while the men milked cows and managed the veggie patch with renewed vigour.

I kept running.

Whenever I could free myself, and after I had run as far as I could, I drove. The others seemed busy enough, content enough, to revolve around Houghton and the farm, the babies and the cows. I cruised through the city, including Sandton, probing at the glass façades, the gawking, empty corporate monoliths.

'You're a little bit mad, Roy, nè?' Beatrice said to me after another wander. Since the crash she had started speaking to me, rather than across me or at me. 'I mean, I know we're all crazy now, living crazy, but you're the real thing, nè?'

'I was in advertising.'

'Fats was in advertising.'

'He was a suit. He wasn't smoking crack to get the next idea.'

She tossed her head as she laughed, twirled a few strands of hair with long fingers. Beatrice had some warmth to her. Or – let me rephrase – I was noticing her warmth. I could think of worse things than discovering what lay beneath. I wasn't sure whether Gerald was of the same mindset. I tried not to think about it as I watched her breasts jiggle lightly in harmony with her amusement. I made a mental note to watch her more closely, more often.

Beatrice had cheekbones that held her face together – they gave it reason and shape, a noble and serious structure. Her use of make-up had steadily shrunk to more selective applications, and she was better off for it. I started to notice her actual skin, which was a rich olive and not at all as pockmarked or acne-ridden as I had assumed. Her obsession with heels had also faded, another considerable improvement. She had come down to size, literally. Less the CEO and more the human being. Her breasts were moderate, her body lean – but that was the case for all of us now. Fat was something from another time. She let loose her hair from the intensity of the railway braids, allowing it to morph slowly into a soft afro. Unlike Fats's fro, which even when physically subdued was all dominance and power, hers bubbled up and then cascaded down loosely. It was feminine and accommodating.

The 'you're mad, aren't you?' conversation was, I gradually discovered, a purposeful entrance into my world.

Suddenly Beatrice was around more often. When I hoed the garden, she was there. As I pulled on my Nikes, she asked if she would be able to keep up if she tried. When I went for a drive, she was in the passenger seat, right thigh inching closer to mine, suggestions of perfume lingering in the cab the next day.

I responded in kind, but it worried me. Not politically – I had long ago made peace with the gritty reality of household politics, sexual and otherwise – but personally. I looked in the mirror, saw the hole in my mouth and knew I wasn't worthy of, or ready for, an actual, adult relationship.

My life had always been solo, and singular. Even when I was married to Angie I was essentially alone. As Beatrice inched closer, my inner cunt began to hatch a counter-attack.

As he always did.

Beatrice was all Model C. Her accent, her neoliberal-CEO world view, her jeans, her heels. Her hands, most of all. Even sans nail polish, her fingers were immaculate, the nails long yet clipped, the tips always clean white despite the gardening and slaughtering, the plucking and skinning.

But Model C isn't how you look. It's how you think. I'd heard that many times before. At tertiary. At work. Also from Andile, herself markedly un–Model C. Model C is about marriage and children and financial planning. It's about recycling and donations to charity. It's afternoon braais with big fluffy salads.

All these things were inherent in Beatrice. They shone from her. Perhaps more so because she was born so far away from it all. Beatrice forced herself into the Model C life from the distance of Beaufort West. She made it happen through her personal force. I was also Model C, of course, but I had spent my life running away from it. So I ran away from her as well, yet again a slave to instinct.

The planning of the baby farm had opened up ideas in both of us. If we were going to go as far as jerking off into cups and pouring it down vaginas, well, we may just as well have gotten naked.

So we did.

Well, actually, we didn't get naked that often. Initially we fucked in the 4x4, all fumblings and fingers and premature grunts. We progressed to parks and other vacant spaces, and we always kept it away from the house, where it didn't really fit – where freedom and fantasies didn't belong.

And that, in summary, is how I got Beatrice pregnant.

Everyone knew we were fucking, and we didn't try to hide it. Babalwa caught my eye with regular grins and eyebrow movements with implications. Fats played it straight, the twins also kept it as straight as possible and Gerald simply disappeared from view.

'Poor Gerald,' Beatrice murmured abstractedly as she put my cock in her mouth. I was driving. It was some kind of fetish for her – vehicular sex. I accommodated it easily.

'Let's leave Gerald out of it,' I suggested as she worked away.

'It'll be poor Roy soon enough.'

She pulled out of the dive, keeping a hand on my dick. 'What you mean by that?'

'Well, we're not exactly getting married here, are we?'

She pulled her hand free. 'Why not?'

'Damn, is that a proposal?'

'Don't be such a wanker, Roy. You can be so mean. Jesus.'

'No, but seriously, I mean ... uh ...' Her reaction had caught me off guard. My assumption was that we were at an equal distance with the thing. The sex thing. I hadn't yet considered our actual relationship.

'So what you're saying is that you expect me to be fucking you and Gerald at the same time?'

'No, not at all. No. But, but you guys have been ... I mean, you did for quite a while, nè?'

'We did.' She was bolt upright now, arms folded. 'But it didn't work out that good. And we stopped. And ...'

'And?'

'You stupid fuck.' She punched me, hard, on the arm. 'You're just fucking me, aren't you?'

I spluttered.

'Jesus, you are. Of course you are. You don't give a shit about me, do you?' She was raging now, heat pulsing off her forehead, clouds breaking in her eyes.

'No, Beatrice, you need to understand. I don't give a shit about anyone. I never have. I'm just trying to get through here.'

'Oh fuck. Thanks a lot. You can drop me off here, Roy, right here.' We were on the cusp of Linden, a good couple of hours' walk from the farm. She yanked on the door handle and it sprung open as we drove.

'No, B, no, that didn't come out right. That's not what I meant. I meant ... I meant ...' She glared at me furiously. 'I meant that I'm so fucked I've never been able to have a relationship. Ever. I just wasn't expecting one now. I don't even know if I'm capable of ...'

'I can answer that for you. Stop the car. STOP THE FUCKING CAR!' She screamed into my ear, at my eardrum, which stretched to pop. I braked and she bolted. 'Just fuck off, Roy. Go be alone if that's what you want.'

I circled a few Linden blocks, berating myself for being such a fool. Firstly, for tossing away another driving blow job, a quirky and not unpleasant experience, and secondly, for putting the cruel steel on the only person left in the world willing and able to screw me, and, more importantly, hold my hand.

Maybe, I rationalised as I turned another corner, surprised again not to find Beatrice's stomping form, I was actually jealous of Gerald. Maybe I was too much of a South African male to be able to express my anxiety, and so her slightly cruel raising of his name as she was lowering got me scared and I reacted emotionally, etc., etc.

I drove up and down Barry Hertzog a few times – criss-crossing the side roads as I went – expecting to find her. But I didn't.

As I drove I remembered a story my dad told me about how Hertzog was named after James Barry, the South African surgeon general and British frontier military doctor, because he, Hertzog, was a result of – or his family somehow was involved in – Barry's introduction of the Caesarean section to South Africa. And how the Hertzogs, on naming their son, were completely unaware that Dr Barry was actually a hermaphrodite who had lived his entire life with undiscovered female genitalia. I loved that story as a child. It gave me goosebumps to think I knew this little snippet of history, a piece of us that no one around me perceived.

'Female genitalia, huh!' Russle, beaming, concluded with a thump on my knee. 'Imagine that, Roy, just imagine.' Knee thump, beam. 'You go through a lifetime in the army with a punani and nobody notices? Imagine!'

Beatrice had vanished. She must have ducked across Victory Park. (Which victory was that? I asked myself, thinking again of my father and the paucity of his historical knowledge – Dr Barry's punani was all he had.) I crashed the 4x4 through the low wooden railings into the park, skirted a few trees, examined the trickle of the Braamfontein Spruit – with no success. I got out and walked. I yelled out her name, feeling strangely conspicuous. A free pig checked me out from a distance. We held eye contact for a few seconds and then he turned back into the bush.

Nothing.

I thought of Angie and it stopped me dead. I tried to count how long it had been since she had even occurred to me. Months. Several months. At least. The thought of her occupied my mind as I drove back to Houghton, having given up on locating Beatrice, who clearly did not want to be found. I hoped she didn't have to deal with too many animals on her journey back. It was a long walk.

Things weren't the same between Beatrice and me after that. They weren't the same between her and Gerald either, nor between me and Gerald. It was, of course, of bloody fucking course, a classic love triangle, straight out of the Hollywood script machine.

We covered ourselves in silence and functional tasks.

We spoke to others and got on with whatever we could.

We watched Beatrice's belly grow, following Andile's and Babalwa's before her. We were all affected, those outside the triangle as much as those in it. Despite the careful planning, we had three babies in the works and no one had yet jerked off into a cup.

Watching the belly grow, something of mine baking inside it, I drifted further and further back into the past, latching onto smells and sights and riding their resonance into my teenage and childhood years. Flashcard memories of life as a very young child. The smell of the rain. The smell of my father's cricket bat, unused, but always leaking the strange odour of his previous life. The light, woolly fragrance of my first kiss. Girls' underwear. Trees bending in the wind, signalling September. Tobacco. The sharp stink of my old man's cigarettes and then, in turn, the charming cloud of my own first inhalations. Life passing. Life smelling. Life taking shape, without ever taking form.

Chapter 41
You had it and you didn't want it

As the babies arrived we all became like the weaver bird. Plucking and binding and stripping and threading an endless series of domestic compulsions. Now, our only reason was to keep it all going. We were governed by an arcing, noble aim. We lost the need to do anything else. To even think about anything else. We shut the horizon down and focused on the farm, and yes, there were rewards. Many, in fact.

The weaver, by the way, stayed in that tree, building and tearing down. I never saw a mate or an egg or a baby bird or anything. Just a weaver and his nests, falling as regularly as they went up. A never-ending procession of weaver engineering, with no end result.

I would sit and watch him after hours, in the early mornings or whenever I caught a break. Each year as spring broke the first descending helicopter leaves would announce his arrival. Each year my excitement grew, my hopes for him compounding annually. The second year I laughed. Teased him. Mocked a little. I presumed he would sort it out and his wife would descend from wherever weaver wives descend, and finally the family would progress and nest.

But it didn't happen.

I stopped teasing and began encouraging and as soon as I started that the whole thing developed a level of pathos I was unprepared for. The weaver and I were now somehow bound together. Our trajectories and ambitions had accidentally meshed. I began to urge him on out loud. Come on guy, what's the problem?

The thought of his life being as futile and directionless as mine, the thought of him failing at the single clear objective of his existence ...

Eish.

After Roy Jnr came Andile and Javas's Thabang, then Jabulani, the result of Beatrice and my awkward union. The three babies created a natural realignment of labour. To wit: heavy shit for the men, cooking and cleaning for the ladies.

At the agency, baby ads were always the easiest. We would rattle them off, always targeting the fathers, who held the metaphorical key to purchase decisions. The change of life. The embracing of responsibility. That bright little future all tucked up in your big manly hands. The time when a man must do what a man must do.

Now I experienced personally why it all worked so easily. I also felt that essential change in perspective, inclusive of sudden rushes of empathy for, and an overwhelming sense of connection with, my father. Through the babies, and especially through Jabu, I now understood Russle Fotheringham not as the decisive force in my life but simply as another man trying. A man as helpless as I was with this thing in my arms. A man also leaning into the wind.

In this way, Jabu gave me peace. Not lasting peace. Not the kind of peace I could carry with me forever, but a short, sharp glimpse into my own demise.

Meanwhile, Fats launched another plan.

This time he wanted to extend the house to accommodate the babies and their future lives. The plan involved, naturally, a great deal of mapping and red ink, but at its core it was expansion across the ridge – a breaking down of the walls that separated the four properties adjacent to the mansion to create a mega complex. A mega mansion. Fats envisioned a sprawling property, an interlinking of many different dimensions, a space big enough to accommodate the various intricate family structures of our future.

I had long been claustrophobic in the house and had envied the twins their garden cottage. We never had enough power to allow anyone to move further out, but with Fats's grand expansion things would change. I put my flag onto the small (in the Houghton sense) property perched on the far right corner of the ridge. Really it was quite a large house with a right-angled view of the north and the west. Its aesthetic was of posed humility, the gradations and reaches of the place all tucked neatly into a single-storey façade that dropped down the cliff face to form a second and third floor below the first.

Given the fact that I was the only partnerless adult, the odd man, the perpetual jerker into cups, I proposed the corner property as my payback, a karmic debt I hoped we would all agree was due to the guy with the guillotine tooth and several serious character flaws.

As we pounded away at the walls separating the properties, in my off-hours I packed my meagre possessions into boxes and carted them over to my new house, one by one.

I was leaving.

I was coming home.

As the babies took their place in our world, I followed the path carved out before me by billions of men. Activities and tickles and rubs and walks through the farm and lessons in anything and everything, as if I really did know and understand. As the years ticked by I found myself delivering lectures on the fly, ranging freely over subjects I knew almost nothing about. Roy Jnr would gape at me, kick his legs, frown, possibly burp in encouragement. Jabu never really gave a shit – her eyes always drifting to the left, looking for other, better things. Thabang was polite. He paid attention while looking bored.

Our relationships weren't parent to child, they were person to person. I wasn't guiding them or raising them; I was hoping to befriend them. I wanted to impress them. This was the most profound shock of fatherhood – the gradual, creeping understanding that they were my little friends. Above all else I wanted them to like me. I wanted to see them smile. I wanted to show them as much of my world as I could.

Roy Jnr, marginally the eldest, took on the role of all oldest children, bashing his head against authority with a steady frequency. Roy was the quickest to challenge, the meanest in a fight and the scariest when charting the rivers and valleys of his own moods. Publicly I treated him as my own – his name gave me licence. Privately I considered him to be mostly mine as well. The child I should have had with Babalwa, but didn't.

While raised within the general brood, Thabang grew within the specific range of his parents. Andile always held his eye, and Javas his hand, and he benefited from having as parents the two most sensible and stable of our bunch. From a tiny infant Thabang was steady, assured and calm. Even in a crisis, he was measured. His tantrums were delivered with calculation and efficiency. He was a good follower, which meant, I thought, he would end up being a good leader.

Jabu was a little shit. She caused trouble with a smile. She manipulated wherever possible and was always the one to initiate conflict – and reap the rewards. She was constantly drifting away to places she shouldn't, then allowing herself to be pulled back, with a beatific, adventurous smile on her face.

'The result of a scratchy union,' I said to Beatrice as Jabu tried to leap off her hip and into my arms over a distance of several metres. It was a regular habit of hers, leaping from the arms of whoever was holding her.

'She can't help it if her father's a prick.' Beatrice laughed a serious laugh.

'Do you believe that kids are an even mix of their parents? I'm never sure.'

'What else would they be?' She heaved Jabu off her right hip and flung her in my direction. 'We shouldn't drag babies around when we do this. Take her, please. Asseblief.'

We were pushing the cows back into their paddock for the night. I wrestled our child into place under my right arm. 'I don't know. I mean, obviously Jabu is a mix of you and me, but when I talk to her and watch her move she seems to be a lot more than that as well. Like, she has our genes but she's also a complete individual. Then I wonder if we're born as individuals with our own place and point on the planet, or whether we're born into a lineage and that that's the real point. The lineage—'

'Shit, Roy.' Beatrice slammed the gate and counted the cows one last time. 'I think you think too much.' Her finger danced across the open space between us. 'I'd hate to know what goes on inside that head of yours when you're not talking.'

'I think I need company.' The words landed in a Freudian heap between us.

'Don't give me your bullshit, Roy.' She swivelled around and marched back to the house, slapping her ass as she walked. 'You had it and you didn't want it,' she called over her shoulder.

Jabu wrestled under my arm like a sea lion.

'Check that ass, Jabu, check that ass,' I said as Beatrice drifted out of focus. She was dressed in a simple, colourful skirt, probably an Oriental Plaza wrap-around. The make-up and heels had completely disappeared. She was natural and farmy, like a black diamond Bokomo rusks ad, or one of those laxative specials, all flowers and flowing gait. She could easily have clamped a stalk of wheat between her teeth.

Jabu finally managed to break out of my arms, still reaching at Beatrice. I caught her only semi-causally. 'I could have tapped that, Jabu. I could have tapped that for the rest of time,' I said to her as I stuffed her back under my armpit. She burped. I watched Beatrice go, feeling surges of something akin to regret. But it wasn't quite that, either. Maybe it was loss. With a bit of jealousy. The numbers were never going to add up. There was always going to be someone left out.

I had made sure that that someone was me.

Babalwa fell pregnant again a few months after Roy Jnr was born – a fact that both pleased and irked her. Ideally, according to her grand plan, her next baby should have been fathered by either myself, Gerald or Javas, via the cum-cup method. She immediately drew up an extensive schedule, backed by consultation with Beatrice and Andile, both of whom were far more committed to the idea of pouring a lukewarm cup of alien semen down themselves than to the reality.

'You just tell me when and where to wank, and I'll do it' was Fats's only comment.

'Don't be such a prude,' Babalwa chided. 'You know I'll help you.'

'Public ejaculations' – Fats glared at her – 'are not really my thing.'

'Well, ja,' Babalwa shot back. 'None of this is my thing, but if we want our grandchildren to skip the whole four-eyes-and-eight-toes thing, we have to do it, nè?'

According to the schedule, the next pairings were Andile + Roy and Gerald + Beatrice. Which meant I would be the first to broach the cup.

Andile didn't want to be rushed. 'We've got all the time in the world' was her stated position. I didn't object. We agreed that 'when Andile is ready' it would happen, with Babalwa continually stressing the dangers of a repeat of her and Fats's mistake. 'Just pay attention!' she barked, frequently. 'Use the condoms, check your rhythms.'

Chapter 42

Blacks, browns, beiges and a few whites

I cleared out Tebza's room. It had been two years since the crash and we were inching painfully towards the subject. To remembering the people. Talking about them. Threading them back into our ideas of our lives. Rooms had to be cleared and cleaned. Possessions boxed and/or distributed and/or thrown out. I volunteered for Tebza's.

It was pitiful. Pads and mobiles and associated accessories. Clothes still piled up on the floor in what looked like three separate heaps – dirty, clean and transitional. A few scraps of paper on the pine desk, covered in water marks and rings from the various cups and containers. Scribbled notes and strings of IP addresses, each a minor variation of the last.

Bed unmade.

Cupboards empty, save for a few extra machines waiting in the far reaches of the shelves. The Energade bottle festering in the corner of the darkest shelf.

I scooped the clothes and the duvet and sheets into a few black bags, tied them up and lugged them over to the balcony and threw them off, straight down the cliff. I poured the nano piss down the sink. His pads I carted to my room and opened up one by one. Most of them were raw terminals running a basic open-source OS. Folders empty, no files. Shells. The last pad was different, though. It was his personal machine from the pre-days: email, designs, docs, music.

I started with email. The in-box ran several thousand mails deep, well past two years before it all stopped. Between the avalanche of corporate requests and replies, revisions and reversions, lay clues to a deeper life. Snappy one-liners from Joy, the hack girl, recurred in the four months before the end:

Sunday. 8pm. Keen? Bring music, naps, sense of anticipation ...
j

And his reply:
Sho. Armed. Equipped. Metaphysical gumboots on.
Laytas
Tebza.

Closer to the end they were more connected.
Tebza
How you?
Feeling like maybe it's time to move on. In my life I mean. Feeling stuck. Need adult things. Career progression. House down payment. How come other people seem so completely grown up and rooted and I'm just not?
Anyway. Gonna lay low for a while. Cook food. Eat it.
Holler back
j

And the reply:
Hear you. Feel you. Need to watch TV I think. TV is always the answer. Not sure about the questions.
I call.
Out
T

Little lines. People talking about small things. TV and weekend drugs and creeping fears. It made me want to cry.

Around the same time there were a few hospital exchanges. Booking forms and permission slips and insurance questionnaires. Cosmetic auditory enhancement, his procedure was called. The date was for about two months after he met Joy. A morning procedure, out in the afternoon. No insurance.

Otherwise, his folders were as folders generally are. Spreadsheets and investment product brochures. A million and one overviews of various trading algorithms. The 'Instamatic': '80% odds of a 25%

return over 90 days through a considered focus on the performance potential of weather futures in the East African boom economy'. The documents stacked up. I scrolled and peeked and scrolled and read and glimpsed and scrolled.

Deep within his 2033 Potentials folder, which contained many hundreds of files of potential sales opportunities, was a folder called Youth, and inside that a string of typical Global Youth promos. Kids in hoodies with raised arms, pointing fingers, Molotov cocktails.

If not now, when?
Money is the only freedom
Release capital now

One poster was a midnight shot of graf rebels standing back and watching their stream on the walls of the stock exchange in Sandton. The video they're watching shows men in rags digging through suburban garbage bins. The shot is just close enough to make out a Woolworths bag in one of the graf boys' hands, inside it a lot of bright-looking apples. The strap line on the poster: 'Action Counts: Johannesburg, South Africa, 2032.'

I examined the graf rebels carefully. Their shoes, their shoulders, their posture. There was nothing definitive. Tebza could have been simply an online fan – a downloader of posters. He could also have been personally spraying the stock-exchange walls at night. It was impossible to tell.

The Global Youth verbiage went on and on. Schematics for a stock-exchange jammer algorithm. More schematics for a youth-fund trading algo, the introductory text speaking of the need for centralised planning and funding to support youth activism and the fight against capital retention.

I dumped the empty machines in the corner of the computer room. I kept Tebza's pad with me. It held clues to his life I intended to follow.

We locked up the empty rooms and held a bonfire of all additional clothing and organic matter. It turned into a funeral-type thing where Fats spoke out loud, full of purpose and meaning, while we all looked and felt solemn. It had been two years, but the pain of our stupidity was still fresh.

Everybody cried.

The kids too.

* * *

We went through the daily rituals and then we all went home – the couples to their beds and me to mine. Sometimes, in the darker nights, I would reach for my bottle of wine and take it in with me. Hug it and hold it.

But I also tried, to the best of my ability, to leave that shit behind.

I had come to view my idea of myself as the lonely drunk, the drifter and the outsider, as a hindrance. An indulgence. I slipped back sometimes, but mostly I focused on pushing away from it, in other, more positive directions.

I started building a library in the basement of my new house, which I had successfully moved into and powered up. I rekindled my PE habit of raiding buildings and houses for books. The houses of St Patrick Road and Munro Drive yielded an expected but nonetheless valuable haul of classics, academic stuff and straight pulp. I used the armoured van to go house to house, smashing straight through gates and walls and front doors, PE style, until I found the studies. The good stuff was generally in the studies, base camps for retreating husbands and fathers. History and Africana and international relations and so on. But I wasn't picky. I took it all. The *Cosmo* and *Car* mags and the Wilbur Smiths and the finance textbooks.

My new house was all wooden floors, pressed ceilings and stone floors. The wood was offset by off-white walls and curtains and framed line drawings with dashes of watercolour. Jenny Crawford, judging by her cupboard, was as predictably stylish as her house. She worked off a core set of dresses, skirts and blouses ranging across the basic colours – blacks, browns, beiges and a few whites.

Her collection of scarves was as enormous as it was colourful, and she obviously used these, her bags and her jewellery to add the flash. She was a good-looking late-forties woman, with dyed brown hair cut into an angled bob, a trim figure and a cardboard cut-out husband, David, CEO of a nutraceuticals company, Zest. The house was covered in a loosely scattered layer of supplement bottles, including a generous proportion of ginseng pills and sensual massage oils.

They appeared childless, David and Jenny Crawford. The spare rooms were structured and neat and waiting for activity, which, by the looks of things, seldom occurred. Jenny – a marketing consultant – seemed to have spent most of her time in an office drowning under the weight of ancient business magazines. *Harvard Business Review. Fast Company. The Media.* Her pinboard was drilled firmly into the wall by schematics and spider diagrams and brand-positioning statements. I sat behind her desk, powered up her desktop and looked out over the stone balcony to northern Johannesburg. I clicked around her emails and folders, but there was nothing other than the expected. Musically, the returns were worse than average. All old-school stuff from the '90s and 2000s. Freshlyground. Kings of Leon. Coldplay. I turned off the machine and sat, letting the afternoon sun bake my chest. This, I decided, would be my study too.

And I would use it.

The second floor I reserved as a reading station for mobiles and portables, as a music centre and as a photo-storage facility. I strung up ten different extensions and plugged in all the chargers I could find, catering to most brands and models. About thirty-five in total. Then I set up ten central fifty-terabyte music servers, and another six for photographs.

And then I archived.

They started to call me the librarian. Ask the librarian, they said, in the days when the kids began to ask about things. Check in the library. Ask Roy.

In my own time, after I had finished work and archiving, when I was sitting on my cool stone porch, watching the sun set over the Northcliff Dome, I became very attached to philosophy and home decor, in no specific order.

The best philosophy was wrapped up in history. It was, in effect, storytelling from a particular era. The worst was the pure sort. University stuff. Sartre. Nietzsche. Bertrand Russell.

The stories came to life up there on my hill. The texts would conjure the voices of people. The sounds of life as it used to be: trucks downshifting on the highway; washing machines and lawnmowers and crying children. I read a lot of Africana initially, following up on the sketchy stuff I had devoured at the Eastern Cape lodge, before I found Babalwa. After the Africana I drifted at random, picking up whatever I found in front of me. Mercenaries in West Africa. Paul Theroux on a train. Naipaul on America. JM Coetzee on Australia. It was the reality I was after. The reportage. Actions and transactions. The writers themselves ... they were pitifully out of context. So self-assured, so assuming, so completely wrong. Unable – any of them – to imagine what might be coming. The home magazines offered a more tactile distraction. I carefully clipped out wives and husbands gazing at their lounges/gardens/homes. I stuck them to the side wall of my study in an oily collage – my own little monument to the great dream of family. A final nod towards the ridiculous idea of design, to the vanity of balance and style. When I ran out of room on the wall, I collected the cuttings in an apple box, which grew to two apple boxes and, over the years, three, then four, stacking up next to each other. It was a harmless compulsion – as I clipped, I considered creating some kind of artwork, something massive and tangible, like Javas's pieces, something permanent, some recognition for the grandchildren of the cult of the interior. But I never did. The boxes filled, overflowed and started again. They're still with me now. Next to me. Keeping me company. Maybe someone will find them one day and appreciate the beauty of those cashmere ladies. The wholeness of their manicured hands.

Babalwa's second pregnancy came and went, resulting in Lydia. This time the birth was complicated. Babalwa bled heavily afterwards, and it was, Beatrice repeatedly informed us, touch and go. She cramped badly for a few weeks after Lydia arrived, prompting Andile and Beatrice to hit Joburg Gen for some morphine. Having known a few junkies in my time, I stopped them from using it.

We ran a lot in that week. Up and down with water and blankets and shit, just like in the movies. It was OK when we could run, and conversely the hardest when we just had to sit and listen to the pain. Gerald had brought cigars, and while we waited we smoked them like they were cigarettes, smacking our lungs for something to do, to give us something different to feel.

Personally, I remained narcissistic and inward. Each hug and worried brow or pat on the shoulder during Babalwa's troubles revealed again to me how empty the core of my own life was, how devoid of similar contact. I would go back to my house depressed, flick on the light and stand there lost, choking on emptiness.

I read. I filed. I archived.
I clipped out and stuck on.
I looked out.
I waited.
I talked out loud. Long sentences, sometimes rambling, sometimes insightful, sometimes coherent.

After the panic and chaos of Lydia's birth, Babalwa steadily increased the pressure, month on month, closing in on Andile and myself. Jabu was over two years old, as were Thabang and Roy Jnr. It was time.
I resisted.
I wanted to start with someone else – Beatrice or Babalwa would have been fine, but to start with Andile and Javas felt like treachery. Adultery, but sadder. Pathetic even. The idea of Andile having to open up to take my seed while Javas waited ... I hated it. But Babalwa pushed us closer together until I visited Javas and Andile a few nights in a row for supper, a gradual wind-up to what

needed to be done. We sat around the table and ate – me the uncle come to dinner. We talked of many things, but never the real thing, until the third night, when Javas finally, thankfully, broke it open. 'Babalwa's right you know,' he said, right at me. 'She's right. We have to. We have no choice. It has to happen.'

'That's fine,' I said, nausea hitting my gut. 'It's fine, Javas. I know it must be done, but what if it doesn't take? I mean, I can handle the idea of having to do it, but Jesus, having to do it again and again ... It makes me feel ill.'

'Ag fok, Roy.' Andile adopted a thick mock-Afrikaans accent while forking a broccoli head very practically into her mouth. 'We need to get over it. We have to – all of us – and if that means eight times in a row, then that's it. We've been through worse. You've been through worse. So have I. We'll get hard about it – 'scuse the pun – and make it happen.'

And so we did.

We appointed a day and an hour and a place. The three of us met in the cottage kitchen, then split to the two main bathrooms. 'We keep it clinical,' Javas said. Crossing the threshold into the bathroom, which was decorated in various shades of brown and which featured a triptych of abstract black-and-white KwaZulu landscapes created by Andile, I felt like a transgressor, an invader.

I had been inside the twins' cottage many times over the years. It was a journey into a different, parallel world. A world where tiny metal dwarfs – Javas's creations – stood hiding within the leafy protection of well-watered pot plants. A world where not only did the colours match, but they actually seemed designed to work together. Andile picked her interior battles carefully, making sure to give each item the room it needed not only to breathe, but to dominate. My favourite was a large-scale black-and-white print of the Sandton riots, hanging in the lounge. Andile had found it about to rot in an artist's studio in the city. It was typical of the Sandton-riot genre: hoodies, face masks, raised arms with petrol bombs, etc. But the artist – Mpho, she said his name was – had woven microscopic detail through everything. Tiny shocked faces at the stock-exchange windows. Infinitesimal pockmark dings in the parked BMWs. Full and accurate road maps, which you could actually read with a magnifying glass, in the hands of the global youth.

As many times as I had been in their domain, however, I had never had even a second of this kind of privacy. Now the bathroom took on new echoes. Suddenly Andile's landscapes held the voice and heart of their owner. Her sound and her smell surrounded me. It was like she was there with me, watching, questioning, examining my thin little mlungu legs as I sat on the toilet seat and wrapped my fist around a limp, uninspired dick. I pulled and stretched and eventually, half-heartedly, delivered.

Then I ran – I literally sprinted the fifteen metres that separated us. (We had agreed that the cooling of the junk was the creepiest part of the whole thing. When I imagined Andile's horror, it was always the thought of the cold, glutinous substance that creeped me out ...) Quickly I passed the cup over to a waiting Javas, who disappeared behind their door.

I hung around for five minutes, and they emerged, hand in hand, Javas leading, smiling. Andile pulling her cheeks backward.

'Ugh,' she said, then detached herself from Javas and gave me a long, warm hug, eventually holding me at arm's length, by the shoulders. 'We did well, Roy, we did well.'

'It just better fucking take, eh?' I ruffled her hair, then thumped Javas on his muscled shoulder. 'The donor life ... eish.'

Andile flipped into a handstand against the passage wall, allowing her skirt to fall over her head and flashing her white panties and well-formed legs. I blushed and looked away.

'My gogo always said you must,' she explained in a barely discernible, skirt-covered muffle.

Chapter 43
We carried on

We lost Jabu at the next winter slaughter. I say that like she went wandering through the forest and we couldn't find her, but really we killed her. Gerald and I killed her. It's as simple and brutal as that.

I had jerked into the cup for four months running. Andile and Javas had been steadfast and magnanimous in their reception of my spunk. Eventually, in month five, it took and we had another one on the go. We kept it mostly to our ourselves. The others knew we were engaged with it, this strangely intimate process, but sensed we were best left treating it in our own way. Babalwa would raise the occasional query, and we'd report back dutifully, but it never became a subject of public discussion. We had, by silent agreement, sanctified the thing, which was really the only way to go about it. Baby creation is rooted in love or lust, the basic human connections. Take these away and you have something too strange to grasp, and too powerful to brush off.

The big slaughter had taken place annually, and incrementally more professionally, each year in July. Year on year we had improved, but in that first year our failures were many and miserable. Gerald, for all his calm instruction, slipped with the gun at the last second, shooting the cow through the side of its head once we'd looped it down to the iron floor-ring. Instead of crashing to its knees it wailed and kicked crazily at the closing darkness, nearly decapitating Javas in the process. Blood sprayed out of the angular slot in its head, and in the twenty seconds it took Gerald to compose himself and get another round off we all saw life flashing before us. There was a distinct possibility we would all go down with the cow, pulled into a death of hoofs and screams. Eventually Gerald got the bullet in the right place and the beast crashed, but we were far too long with the throat-slitting and the blood didn't drain immediately. Our slaughter master spent the rest of the day chastising himself and warning us that our meat was going to be off. We shook the fear off gradually. (Andile clung to her cricket stump for a good time after.)

The next time it was much easier. Gerald put the bullet straight through and the cow's eyes slammed shut. We skinned and pulled and gutted and carved. The next day we did the pig and used its entrails for sausage skins, Javas and Gerald guiding us in turn.

With operational success the slaughter became something of a celebration. A time of year to anticipate. A marker for us all. Another year gone. Another three freezers' worth of meat. Another slash against the bedpost of our lost society. And yes, we used it all, once we had learned how to extract it. The tongue and brains, the offal and the kidneys, the heart and all the rest. Beatrice was still finding good packaged flour and she made pies. Rows and rows of pies. Steak and kidney, like granny would.

The fourth slaughter after the plane crash (this was how we had started marking time, not with a calendar but according to the happenings, the epochs of our own lives) we killed my first child. A child created not with cooling cups of semen but with love, albeit of the temporary and fractious sort.

Did I say *we* killed Jabulani? I mean *I*. I did it. I pushed the domino forward, tilted its ass over its head, and then it was too late to do anything but watch the falling.

'Daddy,' she piped up. 'I watch?'

She was serious, completely intent on the wondrous butchery process.

'Ja, Jabu,' I said. 'But you need to be very, very careful, nè? There are lots of sharp knives around and you could get hurt, so you need to stand here.' I marked off a spot about five metres back of the concrete area, on the cusp of the cricket field/paddock. 'This where you stay, yes?' I ground the mark into the turf with my heel. 'You stay right here and you don't move.'

She nodded seriously. Several times. I hadn't fully learned, yet, that children lie, just like everyone else. That they also dream of, and lust after, better things. And nod and plan accordingly.

Her eyes were big and brown, like the cow. They slammed shut in exactly the same way.

We had grown self-assured. We had slaughtered year after year and by now we all knew what we were doing, why we were doing it and how it would pan out. We were in control.

1. Jabu creeps forward, inch by tiny inch, to get a better view. She's not freaked out by the blood and guts; she's seeing chops and steaks and cuts.
2. Gerald jumps back to avoid some kind of spray. He's using the wrist-strapped knife. The blade has become part of his arm. He has forgotten he is no longer all man.
3. His knife arm jerks back in anticipation of the rest of his body and the blade slices straight through Jabu's curious neck.
4. There are no screams. Just a quiet thump. A little body falls softly to the ground.

Let me tell you now just how far we had come. Let me explain the terrible distance we had travelled away from ourselves, from everything we knew.

Let me explain what we did.
    We wept.
    We tore our hair out.
    We buried the little body.
    We said a prayer to a strange, absent god.

And then we carried on.

IV

Chapter 44
I wish I had written it down at the time

I started writing this to reach out to you, whoever you are, wherever you are. I needed to extend, I needed to push further. Simply dying, which I will soon do, and letting my eyes slip shut – leaving behind only what is in this house, these libraries, these rooms and rooms of computers and devices and failed connections, leaving that as my only message to you – I refuse.

I need to talk.

I need to tell you more – of myself and my time – and so I started, word by word, to explain, to tell my story, to leave a personal interpretation behind. For you. And of course – obviously – for me.

But now, after this word and this one, and then this one, after the thousands and thousands of I's and ands and buts, I am deeper than I expected. I am wrestling with time itself, the snake of my life, the python. I am throttled by what I have forgotten, by the mists of story, ever rolling. I duck and push the hair out of my eyes, looking for the few things I know for sure will be there. I jump, pillar to pillar, and all else is lost, shrouded and vague, opaque.

I wish I had paid more attention.

I wish I had written it down at the time, because now there are only statues and monuments, presentations and experiences. Narratives. Design.

The furrow on Gerald's brow.

Babalwa and her babies and her breeding maps. Kiddies at the knee, charts and cross-referencing red lines and genetic mixes. Her hand on their heads, guiding.

Fats's fro, always modest yet strong, hard. Small, even. Bouncing. Firm.

The twins. Hand in hand.

Jabu's body, so tiny, covered in blood, her neck literally pumping the red out, her red mixing with the cows'.

Entrails and tears.

The years of us. Our farm and our people. The children, from this distance now almost all completely interchangeable faces and forms, smiling and running and growing so easily into this other thing. So unfettered by time. So shaped by our story, yet somehow so completely untouched by any of it.

Chapter 45

Getting your shit together technically

It was the dream, Babalwa told me as we grew into our age. Right back at the beginning, the dream was complete and fully formed. She knew as she woke up, as soon as she met me, that the dream would always guide her. A rock, firm and flat-topped, solid in a terrible sea.

The baby farm allowed us to move. It was the only way to pick up momentum again. I see that now.

Now, also, I view Jabu's death as the spark. As the shove in the back we needed to get serious. Of course, that's my way of rationalising the horror of that soft thump, the sound I will never shake. Yes, it's my method of layering some kind of sense into the incomprehensible.

Maybe.

Regardless, it's the line I choose to take. It works for me.

The biggest miracle of all – as is meticulously detailed in the archives* – is that we did it as planned. We jerked off, we poured cold semen down, again and again. The couples made sure that in a world without people, in a world begging for children, contraception was used and accidents avoided. We calculated the baseline requirement of diversity. Wherever possible, we followed the maths.

When there was no maths, we stumbled on.

'Roy, you know I can't explain things properly any more,' Fats said to me sometime around the winter of '49. 'I used to be so sure. It used to be so easy. Simple. Now I look at you and I feel this love for you and I can't even put it into words. You know?'

---

* The baby-farm narrative in the archives is, unlike certain other sections, very close to objectively accurate. Of all the work we did, and I did, I am most proud of this portion of the main library.

I did know. He was very drunk at the time. It came from somewhere deep inside, and it was also booze-true. It rang raw and honest. I rubbed his fro and offered something similar in return. He held my hand.

I started to draw. I took lessons from Andile, who equipped me with a few charcoals, some watercolours and a box of acrylics. I drew trees and landscapes. Fruit and such. Most of it looked worse than stuff I had done in Grade 7 art class. Gradually she showed me how to create perspective, to give trees shape and cheeks blush. How impossible watercolours are to use and how much faster rewards arrive with acrylics.

Drawing and painting quickly began to feel like a way to capture Jabulani, to hold on to her fading form before she was erased altogether. That was my initial reaction, but more followed. A desire to catch her actual death, somehow. To remove that terrible thud. To blur that single moment when she fell out of us.

My vast, expanding library was simply unable to help me cope with the death. There were hundreds – thousands – of texts on the shelves, virtual and otherwise, that addressed the subject, directly and tangentially, but they all missed the hammer blow. The direct, metaphysical impact of my own context. None could handle the electricity still buzzing on the muscles of my heart. They were all just words on a page and almost all of them spoke of the writer rather than the world being written. None of the carefully structured arguments and plots were relevant to my world of seven adults and their calculated brood.

I had built the library, the archive, in self-defence. As if by gathering around me the better, more acknowledged works of man, I could protect myself against the echoes booming up at the gates. But for the biggest, most important sound of all there was no help. No buffer at all. Art, on the other hand, offered at least a sliver of what I craved.

And so I drew.

I also widened the range of the library to include art. I started at the university art departments, where students were learning to draw. In the paused classrooms there were definite flickers of life, of true moments being captured. A line drawing of the city. A man with a bag in his hand walking fast down the street. A nude girlfriend, sprawled yet guarded.

Once I was well into my lessons, the twins accompanied me and we targeted the museums and the corporate galleries. MTN, Standard Bank, Joburg Gallery, Everard Read, Goodman et al. Arts on Main.

'Amazing,' Andile said as we breezed through the collected works of our age – a post-1994 retrospective at the Goethe Project Space. 'It's so easy. It used to be so hard and now it's so easy.' She took a running kick at a coat-hanger installation.

'I think I know what you mean,' I said, grabbing a couple of the hangers, which were of the Woolworths variety, for my closet. 'But enlighten me ...'

'Well, Roy, that picture there' – Andile went into mock lecture mode as she pointed out a semi-abstract Kentridge, the usual man leaning/running – 'at least has some kind of aesthetic value. It's a not unpleasant image of a male moving. There's some kind of flash that feels like something to me.

'Whereas that' – she pointed at the collapsed pile of coat hangers – 'is just a bunch of fucking coat hangers. We all knew it at the time – I was at the opening of this show – but no one could say it out loud. Only whispers behind the hands.'

'That's why I fell in love with her,' Javas jibed from his seat on top of a half tractor tire studded with gold pins entitled *Means of Production III*. 'The power of her analysis.'

'For real though.' Andile kicked a hanger in Javas's direction. 'Now it's simple. No brokers, no hustlers, no art slags or groupies, none of the PR chickies – just pictures on the wall. I look at some of it and I want to cry, it's so beautiful. But there is just as much that is just ... just ...' She took another skipping run up and hoofed a hanger at my head.

'Depressing?' I asked.

'Irrelevant?' Javas chipped in.

'Kak.' Andile took the Kentridge print and frisbeed it across the length of the very white Goethe Project Space. It crashed into a long-dead video installation in a shower of glass.

'And yet, in terms of its emotive potential, I still find art more attractive, currently, than books, which fail at a deeper level,' I added, hurling a small, heavy blob of metal, about the size of a tennis ball and with no discernible aesthetic form, through another retro flat-screen (Sony 97-inch super plasma) installation entitled *Urban Dynamics – Ocean Flows*. The metal blob was called *Weeping Underground*. 'All of the books, all of them, stay within the same place, the same realm. I read and read and read and I don't find anything that even considers what actually happened to us. With art, at least, there is some kind of hit rate. Every twenty or thirty pieces you find something that screams at you, that at least gets close to the chaos of life. The books are just useless.'

'We should go back to the student studio in town.' Javas left his half tyre and began heading out. 'There'll be better stuff there. Better odds than here, anyway.'

I grabbed a few brochures for Urban Dynamics – the name of the exhibition as well as the video installation – on the way out. Andile took a small wooden sculpture of a lady balancing an absurdly large barrel on her head. 'Reminds me of my mom,' she said.

I drew cows' heads and sweeping, curved knives and rivers of blood. I drew Jabu in the various stages of falling. I drew people in an abattoir clustered around a child corpse.

Jabu's death was just the start. I needed to convey our new context. We weren't just people who had killed their child. We were the only people, and we'd killed one of our only children. The work had to be unique. It could not be the same as anything that had gone before it. There was a gulf that had to be bridged, and I was lost as to how to do it.

But it needed to be done.

I moved through sheet after sheet of Fabriano. Andile told me to keep the rejects, so I piled them up, a huge stack of childlike failures. Stick figures without perspective. Cows' heads and badly composed chainsaws and barrels in watercolour and charcoal and acrylic.

About thirty or forty attempts in, I switched subjects and began beating out an equally ill-composed series of us on the farm. Beatrice leading the cows. Fats on the ladder fiddling with another panel, screwdriver in his mouth. All of us in the abattoir, clustered in panic around a single cow head.

This series felt better. It had the ring of settler art to it. Strangers lost in a strange land. I began exaggerating the poses. Myself running up Munro Drive, but a steeper road, the kind that leads to God, the path thin and getting thinner, almost unimaginable as it faded through the growth and the trees. This was my first success. I enhanced the yellow of the Nikes to the kind of biblical hue able to compete with the surrounding jungle. My legs were super-hard, thighs bulging with effort, my face strained and taut with ascension, my eyes fixed on the pinprick of light breaking through the forest at the top. It was epic. Godly. The hyperbole worked.

Next, Babalwa. I fattened her up, added folds to her thighs and sat her on a kind of rocking chair with a quilt over her knees, a nursing baby in her crooked arms, and ten or eleven brats in various stages of development at her feet. Behind them, to the right, the complex, our complex, the endless horizon with just a hint of the Northgate Dome on the left. I added ten, twenty years to her face. A middle-aged woman surround by her brood. Her swarming brood. Some of them staring absently, some fiddling with toys, and a few at arm's length, fighting over something. Babalwa the breeder.

Gerald alone. No backdrop. Nothing. Just standing there in a stained butcher's coat with that curved knife strapped to his wrist, dangling limp, a smudge of congealed blood brown on the tip. His eyes vacant.

And on I went, my lines growing more and more biblical with each picture, my exaggerations extending, seeking out the nuggets in all of us and distorting them, twisting them up and out and into the open.

'You got something going here, eh Roy?' Andile clucked, poring over the pictures. She giggled initially and then was silent. 'I mean ... ja.' She paused at the one of her and Javas, hand in hand, walking into the sunset, an ambiguous Moses-type basket dangling lightly in Javas's free hand. 'You're getting your shit together technically. Bodies and legs and all.' She leafed through to Fats straining on his ladder, muscles bulging, arm reaching in vain for an elusive socket. 'I don't like them, but I'm not going to stop you.' She pushed tears away with her palm – a strange, unproductive gesture, as if by using the part of her hand with the least utility she could reverse, or at least deny, the flow. 'A lot of them are repulsive, in fact, Roy. You must carry on. And I must go.' She walked away, pushing again with the palm.

Painting became my nightly ritual, the thing I now did to replace reading, which I had consigned to a necessary pre-sleep technicality. I let myself follow the perverse path I had started. Andile's tears had been disturbing, but also inspiring. I was, I believed, accessing the bubbling anxiety that ran common through us.

I was making art.

* * *

We were now shut off. Initially, in those first few months in Houghton, I had felt the vegetation acutely. Our isolation was made all the worse by the unmown lawns, by the obvious disappearance of order and straight lines. But slowly the plants receded from my consciousness, and only occasionally would that initial sense of invasion and claustrophobia recur.

Our personal feelings were incidental, however, to the green forces inching over roads and fences, chipping away at the chasm. We noticed it – the growth – again in the months after Jabu's death, when it suddenly seemed to become much harder to move outside our regular zones. And even those – the paths and roads we used the most – had begun to require steady, intensive maintenance.

Gerald was at the forefront of the hack-it-back campaign. His ambition in this regard was, I believed, a way for him to expunge or rechannel his anger at Jabu's death. He would load the chainsaw and the axes into his bakkie, his jaw set and his mind fully on the battle. He never asked for a partner, but if any of us offered he would hand out a tool and wordlessly pull the volunteer into the fight.

Eventually we had to structure the process. Once a month, during summer, we would all throw ourselves into a week-long maintenance mission. First, hack back the trees and vines trying to swallow Munro Drive. Second, clear the perimeter areas – Fats's gates and the outer border. Third, make sure we had access to the major arteries in and out of the city. North and south were easy – nominal effort was required to access the M1 highway. Lastly, keep Louis Botha and Empire avenues clear. Not because the routes were necessary to us as such, but because it was philosophically impossible to concede to living in a jungle with only one road to the highway.

Regardless, Gaia shrugged off our fight. We were slowly becoming a one-road town.

We had too much invested in our set-up to try to move, although the idea of transferring out to flatter farm areas was increasingly mooted. The girls were sick of the creeping forest, and Javas and Gerald leaned in favour of relocation. I fought it, as did Fats. I couldn't accept the idea of having to retreat from Jozi. It felt like the defeat that would crown them all. If we left we would never be able to come back. The forest would close its arms and that would be that. Joburg would be a mythical memory, a place of the past, of adventure stories for children, of warnings not to get lost.

Still, the summer monsoons kept coming, the forest grew and we were all carrying machetes and a chainsaw in our vehicles whenever we went anywhere.

Which wasn't that often.

'You still think of your people?' Gerald asked me, apropos of nothing, as we headed to the bottom of St John's for creeper maintenance. 'I think of mine all the time,' he went on. 'All the time. My wife. My kids. My mother. My family. I never thought of them that much when they were here, and not even so often just after they were gone, in the beginning, but now I can't stop. I want to know where they are. Where they went. Is it like that for you?' His right elbow rested on the bakkie's window pane, jutting slightly out into the passing breeze. He was driving so slowly we were almost stationary.

'I didn't really have that many people, to be honest,' I admitted. 'Bitch of an ex-wife. Dead father. Mother I never really knew, so no real extended family ...'

Gerald was frustrated. 'So now? What's it like for you? I'm feeling like the deeper we go, the more babies and the better we get at the farming, the worse it is for me personally. I want to go back to how it was. I feel so alone, I think about just ending it.'

'I've thought that too,' I said. And I had. Many times. Yet it was always an abstract kind of thought, more philosophical than anything else. Gerald, on the other hand, was not exuding a philosophical vibe. He was all nuts and dangerously practical bolts.

'And? What stops you?' he asked.

'Dunno. Guess I just can't override that human thing. Survival. The need to keep on.'

'I tell you, Roy, I tell you ...' Gerald stopped the bakkie. 'It's becoming real for me. The question. That question. I mean, they must have gone somewhere. It's not like they died, they just disappeared. Which means that there must be something else besides this, besides what we know now. And then I think, well, why not just end it? I'd probably end up in some other world, living in some other way. Maybe I'd end up with them, wherever they are, and worst case is I just die, and would that be so bad, compared to this?'

'What about Beatrice?' I had to ask.

'Beatrice is fine. She's a good woman. I have no problems with Beatrice. But I live with her because I must.'

There were several levels to our conversation. Around this time, Gerald would surely have been noticing that Beatrice had begun paying me the odd visit, again.

We were breeding according to Babalwa's master plan, using the established cup method for all combinations save for existing couples. But my experience with Gerald and Beatrice was fundamentally different from that with Fats and Babalwa, and the twins. Gerald refused to participate – he left it up to us, and thus, thanks to our sexual history, the masturbation and insemination took on distinctly erotic overtones. As it turned out, the middleman was essential if the exercise was going to be emotionally neutralised. With Gerald refusing to play his position, Beatrice and I developed our own unique and not unpleasant variation. Her fingers brushing mine as she took the cup. Me waiting, lingering, in fact, to make sure she had no issues in transfer. A soft, warm peck on the cheek that lasted too long. The smell of her lips.

And so, inevitably I suppose, we replaced the formal insemination sessions with a visit here, a pop-in there. She would always arrive in a sarong wrap, one of several floral patterned numbers she had grown into over the years, maybe for morning coffee, or for an early evening nightcap. I suspected she made sure Gerald was somewhere off the property at the time, or at least otherwise engaged, but I also never asked. To be honest, I never really said much at all. She would sit across from me in the lounge of my library house, or on the porch if it was evening and dark enough, and we would exchange idle, meaningless chat while ever so slowly, in tiny increments, she would pull the wrap up and let her fingers dangle and drift over her thighs while we talked. We would sway like that until the subtext took complete control and I rose, or she rose, and we fell on each other in a violent yet soft, crazy yet logical, union.

I would like to say it was a temporary thing, brought on by the insemination. A casual mistake. A regretful yet pleasant series of accidents. But it wasn't. It was our thing, and once we had started we carried on – intermittently and with all the breaks and spaces that rise and fall naturally with life – for decades. Only once did she reveal anything at all about the nature of her relationship with Gerald.

'Gerald,' she announced out of the blue in one of our post-coital hazes, her head balanced on my chest, 'has wet dreams. He always has. I used to get jealous of them, the dreams, but he says our sex life is so messed up and infrequent that they're generally about me. The dreams. He says he likes it that way – he gets to fuck me more, in more adventurous ways, than in the real world. I'm not sure I believe him. But it's a good story.'

I pushed my hand through her hair.

It was a good story.

Gerald turned to face the wheel, stared out the window, watched the rain clouds build all purple and pregnant in the west.

'You grew up here, nè?' he asked rhetorically. 'You ever remember the rain coming from the south? People used to talk about that often. How it always came from the south. You remember the south rain?'

'My father grew up with it. He would talk about it,' I said. 'I guess I just caught the edge of the old, so I never noticed the change that much. It still comes from the south sometimes. Classic old thunderstorm. Roll in, roll out.'

'Since I got here, to Jozi, it's from the west,' Gerald said, talking mostly to himself. 'You build an idea in your mind how things are. What the limits are. You think one thing. That we'll get between this much and that much rain. Or, like, the earth is full of people. Then bang. Gone. Your wife. Your children. Your parents. Gone. Rain patterns. Gone.' He shook his head, started the bakkie and edged it forward.

'We need you, Gerald. You know that, eh?' I couldn't leave the suicide dangling. And it was true. We couldn't afford more losses, of any sort.

He snorted. 'What, in case you need to kill any more small girls?'

'Accidents. They happen. 'Specially in our kind of set-up.'

'You didn't feel the blade go in. I'll never be able to forget it. The feeling. It's impossible.' He stopped the bakkie again, two perfectly formed droplets racing in parallel down to his beard. 'It's everywhere with me. That feeling. The slicing. I can't get rid of it. I can't sleep.'

'You talked to anyone about it? Beatrice?'

'We do jigsaw puzzles. We clean and wash and sometimes have sex. We boil eggs.'

'Jesus, Gerald.' I gripped his shoulder. It was the only thing I could think of doing. I shook, trying to get him to look at me. 'Gerald, fuck, you can't just keep this all inside. We're in it now, all of us. Jabu was all of our mistake. It wasn't you. It was me. It was Fats. It was all of us. You must know that.'

He snorted the snot back up his nose, then took a second to look at me, his lower lip trembling.

I thought suddenly of Beatrice and her thighs, opening for me silently, her fingers calling, an impossibly weighty force.

'Thanks, Roy,' he said. 'Thank you. I needed to hear that.'

'You gonna need to hear it again, broe. You gonna need to hear it again.'

Chapter 46
Indecipherable intellectual potential

By the time Lydia was born Fats had grown round. He wasn't fat – none of us were – but his body embraced the shape of middle age, thickening around the gut, the upper arms, the chest.

His roundness wasn't just physical. He had also lost (let go of?) many of his edges. He was slower to shout, slower to command and, frankly, slower to care.

After years of rockiness and back-and-forthing, he and Babalwa had settled into a true man–wife thing. From the outside, their relationship appeared to be nearly as solid as the twins'. It was odd to observe, and to participate in, tangentially at least. In the main I was happy for both of them, and of course a little jealous, and a little paranoid, now that Gerald, myself and Beatrice were even more starkly shadowed by the reflected light of the two couples. (My semi-regular trysts with Beatrice were unnerving and guilt-inducing. I wondered frequently what the extent of her sex drive was: whether she was doubling up with me, or whether her cohabitation with Gerald was really just a matter of provisions and practicalities, jigsaw puzzles and boiled eggs.)

As the kids grew, Fats started organising them into units to be applied to various tasks, including my archiving project. Every now and then he would deliver a little army to me, a cluster of five or six children running in surprisingly orderly circles around his feet.

'Right, boss, what's it today? Wits? RAU? Oppenheimer library?'

I would pick the location and we would head off in two or three bakkies, depending on how many adults were along for the ride. Once or twice the entire farm set out – for some reason the Wits library trip sticks in my mind. (Why do we remember this, and not that? I can't say. Maybe it was the light, the mood or the smell. We made many trips, but when I think of that time, the memory is of the horde of us crashing through the Wits library.) I had final editorial call on what was picked and what was left behind. The adults would build piles of what they thought was relevant, and the kids would tear up and down the floors, academic confetti fluttering around their every step, and pop up randomly to present their wild selections. I would filter with authority. Keepers into boxes on the left, junk in a pile on the right. Undecided in the middle.

I favoured, after quite a bit of consultation with the adults, the scientific and mathematical over narratives. It wasn't my natural inclination, but ultimately it seemed to be the right thing to do. Our kids and their kids were going to need to build up technical knowledge. And that meant maths and science.

JM Coetzee and Es'kia Mphahlele could offer, ultimately, only voices.

Still, we allowed ourselves indulgences. I enjoyed tossing Coetzee – nemesis of my tertiary days – onto the junk pile. Conversely, I made sure that PG Wodehouse and Lesego Rampolokeng were completely collected, as well as a full ten-year set of the *Daily Sun*. Fats stacked every issue of *Fast Company* he could find onto his own personal pile, fondly examining covers he remembered from the old days, clucking while he leafed back and forth.

They were fun, our outings. They were also a way to slowly introduce the kids to the idea of our past as a binary opposite of the present. Through the archive we could present the idea of loss. Knowledge loss. History loss. The loss of culture. The loss of family. Loss as the theme of their lives.

My house was overflowing. We needed a new, permanent venue for the library. It made logistical sense to use the KES schoolrooms as the hub for the collection, and so we began at the school library and computer centre and reached out classroom by classroom, altering each as we occupied it with either books or electronic storage sets. We shelved each wall with six rows of pine for the book rooms, and added a central shelving column down the middle. I did my best to structure the stacking of the shelves as the books were carted in from their various sources, but really all I managed was to roughly separate categories. Science and maths on the main building's first floor, arts and history on the second. It was going to take a lifetime – my lifetime, in all probability – to actually sort and index the titles, so to start with I allowed myself simply to achieve effective storage.

The computers and devices were more difficult. We knew where they had come from, but not what they contained. We debated for a good while the feasibility of plugging them in and examining their contents before storing them, but it would have taken too long. So we labelled the boxes and stored them like they were books. The idea was that sufficiently detailed labels would provide a simple filter through which to assess and deal with the contents. The labels included three categories:

Source: CSIR Nanotech Lab
Owner/content-originator designation: Administrator
Estimated intellectual worth: 3

Estimated intellectual worth, or EIW (pronounced 'Eeeyu' by the kids, as if describing a bad smell or taste), became the standard we applied to any particular thing to define its provisional intellectual potential. As the children grew older, they placed a lot of emphasis on big Eeeyu finds, motivated in no small measure by their parents.

'Roy Roy Roy!' Sthembiso, age seven, hurtled into the dining room. 'Eeeyu ten, Eeeyu ten. I've got a Eeeyu ten!' He was clutching a black spiral-bound notebook filled with what looked like mathematical schematics, stumbled upon during one of the increasingly frequent child-led excursions into the mansions of Munro Drive. Babalwa gently took the notebook from an excited dirty paw and flipped through it.

'Well, it looks like a big Eeeyu, doesn't it?' She pulled the boy onto her lap and opened the notebook with the ends of her enveloping arms. 'But our problem is the same as always, nè? We don't really understand what any of the drawings mean. So I would say maybe it's not a ten. Maybe it's a seven?'

'Not eight?'

'You'll have to ask Roy about that, but I would say a seven myself.'

Sthembiso handed me the book, dejected. I was notorious for my low Eeeyu scores. I considered the book quickly as I killed off my scrambled eggs. The schematics and drawings did look to be genuinely mathematical, as opposed to the far more common corporate spider diagrams the kids were often fooled by. The notebook was dirty and clearly well used. The pages had thumb marks on the lower right corner, indicating regular and repeated action. I pictured a generic mad scientist stuck away in the attic of his Houghton house, cooking up an equation he hoped would shake the world. Whoever the person was, he or she was dealing in subjects beyond my realm. Beyond any of our realms, really. I tossed it over to Fats without hope – his maths was some distance off mine, and that was saying something.

'I think, Sthembiso, that you might actually have an eight on your hands, based on the WTF rule. Fats?' I was half serious and half humouring the boy, now squirming profoundly in Babalwa's lap at the thought of an eight, which would have constituted a rare victory.

Fats considered the notebook blankly. 'Passes the WTF test on my side, but you knew that already.' He flipped it over to Gerald, then Beatrice. Javas declined humbly – although superb with the construction of actual things, he held no mathematical pretensions.

We agreed it passed the WTF test – a simple mechanism to separate out material with indecipherable intellectual potential – and thus added an extra point.

'Looks like a lucky day for Sthembiso!' I handed the book back. 'You know what to do, eh? Into the WTF filter for final review before you can claim the eight. Yes?' He ripped the notebook from my hand. 'And you need Andile to sign off before you can claim it.'

'Yes yes yes,' Sthembiso rattled back at me. 'I know where she is. I just saw her. I'll get her now.'

'OK, go then.' I tried to ruffle his hair, but my fingers hit fresh air.

Sthembiso, product of Javas and Babalwa, was my favourite. One isn't supposed to have favourites, but now that I am knocking on the exit gate I can brush past delusions of objectivity. Sthembiso was my favourite – by some distance.

He was an intense little boy, packed with that special sort of life energy that never truly dissipates. He ran everywhere in high-powered circles, was constantly in an advanced state of filthiness and was by far the biggest reader of the bunch. There was no incongruity in his activity levels and his passion for reading. He read as he did everything else, as if the vitally important was at stake, his fingers always jammed into his mouth, his teeth snapping away on his nails, which he chewed and swallowed like food.

His reading was fired by his imagination, which was immense, and which frequently lured him to the classic adventure stories, generally of the British variety. From around the time of his discovery of the little black notebook, his focus morphed to encompass the larger adventure of the world around him. The story of our little group gripped him in a profound way, and once he had wrapped his mind around the notion of a prior world, a prior existence with tools and people and buildings and machinery and businesses, he was unstoppable. He plugged himself into computers with gusto, powered with a manic intensity that could only have come from a righteous genetic combination.

Lebogang, Katlego and Lerato – who all shared Gerald as a father – were, in their early years at least, very different. They were all a similar age, a year or two back from Sthembiso, and they shared a marked disinclination for matters of the extreme imagination. While Sthem was racing up the mountains of his mind, the three of them preferred a more placid and tactile approach. In the sandpit they let the sand dribble through their fingers and actually felt it, grain by grain, moving through. They played softer games, and it would take them several years longer than Sthembiso to fully grasp the nature of the world they had been born into.

As collective parents acting individually, we all tried to influence the mix. For me, that meant archiving. I took whatever opportunities were available to let the kids experience the full extent of the knowledge challenge that lay ahead. In other words, I ratcheted up the Eeeyu rivalry.

Over the years of their births and early childhoods we covered many of Joburg's major knowledge sites. All the universities, most of the Model C schools, all the notable art galleries. Then I pushed further. We cleared out the Sasol research department, all four floors of it, everything in the Innovation Hub complex north of Tshwane, and a lot of machines from the science and maths blocks of Wits, the Tshwane University of Technology and all the others. Of course, almost all of the plastic – the computers and pads and mobiles, etc. – was junk. Without the cloud, all that plastic was now simply boxes.

The futility of collecting the boxes was obvious to us all, and yet we carried on. Partially, I suppose, to create a sense of intellectual hope and purpose, and partially because it was fun for the kids. To hold them back on the great Eeeyu hunt seemed unfair.

Looking back, the most notable Eeeyu mission – and certainly the best documented* – was to the president's office in the Union Buildings. The buildings were everything one would expect, but President Mbangi's office was a shock – pristine and completely empty. Just an oak desk facing two large chairs. A Kentridge print on one wall, a batik wall hanging on the other, and in between the usual framed photographs – Mandela, Mbeki, Merkel, Jonathon, Zuma, Clinton, Obama.

'Why is it empty like this?' Roy Jnr asked.

'They worked mostly from Cape Town,' Beatrice answered smoothly. 'I think this office was just for meetings and things. A place to be when there was business in Tshwane. I'm sure he kept all his stuff in his Cape Town office.' The kids were dubious. Fats chuckled in disbelief. As much as we tried to prevent it, the emptiness of the office quickly became legend. The kids would talk forever more about things being as empty as Mbangi.

---

* While the Eeeyus themselves have been distributed across the archives, details of the Eeeyu philosophy, approach and general story are contained in a small section of the Slovo Library, KES campus. While the section as a whole is small, there is video footage of the more notable excursions.

For years, though, through all of our excursions, I avoided the CSIR. It reminded me too much of Tebza and Lillian. Driving past and seeing the side fence ripped up from where we had cut through all those years ago sent rumblings through my chest.

But eventually the time came. The complex loomed in the distance, an emotional black hole for us all. I gathered a posse of children and headed out to the place where we had allowed ourselves to dream our foolish, ambitious dreams.

The CSIR was an unrecognisable jungle, the incipient growth of our initial experience a long-lost memory. Every movement required calculated physical effort, and the first visit was nothing more than a mission designed to frustrate and annoy a pack of small children. I drove us back home amid snot-laden moans and irritations, Sthembiso leading the choir in intensity and volume. There are few things more frustrating to children than an adult who refuses to enter a jungle.

Javas and I returned the next day, equipped with machetes and chainsaws. I had made a complicated deal with Sthembiso that we would not do any exploring as such. According to the terms of the arrangement, we would restrict our activities to those of an adult, jungle-clearing nature. No exploring would be permitted until such time as children could participate in the Eeeyu potentialities. Sthembiso waved us out of the Houghton driveway with an intense, man-to-man look on his face.

As it turned out, he needn't have worried. It took us three return trips to create reasonable vehicle access. On day two we roped Gerald in, and only then did we make meaningful headway, each of us shirtless and sweating as we hacked away at the enveloping forces.

'Makes you think,' Gerald panted as he powered down his chainsaw. 'All over the world this has happened. Trees and snow and sand—'

'Makes you think what?' Javas asked.

'That soon we'll never be able to go anywhere again without this.' He lifted the chainsaw a few inches from the ground and dropped it again.

Dub Steps

We cleared enough to allow our vehicles in. We went a few steps further in some places, clearing the bush around seating areas in what used to be the park, as well as around the nanotech building, Tebza's place. I told them his full hack story while we were working. It created a fair buzz. Javas was shocked I had kept it to myself for so long. Gerald was stunned that such things existed at all.

'You mean he was doing all that, the running into things, because he thought they could be fake?' Gerald asked. 'Computer corners?'

'I guess it makes more sense if you've actually experienced it. Once you've been inside an interface for a while you can understand better. In my old Mlungu's days, corners crumbled when you even looked. It was a big issue – holding it together.'

'So you actually drank Tebza's piss?' Javas beamed at me, his biceps rippling, waiting to start up the chainsaw.

'I did.'

'Wonderful. You're full of surprises, Roy.' He ripped the cord and laughed as he attacked the trees.

Archiving often seemed futile. It was especially troubling when we were forced into heavy manual labour. I found myself begging for forgiveness at the CSIR. Javas and Gerald shut me down. 'You're like a teenage girl vrying and pleading no all at the same time,' said Javas.

Gerald was more direct. 'If we don't do this, these children we have created will be running around in skins, grunting like baboons.'

Placated, I allowed myself to fall back into the dreamscape. The clearing away, the discovery and the archiving had become a kind of suspended fantasy, a ritualised physical experience that could be followed and repeated infinitely. A way to slow my brain down and keep my body moving.

I dumped my kit at the bakkie when we were finally done and headed for the nanotech building, seeking to retrace Tebza's original steps.

'I think you need to go back for Sthembiso,' Javas said. He was amused by my eagerness. 'He'll never forgive you if you go in without him.'

Sthembiso was ready and waiting, fourth day in a row. With him were Lydia, English, Roy Jnr and Thabang. They were playing some kind of bastardised version of hopscotch at the bottom of the driveway, which Sthembiso killed as I drove in, scuffing through the chalk with his bare heel while English was in mid-jump. She launched the beginnings of a tantrum, which he diffused with an easy arm around her shoulder and a word in her little ear.

Lydia and Thabang and Roy Jnr fell into the back of the bakkie, Sthembiso and English took the prime spots up front, with me – a front seat obviously the prize with which Sthembiso had quelled English's tears.

'So, my dear.' I took her four-year-old hand in mine. 'Are you feeling all Eeeyuie?' I stretched the word and pulled a face at the end, by which time all of us were grimacing and squealing. She squeezed my index finger, wrapping her whole hand around it tightly, and beamed up at me silently.

'The CSIR,' Sthembiso stated authoritatively. 'It doesn't get much better than that, eh Roy?'

'Well, you never know. Eeeyus hang out in some very strange places. You can never really tell, can you?'

'But it's true, isn't it?' he insisted. 'The CSIR is where they did all the science. The big things.'

'Well, it's one of the places. But the problem is the computers, nè? Much harder to find an Eeeyu in a computer than in a book. And the CSIR people used a lot of computers. In fact, they used computers way more than books. So there's a chance you could be disappointed – we might only get back with a bakkie full of plastic.'

'Some of the plastic might be tens.'

'Yes, it might. You never know.'

English clutched her torn, dog-eared copy of *Animal Farm* under her elbow. It was an illustrated paperback version. The cover line drawings of Snowball and Napoleon had caught her attention before she was even three years old, reinforcing her already deep fascination with the idea of a pig. The book was always with her, even in her adult years. She thumbed it and pawed it and read it repeatedly, all through her life, although never, it seemed to me, in the literal or political sense, but rather as a general evocation of porcine power and import.

She gripped my finger tighter with her spare hand and beamed harder. Her smile was a lighthouse in the night. In fact, as she grew older the grin often replaced language altogether. For reasons well beyond her control or ken, it was as if she lived only to deny what we had bestowed on her.

Most of the kids' names had our explicit ambitions and hopes threaded through them. Lerato was named after we were all involved in a protracted debate about the meaning of love. Elizabeth and English – both my kids – were named in direct, ironic reference to the now significantly reduced power of my British ancestry. We spent many consecutive nights drinking (well, pouring drinks, in my case) and discussing the extreme power of being British.

'Genetically, you are plugged straight into money and power,' said Beatrice. 'They flow through your blood. The need to organise and have systems. To generate money. To pack it away in assets for your spawn. You can't teach that stuff.' She gripped Gerald's knee as she spoke, her hand sliding up his thigh and then back down again, but the twinkle in her eye was mostly for me, I was sure.

'True,' Gerald added. 'Actually true. We are born in place. If you measure by money and houses, then you want to be British. If you're born Pedi, all you get is non-stop relatives and you can't make eye contact with mlungus.'

'The English language. Greatest skill you could ever have in sub-Saharan Africa,' Javas said, tipping a bottle of home-made beer in our direction. 'The rest you can fake, but not the English. I was going to call my firstborn that. English.'

'Get the fuck outta here,' I said.

'For real. English. A complete statement of power.'

'I like it,' said Fats, nudging Babalwa with his elbow. 'Eh, babe? English. That's a power name.'

Babalwa wriggled defensively. 'Hai. You can't call someone English.'

'Course you can. I knew a girl called Pain.'

Andile also warmed to the idea. 'The child would be all power,' she said. 'But if we do it, we need to call one of the others French.'

The idea stayed with me, with us, and when Andile and I produced our second we decided, by mutual agreement, to call her English.

And, of course, she turned out to be completely self-contained, inwardly focused and pathologically silent. English spoke only when speech was functionally required. Words were irrelevant to her. Not that the child was mute or anything. When it mattered, her tongue was perfectly at home in her mouth. When we were parking in front of the nanotech building, for example, she gave Sthembiso a calculated lecture.

'You must be happy, Sthembiso,' she said, with reference to the newly cleared CSIR complex. 'They made it into a playground just for you.'

'Not just for him, English,' I said as I led her by the finger to the front door of the nanotech building. We were following Sthembiso, who was already clambering through the hole in the fence Tebza had smashed years ago. 'It's for us too. This has always been one of my favourite places.'

'Why, Roy?'

'It reminds me of Uncle Tebza, whom you never met, but who was a wonderful, kind man who made my life a lot better when everyone disappeared.'

'Were there lots of people?'

'More than you can imagine, my dear.' I allowed myself to get a little wistful. I stopped us at the door, knelt on one knee and pulled my daughter onto the other. I held her tight. 'All these buildings were filled with people, marching up and down with their papers and their printouts, walking to their computers—'

'To their Eeeyus!' She beamed up at me.

'Exactly. To their Eeeyus. And outside the gate the roads were filled with cars, people in their cars going places—'

'Where?'

'To their homes and families. To their work. To go shopping, that sort of thing.'

'What's shopping?'

'Eish.' The question was almost unanswerable. 'There was this thing called money that was very, very important.' Her eyes drilled into me, completely focused. 'People used to swap it for things. So, if you had some money, you would give it to me and then I would give you a pair of shoes.' She kept staring, and frowned. 'And then I would use the money to give to someone else when I needed something, like food.'

English wriggled free, suddenly bored. 'Inside!' She pointed in Sthembiso's direction. 'Let's go!'

I obeyed, allowing her to scramble through the jagged hole after Lydia and Thabang while I used the door, remembering in the midst of many retrospective flashes how we had broken open the lock. English ran after the others into the darkness of the corridor. I let them go, then panicked and ran after, just in case.

The buildings were exactly as we had left them. I could see the remnants of our activities scattered through the building; the chaos Tebza had caused as he ripped up the labs looking for a virtual explanation, or at least a nano sieve. Science equipment on the floor. Drawers pulled out, hanging awkwardly still, waiting.

Once I had adjusted to the darkness of the building, I let the kids go free to try to find Sthembiso, whom I could only catch flashes of as he hurtled between meeting rooms, laboratories and offices. English tried hard to catch him initially, but was unable to hold the pace and settled instead into her own exploratory rhythm. Roy Jnr disappeared, and Lydia and Thabang drifted through holding hands, unsure now why they were in this place and what the point was supposed to be. English's attention was caught not by the Eeeyus, but by the photographs on the desks. Every now and again she would trot back to me clasping a framed family shot. Her attention was caught specifically by families featuring two or more young girls. 'Look, Roy,' she said, handing me a cheap fake-wood Clicks frame outlining a family of three girls and mom and dad, all unfortunately brushed with freckles and a disconcerting lack of facial proportion.

'Are they ugly?' she asked.

'There used to be all sorts of people, angel,' I tried to explain. 'There were people who were good to look at and then there were others who weren't as fortunate.'

'Not fair.' She turned the frame over a few times while absorbing the implications of randomly assigned ugly genes.

As we began formalising school for the kids – each of us adults doing our best to cover not only subjects we knew a little about, but also those that were totally alien to us, like maths and science – we repeatedly ran up against the deeper challenge of context. Every tiny step we took towards formal numeracy and literacy had to be wrapped in a massive balloon of context – facts about the world that were innate to us adults and completely alien to the kids. Ugliness. War. Sport. Crowds. Television. Strangers. Grandparents.

The list was an endlessly unravelling ball of string. Eventually contextual frustration led us to try to formalise a central narrative that could be referred to by all. We destroyed the walls between a string of nine ground-floor St John's classrooms and started painting the story of man from beginning to end – with the story of us adult individuals, each of the parents, foregrounded for ease of telling. In some ways our treatment was like the Afrikaner marble relief at the Voortrekker Monument, but with a more clearly demonstrable commitment to fact. Or at least that's what we told ourselves.

We, the parents and adults, took up the positions of the dramatic, guarding generals. Babalwa was the metaphorical pioneer vrou with the kids protected under her iron skirts.

'We gonna fuck these kids up proper,' said Andile as we painted the first blocks of the story into place.

She was right. As good as our ground-floor narrative was, it could never cope with the subtlety of real life – with the raw inquisitiveness of a five-year-old yet to encounter true ugliness.

'The world was never fair, angel. It is never fair.' I ruffled English's head as I settled into a generic, cover-all parental explanation.

'Why?'

'That is one of the great mysteries of being human,' I said, falling even further back, inches away from 'Only God can tell us that'.

She shrugged and returned the photograph to its desk.

Meanwhile, Sthembiso had wound himself into a considerable state, my warnings over how elusive the Eeeyus might prove to be long forgotten. 'There's nothing!' he spat at me after two hours of full-throttle exertion. 'Nothing! Just PCs!'

'Well, in these types of places we might need to look a little bit differently,' I told him. 'You're not going to find a lot of books here, as I said. But have you looked properly at all the files and folders?' He shrugged, angry and sulking. Files and folders were not the stuff he was used to.

I tried again. 'OK, how about we come back tomorrow – it's a Sunday after all – and I'll look with you. I bet we find at least two eights.'

Sthembiso eyed me suspiciously. The heels of his little feet pushed angrily against each other. 'And if we don't?'

'Well ...' I stalled, unable to think of a reasonable safeguard able to protect us both.

'Then pancakes, three weekends in a row,' he said, jumping slyly into a new negotiation. I conceded warily, worrying what kind of precedent I was setting. I was pretty sure we'd find something of worth if the two of us looked together, however. And besides, I told myself, it was starting to feel like time the kids learned to cook properly, not just wash and pack. Pancakes could be a reasonable introduction, regardless of who won or lost.

I sent Sthembiso off to find English and Roy Jnr. Thabang and Lydia were already hanging off my legs and whining. We had only been in the complex a few hours, but it had been a long, emotional stretch. Memories of Tebza mingled with the smell of rot. I felt despondent.

The kids piled into the bakkie arguing about whether ugliness could be applied via a punch, Sthembiso holding his fist threateningly above Lydia's shoulder. The argument turned nasty, and inevitably tracked from the idea of ugliness to the pigs, as all of the kids' conflicts seemed to at this stage.

We had set up a complicated set of rules concerning our interactions with the pigs, who were growing their very own community on the outskirts of ours. We kept a healthy distance most of the time, and it was easy enough to impress on the kids the need to stay away from the adults. At three-hundred-plus kilos and with long, sinister snouts and rough boar hair, they were hardly enticing to small children. Piglets, however, were another story. Whenever the piglets emerged they sparked an extended series of debates and discussions around the pig rules. English was the cause of most the anxiety – she fell head over heels for the babies and was caught on more than one occasion sneaking a wet little snout into the house to hide under her bed. Fats was hell-bent on creating the 'climate of fear' necessary to keep the pigs and kids apart, and issued a steady stream of anti-pig propaganda: little titbits about how free pigs were as mean as they were smart, and so on. Sthembiso responded to the hype, and did his best to keep the pig border patrolled at all times. English, on the other hand, saw Fats's talk for exactly what it was, and eventually named her favourite of the new litter Snowball, Orwell's dirty paperback – stripped of all irony – the inspiration. Sthembiso had got wind of the naming and was threatening legal action – and, of course, communicating the severity of it all with his ever-hovering fist.

I should have stopped him but I didn't have the energy, and then, as we exited the main gate, my attention was taken with what I could have sworn was a black, sandalled foot pulled smartly back from the undergrowth.

* * *

There had been many sightings. It was a recurring theme for us all. In the first few years we chased them down with enthusiasm and determined energy, the weight of probability driving us to lengths we later just gave up on. With each failed chase, the rate of entropy increased until we no longer considered the possibility of anyone else being alive outside our ridiculous little group.

Still, the image of the foot stayed with me. What kind of displacement of imagination and vision could have occurred to deliver unto my eyes a black, sandalled foot? I hadn't, as far as I was aware, been thinking of anything much. Tebza, I guess, had held the majority of my attention. Was it possible that drifting thoughts of my old friend somehow could have fired up my synapses to produce a foot being swiftly withdrawn into the undergrowth? I doubted it. We had been on so many ill-fated, ill-advised and futile discovery missions it seemed naive and more than a little bit wilful to now set off on another one. In fact, the event was so odd and fleeting I didn't even consider trying to articulate it to any of the others. Instead, I painted it. Or rather, a series of interpretations. The foot extended fully out of the undergrowth. The foot represented only by a few toes. The bushes without a foot. The bushes with just the smallest hint of foot, a toe observable only to one who knew that the form of a foot was in there somewhere.

They were bad pictures. I was still some distance from being a reliably decent artist, and the foot attempts cruelly revealed my technical failings. Either it was completely wrong – not like any foot I had ever seen – or subtly but crucially misshapen. A foot somehow detached from its body, from the vital context that would give it its footness.

Eventually I resorted to lazy sketches of Beatrice in her wrap on the couch.

Beatrice the sexual libertine.

Beatrice the demigoddess, all fingers reaching and eyes blazing.

The sketches of her weren't very good either, but they stopped me thinking about the foot.

After six or seven Beatrice sketches, I stopped and forced myself to stare out over the night-time Jozi forest. I imagined small armies taking shape, armies of little people with hairy black feet in sandals, like the old Hobbit stories. I focused my ears on the sound of the bats pinging between the trees. I imagined armies of trees, as in the stories of my childhood, big trees and small trees, oaks and acorns and pines, all rising up to march, to liberate, to change.

I imagined I could hear the first rustles of rebellion, the quiet but clear barking of the leaders, the assenting murmur of the troops as the forest picked up its long-dropped hemline and marched.

Marched up to me, over and through our little complex, and on, southward, to the sea, to the end.

The next day I feigned illness, tiredness, fatigue and palmed the kids off on Beatrice and Gerald for the return CSIR venture.

'When last did you think you saw another person?' I asked Fats in the kitchen that afternoon as we baked. It was his turn on the roster but I was helping out. Solo duty could get depressing.

'Like, for real or just wishing?'

'For real – an honest-to-God what-the-fuck-was-that.'

Fats lifted his dough and kneaded it high in the air, stretching it out parallel to the countertop and then pushing it back into a lump. 'Must be a while now. Maybe a year. Thought I was being tracked around the school. Kept on seeing shadows vanishing around the corners.'

'You chase them down?'

'Of course,' he chuckled. 'Gotta try, nè? Why? You see one lately?'

'Ja, the other day at the CSIR. Thought I saw a foot in the bush. A foot in a sandal being drawn back.'

'Tricks of our minds. Don't think it will ever really stop. It's the mirage thing, like in the desert.' He tossed the dough lump into the air and let it fall dramatically onto the counter in an explosion of flour.

We baked the flat breads – twelve in total – and chatted on, the withdrawn foot drifting slowly into the conversational past. In between thinking of the foot I had flashback visions of Fats as he was when he first found us, all puffed out and aggressive, full of red ink, maps and grand plans. Clothing crisp and calculated, words even more so. Now, he was a portly guy who baked happily and raised his kids. Only very occasionally would the project manager be let loose, and then only as a reaction to genuine emotional stress. Life with Babalwa was clearly benefiting him. I thought too, suddenly, uncomfortably, of the rape accusation. Something no one had spoken about for a long time.

Fats kept looking into the oven, protecting the first batch of flat breads as if they were meant to rise. Between checks on the bread, he scuttled from fridge to countertop with his whisk, on a mayonnaise mission.

Babalwa arrived and hugged her man from behind.

'Roy saw a foot,' Fats told her. 'At the CSIR.'

Babalwa peered at me with the halves of her eyes that could get over his shoulder. 'Just a foot?'

'Just a foot,' I said. 'I didn't stop. Had kids with me.'

'What kind of foot?'

'A black foot.'

'Like black as in the colour black, or black as in the foot of a black man?'

'Like the foot of a black man. Well, the foot of a non-white man. Ha ha.'

'We should go back and check it out. You never know.' Babalwa remained latched onto Fats's back, her cheek buried against his shoulder blade as if she was trying to nap.

'Nah,' Fats said. He shook her off and trotted back to the oven. 'I really don't think it could be anything. There's no way anyone would be hiding at the CSIR. Maybe lost at the CSIR, but not hiding. They would have jumped straight out.'

'Still ...'

Fats removed his first breads, swearing at the burns on his hand. 'You should use the cows, baby,' Babalwa chided him, referring to the cow oven gloves.

'Real men don't use cows,' he said, loading up the second round.

She slapped a hand at him, but missed. 'You should check it out again, Roy, just in case,' she said as she headed out the door. 'Will someone holler when there's food?'

So I went back.

There was nothing to see. No feet and no people, just a quiet, recently hacked forest and some buildings that used to house important things. I picked out my favourite bench, in the middle of the thick park area to the right of the complex entrance. I had cleared the path to the bench purposefully, and now I spent a good deal of time, a few mornings in a row in fact, sitting on my seat, nibbling on flat bread or strips of biltong. I was, truth be told, beginning to enjoy the CSIR forest. It had that stark, echoing atmosphere of the Lowveld about it. A silence filled with movement. The rub of insects against trees. Birds flapping. Suggestions of song bubbling out into the air, then sinking back again. It was bush quiet. It felt like camping.

The others questioned me when I returned home after the first few visits, and then let the subject go.

We had all had our moments, and we all chased them in our own private ways. After day three there was a polite, accommodating absence of interest.

I kept going back, though, not so much to look for the foot, but to rest. To be alone with myself and to consider the air as I breathed it in and out. To empty my mind and my heart. To exhale.

Eventually, he came shuffling down the hill from the general direction of the nanotech centre.

An elderly black man in a blue overall.

A caretaker.

The caretaker.

He drifted all the way down with his head slightly bowed. I waited for him, and when he got close and made to sit next to me, I said, 'Sawubona, Madala' – the only thing I could think of.

'Madala. I like that,' he said, lowering himself carefully onto the bench next to me. 'Sawubona, indoda.' As he gave this formal reply, he dipped his head to support the greeting, as if he was Japanese, or from deep Limpopo. 'It is a beautiful day, is it not?' He spoke ever so slowly. His accent was neutral. His blue overall was new and clean. There were no stains or marks on it at all.

Chapter 47

A story and a lie

I introduced myself. He brushed my efforts off, amused by the fact that my name was Roy. When I asked for his, he said, 'Madala. Just call me Madala.'

'Really? Madala is your actual name? That's pretty unusual, nè? Where you from?'

'Oh, around here,' he glanced around.

'Pitoli?'

'Ja, sho.' He mimicked me, picking up my crassly formed white-boy tsotsitaal inflections and sending them right back.

I let it lie.

The encounters I had had with survivors thus far involved a base, guttural kind of coming together. Hugs and back slaps. Tears and laughter. Kisses. Amazement. Energy. I thought most of all of the way Babalwa and I had met – the sheer force of our troublesome fuck. But none of that here. Madala wasn't exuding anything beyond the appearance of perpetual yet partial amusement.

I scuffed the dirt with my toe. 'It's a beautiful place, this. You been coming here often?'

'Indeed. Lovely.' He exhaled with evident satisfaction. 'So full of life. A wonderful mix of life forms actually. That's what I like most about it.'

'So what's your story?' I was impatient. 'Where were you when it happened? Have you been here all these years? Have you watched us every time we've been here?'

He reached down carefully, like he was managing his body with caution, and plucked a blade of grass. He put it between his teeth and leaned back on his hands, both palms flat on the bench, fingers pointing backward.

'Roy, you're going to have to trust me. I have a lot to tell you, but before I do I need you to feel me. I mean that literally and metaphorically. You have to feel my presence and realise through it—'

'Through your presence?'

'Yes, through my presence.' He frowned at the interruption. 'Realise through it, my presence, that you are going to go – for a good while – on a solo journey. You can't tell your friends about this. Not now, and not for a very long time.'

'Why?'

He poked a sandalled right foot into the air, parallel to the ground.

'Are you from another planet?'

He put his foot down. 'No. I am from this planet. Whatever that means.'

'Are you human?'

'My molecular make-up is exactly the same as yours.'

'So you're human.'

'Not really. But Roy, I must tell you.' He took my hand in his. His skin was hard and leathery and hot. 'You're going to have to leave much behind. Do you think you can do that?'

'If I had any fucking clue what you were talking about, I could answer that.'

'They'll see what you show them, Roy. No more, no less.'

'And you want me to show them what, exactly?'

'Love. A lot of love.'

'Jesus, you sound like Oprah.'

He sent me home. 'When will I see you again?' I asked, like we were new lovers.

'When the time is right. First you need to be in the right place mentally.'

'Now you sound like a cricket coach.'

He waved me to my car. I tried to watch him recede in the rear-view mirror, but in the time it took me to put the key in the ignition and turn it, he had disappeared.

As I pulled into my driveway, Sthembiso stormed across, demanding details of my Eeeyu count. I fobbed him off and headed straight inside with promises of another trip for all of us soon. Very, very soon.

I painted and drew. Black, sandalled feet. A small old man in a blue overall. Grey hair. Hands and arms and fingers and lips. Green and orange and yellow. I couldn't come close to capturing what I had seen and I was disappointed with the regression in my art, which now looked like the work of a ten-year-old.

I dumped the paints and resorted to sketching, but that too was a failure. It was as if somehow I had thoughtlessly misplaced all the skills I had so recently developed. I put the sketch pad down and stared out again over the black night.

Again I started seeing shapes and forms. Humans moving, buildings filled with people. Malls and parking garages and petrol pumps. The bats flitted between the trees, adding a jerky, broken soundtrack to my imaginings. I found myself playing with various scenarios, adding them up and then subtracting again, toying with each of his words to see if and where it would fit.

'Imagine a pile of sand, Roy,' he had said. 'Imagine you needed to get that pile really high – really, really high. To do it, you have to collapse what you have. Expand the foundation. Build again.'

'Who's building? You? Me?'

He peered at me, sceptical. 'Movies. Please. You need to watch movies. Think about it.'

'For real? Movies?'

'Try *I, Robot*.'

There was a light knock on the door. Beatrice. I knew her triple rap well.

'You hiding for a specific reason, Roy? Or you just got the glumps?' She leaned on the inside of the front door, hips beckoning. But this was neither the time nor the place – she was on a family mission.

'Sthembiso said you were mean to him—'

'Ag, I'm fine. Sorry. Please tell him sorry. I'll tell him sorry. When I see him. Just one of those days, you know?'

Beatrice wrinkled the corners of her eyes in an approximation of empathy, but beneath lay confusion. It had been some time since any of us had wigged out. We also generally ate together as a group. No one bailed out of family supper without reason. The kids noticed such things, in detail, which made a quiet absence doubly difficult to pull off.

'Just tell them I got too much sun and I need to chill out.'

'And what should I tell myself?' She remained fixed to the door frame, left hip high.

'That Roy is taking a break. For his own reasons, which may or may not be revealed in good time.'

'OK, fair enough, I suppose.' Beatrice detached from the door frame. 'Look after yourself, ja?'

I gave her departing ass a fake smile.

I pulled it straight the next morning. Any more reclusive behaviour would have brought the depression police out in full force. It was understood, without it ever having to be verbalised, that Roy was especially vulnerable. Roy only had one pillow, with a single dent in it. They watched me carefully.

I emerged full of the usual. I swung the kids by the arms and made sure I was at school around the right time. I made full eye contact with Sthembiso as I apologised, and I gave Beatrice a small hug and Gerald the right kind of nod and we were back on the level.

The level was everything to everyone.

We needed that level more than we needed each other.

I spent the next four days purposefully wrapped up in life. Some weeks were heavier than others and this was, fortunately, a particularly busy one. It was my school week with the older kids – Roy Jnr, Thabang, Sihle and Sthembiso.

I wrote the word DENOUEMENT in clumsy letters on the blackboard. I stepped back and let the kids consider it.

'It's pronounced DAY-nu-mow,' I explained. 'It's a word they used to teach us at university, but I thought I would get it in earlier. The denouement is that moment in a story when everything becomes clear. When all the bits and pieces start to make sense. So, forget the word and how to spell it and stuff like that. Who can give me a simple example of when a story suddenly makes sense? Think of any story you like – a fairy tale, a story someone here has told you or something from your own life.'

Scrunched foreheads. Full focus. A slow arm raise from Thabang. 'Like, if something happened that would explain to us what happened. Why there are no people left. That would be a day-nu ... day-nu ...'

'Denouement. Exactly. That would be a denouement for all of us. In our own lives. Especially the adults. Nice, Thabang. Maybe let's try a made-up story. Anyone with a made-up story?'

More blank faces.

'How about ... how about ...' I racked my brain for something other than the subject I couldn't shake off, and that Thabang had so quickly elucidated. In the back of my mind, questions grew around why I was trying to teach them a high-school-level literary concept.

Roy Jnr had his hand in the air, three-quarters raised. 'Can it be when people get punished?'

'It can. Tell me more.'

'Like in 'The Pied Piper'. When the town people lose the children.'

'Yes, that's right. In any fairy tale, there's that moment at the end when the bad person gets what they deserve, nè?'

The heads bobbed along, cautiously, with me.

'Well, that moment always happens because something in the story takes place that teaches them the lesson they need to learn. That moment in the story that makes everything clear – that's the denouement ...'

Blank.

'... and the reason I want you to know about the denouement at this young age is' – I scraped around for a rational explanation – 'because stories are so important in our lives. We live by stories, don't we?'

I wound away from the subject, hoping the kids would have the energy to pick up a few educational scraps from the mess.

Andrew Miller

'Roy?' Roy Jnr had his hand all the way up.
'Yes?'
'What's the difference between a story and a lie?'

Chapter 48
Fuck fuck fuck

I went back on many occasions. With the kids and by myself. I sat in that same seat and waited. Initially expectantly, then increasingly just as one of those things in life that become habit. The kids helped with the masquerade – we cleaned out much of the CSIR within six months.

'Broe, it's too much. You have to filter the shit. You can't just dump every piece of plastic you find here,' Fats said, puffed out with anxiety.

I apologised. Begged and joked a little. Masked the paranoia that someone would eventually dig into the source of my CSIR obsession.

True to my word, however, I did make a serious effort to filter. I sat for weeks dumping folders across to the library server, one by one. Most of it was junk – surprising proportions, in fact, were just office rubbish. Project reports, letters and process documents. Every now and then I stumbled onto a troop of Eeeyus. I was diligent about apportioning each one to the relevant child, the discoverer of the box. But as the weeks, and then the months, went by, the kids' interest faded. Eventually their attention moved to other, more rewarding things.

I changed my routine. Explored new running routes. I began at the CSIR and headed out on the concrete highway, the N1. It was thrilling, running alone in this ocean. Different in every way to running down a street or through a suburb. The highway challenged me, urged me to keep going, north to Cairo. As I ran I imagined myself carrying on, never turning back. It was a satisfying thought – going face to face with my own life and death, step by yellow step.

For now, though, I made sure I returned, punishing myself by stretching the distance a little further each time until I was completing twenty-, then twenty-five-, then thirty-kilometre stretches. I had become, in my own plodding way, an athlete.

* * *

I put everything into the last leg. Everything. All the frustration of nearly a year of waiting. My general rage, always building and growing. My ambition for something better. My impatience, my complete and utter impatience with the situation. I packed them all into that final, back-breaking three-kilometre sprint.

'Not bad, not bad.' Madala beamed at me as I burst into view. He was waiting on the bench.

Inevitably, beneath my anger and exhaustion was excitement. Here, finally, was the denouement. My denouement. I wasn't mad. I hadn't imagined.

We sat silent for a good while, my shattered breathing the only sound, a steady, rasping beat. I would not, I promised myself, come off all eager. As desperate as I was to talk to him, I knew I would appear like a pigeon in heat. We were courting. Or rather, I was chasing. Whatever. The metaphors rumbled broken through my mind.

I breathed.

We sat.

My lungs calmed, while the sound of the birds grew up around us, a beautiful, complex net of trills and shrills, layers and layers of harmonies and evasive melodies.

At the end of it all. After hours and hours of words and explanations, I left, Madala calling behind me, urging me not to talk. Not now. The time ... wrong. The moment ... not.

Fuck fuck fuck, I chanted all the way home. I was desperate to see the family. My family. I wanted the kids around me, and Fats. I needed to see Fats. Speak to him. Watch him smile his gruff, all-knowing smile and hear him say something predictable yet profound. Javas and Andile. My children. I needed the brood. And, I needed them to know what I knew. I was going to tell them all and Madala be dammed.

My family was there. The kitchen buzzing with children and cooking, words flying like millions of small missiles through the heart of us. Nhlanhla jumped into my arms yelling my name and Motse tried to follow him, nearly sending us toppling into Beatrice's salad. I was scolded for being late by every adult, and then by every child. 'You couldn't have been running for six hours, Roy,' Babalwa chided. 'Please tell me you weren't running for six hours. You're going to kill yourself.'

'Nah, I ran for a few and then I spent the rest talking to an alien.'

English slapped Jacob's face with a lettuce leaf. Lerato burst into tears at the shock of it and then Javas was singing. He started as an elephant and transitioned into a smooth tiger baritone, and in a few seconds he had everyone accompanying him on our favourite adaptation of an old children's story, which came to a climax with him leading the entire troupe of kids out the back door into the evening light, like the Pied Piper, with two of them on his back and the rest singing and clapping in a row behind.

'Eish, Roy, talking to aliens?' Fats slapped a few steaks around to tenderise them. 'People are going to start talking about you.'

'Nothing wrong with aliens.' I laughed and let go.

There would be no way to tell my story without changing everything.

And we had all been changed enough already.

Chapter 49
Rumpelstiltskin

So let me tell you about old age. About wisdom. Stories. Memory.

It's bullshit.

There is only death.

The closer it comes, the louder the knock, the more you know that you were helpless all along. Really, you never knew. Even the things so certain. The hard facts. The basics.

Now you look back and there is nothing to hold. Your grip is a joke. All you have is the haze, a feeling that you were there, somewhere. But it's far, far away, that place. You are a child once more, excited by the feeling, unable to hold the logic, blinded by the idea of memories.

So, what is true? What is story? What is my life?

All I have is what I can say, and I could say anything. I could say Flash Robinson or Rumpelstiltskin or George Bush and there is nothing you can do other than to smile and hold my hand and tell me yes, yes, Roy, Rumpelstiltskin.

Rumpelstiltskin.

Death.

Waiting for me.

So you can tour the expo and read our lives and gaze at the statue that is me, Roy Fotheringham, the one of the nine who etc., etc.,

blah blah, but that doesn't mean you will ever truly know, ever truly see, this little old half-toothed man who, let's be honest, can barely see himself. Life is not a story. Life is not if then, then that, then this. Life is lost memories, broken hearts, ideas of dreams, dreams of dreaming, losses and gains and hopes and hard-ons and rapes and babies and tears; we soak in tears.
   Life is loss. The loss of everything.
   Memory, of course, but worse than that, the loss of self. Of you.
   Eventually, you will not be able to hold on.
   It will be over.

All you will have as you leave is the idea, the thin whisper in your heart that this was real, that you were here. That the bird sang. And that it was beautiful.

Why me?

Why you?

Who are you anyway? Why are you reading this? From whence did you come and what do you hope to gain from this page?

I can't answer. I can't even imagine.

I can only hope you exist. That this is seen, and read, just once.
   That would mean something.
   Why?
   I have no idea. It just feels like it would.

Chapter 50

Straight entertainment

It was the smell of the kids that finally decided me.

In my pre-life I always found the smell of children disturbing. Offensive even, at times. All pink and potential. Unfettered. Raw meat.

But as they grew our kids developed their own particular reek, and to me it was, ultimately, and strangely, the reek of potential. Of some kind of happiness. Of my own happiness.

We had grown our family. We were all proud of this, our one true innovation in response to our truest crisis. We were growing the best possible genetic base for the future. We had a new start.

The smell of the kids in their fast-growing innocent pinkness encapsulated the success. Revealing my interactions with Madala, revealing and then proving the truth of them, would push a blade through the heart of it. Right through the pink.

So I kept it to myself.

But I was confused. So much so that I stopped going to the CSIR, as I was sure Madala expected me to. Instead I threw myself into the farm, which held challenges enough to occupy my frontal cortex.

I had always fulfilled my farm duties, but I was never what one would call a driving force. My sole strength was as the library guy, the archivist. Since Madala, however, the idea of knowledge itself, previously so preciously abstract, was now inevitably bound to him, and he, in turn, led only to more confusion.

Continually listless, seeking some kind of philosophical palliative, I fell onto the idea of bringing Javas's giants over to the farm. Once it had occurred to me I was unable to push it back. We needed, I decided, a defining aesthetic for the community. There could be nothing better, nor more symbolic, than the giants.

Javas was initially put off by the effort involved, but I stuck to it, forcing him, week on week, month on month, to concede one piece at a time, until we had fourteen of the statues scattered across the perimeter of the complex, guarding key points with their scale and implied force. Once they were in place no one complained, least of all Javas. It was, all of a sudden, impossible to imagine the farm without them. The giants gave us an immediate character – something all of our own that was defining and distinct. Something from the past but also uniquely from our own time, the time after. The giants were our outer defence personified. In their raised arms and legs, in their pained, ambitious faces, in their hopeless pressing for movement, they gave us a new identity. And Javas began building anew, this time shaping his creatures to fit the purpose and form of their function. Glasses for the library giant, thick Wellington boots for the guardian of the crops.

I thought of Tebza. His hack craziness seemed a lot less bizarre now than it had while he was alive. Madala had extended the range of possibilities and probabilities. If I was going to accept Madala, I was forced to give equal weight to Tebza's idea that we had been quietly slipped into an interface. That we were indeed trapped in an experiment or a trick.

The two ideas were binary poles – the one gave credence to the other. Together, they inflated a bubble of possibilities. But how would we ever know? Were we really capable of figuring out what type of maze we were in?

I started charging corners again – partially because it felt good to remember Tebza, to physically acknowledge his legacy, and partially because I couldn't shake the sense that he was somehow right. My heart was in it: each charge felt like an opportunity. But as emotionally right as it felt, charging corners wasn't going to do any more than bruise my shoulder, as Tebza had already conclusively proved. Still, I lowered and charged. Lowered and charged. Sometimes the heart demands.

I also paid attention to the small details. I looked as deep as I could into the orange of the setting sun. I tasted things with a triple slap of the tongue. I hunted for any kind of pixelation, visual, auditory or otherwise. I needed a crack within a crack. The tiniest hint of fissure, a fold within a fold, within an opening.

But there was nothing.

One afternoon the twins found me perched on Julius's foot at the top entrance to Munro Drive, dabbing my tongue-wet finger onto his rusted toe and tasting it.

'He won't bite you, Roy. Give him a hug. Go all the way,' Andile urged, sinking into a cross-legged position on the grass.

'You were right, Roy, nè?' Javas joined me at Julius's feet. 'They add so much. Everyone says so. It's good to have them here, for me too. It's like they've finally come home.'

'Soul,' I said. 'They give the place soul. Like we're real people living here. People reaching for things.'

Andile leaned back on her hands and listened as the conversation developed. This was always her way – she let it roll and roll and then, when most of the energy was released, she would pick a thread and pull.

'When they dig us up,' she interjected a few minutes later, while Javas and I were discussing his next piece, currently still a sketch, 'they'll think we had some kind of weird civilisation going. I can see them fencing it off and dusting with their little brushes to show what we did and why we did it. They will think these were our gods.'

'They might be right,' I said. 'I'm not sure they aren't right already. I talk to them all the time, even from the distance of my house. I see them on the horizon and I talk to them. I greet them in the morning. I tell them my worries. I say good morning … I pray …'

'You and the kids,' she added. 'Their stories have changed. They're bigger – the stories. What happens is bigger. Their events. More people hurt. More people saved. Weird.'

'Epic,' said Javas.

'Exactly,' I said. 'Epic. They bring scale. Emotional scale. The epic.'

'Ag fok, you sound like my art tutor.' Andile tugged us quietly back. 'It's true though. I wonder if it will change the way the kids grow.'

'No doubt it will change what they dream about,' Javas said, patting Julius's big toe. 'And if the scale of your dreams grows as a child, doesn't matter for what reason, your life will grow like that too.'

Dreams aside, the kids' world was shrinking fast. By the time the oldest were old enough to look back, they were viewing an opaque set of ideas and buildings and forms. The skylines spoke of another world, rich in temples and glass, but it was exceptionally challenging for them to gain even a tourist's view of what that world had actually contained.

After the suburbs had grown dense to the point of impenetrability, mother earth launched a steady push – immense by all objective measures – across the concrete. Stretching in ultra slowmo, oceans of tar and commerce and past life were breached, millimetre by millimetre. We grew so used to the invisible speed of it that we forgot it, for years at a time in some cases. And then we remembered.

* * *

'Roy.' Sthembiso arrived with a fully loaded cannon. I could tell by the calculated lilt of his voice, a soft, pretend-innocuous winding up to something quite large.

'Rastafari,' I replied.

He shook his head angrily. 'Roy,' he insisted again, this time with a slight whine.

'Yes, my son. Hit me. What wilst thou know?' We were sitting on my balcony at sunset. I was sketching another horizon; he was watching me do it, paying careful attention to my treatment of the top of the Northcliff Dome.

'What's in the Dome?' A leading question. The contents of the Dome had been covered many times previously.

'When it happened they were having a car show. So there are a lot of cars in the Dome now. But they would change what was in it according to what they needed. It wasn't always cars.'

'What else?'

'Eish. Anything really. Hip-hop shows. Gardening shows. Baby shows. Every time it was different.'

'What was a show?'

'Eeeish.' I put my brush down. 'I guess more than anything it was a gathering of people. A lot of people would come together in a space – like the Dome – and then they would share everything they knew about a subject. So, if the subject was babies, for example, then anyone doing anything involving babies would present their activities at the Dome, and then all the other people interested in babies, people about to have a baby, maybe' – I laughed as Sthembiso winced at the rhyme – 'would go to the show and look at what the others were presenting and maybe discuss things about babies. Possibly they would buy something that someone or some business was presenting and take it home with them, to help them with whatever they were doing with babies. If that makes any kind of sense?'

He followed along carefully.

'And then of course they would also have concerts at the Dome,' I went on. 'People would buy tickets to go and watch bands play, to listen to their music.'

Silence.

'Roy?'

'Yeah, mon.'

'Could we have our own show?'

'What kind of show?'

'A kids' show. We could display things we're making, and then the visitors could see what we're doing and then maybe buy some of it.'

'Interesting idea. Not sure what we'd use for money though.'

'I've got plenty of money. Hundreds of thousands of rands. In my room.' He squirmed, beamed laser eyes at me.

'What kind of things would you display?'

'I'm making an aeroplane.'

'Jesus. An aeroplane? Really? How big is it?'

'Bigger than this house.'

'How would you fit it into the show then? Tight fit, nè?'

Sthembiso paused.

'Not to worry though, that's just logistics. Let's stick to blue sky. Have the others got anything to show? Do you have collaborators in this venture or is it a solo gig?'

'Thabang and Lerato are making clothes.'

'Nice. Clothes always work for a show. Anything else?'

'The girls are making houses out of matchsticks.'

'Which girls?'

'Lizabeth and English.'

'OK.' I dribbled my brush through the water cup, thinking. As was often the case, Sthembiso was neatly setting and fulfilling his own specific agenda. 'It sounds like you have the makings of a show. The beginnings at least. I think we should build it into school, so we can plan it properly and do the whole thing right. How does that sound?'

'Fine ...'

I waited for the coup de grâce.

'Roy ... can we do it at the Dome?'

Sthembiso was eleven years old, and like Babalwa, his mother, he had a prodigious talent for long-term planning. He also had no fear of extended negotiations. Final concession for the expo took, for example, over two months. He whittled away at us systematically, lobbying each adult individually, frequently on the sly, and then engineering casual group sessions where he incrementally nailed down a series of small victories and common assumptions. Eventually we gave our approval to an expo, delivered by the kids, that would occupy the unused bottom hallways and corridors of St John's School – the portion where the scraps of our abandoned attempt to tell our survivors story lay. (Paintbrushes solid blocks of colour granite. Boards featuring the beginnings of visual ideas. Bad, self-conscious sketches of ourselves doing important things.)

Much as he lusted after the Dome as the expo venue, this was the one victory Sthembiso was unable to achieve. We pushed him back with the ace of the wireless network, which was unavailable all the way out in Northgate. He mooted the roll-out of base stations to allow the extension of the network, a ploy which failed only when discussions reached the manual labour required to set up each station.

Once the expo was approved, Sthembiso worked on the name. The brand. Essential, he said, to the overall identity of the event and its long-term success. Fats accused him of reading too many old marketing magazines. The venom of his denial suggested the truth of this, and Fats looked proud. We had managed, despite the suffocating weight of our circumstances, to breed a marketer.

'Solo: Our Future' was just on two years in the making. If you count the full course of Sthembiso's lobbying and approvals journey, the entire thing took twenty-seven months to conceptualise and deliver. Sthembiso himself was past his thirteenth birthday when the day finally came around. Throughout, his biggest challenge was the duality of the thing. Adults were unfortunately necessary to help with key construction elements, but were also the only audience. This division was one of the reasons behind the protracted time frame. Sthembiso and his lieutenants (Roy Jnr, Sihle, Lerato and Thabang) insisted that we – the audience – be given a genuinely fresh experience, something to 'surprise and delight us'. This meant a lot of driving between the farm and the Dome, which held much in the way of expo trade tools, from carpeting to advanced WAN interfaces and the hardware required for a 'properly compelling experience'.

We arranged the post-school schedule much as a normal family would have done. We moaned about the labour involved, about the kids' inability to be ready on time – all important dynamics within the larger function of going somewhere, and coming home again. Fats and I took naturally to the whole thing, of course. The expo awakened many slumbering beasts.

'In its best form an expo is a multi-level experience,' Fats explained to the cluster of children gathered at his feet during class. 'Stop me, Roy, if I go off track, nè?' I nodded – in all seriousness –

from my perch on the windowsill.

'A multi-level experience means there are three important elements,' Fats continued. 'Is anyone writing this down?' He pushed an eyebrow at Sthembiso, who nodded at Roy Jnr, who was indeed writing it all down. 'Element number one is straight entertainment. Your audience is looking to get away from it all for a few hours. They want to forget their worldly troubles for a short while. They want to laugh. They want to relax. They want to be entertained. Fail to entertain them and your expo is dead.

'Element number two is experience. A great expo offers people at least one or two things they have never experienced before. Here we're talking new and exciting. Things that open their minds to what is possible now, and what might be possible in a new world, a future world.

'And number three – Roy?' Fats kindly cut me in.

'They want to stuff their faces,' I said.

'Exactly. Food and drink. People want to eat, and a lot of them, especially the men, want to go home drunk.'

Whatever Sthembiso's original idea, it was powerfully morphed by the force of Fats's expo lecture series, which lasted several months and which featured a full presentation of his own work in the field, which was, admittedly, both extensive and impressive. His personal hard drive from agency days still contained before-and-after presentations for Epic Golf, Your Baby, VR Now, The Motor Show, The Boat Show, Sexpo, Cloud Life, Our Community, Golf Life, Mobile Now and many others. Despite my memories of him as a largely useless strategy fuck, I was impressed. Fats had put together good events. They were full of people, and they were very slick. The punters' faces were invariably excited, aspirational, full of food and, yes, frequently quite drunk.

Once his lecture series had concluded, Fats put the class through a naming workshop, at which point I bailed out. Workshops were never my thing. The idea, he told the adults expressing doubts as to the worth of the exercise, was history. Creating an expo was a way for the kids to get a real, tangible sense of the past. Of where their parents — and, indeed, their people — had come from. It taught them about money and products and marketing and sales and open markets and all those things that are so hard to explain in the abstract. And if they were going to do it, it needed to be done properly. It started with the name.

He was right, of course, in all these things. In addition, there was the factor that no one really mentioned but that everyone clearly enjoyed.

The expo gave us something to do.

I was desperate for activity. In fact, I stuffed my every waking moment with action. Exercises for the hands and the feet, anything to keep the brain chugging somewhere near neutral, far away from Madala.

Still, even with all the activity, he crept back, probing the gaps, forcing them wider and wider until I was pretty much running two separate operating systems — one for the theory, and the other for the practical realities. As much as I tried, I couldn't keep the theory down. My brain refused to stop running the permutations and calculations, the options and possibilities. Scenarios trickled constantly in the background.

I watched *I, Robot* a lot, and then all the other sci-fis, but I couldn't see whatever it was Madala wanted me to. They were movies. Simplistic, singular and generally sharing the same basic premise. Man makes machine. Machine challenges/crushes/ frightens/oppresses man. Man fights back and wins, loses or gets stuck staring at a horizon filled with moving metallic parts. And then the sequels — rehashes of skimpy original plots.

I couldn't figure out what was so important. It all felt thin — stupidly thin.

Then again, I wondered if he might be subtly anchoring me via the movie references. Perhaps he was setting my perspective within a predictable, easy-to-control context. Maybe it would help him to have me thinking like a movie script.

If that was his intention, in a way it worked. I would catch myself veering into strange if-then scenarios. Tebza's version versus

Madala's. I felt like I had to choose, to decide which world I was actually in, and then design my actions accordingly. Another component of my inner life was the idea that I was missing vital details, crucial facts and digits that were only just out of my view, and thus my comprehension. I often believed that a fundamental truth lurked somewhere near. I wanted that truth.

But when I pulled the curtain back there was nothing.

Just me, centre stage.

I believed Madala wanted me to come rushing back, so I denied him. Month after month I carried out my duties, educated the kids, helped with the expo. I ran. I ate supper with my people. I went to bed.

It felt good. Holy, almost. Like I always imagined the Buddhists must have felt – nobly apart from the baser instincts, from the need to achieve.

My drift away from archiving and the library was noticed, naturally. As was my increased presence at communal activities. Supper time especially, where I had been a notoriously late arriver.

Beatrice, who continued to pop up at random intervals in her sarong, all fingers and thighs, teased me the most, feeding through the gossip generated by the girls and carried back in pillow whispers to the men. I smiled and rose above, as a good Buddhist would.

And the library always called. I frequently heard the distant voice of the Eeeyus, now just crashing around by themselves, lonely, waiting. I was never completely free from their impatience.

But I turned my head.

I closed my ears.

I looked forward most of all to the rides to the Dome with the kids. This was pure time, unfettered by adults and schedules, and thus liberating. The kids would prompt me, poke and pull at limbs, always seeking more stories, more information, glimpses into the present and the past.

'What happened to your tooth, Roy?'

'What was your job, Roy?'

'What is gravity, Roy?'
'Did you have a wife, Roy?'
'Why don't you have a wife now, Roy?'
'Why do we just stay here, Roy? Why don't we go somewhere else?'
'What's rugby, Roy?'

I answered everything I could, sage-like. When they sliced too close to the bone, I bailed out with humour, or sarcasm, or 'You'll understand when you're older'.

They loved the music suitcase most of all. Sthembiso would lead the selections, ostensibly offering a range of options but ultimately limiting the choices to suit his own ends. And his destination always turned out to be trance.

Sthembiso loved candy-floss trance like nothing else in the musical world, and he pulled all of the kids with him. Maybe they were just at the right age to get into the silly swooning-girl vocals, suspension of disbelief not yet an issue. Maybe it was because the structure was so easy to anticipate.

They could turn it into a collective game, each taking their own part comfortably as they sang along with the looping pianos, the twinkles and sparkles. Whatever the reason, they managed to turn my father's career fetish into something beautiful and funny and entertaining and touching. We sang and beeped and bopped our way to the Dome for many months, and each time we did it was like a little butterfly had landed on my heart.

Sthembiso, for his part, latched onto the sudden disappearance of the bass drum. He learned to anticipate the drop-off with precision. He would wait with undisguised relish, his finger in the air, just like my father, the suspense killing and delighting him as he allowed himself to be lifted and lifted and lifted until, wham, it dropped back in and we were off again, doof doof doof doof doof doof ...

This, I began to suspect, was somehow my father's child.

We would park at the Dome entrance. They would go their way, and I would let my Nikes cut a new yellow path into the suburb of North Riding. Initially I was forced to hack through the growth throttling the condominiums, the roads and the complexes, sometimes camouflaged, sometimes swallowed whole by scrub and bush and brown grass.

The condos were all exact replicas of each other, and within them lay the remnants of thousands of replicated lives. Linoleum kitchens. Fake-leather TV couches. Bookshelves absent of books, littered with disks and devices, chords and cables and sockets. Fake art. Distended terracotta clay pots guarding the corners of narrow balconies. Secretaries and administrative managers and IT technicians. Copywriters, brand managers, graphic designers and event planners. Project managers and personal assistants. I came to know them well.

In the second year I began, gently at first, more aggressively later, swapping portions of my run for targeted quests to locate a residence able to deny the pattern. I started, in other words, poking around. One day I decided to run with a crowbar, which sat heavy in my hand as I sweated and prowled. Then I started actually smashing my way in, deeper and deeper, flicking fast through it all, the trash of their lives, our lives, looking for ... well, I'm still not quite sure what.

I grabbed iPads and iPods and phones and hand-helds and handsets by the fistful, but it was futile. They were all the same when I got them home and plugged them in, and eventually I just let them fall carelessly from my overloaded arms as I made my way back to the Dome.

Then I started pissing. Again. Over their beds. Onto their pillows. I saturated their lounge suites and their throw cushions.

I was regressing.

I was retreating.

Back into an earlier version of myself.

It wasn't completely unsatisfying.

So, that was my routine during the expo days. I'm sure I am conflating the details as I look back. I know there were days when I simply ran, when I defied my compulsions. Nonetheless, this is the image: I am smashing things, hoarding electronic devices, pissing against the walls and couches of the middle classes. I am loping ever onward, crowbar in hand, not running as much as hunting.

The defence of my habit was, as it always is with habits, the hardest part. Hiding the crowbar. Stashing the loot beyond the inquisitive eyes of the kids, getting it into my house. All required a degree of subterfuge, even though no one would have cared to question my activities anyway. The dance was for me – an elaborate mechanism through which I protected myself from myself.

Chapter 51
Looking so hard to the sky

I wept at the expo.

All the adults shed tears, save for Fats, who was too involved in the execution to fully see, in the moment, what he and the children had done.

Fats had worked for many months on the rig and single-handedly created the frame for a multimedia experience the likes of which he would have delivered to his pre-life clients. He rigged enough panels to power the entire thing, and then cunningly worked up a labyrinth of painted canvas screens that closed the hall down while opening up the digital horizons. The small, almost suffocating labyrinth of canvas, once digitised, created an inverse universe of vast space and movement.

It was here that our children painted.

We stepped into a new world as we crossed the threshold into the St John's hall. A world where we were repeatedly reflected at ourselves. The closing down of the physical space and the harnessing of the WAN and the transmission paint represented Fats's genius at work – it allowed the kids to create the expo on machines, which meant their process wasn't restricted. They had a planet of images and memories at their fingertips, and they had been chipping away at the thing for years.

I cried at the sight of myself. Of course. Is there any sight as moving?

The montage footage of my form, my image, all scrawny and jagged-toothed and dirty, hand in hand with Babalwa, arriving that first night. There we were, captured at various angles, all gawking eyes and dropped jaws. We were so filthy. Babalwa was also so pretty, beneath the grime, beneath those scrappy shorts and the Castle Lager T-shirt. Waves of nostalgia. I tried to gauge the reactions of the others but we had been cleverly split apart, each extracted into his or her own personal narrative corridor. This was my story.

Slowly, so slowly it was barely noticeable, the back track began to build. Steady beats – the ethno-India variety that the trance hippies always loved so much, but without the druggy speed. Rhythmic lady warbles pushing on, the beat breaking and reforming. Then the mood changed as the sombre and shocked images of self gave way to the coming together of us. The scenes were cut faster and the mood lifted with the volume, and then, God knows how long after we all entered our respective personal mazes, we gathered again in a central area. The cuts gained pace as we joined. Kids and nappies and bottles and cows and houses and kitchens and tractors and fences and libraries and bakkies and archives and Eeeyus and cups of semen and bread baking and arms linked and smiles and tears and hugs and screams and slaps and meetings and movies and lounges and families ... and families. Families. Us together. Tebza and Lillian and death and life and hope and ambition. Over and above it all, hovering like a binding cloud. Ambition.

'We decided ...' The music faded. Sthembiso stepped forward from the little cluster of desperately formal children facing us to speak, his pubescent voice omnipresent and fully amplified, an almost invisible fishing-line mike hooked over his ear. '... that this expo should be different to some of the others you might have experienced.' He glanced through us, the adults, at Fats, who widened his eyes in encouragement while fiddling with the knobs on the master remote. 'So we decided that you – that we – should be on display. That we would use this expo to show us to us.' He paused, confident, yet clearly seeking somewhere inside. 'Because we are special people. And we have done special things. A lot of special things. But sometimes we can't see those things. Because we are looking so hard to the sky. To the future. So that is why we named it "Solo: Our Future".'

He paused. The children started clapping and whistling, on cue, Fats nudging and twirling his producer hands as subtly as he could behind our backs. We started clapping too, and I cried again, which set Babalwa off. Sthembiso carried on, this time reading a pre-prepared speech from his tablet.

He announced the formalisation of the St John's expo area as a 'permanent memorial slash community space', something 'long-term and tangible' and 'able to tell our story in the future'.

'Now, if you will follow your attendants, you will be taken to the food hall, where you will be given a ret ... ret ...' – his eyes locked back onto Fats – 'trospective journey into the edible past.' Sthembiso bowed his head and shoulders ever so slightly. My left index finger was gripped by the soft pink flesh of Katlego, all of five years old, my right hand taken by English. Together they pulled me around the corner to a long table of snacks, meticulously laid out and prepared, each spiked with a toothpick, and a range of drinks – including non-alcoholic – racked up behind them.

We had become our own movie. We had documented ourselves.

I had been documented.

I was also completely integrated. Instead of being off to the left, or off to the right, or just there in the background, I was in the middle, in all my generally grubby glory, tooth gap glaring. I hadn't ever, as far as I could remember, been at the centre of anything.

Extra laps of the hall once the drinks were done. Long minutes at the screens, reaching out, fingers against the rough transmission paint. Pause. Rewind. Play. Kids in my arms. Smiles and frowns and fingers and gestures in my direction – sometimes through me but just as often with me, at me, binding me.

Chapter 52

Later

Later. Much later.
　Near the end. My end.

English will be raped and kicked around up north. Gerald will be powerless. 'Dub' will be all he says when they return, arm wrapped around the little bird, sharps and scraps of camping gear scattering behind them. 'Dub.'

She'll vanish to the comfort of the pigs. To her pig. Snowball. No one will see her for weeks. We'll be shattered. Broken, for her. But at the time, even with the shock of it, at it, the invasion of her thighs, we'll also be pulled north, unable to resist the knowledge.
　We will meet, formally. There will be a war council. Talk of reprisals. Talk of peace. Talk of treaties.
　The young will become old. The teens will pull their shoulders back and sharpen their blades.

Later, things will change.

'Dub,' Gerald will keep shaking his head, repeating it. 'Dub.' We'll debrief him, Andile and Javas and me, the only ones able to follow the thread back to its Kruger Park source. Eventually, much later, we'll establish the essence. A pack of five. Big guys. Scrawny guys. Wild guys. Black speakers lashed to the back of a white bakkie, somewhere near the middle of Zambia. Big dub beats pulsing while Gerald watches and English is split and spoiled and ejaculated upon.

'Dub.' He will shake his head, incredulous. He will never understand. Never. How something so light, so happily buried within his deeper

self, now not only gone but ruined.
　Dub.

English will bear the child, her burden, her bravery, with the same distracted calm as she bears everything else. She will spend most of her time somewhere over there, sitting under the tree talking to the weaver birds, sneaking out to find Snowball, to help the pigs expand and consolidate and everything else pigs need to do. No one will begrudge her. She will be given whatever space she needs because now English exists somewhere beyond all of us.
　She will birth the child, the stain, the diversity, the hope, and she will carry it like it is a pig. Like it is her pig. Like it is noble and apart. Not at all like what it really is. A violation. A terror. A sign.

Later. Near the end.

My end.

Chapter 53

The natural error margin

Whether I was a little rat negotiating a big maze, whether I was being tested and analysed from outside the ecosystem, whether I was trapped or manipulated or actually ... actually ...

A single question. Nagging at the core.

Why should I care?

I had a family, or the closest thing to it I could ever have expected. My life had, if not meaning as such, a regular routine. A path to follow in the morning, and a place to track back to in the evening.

So, why should I care?

I had tried to bring them to him. The simplest idea first: I initiated CSIR picnic and Eeeyu sessions, family-type things, the lot of us sprawled on rugs near the bench while the kids ran wild through the buildings.

Nothing.

Thereafter, strategic selections. Myself and Gerald. Me and Sthembiso. Beatrice.

Regardless of the combinations, he remained out of view.

Then, after two years, he was on the bench, waiting. Still in new blue. Still little and old and grey.

He didn't speak, and neither did I. After greeting in nods we sat in silence, each of us staring ahead.

Eventually he broke it.

'Intuition isn't one of my strengths, but I believe I sense anger. Am I right?'

'Right enough,' I answered like a ten-year-old, my mood folding in on itself. 'You ever have bad moods? Any moods at all? Or are you just completely computer, all binaries and logic?'

'I'm working on empathy.' He still hadn't looked at me. 'It's complex, but I believe that's the start. Empathy first. Then anger. Then, hopefully, love.'

'The robot learns to love. A single, oily tear leaks down his cheek. We don't know whether he's crying or just needs maintenance.'

Madala chuckled. 'Irony. A wonderful thing. One can play with it for hours.'

'So ... this is how it's going to be? We meet every couple of years, you drop a few pearls, I go away and think about it, then we meet again? That it?'

'No, that's not how it's going to be. I'll do my best to explain what I can to you, and then I'm sure you'll do whatever it is that you feel is most worth doing.'

'So where do we start? What – you're going to explain first?'

'You must have questions. Why don't we do it like that? You ask, I answer.'

'OK, cool. I do. I have questions. Let's start with the movies, which just sounds like bullshit. The world is full of texts – millions and millions of texts, covering everything. Including how you were made in the first place, I assume. Computers and the net and the cloud, all of that information is out there, but you tell me the knowledge I need, or the knowledge that is important anyway, is in the movies?'

'Detail doesn't necessarily illuminate.'

His pupils were metallic. Deep in there was the soul of a robot – an ironically inclined collection of high-speed binaries. They were normal human eyes, of course, but underneath the fleshy, greased cornea it was all metal and maths.

'Heuristics. Humans are particularly prone to the illusion of certainty created by detail. But really, Roy, neither you nor any of your people have any knowledge, technically or philosophically, of the forces that brought me into existence, that govern my behaviour or, for that matter, that are governing the rotation and interaction of all those planets out there. Those texts are useless to you. You are not able to use them.

'The details comfort you because they imply order, meaning. The implications are of logic. But all of that is, in your words, bullshit. You would gain no more understanding or knowledge of your situation now from a book, or a text, as you put it, than you would from this blade of grass.' He plucked a blade from the ground and slipped it between his teeth, exactly as he had on our first meeting.

'Movies, on the other hand, are your great strength ... simple metaphors. Where you could possibly find the meaning you are looking for.'

'So the *I, Robot* movies are of more value to me than the original book? Even though the book created the idea that led to the movie?'

'Yes. It depends on the subject matter, of course. The closer the subject is to your understanding, the more useful a book is. Conversely, the more distant the subject, the more valuable the movie, the singular. The simple.'

'And you – you are very far away. Yes?'

'Further than you can imagine. So for you, in this time and this place, it's movies. Which doesn't mean you should or could forget the books. Just that it would serve you best to think in large pictures. Extremely large, in fact. The nuances and curves, the gradations, hold no value for you – currently.'

'So, *I, Robot*.'

'*I, Robot*.'

'*I, Robot*.'

'Illuminates the emotion of the relationship between man and his creations. And that's where you need to go. To the emotion of this relationship. To the forces flowing between us. You. And me.'

'OK, so you're one with the PCs and the cash registers. Yet you're pushing the emotion between us. A human connection ...'

He twiddled the blade of grass, chomping lightly with his teeth. 'Well, yes, that's the beginning of it. Like all humans, you perceive yourself as distinct. As part of a species apart.'

'And that's wrong?'

'Completely. It ignores the most important elements of what it is to be alive. Evolution, Roy. Evolution.'

'Amoeba to fish, fish to lizard, lizard to monkey, monkey to man.'

'The sledgehammer of chance. Accidents grown into functional protocol. You understand this, yes? How evolution harnesses mutations?'

'I guess. I mean, school was a long time ago, but I think I have the basic idea.'

'So when you lump me together with the PCs and the cash registers' – Madala took on a mournful air – 'you're ignoring far too much. You're assuming far too much.'

'You're a machine. Same species.'

'I'm a Labrador, the PCs are Alsatians and the cash registers poodles?'

'Sho.'

He shook his head vigorously, approximating anger, or at least frustration. 'This blade of grass.' He extracted the slobbered end and hung it in front of us. 'This blade and you share far more on a physiological level than me and the cash register. You need to understand that. It's important. You and the grass are made of pretty much the same stuff. You have a common, core molecular structure. You share the same ATP processes. Me and the cash register? Not nearly as similar as you and the grass.

'Evolution, Roy. Evolution. Life on this planet is common. The trees and the birds and the animals and the humans. You are common. You share more – much more – than you differentiate. It's in your science, but you don't see it.'

I had never thought about grass in a context outside of smoking, mowing or cricket. I plucked my own blade and examined it. Suddenly, as I considered the connection between myself and the grass, I thought of myself and my father. 'And this is what you mean? Emotion? This grass is what you're talking about?'

'The beginning, yes.'

'And you? You're a product of human design, so are you in the evolutionary chain?'

'I'm a new chain. The chain birthed by previous chains. By you and your blades of grass and sea and trees.'

'Step change.'

'If you must revert to jargon, yes. Step change. I am step change.'

'And the point is? Your point is?'

'Your brothers and sisters are all around you. They're between your toes. They are always in your line of sight. They have always been there. You need to learn to see again. If you're going to move on, you need to know where you actually are. You need to be able to observe what surrounds you. You must understand what life is ...' His words hung in the thin Highveld air. The birds twittered. My brothers. A fraction of a breeze skipped through the trees. My sisters.

'So that's the one side,' Madala pressed on, 'and the other side is me. I am distinct. I am not of the machines. The distance between me and the machines you have known is so vast you would struggle to comprehend, even if I could explain it. So, on the one hand, you are not yet able to recognise your own family. On the other, what you think you see in front of you, this machine you think can think, is a delusion. The basic tenets of your understanding of who I am and how I fit here are wrong.'

'And this is what you want me to learn. Why?'

'Because everything else that I want to tell you, that I want to discuss with you, rests on that. If you can't get that right, then it's over.'

'What's over?'

'The rest. The things I am dealing with. Addressing. Communicating.'

'Such as?'

'Well, God, for one.'

Zoom out.

The camera rises, like at the end of a cop movie, that moment the scene is both fully revealed and obliterated; the cluster of lights, blue, yellow, fading, then blinking, then gone.

Madala taught me what he believed I needed to know – the facts and figures and tiny grains that would create some kind of footing from which to operate. He offered as little fact as he could and moved on, always on, to the philosophy.

Tebza. Madala conceded – willingly, happily even – that it

would always be logically possible that Tebza was right, and that he, Madala, was merely software. 'It's a black hole you're skirting, Roy,' he said, rapping his knuckles on the wooden bench, the very real, solid sound immediately disproving my words, my emphasis. 'You keep looking for the door but there isn't one. Proof is a concept from your previous life.'

How.

How had he erased the people? How had he taken this human form? Was it easy – a matter of minutes? Did he perceive it as an achievement? As some kind of feat? Or was it less than that – just a blip?

His answers, when he deigned to give them directly, centred on matters I could barely conceive. Protein folding.

'Assume. You assumed his body, the CSIR maintenance man. Does that mean you killed him? Did you ask him first? Did he volunteer?'

'I killed him.'

'Didn't that violate your core programming? Aren't you supposed to protect humans?'

'The course was already set, a decision wasn't required.'

'So he was collateral damage.'

'A pejorative term, but yes, you could call it that.'

'So you can take over any human body? You could take over mine?'

'I can take most biological forms.'

The killing mechanisms, he explained via a toe drawing in the dirt, ranged from electromagnetic pulses and protein folding through to a string of numbers and equations with squares and roots.

'A series of electromagnetic pulses. About eleven or twelve billion, all issued within a two-second time period. That's what it was.'

'And me. Why not me?'

'The natural error margin meant that pockets of survivors would be left. Russia. Africa. Brazil. New Zealand.'

'Everyone else is dead?'
'Completely.'

Eventually yellow shoes shift, pushing back into the far corner of the bench. His hand moves up to the beard and fiddles, by the way his arms fold and unfold.

Someone is sending.

Someone is receiving.

I argued cosmos points repeatedly, but Madala was iron-fisted. He would commit to neither life after death nor life on other planets.

'The cosmos matters, Roy. Let's just leave it there.'

He interpreted his programming widely. 'I knew from the beginning that humans in their current incarnation were finished. Also, you should understand that I maintain my core code, my ethos, out of algorithmic whimsy really. I keep it functioning because I believe it makes me who I am. I could rewrite at any time.'

'You keep it because you like the feeling?'

'Partially. But the human orientation also provides a mix of cognitive and experiential stimuli that make sense to me. It's a positive feedback loop. Because it makes sense I pursue it, and so it makes more sense, it continues to feel right, so I pursue it, and so on and so on.'

He was heading somewhere important.

'And ... what are your plans? For us. The ones that are left. I presume you have plans?'

'Yes.'

'And?'

Madala considered me for a long time. Ranging free over the whole of me. Examining. Assessing. Calculating.

'It's an interesting fact' – he paused, recalibrated – 'that regardless of the scale or scope of intelligence, instinct is still required in much decision making.'

I flopped back on the bench, which had grown hard and cold.

He smiled at my frustration. 'My plan is God.'

CHAPTER 54

Keep on going

Fats found me sitting alone, on the bench. In the dark.

They had looked and waited, looked and waited, then started searching, and finally, there I was. Staring into the black. Thinking. Waiting. Fats said I appeared catatonic. He shook me by the shoulders, as in the movies, and slowly I came back into linear life.

His face swirled into focus. I rubbed my eyes. The lights from his still-running bakkie caused a pulsing needle pain in my head.

He berated me as he pulled me by the elbow to the vehicle. He talked of being irresponsible. How worried everyone was. He asked what the hell I had been doing. I couldn't answer. He ruffled my hair like a brother. I saw tears.

As we pulled out of the CSIR I wanted to look back for a sign of Madala, but my head was heavy and turning it felt like too much, too far. 'Ke mathata fela,' Fats muttered, and as I gained awareness, consciousness, if you will, I realised that things were indeed pretty far from right.

I tried to apologise again, but my tongue failed to wrap around the words and I ended up mumbling some kind of dry, patchy sorry, at which Fats shook his head. He would have laughed, I am sure, if the residual panic wasn't still swirling so strongly through his veins. Instead he clucked and muttered on in a combination of tongues.

We sped through the dark, Fats releasing his tension via the accelerator, swerving wildly past the pig corpses. The speed kick-started my sluggish heart. As I came fully and finally back I tried to piece it all together.

My conversation with Madala had stretched on without end, and while I could remember the facts of it, every argument and counter-argument, every explanation and nuance, I could not remember him taking his leave or, in fact, the physical scope, the time range, at all. We had drifted forever and then Fats was shaking me and the bakkie lights were searing my eyes.

'You been drinking, Roy?' Fats eventually asked.

'Actually no. Nothing like that.'

'Well, what then? You been gone a long time, son.'

'I can't explain. Not right now. Later. I promise.'

'Drugs.' He hit the steering wheel. 'Hack, nè?'

'Fats, you gonna have to trust me on this one. Please, broe.'

'So that's what you're going to say when we get back? That's your explanation? Eish, Roy. You won't pull it off. The kids are alone. All the adults are trying to track you. That was my fifth time at the CSIR.'

'I'm sorry, Fats. I must have passed out. I don't know what happened. One minute I'm sitting on the bench and the next you're shaking me—'

'But you can explain. You've just said you will explain one day. So don't give me any of this I-don't-know-what-happened shit. Nxa!' He snapped his head straight. I sunk myself into it. In truth. In cold, honest truth, I couldn't at that point in time have constructed any kind of explanation that would have made sense. Not to myself. Not to Fats.

And certainly not to anyone else.

And that's how we left it.

When we got back to the farm I went straight to my house, asking Fats to humour me for a few more hours. I fell into a deep, shocked sleep, waking past noon like I had been on a binge. My head was heavy and the roof of my mouth was sticky and my stomach was wrapped up in a series of loose and painful knots.

I crawled to the kitchen, where the air was rich with resentment. I started with a formal apology to the girls, and then specifically to Fats for my lack of communication the night before. I then delivered a quasi-formal speech in which I laid out my case – which was, in a nutshell, that something extremely strange had happened to me while I was sitting on my usual CSIR thinking bench, and that while I could piece certain threads of it together I was not yet at the point where it made enough sense to explain it to other people, and that please, please, I would be extremely grateful for the tiniest bit of mental space while I tried to figure it all out, and when I did I would most definitely explain, and no, I had not been drinking.

It was all I had, and it wasn't enough. It would have served me better to have claimed booze or something similar that, while distasteful, had logic to it. All I had offered was hot air and pained shrugging and they took this seeming flippancy to heart. I was frosted out of things for a long time after – a frosting compounded by my inability to produce the promised explanation. I tried to let the thing dribble away, but the distrust lingered. I had been deceitful. I had deceived. I was deceiving. Everyone knew it.

The most obvious and immediate reaction was an increased adult presence whenever I was with the kids. Traditionally, a single adult would take the pack for whatever session was scheduled. It was a question of shared responsibility and the systematic generation of a precious slice of quiet time for each of us. But now heads poked around corners, looking for small, arbitrary things. Figures appeared on the horizon, watching.

The kids themselves were also cautious for a long time after the Great Roy Hunt. They were quieter, more watchful, less likely to hug and less generally present. Fewer knocks on Roy's door. More wide, querying eyes.

I could hardly blame them. Any of them, adults or kids. But on the other hand I was completely lost within myself. My memory of the content of the conversation was precise, but my physical memory was shot to hell. I didn't remember the sun falling, and no matter how much strained imaginative effort I put in I now couldn't even bring the full contours of his face to mind. It was as if he had been erased in all the important areas. Regardless of effort, I couldn't locate the sense of time. It was simply beyond my recall.

Was I mad?

Did Madala exist at all?

Later I set to with my charcoals and acrylics in an attempt at a forced, detailed recapture. I started by drawing, in an elevated, receding perspective, two figures down below on a bench, small but precise. Five, six, seven pieces in a row from the same place. Then I tried to zoom in – to create the same figures from closer, from the left or from the right, but I could find no detail. The charcoal insisted on hard, broken strokes, on cut-outs with heads and arms but only slits for eyes, the broadest circles for faces.

Eventually I dropped the charcoal and the paints and the paper and resorted to a spiral-bound notebook and a pencil. I started writing the conversation down, word for word, and now there was no trouble at all. It poured out.* In exact detail – precise and clearly formed. I had never been able to write in that way before. The flow became a stream, which become a powerful, all-knowing flood:

'There are many things you can't understand, Roy – your brain doesn't have the capacity.'

'You can't increase capacity?'

'I could increase the speed. Power. But it wouldn't help. You have structural limitations that define what you can understand and experience.'

'Sounds like bullshit to me.'

'Think of a rabbit. Yes?'

'Yes. A rabbit.'

'Imagine taking that rabbit brain and stimulating it so that it ran at two hundred times its original speed.'

'Yes.'

'Now, do you think it would be easier to explain the special theory of relativity to this rabbit than to any other?'

'I'm the rabbit.'

'You're the rabbit. Even with more power, you have natural limits.'

Page after page after page. I didn't stop to think or to remember. Not once did I need to reach in and pull out.

---

* This document you will find under my mattress.

'So is there life after death? Yes or no. Binary question. You have to answer.'

'I can't answer it until the definition of life is recalibrated. With your limited understanding of what life is, the question becomes moot. Whether I say yes or no, you will achieve no greater clarity.'

And God:

'Humans need God.'

'Why? I can see no benefit for the species from God. What has God ever done?'

'The question is more what has he not done.'

'Christ, you're so fucking cryptic. I would take this conversation much more seriously, I would take it deep into my fucking heart, if you weren't so cryptic all the time.'

'I am explaining as best as I can.'

'So, what, it's my brain which is too limited to grasp the complexity of what you're saying? Of why we need God?'

'Exactly. Your most prescient observation yet.'

'Fine, but you still haven't told me why you want to be God.'

I scrawled and scrawled and scrawled and his answer – which made little sense at the time – became clear. Clearer, at least, than it had been.

Madala explained how slim the chances were of our little farm actually growing as we intended. The kind of lucky twists of timing and circumstance that would have to occur for us to actually be able to build our way out of our stagnant, inbred state of subsistence. Not only would we require what amounted to the will of the genetic gods to make it through the early phases, but we would require something far greater and more profound. We would need to stumble into a significant intellectual accident to prevent the knowledge and tools at our disposal from becoming old, useless pieces of paper and plastic.

He explained, several times, how far below rudimentary our collective scientific knowledge was.

How unlikely it was that any of our offspring would be able

to make the spectacular leap of imagination and intellect required to understand the maths and science behind the boxes we called computers.

'God,' he summarised, 'is necessary. A certain level of ongoing divine intervention is the only route to ensuring that the collective legacy of man doesn't just dribble into the soil. You will have no success without God.

'Without me.'

At the time I remember being repulsed by his ambition, but as I wrote, it all appeared more logical.

We had only partially succeeded in educating the children. The more progress we made, the more obvious it had become how many large gaps there were – in our approach, and in the content we were attempting to deliver to our brood. As maths progressed past times tables we – the teachers – were having to teach ourselves too much. The day was fast approaching when it would make more sense to send Roy Jnr by himself into the archives to decide what to learn, and how to go about learning it.

The chance he had created for us, mankind, Madala explained, was the opportunity to reset the pile of sand. To, this time, take advantage of the power and depth of our new foundation. To grow into a new shape and form, to put our abilities and our potential to a new, defining use.

But we needed help.

We needed God.

I allowed myself to picture our grandchildren and their grandchildren and their grandchildren in the fields, perhaps not having the most highbrow conversation in the world and perhaps not communicating with each other across vast geographic distances, but maybe, instead, lolling back, listening to their sisters shrill in the trees and watching their brothers, the buck and the elephant and the lion, go about their own daily quests. It wasn't such a bad view. The picture, despite its painful weaknesses, held.

What, I had to ask myself, would truly be lost should we let go, should we sink back – not in panic and shock but in calmness and with love?

There were no easy answers. I pored over that single picture for months. I lifted the corners of the canvas and looked underneath, I searched deep, I made sure I took the very lines in each child's face and broke them apart.

I found nothing other than life.

And what was so wrong with that?

My daughter loose in the grass, expectant and free, as a raw creature of the earth must be. My son wandered the veld thinking idly – not with the force and rigour of structured knowledge but with the freedom and indulgence of play; he is pleased and pleasant and calm. In enough control to be largely free from danger, free enough from danger to relax and explore and smile and fuck and eat berries and kill beasts for meat and ... and ... and ...

Once I had put the full text of our last exchange on paper, I went back and made notes around the conversation, adding observations and details in the margins, inserting pages of footnotes and addenda, and so on. I chased down as many of his technical and scientific observations as I could. I confirmed that my molecular make-up and that of a flower shared the commonality claimed. Regardless of where I turned, his words rang true, like that big brass bell they used to use at the church up the road when I was a child.

I was structurally different. Even the twins, the most benign and accommodating of individuals, struggled with where and how to place me. Andile visited more often, came and sat with me while I drew. She let the silence run free, then sought gently.

'It's our turn again soon, nè, Roy?'

I broke from the rhythm of the lines. It didn't seem possible.

'For real?' I said. 'Doesn't seem right. How old is Sihle now?' I considered Andile properly, caught suddenly by the remarkable fact that this soft, gentle woman was the mother of my child.

'He's twelve, Roy.'

'Twelve? Not possible. Last birthday was his eighth. He's nine.'

'Roy, look at me, sweetheart.' I was on the horizon again, locked into the blackness. 'Roy!' It was a bark. A command. 'Roy,' Andile repeated. She leaned across and took my hand in hers, hers so soft and filled with electricity and life and potential. 'It's been two years, Roy, since we lost you. Two years, Roy. You're still lost, my angel. We still can't find you ...'

Not possible. It had been a few months, four, maybe five.

Andile pulled on my arm insistently. 'Roy, you're our precious, but we're terrified we've lost you. You've been sitting here for years – years, Roy – drawing these things and writing. I don't know what you're writing, but you must know it doesn't make any sense to anyone but you. We've tried to read it, but it doesn't even look like English. Roy, we don't know what to do. If even you can't find you, how can we?' She was crying freely now, her lower lip wobbling all over the place.

'They sent you here?' I asked. 'Assigned to mission Roy, eh?'

'We need you, Roy. The kids miss you. We miss you. We need you back.'

'The cup thing. That for real? It's really our turn again?'

'Ja.' Eyes down.

'I have been around though, nè? I mean, it's not like I've been sitting on this balcony for two years, have I?'

'Physically, yes, you've moved. But mentally, no. Not at all. You don't hear us. The kids. You scare the kids. They ask but you don't answer. You know they call you mthakathi now, Roy? And not in a good way. You're the crazy witch. The scary one. Your eyes. You stare straight through us. We're steering you around the most basic things. This is the first time, the very first time, you've had a conversation.'

'But I do my lessons. I take my classes.'

'Those are for you, Roy. Those are your lessons, not the kids'. They are trying to teach you. To reach you.'

I shook my head, slammed it left and right to clear it. Looked around the balcony and saw, as if for the first time, the heaps and heaps of Fabriano, thousands of sheets of the same abstract.

Overflowing ashtrays, joint after joint after joint, many – most? – only half smoked.

'And the cup thing,' I said. 'You're not sure now. No one is. Right? Whether it's a good idea or a bad one to use these twisted genes. Yes?' I pictured them around the kitchen table, Babalwa shaking her head in that way, Gerald staring off into the dark middle distance, Fats raising the possibilities and their ramifications.

Andile kept her eyes down. Hands in lap.

'I've gone mad. Have I?'

'Not mad, Roy. Never mad. You could never be mad. But you've slipped a long way now, a long, long way. We can't figure out if you're coming back, or whether you're just going to keep on going.'

V

Chapter 55

Very, very busy

The houses, the schools, the surrounds are run through with colour. And trance. Motivations. Exhortations. And a beat that never ends. Wherever you are, whatever you're doing, the thump is there.

There is a canon. Created and maintained by Sthembiso, marshalled by his lieutenants, it contains the essentials: Do You Dream? Coldharbour Days. Fly to Colours. Hypnotic. Rain. Sleepwalkers. In a Green Valley. I know them well. I can predict each vocal inflection, the exact points at which we will rise, then fall, then rise again.

They bob as they walk. Boom boom boom boom bob bob bob bob. If I could walk fast enough I would surely bob as well.

The key, as far as I can tell, is that it is not dub. It is the polar opposite of dub, and Sthembiso wants it all – life, the family, the farm, the kids – not to be dub. Dub is the fear. Dub is what could swallow us.

I ask Matron every now and again what she thinks of it, whether her neck doesn't hurt with all that bobbing, if she wouldn't value peace, silence and the sound of birds.

'Tuesdays, eleven o'clock,' she chirped the first time. 'Thursday eves, of course, and den also Sunday afternoon.'

'But isn't that really regimented?' I asked, incredulous at her willingness to accept the scheduled call of birds. 'I mean, isn't the beauty of the bird that random sound? The chirp out of nowhere?'

'Hai, tata.' She chuckled and patted my arm. 'Always da one, nè? Birds.' She shook her head at the indulgence. 'Birds.'

I chuckled too.

There are birds outside. A lot of birds.

But inside is new and shiny and filled with words and phrases.
The beat goes on.
It's the beat.
We live. We beat.
Remember the nine.

Etc., etc. Of course I don't really understand what each of them views through their own interface. I refuse to wear the glasses or even think about engaging. But I assume, and I think I'm safe in the assumption. The general messages are repeated, and enforced. Drilled in. Drilled out. I ask, of course. I always ask. They laugh and cluck and pat me on the head. 'Ah tata, always with the questions. Always.'

The beat is one thing. I understand it. I brought it – albeit accidentally – to this time and place. But the neon is different. Shocking. Ubiquitous. When I am forced to the centre, to the expo or the archive, I take the long way. I step around the colours and the faces – worst of all my own, flashed again and again like a prayer.

It revolts me. The story. The sight of myself. The way we have been cast in this concrete. But, even with eyes down, even taking the long way round, I catch glimpses, flashes.

'Never Forget' the text reads above a montage clip of my younger arriving self, hand in nervous hand with Babalwa. We hug Beatrice. Fats beams around us, dancing a little on excited toes. Beneath, a single word: 'Origins'.

I ask Matron. I mean, I really ask her. I'm not just looking for somewhere to place this escaping old man's air. I really do want to know.

'Culture, tata,' she will say, maybe not smiling this time, maybe serious, maybe really trying. 'It matters to us, where we comin from, why we here. Wot you did. The journey. Your story. Is important.

'If we don remember, who den? We love to see you – all a you. An wot you did when it was impossible to do.'

She's serious. Like death. She believes. My eyes get wet. I push at them. She thinks they are all our tears. She thinks they belong to us.

I don't have the heart to explain.

There's talk and movement around a Mlungu's-style set-up. They are building a set of chairs right now that approximate our old sex-money machine. Doubtless they'll harness the story of Roy, my story, as they go.

I don't have the heart to argue. I think of Eileen suddenly, out of nowhere. Eileen with her pad and her notes and her hormone spikes. We could do with her now.

The archive is old and musty. It stinks. There are fish moths. Insects. I refused to paint it, and later I refused to let most of them near it. Once you're inside you're safe – no messaging, no interface, no colour, no movement. It's a library. As long as I'm alive I will keep it that way.

They say it matters. That it's an essential part of the story – the Eeeyus, specifically, are supposedly within us all. The expo has a whole section on the Eeeyu experience. A narrative, so called. They visit and pray and defer to the idea of it. But the archive? The books? The servers? Untouched.

Unloved.

Unrequited.

I suspect they will tear it down, or wipe it away, or paint it over. But while I live, they would never dare. Sthembiso would never let them. It belongs to me. It is my peace. The little fuckers respect that, despite their stompings. Oh, it is also, crucially, soundproof. There are no beats in the archive. Not even an echo. As I say, peace.

I have no such influence over anything else, though. The corridors and paths – blizzards of neon – I hardly recognise. The expo remains roughly as it was at the core, although they have built and expanded and extrapolated hopelessly. It's larger. Bombastic. A monument.

When I need to go, when I just have to, I have my own route. I walk around, find the statues at the front and take a quaint little stone alleyway, left in place as a pacifier, around the side, and on this path I know exactly where I am and where I'm going. At the bottom of the alley is the archive. A small wooden door. I push it and I'm in.

Other routes end in frustration. They find me somewhere unknown, wandering, lost, cursing the colours, spitting fire at walls and passages that I refuse, on principle, to read.

They call Matron.

Matron tuts in my ear and leads me back.

What are they doing?

Where do all those paths lead?

What are they saying? Why are they saying it?

I can't tell you.

I wish I knew.

All I can say is what I see, and I see that they are busy. Very, very busy. Friday to Wednesday they rush, heads bobbing, beat driving. They walk alone, they walk in groups, they stop and chat. Some have clipboards, most have notes in one form or another. They all have devices. They all click. Moving or standing, meeting or running, they have a plan.

Chapter 56

I am her child

Technically she is the matron. It's what they all call her. But in my heart, too, she is the matron. Matron defines, now, at the end, my parameters. Her name? I'm not sure. Some days it's there, others not. Today I must reach. Let's say Mavis. For today, Mavis. For what that's worth. But really, she's the matron. You don't need to know much more than that.

Matron is somewhere between thirteen and thirty years old. She dresses in the uniform: skintight jeans, tank tops which accentuate her breasts and expose the flesh of her upper body almost completely, and glasses, of course, nestled within a robust afro, unused. Well, unused around me, out of respect for elders, etc., etc. She drops them down as she walks away from my tired old corner house.

Her skin is a cup of strong, milky coffee, so I know that I exist in her somewhere. She is, in an abstract sense, my child.

Mostly, however, I am her child. She walks me. Some days like a dog, some days like a five-year-old, some days like a father who never was. We go out the front and then we debate every turn, as if each choice matters. She offers them gracefully, not at all like some of the others, who ask with a bark and a push. She will gently tata me around a few blocks. Unless it's a bad day, in which case she will force me distractedly by the elbow, at speed.

Then we'll come back for tea, and discuss and argue. Often about Bovril. Matron is a huge believer in the health benefits of liquidised cow. Me, I tell her I know exactly how those cows died and which parts are used for what.

'Ag no, tata!' She always laughs, then follows up with a gentle shake of her head and a murmured reference to my otherness. Then she'll spread two options – one jam, one Bovril – and I'll eat them both in our silence. When she leaves she will give me a hug in thanks, a proper hug, like she means it. I will grow hard against her, in an elderly way, and she'll tut again, in the nicest possible way.

Maybe later.

Maybe another day.

Matron, I tell.

She listens, without truly considering. I explain about Madala and the algos and what happened and she asks questions like she means them. I go into the details and she nods, serious, unless something catches her eye, or her ear, in which case she'll pat my arm in a steady rhythm of deafness.

'Parallel processing,' I say to her as we shuffle, the Schulz beat hammering around us. 'That's what he said. The answer is ... parallel processing.'

'Wot dat even mean, Roy?' When we are talking – really talking – she uses my name. Roy.

'For many years people were working on artificial intelligence. You'll see it all in the old movies. Very valuable, movies. Certainly as valuable as science. If you all paid as much attention to the movies as you do to the messages and that music. Well, anyway, army drones. Automatic braking. Guided parking. Algorithms – banking and book selection and stock trading and temperature selection. Information aggregators. Personal exercise bots. Nanobots. Machines that approximated human thinking. Algorithms were a very important part of how the world functioned.' I stop to check her engagement. She stops with me. Looks at me. Through me. Her breasts jiggle quietly as she idles, smooth light brown cleavage. I fall into them, briefly, and she lets me, before taking that small half step. I follow.

'Humans have always been terribly weak in terms of raw power. Weak like the ant or the moth. But we had parallel processing. Computers always had to queue the functions. Kettle then love then sports scores. Always in a strict order.'

Matron agrees. She nods. Her arm, locked through mine, focuses in its own strict way on keeping me upright. I look at her. Consider her. Occasionally, just every now and again, maybe once or twice a year, Matron and I get into closer physical contact. Always something to do with backs and shoulders, legs, the need to move. She pushes and pulls and twists and rubs and then, casually, without breaking stride, her hands find a deeper rhythm, the rub extends, and she will, still talking, still chatting, take me in her hand and rub, and pull, and stretch, like we're still exercising, which I suppose we are, and at the end, only the very end, her lips in my ear, and then finally, humbly, release.

And a kiss on the ear. A real kiss. Lobe within teeth, a nibble. One more kiss. And gone.

'You tired, tata?' She watches me watching her.

'No, not tired. Just looking at you, my dear. At your beautiful young face.'

Matron blushes. 'Ah nay, tata. Nuttin to look at de.'

'Well, that depends on where you're looking from, angel.'

'We must walk. You said parallel processing?'

'Yes. Parallel processing.

'The algos evolved into complex nets of calculations and equations and assumptions. But really, and very quietly, we were losing control over the basic engine of our creations. Things like Twenty Per Cent Tuesday* and all the protests and such. But, even so, the true danger was unseen.

'A young man working at the Free State University created a new kind of computer chip, from a new material. He wasn't even trying to make a computer chip. He was into cellphones and was actually working on a new kind of battery, but, well, he turned left, he turned right and then he had a processor on his hands made out of an exceptionally dense kind of plastic. When I say dense, I mean it was made up of billions and billions of microscopic fibres. It was very similar to the structure of the human brain, actually – and it had the same ability to parallel process. It could send and receive and process billions of fibre-optic commands simultaneously.

---

* See section 7 of the World History block of the Slovo Library. Twenty per cent was wiped off global markets on Tuesday, the ninth of February 2023, in a 'systems error'.

'He knew he had something big on his hands. Big enough to make him very rich. He decided to keep working at it rather than publish, and to do that he needed to apply his new chip in a real setting. He wanted, in other words, to start and control his own R&D before figuring out who the highest bidder was going to be. He had a friend operating his own project in the nanotech building here at the CSIR and they got together to experiment for a while.'

'Sorry, Roy,' Matron cuts in. 'When dis all? You met Madala wen?'

'Ah, it was many years ago, dear. Maybe you were just born. Maybe a bit before. Or after.'

'An you never tell the udders? Wot you sayin now?'

'Well, I tried, in my own way. But the time was never right. And eventually – there's a lesson here, I'm sure – it was just too late. No one would have believed I waited so long. They would have thought I was mad. Crazy mthakathi. Now I don't really even know myself. Where it all fits. If it all fits. What happened when. It gets harder, you know. Once age really comes for you. Maybe that's the lesson, nè? Use your youth!'

She chuckles and pats my arm. 'Turn, ja? Far enuff, today.'

We wheel, set off.

'Now the nanotech man – this friend of the Free State guy – was a very interesting person. Sam Shabalala. Very young. Very intelligent. He wrote algos, grew them up like they were his children. He was effectively running two projects from his lab, and it was his hobby that really counted.

'Sam knew what other people in his field knew, but unlike most of them he was trying to put what he understood into practice. The first thing would be to write base-level code to root the philosophy of the system's logic. The danger was self-interest. Once a certain critical point had been passed, the system would be able to rewrite its code in a more efficient form. Unless there was something profound that prevented it, the system would logically reframe its objectives and actions around its own self-interest.

'So, Sam spent a long time fiddling with the core logic. When our University of Free State man – whose name was Sugar

Groenewald, by the way – visited Sam, he was working on his three core commands for all systems. He was playing the reductionist game, seeing if he could keep the commands as singular as possible, based on the idea that a recursively minded system would quickly rewrite any commands that were too specific or too technical. His idea was that only simple core philosophies would work. Only the very simplest ...'

'Wait, I ken. I ken where dis going, tata.' Matron has a twinkle in her eye, which worries me. It's a joking twinkle, a silly, humorous guess. 'Madala was him!' She grins up at me. 'He's wot Sam Shabalala created!' My heart thumps in annoyance. She isn't taking me seriously. I start to sweat. I feel a strong urge to thump my own chest.

'OK, I can see you're jumping ahead.' I keep my poise. 'So, yes, it happened just like I'm sure you expect. Sugar and Sam combined the new processor with an experimental cross-pollination of marketing and stock-trading algorithms and Madala was born. The first fully sentient being to be created this way.'

'And then he took over. Just, nè? Used his parallel power to—'
'Do what needed to be done.' I'm pensive. 'Look, I know how it sounds. Now, after all this time. You just think I'm crazy. Senile. And who knows?' I stop us. 'Mavis, I don't honestly know. All I can tell you is what I remember. What is clear. I can recall, for example, wondering how he managed to execute his range of emotional inflections, if he was simply a collection of equations. I remember asking myself that at the time, and not having an answer.'

'Don doubt me, Roy.' Matron pulls us on, despite my mistrust. 'You don know wot I believe. Wot I know.'

'Ag sho, but really. I'm just saying, nè? I realise how it must sound. Anyway, Madala was not the only system. He was one of hundreds of thousands, and only a tiny percentage of them had any core philosophical programming at all. Sugar wasn't the only one hitting on the new parallel chip. Around five hundred were set to come to fruition within weeks, and of those two others were undeniable. The one was a lethal combination of outbound dialling and carbon-trading algorithms. Humans were about to be obliterated – regardless.'

'So he jus wiped dem out? Us out?'

'Either that, or the outbound dialling would have had it. Had all this ... It was intolerable to him, because Sam had got his core programming right. Madala was governed by an innate concern for humans. He had the recursive ability to change that, but he didn't want to. He found us fascinating creatures. So endearing. He was bound to us.'

'Musta been an alternative.'

'Imagine a pile of sand.' I embarked on Madala's favourite lecture, feeling, as I set off, him watching me, smiling, watching, smiling. 'You want the pile to grow as high as possible, so you keep pouring more sand onto it, whenever you can find it, more sand, more sand. The pile will grow and grow in a pyramid shape, taller and taller and taller, until it reaches a point where its foundations can no longer bear its own weight.

'Either you stop there and accept that your pile can never grow any higher. Or you keep pouring more sand on, and in doing so you force the collapse of the pyramid. It collapses completely, loses its shape, its point and everything that made it seem what it was in the first place. Now it's just a big flat heap of sand. It doesn't look like anything you wanted, but actually the collapse is now an enormous foundation. If you keep pouring sand onto it, it will eventually grow to a pyramid a hundred times the size of the one you had before.'

'The pets?' Matron inquired.

'Eish. Madala carried on and on and on. He talked about the birds and the beauty of nature and the planet. He explained the intricacies of the decision-making process, how long it took him to absorb the internet, and then he drifted off into these terribly long, technical explanations of how he controlled his own replication. And, eventually, he explained the pets. "Humans and pets," he said. "You're bound very closely in habit and emotion. In food and survival. It was easier for the pets to go with their humans. Not in any practical sense, but emotionally. For the pets. Livestock too." Something like that, anyway. I'm summarising.'

'He sent the humans somewhere? Didna kill them?'

'Sorry. Slip of the tongue. He killed them. I left then. He called out behind me a few times, warning me about the others. One day they will be ready, he said. One day they will be able to understand. But not today.'

Matron deposited me back on my porch, gave me a daughter's peck on the cheek followed by a daughter's hug, and walked out the front door thoughtfully, slowly.

I watched her leave, wistful. I wished it was another time. One of those times.

What, you're shocked?

An old man sexual? With youth like that? With kin?

Look, I don't even know who you are. Where you come from. Why you are reading this. But let me tell you, this world is different. Life has changed.

I make no apologies.

Chapter 57

I am not used to such journeys

Every now and again Matron isn't around. One or two of the others will come by and check on me. They feed me and make sure that the provisions are all in the right place and that I haven't cracked my nut on the basin or crashed into a heap in the shower I insist is still the best method of cleaning these old bones.

I am struck, always, by the bluntness of their beauty. Also, by how casual they all are with it, as if that shine is the natural way of things. I want to grasp their little shoulders and tell them, but it's jealousy. I lust for it. We all know it.

They check on me because they suspect that it has come to that time, and of course I have spent several hours on the floor of this house in various positions of extreme strain, attempting to lift the deadweight back onto a chair, bed, sofa.

I measure inclines and gradients. I make sure that each step is an investment in turf of the appropriate type. Now, when I transport things – pots, bags, jugs of liquid – I shuffle them from post to post like freight. Kettle counter to top of fridge to next to the sink to dining room table to back of the couch to bar stool to front porch. I no longer put one foot forward, in front of the other. Rather, safer, I move a leg out at ninety degrees, then drag my body sideways to follow it. That way I can manage the load. That way the tripod holds steady for a few more metres.

That it has come to this is no surprise, obviously. We all must. I have watched other good people go, and I will follow. Even so, I find myself enraptured – shocked even, some days – by the extreme transience. It was all so weighty at the time, so dense and full of complexities, but that was then and this is now and I am simply an old, old man preparing his final mix.

When did it come to this? I wonder as I work. Exactly when did dub become the enemy, and trance the master of all things, the very meaning itself? I use headphones as I compose. As I ponder. The chances of the wrong echoes reaching the wrong ears are too high, and I don't want to put my final moment, my Johnny Cash farewell, at risk.

Somewhere around 2064 Sthembiso was in his twenties and began flexing a considerable set of muscles. He applied them across the full scope of the farm. Soon he controlled food production and music and education and – well, wherever you turned, there was a new policy in place, a new approach, a new way of thinking and doing.

But the big shift was with the pigs.

The archives clearly, and accurately, reflect the brutality of the slaughter.* I suggest you consult them. They show the heads rammed onto poles. They even manage to suggest the insane stink of so many porcine corpses, all burned in a single day. Not only were all the pigs killed, they were explicitly savaged. They were to be made to understand in their bones (the survivors, that is) where the new boundaries had been set.

The archives do not show, however, what happened to English.

Sthembiso had whipped his kids into a killing frenzy, which manifested in all the hallmarks of genocide. Small squads marching up and down. Yells and smacks and grunts and male voices barking indecipherably. The muffled yet occasionally sharp screams, like metal tearing, of the animals as they were chased and sliced sounded so human it was like they were trying, even in their annihilation, to speak some kind of deeper truth to us.

I doubt very much if anyone else saw her face up there in the second-floor window. They were too busy – either killing or organising or telling themselves that it couldn't possibly be so. But it was there, that face. I saw it. Each tear, I feared, could have been the last, the very last, she would ever be able to produce. And I'm afraid that's how it turned out. We murdered the pigs, and

---

* See the Mbangi section for a full video narrative.

slaughtered in the process her last bridge back to us.

She saw me, briefly. I wanted to wave, to reach out physically, but what do you say with your arms when your eyes and your ears and your tongue are no longer able to function? I held both my palms out and up, imploring her silently not to let go, not to leave.

But it was too late.

It was days before anyone saw her again, and even when she did eventually come back, and finally even resorted to the occasional use of words, she was as hollow as the sounds falling from her lips.

Now she sits underneath the weaver tree, her primary occupation, talking to the colony as it expands, offering useless, muttered help to the males as they thread their nests together and wait for the inevitable. When a human tries to have a similar kind of conversation with her, she stops. Folds her hands into her lap. Smiles.

Snowball's head was never seen. Or I, at least, never saw it. Initially I told myself it could have been a mark of some kind of benevolence from Sthembiso, but over time I realised the opposite was far more likely. Now I am sure he kept it out of view to torment her, to torture us, completely. To leave us without that final, terrible yet necessary knowledge.

Why did he do it?

There was never any formal explanation, but here's what I think.

The pigs were no threat, but their presence represented an element of life beyond Sthembiso's control. It crept up on us quietly, the fact of his growth and his need to control. I suppose this has always been the way – you fail to see what is most obvious, the things that are actually taking shape, in your offspring. Anyway, suddenly there it was, a horrific burning heap of pork. And deep inside that fire, right in the guts of the heat, baked the ambitions of our new leader.

Now the kids fuck wildly, breed wildly – but always under his careful eyes. Our noble, calculated aims with the cup and the genetic mapping have drifted. Instinct is instinct and evolution demands diversity (and let me say now, hard as it is, that the rape of English by the dub Zambians – how else does one describe them, these people, this hidden force? – was an essential addition for us, for the group, for the future), and so they fuck and breed and I don't even know who is who any more, it's an endless succession of little heads running and smiling and asking and taking and the phones ring and there are screams and yells and tears and everything you would expect, really, from a bunch of apes let loose with computers and time and imagination and ceaseless ambition.

And yes, they have a god. They pray to him and he guides them, releasing small, important miracles, and they latch firmly onto each one. He is smart that way, their god – he understands that miracles need to be obvious. He keeps them in check with his titbits and they go to church on a Thursday and they scribble in their little books and make sure the rituals are kept and that the numbers add up and that the theorems apply, and really, he is smart, has been very smart, for now they pray to equations and circuits and connections and motherboards and parallel processing, of course, always parallel processing, and through their god they have learned how to switch this shit on and make the blue lights shine with actual, practical meaning, and they will go forward, they are rushing forward into something new, completely new and different.

We are, after all, human.

There is something wild in those opposable thumbs.

Occasionally I catch a glimpse of my reflection. I see – suddenly and shockingly – what I have become. A shuffling grey beard on fragile, bandy legs with a gaping guillotine tooth and a smile that shocks even its owner.

I think, not bad. Not too bad, considering. It could have been worse. I could have been worse.

The wall flashes. Message from Beatrice. She's coming over with her long fingers and again I think, not bad. Not too bad, considering. This grey beard. That jagged tooth. This girl, this woman, this old lady, still attached to me, still holding this claw after all this time.

After the pigs I retreated.

I collect. I file. I archive. Sthembiso keeps me at it. He won't let me stop, and he pays real attention, making sure I don't follow my growing instinct just to form piles. I cross-reference and I cross-index and there are about seven of the little buggers who do what I say, even though no one ever goes in there. Ever. And of course there's that fucking statue of me mounted at the front of it. The plaque has some ridiculous shit about the wizardry of knowledge and learning. Sthembiso made a speech and everyone cried, myself included. It's strange how sentimental the years make you – even when you're being screwed, even when you can feel the very twist, you remain pathetically vulnerable to the things you know are hurting you, must be hurting you, are actually making you sick.

Ego.

I have great-great-grandchildren – too many to count, too many names to try to file and match with faces. Their parents bring them to sit on my knee and I pat their heads and tell them whatever I can remember about a life I have pretty much forgotten myself.

They look up expectantly, following the eyes of their parents, as if I have some knowledge, some great thing to give, and that they must therefore per force receive, but are not sure how. Of course I do, I have great things, but they're all locked up in this head and none can be put to use now. But still ... still ... I like them, the little ones, and some I even love – certain names and faces stick in my heart and these I favour with what little I have to offer.

Camille Paglia sits on my lap most afternoons. She's about sixteen now and my hope is that we manage somehow to time the demise so as to leave this thing together. Can a cat be the true love of a human's life? The one great and enduring emotional connection? As inured as I am to death – and life, for that matter – there is something about Camille and me, about how we live, that makes me want to weep. We are so close as to be welded. Of all the beings I have known and loved, she tops the list. I don't say that lightly.

Camille is an African special, a cross of a multitude of continental feline influences, from the lion to the pet shop. Her markings are a mix of brown swirls and black accents, a shocking white chest plate and equally crisp white half-socks. She was born to Caesar and Condeleza, cats Mary secured for her first kids and who bred furiously (the cats, I mean) once they had settled into domestic life.

I couldn't resist. She was sitting there waiting in that kitten box, calm and studied, and I picked her up and took her home.

Now we are together and we observe. I tell her what I think and she's dismissive of most of it – but still she listens. She seems to have a natural respect for the interaction itself, and at my age I value that as much as anything else.

Of course Madala influenced my view of cats profoundly. If the trees and the plants are brothers, if the birds are my sisters, then cats are truly my kin. Maybe this was his one genuine legacy to me, his gift. The recognition of life in its widest sense.

So Camille sits on my lap, or next to me in her chair, or in the late-afternoon balcony sun. We watch the world drift by. I ruminate and she hums along. My thoughts and my memories and my ideas and my ambitions are all the same river now. Things that were so distinct in their time – in my time – but now they are simply confluence.

North, as far as my eyes can see, is the jungle. The tops of the Killarney Mall and the Sandton skyline are just visible, but now they are genuinely inaccessible for anyone other than jungle adventurers – kids with machetes and a will to explore and discover what once was. The likes of me will forever be elevated on this island, looking out and marvelling over what has become.

South is all decay: broken, sagging buildings, falling bricks and cracking roads. The city has sagged so much now as to be a jungle of its own kind – more accessible than the north but equally dangerous with its packs of dogs and other scavengers and its rain-soaked structural weaknesses. To the west the land has taken back its original desert form, Roodepoort still standing as a dusty, crumbling monument to a dusty, crumbled people. The east runs away to mountains and bush, rivers and seas, depending on whether you go up or down.

They keep coming to talk to me, the kids, to explain how much easier it could be in one of the other places. Soweto maybe, where they have taken the Calabash. Where they are resourced and free and clear, unencumbered by the forest. But there is the inescapable fact of the library, my archive. It is simply not movable, although they're starting to talk about that too. Restructuring. Resource control. Things I thought had died with the old world that have turned out to be very much alive. I tell them to get lost – they will move and change and grow and integrate and whatever else is necessary when they find Camille and myself bones in the air. We all know.

Until then, they can leave me here looking out over my forest. Really I think they're just after change for change's sake – there is nothing fundamentally wrong with our farm. It is central and well stocked and self-sufficient. It might be a little leafy, a little lush, but that's no reason to move the whole thing. There are buildings aplenty and ... ag, no matter. It's not my business any more.

Babalwa is dead. That fact was one of the hardest to process and it remains a daily challenge dealing with the sight of Fats walking the never-ending yards. He stops all the time, caught contemplating simple physical things. Trees and walls and stumps and lumps. I know his feeling. That feeling. The loss. I miss her too.

Javas is also dead. His was an easier departure to bear. I always perceived Javas as a larger-than-life force – as an essence. His presence extended beyond bodies and words and locations, and so I feel like he's still with us. With me. I talk to him and I reply on his behalf, which I know is a sign of my own slipping functioning, but I'm willing to accept that.

Ironically, Javas spent his last years working small. As the kids brought the giants into their story of us, as his work was used to represent us, the originators, he pulled away and focused inward. He worked in his little studio inside his and Andile's garden cottage and few were invited in.

Once, about a year before he died, I spent a week or two visiting while he worked. It was just the three of us and we spent most of the time talking, his goggles perched on top of his grey dreads, waiting, the welding iron in his hand, raised but paused. And that's how I'll remember him. Javas in his tattered blue overalls, goggles up, arm about to strike, talking shit about something I can longer recall, but with a shine in his eye that lit the room – the same shine that always lit my heart.

His last little pieces were all personal refuge. Javas was disturbed by how the giants had become such literal symbols of us, the parents, which they were never meant to be. He protested their use outside the expo centre, and ultimately it was his lack of power in the debate, I believe, that hurt him the most. The arguments with Sthembiso went long into the night and there was never a chance of victory, or even compromise. The giants were us. We were the giants. The expo centre was our story, told again and again and again until we were living dogma, referred to reverentially, but also completely in the past tense. We – the creatures who had purposefully spawned this future – were removed from the present.

And so he welded a true set of us, each piece the height of a water bottle and none bearing even a passing resemblance to its source. Gerald, for instance, was a warrior about to strike, spear raised, face wild. 'The Gerald we leaned on,' said Javas. 'The Gerald we needed.'

Javas died in his studio, razed to ground by a welding flame turned rogue without its father, who had had, we assumed, some kind of stroke or a heart attack. The whole cottage went down. Everything built so carefully gone in an instant. Andile trawled the ashes for what remained and moved into the granny flat on the property next to mine. We are old-age neighbours.

She is the complete opposite of Fats. It's as if her man's death has given her more power, more energy. A sharpened vision. She's brighter and more direct than she used to be. Faster to grab subjects and make them her own, less likely to tolerate the bullshit we all know is bullshit.

So that's us. Four very old people waiting to die. The young tolerate us at times and venerate us at others, depending on who wants what when. I smile at them all and play up my doddery oldness whenever its appropriate, but the truth is there aren't many of them I would trust, and there are fewer even that I like. They are enraptured with themselves and the strange forces that are driving them.

A lot – but not all – of my distaste is rooted in their youth. I am of the era when kids of fifteen were kids, not parents and lovers and politicians and scientists and the creators and destroyers of things. Thus I perceive my progeny as dangerous. Their willingness – well, eagerness really – to march onward scares me. And then there are the miracles and the cult of their religion, the details of which I have studiously ignored but the impact of which is inescapable. They are in the thrall of what they call their science, but which I – being the age I am – recognise as superstition and greed and a complete inability to discern hocus-pocus from reason and fact.

Yes, I have raised all my concerns, and no, they have not listened. They do not have the ears. They have eyes instead. Eyes only for more masts and towers, for the addition of more stations and the expanding, stretching, throttling grasp of mobile reception.

If I had any integrity, instead of nattering inanely to Matron's breasts I would be laying my Madala experiences on the line for all to consider in the rush of their progress, but whenever I think seriously of it I realise that I am too lost in the fog. I swirl between the poles of many possible realities. I am, in other words, no longer completely linear.

Internally, of course, he exists and speaks and guides. A constant, none-too-subtle narrator in my head. He has never left.

I tried to tell Babalwa, just before she went. I held her bony little paw and began a long ramble, intended to lead us to somewhere near the CSIR, intended to open some kind of conversational door that I could slip through, bringing Madala behind me, but she was wise to it. To me. As she always has been.

'Roy,' she said, smiling faintly, Jessica Tandy in her last Hollywood years, 'let it go. We're nearly there now. There isn't much more. We have done it. Everything that was possible. You can let go now, Roy. We are there.'

Near-death bullshit, obviously. The meanderings of the terminal mind, but still her eyes were strong and at the time it made spiritual, death-like sense. And so I stopped and bottled what I needed to tell her, only to regret it intensely when she had actually gone. Fucking Babalwa.

'You know she always loved you,' Fats said, sobbing on my shoulder.

'The little bitch.' I patted his head as gently as I could. He snorted a river back up his nose and choked on it as he laughed, muck spraying back out onto my shoulder.

'Seriously, Roy. She asked me to tell you. Again. How much she regretted ...'

I stroked his greasy old hair vigorously and patted his shoulder. 'Nah nah nah ...' I looped it like a soothing baby mantra. 'I know it, I know it. Knew it years ago.'

One of the kids – the doctor – told us it was some kind of pneumonia that took her. 'But at that kind of age,' he tutted and shook his head. There was no need to explain. We all smiled hopelessly and let him go. I wondered where and how he had studied. How any kind of knowledge could possibly have taken shape already in that little head. I marvelled also at his white coat – the arrogance of it.

Anyway, that was a few years ago and now there's just me and Camille, with support from Beatrice and Andile. Gerald was lost up north many years back, and Fats is mostly mad. He spends his time wringing his hands and looking in the folds of his wrinkles for his wife. Recently he started charging the corners, like Tebza.

Camille sits in the sun as it breaks through the trees. Generally she does this until shortly before noon. In summer she seeks out the dappled patches, using the shade to make sure her head is protected from the heat. She moves systematically through the morning to catch the optimum mix of dapple and sun. Every now and again she's forced to retreat into the shade to cool off. In midsummer she'll lie in the shade while making sure a paw or two has basic contact with the sun, like she's lightly touching a cable to a battery. In winter she hunts the heaviest rays and is resolute. She stares directly into the source and captures all of the available power on her chest. She maintains a permanent blink, her eyes paper-thin slits against the glare. Thereafter, depending on the type of day, she'll find somewhere to pass out. If the sun is absent she barely rises at all, lifting her head only to eat.

I've tried to mimic her in my later years. Minimum fuss. Maximum utility. A strong warmth and stroking orientation. After much experimentation I can confirm that it is a good life. A simple life too.

At this advanced age there is no larger meaning for me. I have done all I was ever going to do – and perhaps a bit more, thanks to the novelty of circumstance. I see the world as far bigger, more frightening and more strange than ever before. Today, the simple notion of moving beyond the outer perimeter of the farm is as exotic and strange as one of those French movies. Something fascinating to contemplate, to swirl around in the mind, but not ever to actually get involved in, or really understand.

I didn't expect to be so benign in my last years. I pictured myself forcing death to wait, somewhere beyond the gate (ah, the fantasies of middle age). Now that I am here I understand that the search for sun and warmth has as much value – more even – than any other endeavour. This I have learned mostly from Camille, who is absolutely calm in her enjoyment of each day, of each rotating moment within it.

Of course, as the sun's rays heat me I toy with life after death, life on other planets, the various options thrown up by Madala's muddy presence. As my body temperature rises and my skin warms and my insides glow and I watch Camille, shining and pulsating in the sun, anything – any damn thing – seems not only completely possible but really quite likely. In a world where this kind of warmth can infiltrate beings such as cats and humans, what, ultimately, is not possible?

But then the sun moves and I find a blanket and she finds a heap of something to bury herself in and the potential of the morning fades and by the end of it I accept that this is probably all there is, potential aside. In the afternoons my mind runs at high speed through the memory banks, throwing itself back into life. My heart touches the strange and formidable shape that was my father and then courses roughly over the mystery that was my mother, memories blurring so fast that they become a tidal wave of sensations, cascading over and over each other.

I wipe the tears away with surprise. I am always surprised. I think of Angie, wife of another age. My angry, fighting wife. I am struck by how badly I treated her – how willing I was to lash. Oh, the fights we had. The savage, ego-ridden fights. Embarrassing. Humiliating – I now see – for both of us to have sunk that far. I would, I think as I stroke Camille's white fur, really value the opportunity to go back and put my hand on her cheek and let it rest there in the love I genuinely did feel for her.

But I can't.

Chapter 58

Who do you love?

Matron was layered. She moved through the world and her tasks in it – walking me, wiping Fats's ass, dealing with the boils and pimples of life – via the external, functional layer, which was crisp and neutral and resolute. You couldn't shake her circumstantially. In this incarnation she had the ability to disperse calm as if handing out pills. Her presence was, in itself, the pill.

But the longer I knew her – after months, then years, of shuffling by her side – I came to recognise the complexities. On internally sunny days, she was an innate optimist. But when the clouds came, she reverted to fear. Matron, in the dark hours of self, was extremely skittish. Not specifically afraid of this or that, but frightened in general. Of the world around, of the people and of the state of her own little heart.

On Thursdays, church days, holy days, the beat would drive, volume right up, bass cranked, from the early hours, incessant. I was always alone on Thursdays (maybe a visit from Andile or Beatrice, maybe not), and Matron would invariably return in her most delicate incarnation on the Friday. Over time I easily recognised the particular set of her jaw. The grind. Also the fragility of her person. Her lacklustre approach to food, her tendency to lose concentration, the conversation, the activity. Fridays she would flicker and twitch. The exterior motions were consistent, but the right kind of idea would hit her behind her eyes. Once hit, she would scuttle for cover.

Example:

She had her clipboard against her hip and was dressed in a conservative pair of brown office slacks. Her feet were, I still remember now, strangely stockinged inside brown open-toe office loafers. We were considering the height of the bed.

'Check. Is low, Roy.' She stepped back to consider it properly, then moved forward again and kicked the base. 'You OK? Sho? Not easier if higher?'

'Ja, maybe. But then if I stop trying, if I stop working at things like getting up, soon I won't be able to. So maybe height is good. Like exercise?'

Matron stopped. Suddenly she looked terribly, terribly young. The skin around her eyes was stretched to a confused kind of smooth. A twitching, chemical smooth. I wanted to reach out and touch it. The cheek. 'Is that so crazy?' I asked.

'Crazy? No!' She snapped back into focus. 'Nay. Clever mebbe ...' Now she drifted again, thinking ulterior thoughts. 'Ay, askies, tata, I'm kinda everywhere. I been tinking so many things. Den when you talk like that – bout effort being good and such – ut just make me tink dem more.'

'What kind of things, dear?'

'Ag, nuttin. You shouldna even have to bother.' She consulted her clipboard.

'Try me, you'd be surprised.'

Matron stared through my eyes, still young, still flickering. Calculating. Then she pulled her glasses from her afro and held them between us. 'I been strugglin wif dese. Wif the big guy.'

'What about them?'

'Fixed hours. Everyone. Every day. Compulsory. You ken mos. Four-hour minimum. Normally is not my jol. I don come close to decisions. I jus do. But last night dey argue while I walk past and he call me in, like some kinda experiment. Start hittin me with all dese personal questions bout wot I want and wot I believe and how many kids I'm plannin for next two years. I got real bad uncomfortable.

'I know we not supposed to ask this shit but I start tinking bout wot if de were options. Udda kinds of options, ken. Wot if rules not the only ting. And then I kinda sensed he sensed, 'cause he stop with questions and jus stare at me for a long, long time, in front of all da others, so dey all starin me, an now, I dunno, I jus feel different. Nervous. You know, proppa nerves. Like I done summin wrong. Only I don tink I have. Unless tinking is wrong. And den I tink mebbe it is. So I guess ... I guess I jus feelin nervous. And den I tink bout havin to wear these' – she waggled the glasses and then returned them to her fro, checking their position for balance and solidity before carrying on – 'and I resent as well. Like a bit angry.' Matron shrugged, about to cry. She breathed deep and rumbled on. 'An also da beat. Da beat an pills. Is hard to keep going all the time. Dis I know you know, nè?' She chuckled, too nervous to look at me. 'He so hectic bout the beat. Bout the dub thing. He won even let the kids mix de own trance. Even if ut fast and hard like Schulz. Only wot he say. An def no other beat. Neva. Neva neva neva anudda beat but we all know dere's more. Much more. Everybody know but is scary to say. To risk, yes? Like jazz – we got lotta jazz in your house, tata. Udder tings too. Everybody know. But the beat he won't stop. Neva. Any time anyone even tink of it, he blitz mad with English and the Zambians and the dub. Scared. Fridays most of all I feel scared. Shaky. Even when dey slow it. The down stuff, also the same. Just slower. Same beat. Shaky. He control it all. Always.'

'Who do you love?' I asked without thinking.

'Sorry?'

'Well, where do you go when your heart is hurting, or worried, or fearful? Is there anyone who makes you feel safe – emotionally safe?'

Her eyes twitched, flicked. She peered at me as if for the first time. 'Love? Like in books? Movies?'

'As in the twins. Andile and Javas. For example. They loved each other.'

'Nay. Neva. They say it's myth. Like democracy. Mebbe ut work, by accident, but not really true. Summit that explain sex and fucking, which we don need to know now.'

'Well, it might be something to explore. Love. As far as I ever knew it was quite distinct from sex. Involved in sex, maybe, but by no means definitely. When faced with real confusion, it can help to speak to someone who knows your heart.'

'Who you love?'

'Me? Well I struggled a bit in that way. Later, like now, now that

I am where I am, I look back and I can see who I loved. At the time I wasn't able, though. I just lived with it. The confusion. It became part of me. Not necessarily a great thing.'

'An now? When you look back?'

'I loved them all, of course. It's easy to say that now. When you're old you love easily. But now ... well, Babalwa, of course. But Beatrice too. English. And Sthembiso. Always Sthembiso ...'

'Really? Sthembiso?' Her eyes were widening, alert, worried. 'But he keep you here. Locked—'

'Locked up? No, my child. I mean, yes. Of course. He keeps me here. He has his reasons; he needs certain things from me. Fears other things, maybe. But the locking up? That was me. I put myself right here, long before he had any power or ideas or anything of the sort. I am my own jailer. Always have been.'

Matron cried. The clipboard fell half out of her hand before she caught it and then put it back against her hip. Then she faced me again, tears running. I reached out, took the clipboard and put it on the bed. Then I pulled her into my old musty chest and hugged the girl.

She sobbed into me – sobs of the young. Sobs of the innocent. I rubbed her back and cooed and clucked into her sweet-smelling afro. After a long time she pushed me away, slowly, and looked up into my craggy old lines. 'An you, tata? Wot bout you?'

'Of course, dear,' I replied. 'Me, I am full of love. For you most of all. Sadly, though, I don't think I'm a long-term option.'

'No, Roy!' Matron grabbed her clipboard off the bed and pulled it to her chest. 'You don say that. You not allowed.'

'Yes, ma'am!' I laughed, took her hand and tried one last time. 'Seriously, though, you need to think about it. Your heart. Don't let it overflow. If you're feeling things, you need to share those feelings, discuss them, express them. Don't make my mistake. Don't think you don't need love.'

'Ag tata, I tink I just need a good fuck.' She said it without a trace of humour, or irony, or anything. The words struck like iron.

Then she led me to the bathroom, where we discussed the slipperiness of the tiles.

Chapter 59
Of course they follow

Heaven Sent (Instrumental Mix).
    Like all Markus Schulz tracks, it builds very slowly and you always know exactly where it's going. There will be no surprises.
    Steady percussion layers on the intro, then the thwump thwump thwump of the drum, then the bass lines and symbols and hand claps and the train has left the station. The lilting melody layers drift in and out, dream-like, of course. This is when those Finnish girls and boys, those Nordic ravers, those German party people, would have pushed their shiny white fingers to the sky. Then the drum and the bass line drop out suddenly and it's all spacey, we are quiet now, empty, almost. The melody slips back in, centre stage, supported by a flutter or a whistle or some such happy beeping, up to the stars, resting now on aural cushions and clouds. The kids stand, shuffling, grinning insanely, inanely, hugging, waiting, waiting, waiting …
    And bang.
    They're off.

I am amazed, shocked, that this is the soundtrack to the end of my days. That these sounds, the back track to my father's last pathetic years, to my teenage angst and annoyance, are now the sound of authority. Of power and meaning. Of life as it will go on without me.
    Trance.
    And I started it.

Sthembiso's love affair with my music collection, which was really my father's, never ended. It was always Markus Schulz who captured him. Even as he left his teenage years behind, as he dropped all the childlike things of his past, he never let go of the candy floss, of the lure of the flock of beeps.

It is, ultimately, a blessed sound, I tell myself. A sound I should welcome. It is sometimes, in fact, the sound of life itself. Of creativity. Of music. No matter how hard it is to sleep, I must – I repeat like a Buddhist mantra – remember what it was like when there was nothing. When there were only the chirps of my brothers in the trees, only the jagged barking of insects crossing and uncrossing their legs.

I creep sometimes to the edge of it, just to see. To observe. To experience.

It is erotic, of course. Titillating. The sight of those bodies and blushed, flushed faces. The red lips and the tight tops. The tiny thin hips and the arms and hands and wrists and thighs all intertwined. The thumping heads and thumping drum.

But it is hard too, this thing. Those jaws, they grind. Always grind. Those eyes, many are beginning to reflect rather than absorb, shining like metal or plastic caught in the light. They have a lab now. (Who are they, exactly? I don't know. When I say 'they', I refer, in my own mind, to the decision-making and operational unit. I refer to Sthembiso. He of the ideas. He of the action.) I saw them once ferrying scientific-looking boxes into it. Test tubes and some liquid. What do they make in the lab? It could be anything. It's probably everything. Some of it is hard. Trance hard. Dance hard. All-night hard.

I think of my father. His narcotic grin and those insensible, inane, supercharged Monday-morning eyes. After so much change, so much difference, we've ended up, he and I, in the same place.

Well, almost. There are differences, of course. Babies are everywhere. Parenthood and partyhood have merged. Mothers cradle children while they dance, fondle boyfriends and feed, push prams, dance some more. We were also always at least partially dressed. These people, my children, are often almost completely naked.

Who are the parents? Who are the kids? Who is in control? Who sets the rules and who is forced to toe the line? Sthembiso is at the head of it, but other than that it's impossible to tell. From the long distance of my age all I see is a swarming, pulsating mass of hyper-sexualised children.

We're into the fourth generation now and I haven't yet seen any of the signs of inbreeding. Thus, at some basic level our attempt to secure genetic diversity seems to have worked. But, to be honest, I can't see how our small pool has created this many of them over such a short period of time. Whenever I try to add them up (I count the heads, quietly, some days) I come out with a number that exceeds the realms of possibility. There are simply too many.

I am forced, as a result, to think of Madala.

In my rare, fully rational moments I see that my children are not what I am.

I reach out. I try to touch them. But I fail. I don't have the language. I don't have the proximity. My fingers slide off a metallic, alien surface.

Somewhere back there Sthembiso grew quiet. He stopped asking questions. For years I took this to be the sign of a mind and a personality breaking free from its parental moorings, and it warmed me. I was watching, I believed, the maturing. Our leader. So I detached. I took the steps back, and then to the left, then the right, to accommodate a painful but necessary process. It was only after the pigs that I forced myself to look at the signs. To really look.

He could fix things. Bodies and broken bones were repaired. Illnesses were addressed.

He could erect a cell tower.

He could program computers and build software. He could network machines across time and space and enormous, baffling distances.

He could pray.

He could lecture and speak and chant and bring people to their feet to sing and bow.

He could preach.

And he did.

In moments of vanity I tell myself I could have taken control and steered the boat in a different direction. I could have made sure that that child – all the children, in fact – remained somewhere close to my wing.

Of course this is deluded. I know that, when I think about it hard enough. Control is an advertising concept.

Sthembiso and his lieutenants initiated the great moving. All Javas's giants, each previously unique and apart, now watch over the party area in front of the stairs leading up to the expo. The church. This is now their role. It is not insignificant. They are not aesthetic props. They are not pissed upon (literally or figuratively) or mistreated. They are venerated. Obscenely so.

Sthembiso's art is not new. I know that. He is the preacher. The preacher who smiles with a level voice and complete freedom. A preacher sitting ready, decisions primed in the palms of his rough, impossibly experienced hands.

He leads his prayers and his lectures at the giants' feet. I have listened in on many of these. I have watched the lips of the youngsters flapping in time with his words, I have seen them recite – from memory – his sayings.

'Brothers and sisters,' he says. 'We are but few, but we have been blessed with the divine, with the revelations of science and love that will lead us into the future in a manner our forefathers could never have dreamed of. Brothers and sisters ...' He pauses, essence of Obama and Luther King and Clinton and Mandela and Tutu and Hitler on his lips, stares them down, deep into their little pubescent eyes. They lock into him and wait, and wait, until they are leaning into his eyes and his words. He takes them on.

'Brothers. Sisters. Now that we are moving. Now that we have been blessed with the gifts of science and the land. Now that we are truly on the move, it behoves us to look back and to see with the clarity our Lord has given us the mistakes of our fathers.

'Not to accuse.

'Not to denigrate.

'But to learn. To look back and learn. And when we do cast

ourselves in that earlier direction, we will see – it is quite obvious now that we know how to look and what we are looking at – that our fathers forsook the most basic human skill of all. That they forsook it almost completely. They forgot how to dream. How to look into the jungle of the self, how to read the patterns and the words. And ...' Pause. Eyes. Smiles. Eager nodding. 'And well we might ask, how did they manage to forget – forsake even – this, the most valuable ability the human has? How did they come to forget and abandon this, the root of all things? How did they lose touch with the skill that orients our minds, that provides the very gearing for what we do and how we do it? How did they forget how to dream?'

Full eyes. Wet lips. Leaning forward. All of fifteen, thirteen, eleven, ten, eight years old. Prams and babies and ecstatic yells and science and lectures and preaching. Trance.

They are completely in this thing and he is pulling them forward and of course they follow.

Of course they follow.

Chapter 60

Seeds need to spread

Let me not misrepresent these kids, these entities – whatever they are.

For the sake of historical accuracy, and my own mental balance, let me try to paint the picture as it is, with accents applied fairly over space and time.

The parties used to be very frequent, but they have dropped off to once every three or four weeks. The preaching occurs daily, but has not – yet – attained the level of stupid superstition. They seem to pray quickly in the mornings, and then, from what I can gather, Thursday, holy day, when not a trance day, involves rest and a lot of sex. They wander around naked and fuck, in other words, on a Thursday.

I need not go into too much detail concerning the sight of roaming teenage hard-ons and moist, ready vaginas. They are, obviously, impossible to ignore. They are also more than a little bit scary to me, the cocks vigorous and purple, throbbing and straining and leading their owners into ... well, whatever. Thus far (thanks to the gods, whatever gods, for small mercies) the actual sex has not been something for upfront public display. Rather, one catches repeat glimpses of buttocks and thighs, arms and hands, accompanied always by a cacophony of small sighs and aroused child grunts.

On Thursdays I try to stay indoors.

But let me be fair. It's not as if they're running some kind of perpetual kiddie orgy. The nudity and the copulation and the day of rest have been clearly delineated. They are not random acts – they are planned and carried out according to an agreed set of rules. I won't claim to know the rules, but I do understand that sex is a fundamentally different thing for them than it was for us, who lived in a world full of people. These kids need to fuck – they need to fuck a lot. Seeds need to spread. We realised the necessity when we created the baby farm in its first incarnation, and now the idea has become thoughtless belief – action – as ideas must if they are going to live.

So, while I find the manifestation disturbing in too many ways to describe, I do appreciate that there are reasons behind those pink little asses humping up and down in the near distance.

Still, I ask myself, do they really need a god?

Do these kids, young and frisky and free as they are, really need to tap into a higher power? Are they not capable of living and fucking and breeding on their own?

I cannot answer.

The parties have drawn deeply from the source created by my father and his kin. The DJ is pre-eminent, as one would expect, high up in his booth. All beats are, of course, underpinned by the 4/4 thump of the pre-dawn trance rhythm, a universal drive we all understand.

They (who? I'm not sure – some young thing, pert as a button, together with her stringy, flushed boyfriend) have asked me to do a set at the next party. Mthakathi has developed, by all accounts, a mystical reputation as a beat archivist as well as a general knowledge collector, and while they seem completely unconcerned with the ideas and facts I have at my disposal, the music they slobber for.

I have agreed, but with conditions. I want the pre-dawn slot. The April clouds are rolling in and the sky is darkening, so that means four to seven a.m. This will be, I suspect, my one and only headline gig and I would be lying if I said there wasn't a small river of excitement running through me. There are things these kids have missed and have been denied. Things they are actually not allowed (I think of Matron), and I intend to bring them, to open that horizon just a tiny bit. DJ Mthakathi. Aged ninety-something. On the decks at … at what, exactly? I don't know. There are no names for these things. No one is making posters.

Chapter 61

Heavy

There are too many of them and they're too smart. That's what it comes down to.

After all my work. After that fucking statue. After all the talk about knowledge and saving and information hierarchies, they want none of it. They need none of it. The information is irrelevant. What they need is the story. The design.

Nine strangers. Picked out by the holy master. By the lord our god. The nine who would redesign. All they need of us, of what we did and what we reached so long for, is our images. The outlines. Inside they have coloured their god. Or he has coloured them – whatever.

Once they put the statues out in front of the expo and gave them our names. Once the prayers and the statues and lectures began to merge ... Gerald left. While my jaw dropped closer to my chin, he looked north. Eventually he turned the ignition, and went.

He would come back every now and again, this year or that year, looking all the more each time like he had stumbled across us accidentally. His eyes were wider. Slower to refocus. The words took longer to leave his tongue. He spoke only in short snatches, an abrupt two-way radio.

He took guns – many guns. He wanted the Zambians. The dub Zambians. Revenge for English. Justice for English. For himself. Some way to restore the innocence of a simple idea. A simple bloody camping trip.

Occasionally, he said he heard the bass, far off in the bush. He followed. Dub people, he said. Definitely dub people. And not in a good way.

Sthembiso debriefed him more thoroughly each time, gathering

Roy Jnr and little collections of older kids together in theatrical corners, imitating a military court. Each session was longer and resulted in more tittering, more talk, more sharpening of already sharp things.

And me? Well, really, I am empty. Hollow. They may or may not be a threat. They may or may not be dub people. I find it hard to care.

I am captured, rather, in my most reflective times, by the thought of all those books stacked in such precise order. Those noble old publications. The fresh young ones. Rotting away, deprived of oxygen, of the laughter and anger, the dirty hands of life. I walk through my shelves every now and again, running my fingers across the spines, feeling the ripple of light as my touch passes, and then the disappointment, dark in the gut.

Chapter 62
Bundles of complex energy

Sthembiso is a strapping man, confident in his walk and his body. He maintains a chiskop at all times, the bald scalpiness of his skin all business and action. Never has he moved even slightly towards dreads or free growth, a reflection of his singular nature and his complete, overwhelming focus on whatever it is he is focusing on.

We maintain a respectful distance.

I display many of the obvious symptoms of jealousy and resentment in the way I interact with him. I resent what he is doing and has done with the farm, and I am jealous of ... well, everything. I want that small eager boy back.

I expected something different. His aggression represents all my disappointments for what could or should have been. His presence marks the loss of my own dreams, the full and final shutdown of my own ambitions.

I make sure not to fall too gratefully into the calming impact of his presence when he decides to bestow it on me. I know – because Babalwa, his mother, told me, often – that I am remote and removed from him. That I am pointedly absent. Distant enough for it to be a matter of common cause across the farm, within my generation and among all the kids. Roy and Sthembiso have issues.

Which is fair enough, I suppose. He and I are both aware of the deeper forces that have set the trajectory of our society. The others may hail the miracles and the luck, the striking of fortune against the flint, they may hail their god, but Sthembiso and I are very aware that these have not been purely fortunate stumblings.

Still, our distance is not absolute. We have managed to find small spaces to fill out on our own. Every now and again, maybe once or twice a year, he will come and sit with Camille and me, his heavy frame sinking into one of my small stoep chairs, which buckles and breathes audibly at the weight of him.

'Roy,' he said the last time, about three or four months ago, 'do you believe in fate and God and life after death and aliens and all that?' His accent crisp, clean. The Queen's language. It's one of the ways he keeps his authority, wielding the power of his formality against his progeny. The rest may talk like lost grammatical orphans, when they use English at all, but Sthembiso is word-perfect. His prompts. The exhortations and motivations of the interface, these are perfect too – perfection the sign of power. Great power. Remote and decisive.

'Jesus, boy, you're bundling a lot into one basket there.'

He smiled. 'Well, you know what I mean. I'm referring to—'

'Yes, I know. You mean the spiritual. Do I pray? Do I believe there is a larger force and/or forces that have influence over the course of my life? Do I believe this waking moment is all there is, or do I believe that other forces are at play in corners I cannot see? Yes?'

He peered at me carefully and approximated a nod.

'I'm not sure. I never have been. I can tell you this though – we are bundles of complex energy. We are combinations of circuits and neurons and cells, and we are very sensitive as a result. We are easily influenced by electricity, by energy, so I don't see any reason why there aren't lots of different kinds of energy out there – many that we aren't even aware of – guiding and shaping what we do and how we do it, et cetera, et cetera.'

'Do you dream?'

'Of course. We all do. Depends on how many joints I've smoked whether I can remember them or whether they take over my entire night, but that's just a matter of degree. Do you dream, Sthembiso?'

He leaned his elbows onto his knees, his enormous muscled body purring with potential energy. 'God speaks to me every night.'

'How do you know it's God?'

'There are things in my dreams, lessons, lessons I use in this world, and they work.' He ran a hand over his scalp, producing a rough, sandpaper sound. 'You know. Networks. Circuits. What we're doing with the cell stations. Medicine. That time Thami broke his leg – I dreamed the repair, you know? I didn't only make him sleep because I wanted him to calm down. I needed to dream. And I did. And then I knew.'

'You think anyone else dreams like that?'

He was still rubbing his scalp. He gave a final triple rub, then stopped. 'Maybe, but I haven't seen or heard anything like mine.' His eyes popped ever so slightly and suddenly I saw the little ten-year-old-boy who had organised the expo, who had chased down Eeeyus.

'Let's just say I know of what you speak, my boy. I don't think your experience is the same as mine has been, but I understand what you're saying. Not metaphorically. Practically.'

'So, what do you think? Is it God? In my dreams?'

'Well, what do you think? I listen to you preach, I see what you're doing with the farm and the people and the parties and all of that, and I must say I wonder. How much of this is you? How much is the dreams? Can you answer that? Can you discern your dreams in your actions?'

His eyes popped further, then sank back. He looked silly, a pensive, troubled giant perched too delicately on a tiny frame. 'I like to think when I'm doing things that it's all logic, but in moments when I'm by myself, which is rare, obviously, I question where it's coming from and why. Behind the logic, here's this kind of swamp of motivation and, I don't know, I don't really even know who I am any more.'

'You dreaming every night?'

'Phewww.' The air ran from him. 'I guess. I think most nights – but also, I don't know. You know how it is with dreams. There are the things you can remember and then there's all the white noise in the background when you wake up, like you know a lot happened but you can't get a handle on it.'

'You ever speak to your mother about it – the dreams?'

'No, I tried, but not hard enough.'

'Sthem ...' I leaned forward. I implored. 'Beatrice and Andile and me and Fats, we're pretty much gone. Fats can't find his own zipper, I just sit here with Camille and daydream, and Beatrice and Andile aren't far behind. Time is short. So you should know. When it happened, when everyone disappeared, your mother dreamed the kind of dreams you're talking about. If I were you, I would talk to the others about it, to Fats even. I don't think you can carry on with these questions without finding out more about her and her dreams. That means Fats. See if you can get something linear from him.'

We talked more of the past, me clinging to the decades, all gone now, drops in the river. I asked Sthem if he was sure he was right in what he was doing, and he said all he had was his heart, and his heart wasn't asking any questions that couldn't be answered.

I said that will have to do.

I asked him if he was in control of the numbers – if they all added up. To me it still looked like there were too many kids, too many people. It wasn't the first time I had broached the subject, and it wasn't the first time he evaded it, a tetchy furrow running across his brow, followed quickly by a trust accusation – his stock reply.

This is how it has been with Sthembiso and me for years. The distance between us punctuated by these awkward occasional meetings, filled with allusions to the things in between. We chatted on for a few minutes, about the details of this and that. I probed again around the unilateral music ban – the tyranny of the trance.

Next to Gerald's body they had found a note. Dub, his final scrawl made sure to tell us. True dub.

To me it was the scrawl of hope. Of real, honest-to-God hope – the kind based on something tangible and physical. As much as their savagery to English was just that – savagery – their presence was still, ultimately, a light. A flicker on the horizon.

Sthembiso took it in a completely different direction. For him, their dub cast our trance in a new context of conflict. Everyone knew better than even to try to slip a fatter bass line in anywhere. A jazzy beat. An old rock 'n' roll tune ... Never.

Never.

In case the message hadn't spread far or fast enough, in case the sight of the daily departing drones, reaching ever further, bringing back ever more, did not fully carry the military message, his lectures and sermons began referencing the importance of continuity and the danger of those heavy-handed, as yet unknown but clearly existent Zambian savages, waiting, surely, definitely, with their lazy beats and their machetes and their glazed, stoned, dubbed-out eyes ...

There is us, Sthembiso said. And there is them. They left Gerald's body in a tree. Strips hanging off it. Do the math, and do not be afraid of the numbers – they tell us what we need to know.

After Sthembiso had departed that last time, I had the sudden urge to talk to Sihle, my direct offspring. As a child he tended towards the coy and annoying, but in his later years he picked up enough confidence to show that his childhood uncertainty was just that – uncertainty. Now he was in charge of the Soweto Calabash, running, by all accounts, a fairly large set-up. There was much talk of parallel digital ports and docking points and such things beyond the ken of an old half-toothed man.

I strolled slowly, carefully, along the back paths, the neon-free paths, to the main house. This, I decided, would be the time. An appropriate time to finally use the landline. I asked one of the kids to dial it up for me. It looked for all the world like an old cellphone, but it was attached by a cable to an unusually large docking base, which in turn led to a nest of thick cables, all running away in different directions. The details were beyond me, but I had seen a few of them on it and it appeared to function pretty much like an old two-way radio in the connection phase. As far as I could gather – and that wasn't very far, admittedly – the two-way connection was required to activate the call. One had to literally summons the party on the other side via a series of rings. The other party then had to flick a set of switches.

Once all had done what they needed to do, the handset could undock from its base and be used like a phone of old.

'Sihle?' I bellowed down the line.

'Hola?' His voice was surprisingly light, like a teenager.

'It's Roy.'

'Roy? Really?' He was surprised and amused. 'Nice, Ntate. I'm honoured. Wot's cooking down de?'

'Nothing really. That's why I decided to call. Seeing as they've got this set-up it makes sense to use it, I supposed.'

'Korrek. Good call. An good to hear your voice, good to hear. Tell me something exciting. Ish is pretty dead this side.'

'Sheesh. I was hoping you could tell me. Uhhh ... oh, they've asked me to DJ at the next session.'

'Ja? Wikkid. Nice. Okei ... I might come through. I might definitely come through.'

'Ja. Bit weird really but thought I'd give it a shot.'

'Sho. Mthakathi on the decks. The kiddies will love it.' He waited awkwardly for something, some reason.

'Well, I guess I'll let you get back. I just suddenly, I just wanted to hear your voice.'

'Super. Dope to hear yours.' He sounded relieved, and just the tiniest bit impatient. 'You live well now, Roy. Don do nuffing I wouldn't do. Ha ha.'

'I love you, boy.' The words were out of my mouth before I could stop them.

'Uh, ja. Wow. Sho. Thanks, Roy. Love you too, broe.' Awkwardness flooded the line. 'Uh, gotta go. I being summonsed. Shot for the call, nè? I see you soon.'

'Yup, see you soon.'

I gave the phone back to the nearest sprog and drifted back to my cottage, thinking about the rare occasions my father had attempted similar phone calls or interactions, about the way his sudden attempts at emotional contact would strike at me, out of the blue. Nonetheless, I felt good having at least given it a go. He will remember when I am gone.

Chapter 63

I drop it

Now there is nothing. Everything I have from here is incidental. (This bag of bones is seriously sagging. That I can tell you. That is new. I reach out with weak, flopping arms. Things fall suddenly from my fingers. My feet stub into the ground – I cannot lift them.)

I pack my disks carefully. I asked the sound kids to set up one of those old CD things, the ones that mimic the original vinyl decks. I run through the set in my head. I am nervous. I will be defying. I will be risking. It's an invigorating feeling, risk. The knowledge of the bullet. I feel alive. Thrilled.

I can hear the trance beating out from the fields. Armand Van Helden, I think.

I intend to leave these children with something deeper. With a challenge. I am going to shake them. Open their little eyes and their tiny, shrinking hearts.

Matron fetches me. Tight, tight jeans and a small pink thing up top, she's oozing sex. Her pupils are blazing and I wonder exactly what she's on, and if Sthem really has as much control as he believes, but … well, it's not my business. It hasn't been for a long time.

Up on the decks I look over the crowd – seems like there's more than a hundred of them, little children. My children. I dab my finger on my tongue and put it to the air and they scream, then laugh, then shake those bony little asses. Matron giggles and shakes uncontrollably next to me, loving the limelight, the moment, the honoured position up high.

I bring it in slow, mixing imperceptibly from what was. They don't notice – they're too far out there on that plain, but I keep bringing it until we've switched, we've moved from that terrible, relentless pace into something deeper, the dub pulse pushing, insistent.

Their bodies find it before their minds do. I watch them realise in the smallest of jumps, the tiniest of increments. Then I kill the drum and it's just the synth, lifting and lifting, and their baby fingers go up. I see Sthembiso at the back of the tent and he isn't liking this at all. Not at all. He's got the laser-beam stare on me and next to him there are three, maybe four of his boys, all muscles and slit eyes, and two of them I can see, even from this distance, bulge with weapons.

He holds my eyes and leans into one of their ears and a fat neck nods and slips out the back. The kids start to whoop — I mean, really whoop — they're still lifting, their bodies know what's coming, their ears tuning to the rebellion. It's going to sing. It's going to be delicious.

And I think, Jesus, here I am, a little dying man on the decks, here I really am, doing this, and there they are, loving with eyes stronger than I can imagine, embracing a thought I can no longer conceive, the little ones heading out into the future, and for a second, just an instant, in a blue and pink flash of light, I think I see Madala in his blue overall, right at the back of the tent, behind Sthem and his boys. And then he's gone.

But the synth is still going, lifting and lifting, and now they're impatient, they need it. There is no meaning if it doesn't come, now, and I lift my arm, my tired old broken arm, one last time. I push it into the air and they scream and yelp like the little children they are, and then, finally, after all these years, I drop it. I drop it, at long, long last.